QUEEN MOVE

ALSO FROM KENNEDY RYAN

ALL THE KING'S MEN DUET
The Kingmaker (Book 1)
The Rebel King (Book 2)

HOOPS Series
(Interconnected Standalone Stories)
LONG SHOT (A HOOPS Novel)
BLOCK SHOT (A HOOPS Novel)
HOOK SHOT (A HOOPS Novel)
HOOPS Holiday (A HOOPS Novella)

THE SOUL SERIES
My Soul to Keep (Soul 1)
Down to My Soul (Soul 2)
Refrain (Soul 3)

THE GRIP SERIES
FLOW (The GRIP Prequel)
GRIP (Grip #1)
STILL (Grip #2)

THE BENNETT SERIES
When You Are Mine (Bennett 1)
Loving You Always (Bennett 2)
Be Mine Forever (Bennett 3)
Until I'm Yours (Bennett 4)

Coming Soon!

The Killer & The Queen
(co-written with Sierra Simone)
www.subscribepage.com/TKandTQ

QUEEN MOVE

"Romance is about the possibility of a thing."
— *Love Jones*

By Kennedy Ryan

Queen Move
By Kennedy Ryan

Copyright 2020 Kennedy Ryan
ISBN: 978-1-952457-03-6

Published by Blue Box Press, an imprint of Evil Eye Concepts, Incorporated

Photographer: Sophia N. Barrett, Sophia Barrett Studios, https://www.sophia-barrett.com

Model: Lashae Dennie
Makeup: Nakita Lochard of FaBelle Inc.

Cover design by Asha Hossain

Acknowledgments from the Author

There are always so many to thank, this part is nearly as hard as writing the book itself. Not really, but it's hard to not leave anyone out. LOL! I first want to thank Liz, Jillian and MJ, the Evil Eye Team, for this incredible experience working with you and bringing Kimba's story to life. You believed in me, in *her*, every step of the way, and that means the world. I have to thank my publicist Jenn from Social Butterfly. You always stretch and pull with every one of my new expectations. Every 2am email and midnight text—you never complain. Your friendship is invaluable. Tia Kelly, thank you!!! You cared about Kimba as much as I did. Maybe sometimes even more! Hahaha. I appreciate your honesty and determination and your "spidey senses." Most of all your belief in me and encouragement have been a lifeline more than once. To my alpha reader Joanna, I can't really thank you enough for never settling; for not letting me get away with mediocrity. For being ruthlessly honest, even when it's the last thing I want to hear. For pushing back when I don't want to listen because you care so much about the story. I've said it once and I'll say it again. You're my safety net and your friendship is so precious. <3

I'm so grateful to my sensitivity readers Sylvia and Hannah. Thank you for sharing the richness of your heritage to help me write this story. And to Felicia Grossman for answering all my questions and having candid conversations to help inform this journey. Anything I got wrong is on me, not on these amazing women who helped me understand so many things as I wrote Ezra's character and experience. To my beta readers LaDonna, Cordelia, Terilyn, and Sarah, THANK YOU for the feedback. You helped shape this story more than you could know. Even one of your questions led me to ask myself several more, and the answers contoured these characters.

Thank you LJ Shen for answering all my obnoxious questions, (and asking your husband the ones you didn't know! Hahaha!) for reading early when the book was not at its best and giving me insight to make it better. That means a lot. *You* mean a lot, my "tell it like it is" friend, and you'll always be my Molly.

Thanks to my promo team! (*Kennedy's Krew, BlockStars, Pinkballerz* and *Kennedy's Crusaders*). You guys are the best in the game. Your hearts are huge and I'm humbled by your support. To my Kennedy Ryan Books group on Facebook, THANK YOU for being my virtual soft landing. You keep me encouraged and give me a safe place to celebrate every single day. I love you! To Melissa Panio-Peterson, THANK YOU for being my right arm and left flank. Hehehehe. I ask a lot, and you never complain. I don't tell you enough how much your presence in my life makes things easier. I love you.

To my mama, Aunt Evelyn and Aunt Joyce, the first queens I ever met. The women who showed me as much as they told me. Who put compassion and character on display and taught me what real power looked like—the power to help others and make the world better where and when you can.

Dedication

For all the girls who have to work twice as hard.
You know who you are.

PROLOGUE

Kimba
Two Years Before Present

IS THERE ANYTHING SADDER THAN A DADDY'S GIRL AT HER father's funeral?

My mother's quiet sniffs a few seats down give me the answer.

A grieving widow.

"He was a good man," someone in the long line of mourners offering condolences whispers to her.

Mama's head bobs with a tearful nod. In this day and age, she still wears a pillbox hat and veil. It's black and chic like Mama, channeling tragic Jackie Kennedy or Coretta Scott King. My father was not just a good man. He was a *great* man, and everyone should know he leaves behind a widow, grieving deeply, but ever-fly. I squeeze the funeral program between my fingers, glaring at the printed words.

Joseph Allen leaves behind a wife, Janetta, three children, Kayla, Keith and Kimba, and six grandchildren.

He leaves behind.

Daddy's gone, and I don't know how to live in a world my father does not inhabit. The casket is draped with sweet-smelling flowers in the center of the funeral tent. When we leave the cemetery, it...*he* will be lowered into the ground with unfathomable finality, separated from us by white satin lining, six feet of dirt and eternity.

Kayla, my older sister, sobs softly at the end of our family's row. Her four children watch her carefully, probably unused to seeing their unshakeable mother shaken and reduced to tears. Even I'd forgotten how she looks when she cries—like she's mad at the wetness streaking her cheeks, resentful of any sign of weakness.

It's not weak to cry, Daddy used to say. *It's human.*

"But doesn't the Bible say even the rocks will cry out?" I'd challenged him when I was young, loving that something from Sunday school took. "So maybe tears aren't just for humans."

"You're getting too smart for your britches, little girl," he'd said, but the deep affection in his eyes when he kissed me told me he was pleased. He liked that I asked questions and taught me to never accept bullshit at face value.

I miss you, Daddy.

Not even a week since his heart attack, and I already miss him so much.

Humanity blurs my vision, wet and hot and stinging my eyes. I want this to be over. The flowers, the well-dressed mourners, the news cameras stationed at a distance they probably deem respectful. I just want to go to the house where my parents raised us, retreat to Daddy's study and find the stash of cigars that only he and I knew about.

Don't tell your mother, he used to whisper conspiratorially. *This will be our little secret.*

Mama hated the smell of cigars in the house.

"Tru."

Who would call me by that name? Now, when the only people who use it, my family, are all preoccupied with their own pain? A tall man stands in front of me, his thick, dark brows bunched with sympathy. I don't know him. I would remember a man like this, who stands strong like an oak tree. A well-tailored suit molds his powerful shoulders. Dark brown, not quite black, hair is cut ruthlessly short, but hints at waves if given the chance to grow. His prominent nose makes itself known above the full, finely sculpted lips below. His eyes are shockingly vivid—so deep a blue they're almost the color of African violets against skin like bronze bathed in sunlight. No, a man like him you'd never forget. Something niggles at my memory, tugs at my senses. I'd never forget a *man* who looked like this, a man with eyes like that...but what about a boy?

"Ezra?" I croak, disbelief and uncertainty mingling in the name I haven't uttered in years.

It can't be.

But it is.

In place of the awkward boy I knew stands a man exuding self-assurance in the confident set of his shoulders, the proud bearing of his head. If adolescence was the rough draft, this finished product is a masterpiece of symmetry and beautifully sketched lines.

He nods, a tiny smile relieving the sober line of his mouth. "Yeah, it's me."

Maybe it's the emotion, the vulnerability that shatters the guard I always lock in place. Maybe it's the compassion in his expression. Or maybe it's finding in the eyes of a stranger the comfort of a long-lost friend. It could be all of these things, or maybe it's none of them, but I surge to my feet and fling myself into his arms. He doesn't seem as surprised as I am by this ungoverned physicality, his strength tightening around me right away. He's much taller than I am, much taller than the last time I saw him, and he dips a little closer to my ear.

"I'm so sorry, Kimba," he says. "He was one of the finest men I ever met."

His words and arms warm places left frigid all week, and this moment melts into a million others I thought I'd lost forever. Ezra and me tracing our names into wet concrete with sticks. Riding our bikes through the streets, shouting and laughing at summer dusk, racing the sun. Pumping our legs to propel us so high on swings at night in a deserted park our feet seemed to kick the stars. Ezra Stern was the axis of my childhood.

"Ez." I pull back far enough to look up at him, scouring his features for the changes twenty years have made. "But you...what are you...how—"

"I moved back to Atlanta a few years ago. I ran into your father and we..." He swallows, releases me to shove one hand into the pocket of his dark slacks. He used to do that when he was unsure. It's one of the few things remaining of the boy I knew. And those eyes.

"We talked," he continues. "We kept in touch. He helped me. I hope it's okay that I'm here."

He spares a quick glance to my mother at the other end of our row, still elegant and too devastated to really notice those standing in front of her, much less the man standing in front of me.

"It is." I squeeze his free hand, connecting our gazes. "*I'm* glad you came."

Something like relief loosens his tight expression. "Good. I didn't want to—"

"Dad."

The voice comes from behind him. I glance around and see a handsome kid with African violet eyes. His skin is a few shades lighter than Ezra's, his curls less coarse, and there are traces of maybe Asian ancestry in his features, but there's something of the boy I knew years ago in this one, and my heart contracts.

A son. Ezra has a son.

Of course he does. We're in our thirties. He's probably also got a—

"Noah, I asked you to wait with your mom." Ezra brushes a hand across the boy's hair.

"I was," Noah says, his eyes wide and locked on his father's. "But bà ngoại called. It's an emergency. Mom says we need to go."

Ezra and Noah both look beyond the tent and across the cemetery's carpet of grass. A petite woman paces in a tight circle, a phone pressed to her ear, distress on her face. I see the other parts of Noah in her. A sheath of dark hair hangs to her waist and, even at this distance, she's obviously a beautiful woman.

Ezra's wife. Ezra's son. I haven't seen this man in more than two decades, but my breath hitches when faced with the life he made apart from me. We were just kids, and of course he made a life without me, just like I made a life without him, but my heart still sinks like an anchor to the ocean floor.

A family. Ezra has a family.

"I saw you on TV," Noah says, studying me closely.

I frown, for a moment so removed from the reality of life beyond this funeral tent and the cloying scent of flowers that I have no idea what he's talking about.

"The campaign," Ezra says, a small smile lifting the corners of his mouth. "You were doing an interview on CNN."

"Oh." I nod and manage a facsimile of a smile for Noah's benefit. "My job has me talk on television sometimes, but I'll tell you a secret."

His eyes glint with childish delight.

I bend to his ear and whisper, "I get *really* nervous, and it's not as easy as it looks."

Noah nods, his face sobering. "I'd be nervous, too, but Daddy said you're the smartest girl he ever met."

I zip a glance at Ezra, who looks self-conscious for a moment before meeting my eyes. "Still not smarter than me, though," he deadpans defiantly. "And don't you forget it."

I thought there was no way to laugh, not on the day I buried my father, but a chuckle rattles in my throat. "You're just mad because I beat you at chess."

"You beat *Daddy* at chess?" Noah's eyes stretch to full moons. "Nobody ever beats him."

"Once," Ezra interjects with a heatless glare. "She beat me once."

"Now the excuses start," I tell Noah.

Ezra smiles, but his gaze flits back to where his wife stands and the brief flash of humor disappears. "We better go, Noah. Let's see what your mom needs."

Noah takes off, dashing from the tent and across the grass to his mother. When he reaches her, she pulls him into the crook of her arm and kisses the top of his head. What a beautiful family. I'm happy for him.

Ezra turns his attention back to me. "I just wanted to say how sorry I am. Pay my respects."

A dozen words idle on my tongue at the prospect of him disappearing again.

Don't be a stranger. Let me get your number. We should stay in touch.

He looks down at me, and the words lodged in my throat seem to burn in his eyes, too, fueled by regret. And hope. All the things clamoring in my chest play across his expressive features.

"Kimba, we could—"

"It was good seeing you again," I cut in with soft politeness, dropping the hand I didn't realize I still held until now. "Thank you for coming."

He stares at me for long seconds, and despite my best intentions, I stare back. When I was a little girl, no one was closer to me, no one knew me better than Ezra Stern. It was the kind of closeness you cherished as a child—the kind that between two adults could be nothing short of intimate.

"Goodbye, Ez," I whisper, blinking at fresh tears.

"Yeah." He looks out across green grass and headstones to where his family waits, and nods. "Goodbye, Tru."

Long, swift strides take him to his wife and son. They disappear over the crest of a hill, hand in hand and then out of sight. They were here only a few minutes. I doubt Mama even realized he was here. She's still trapped in her worst nightmare where the love of her life is gone.

"Goodbye, Daddy," I say, loud enough for just myself and him to hear, like the little secrets he and I used to keep. The casket in front of me breaks my heart for what I've lost.

I glance over the hill and shed a tear for what I never had.

PART ONE

"We are stardust brought to life,
then empowered by the universe to figure itself out—
and we have only just begun."

— Neil deGrasse Tyson, *Astrophysics for People in a Hurry*

CHAPTER ONE

Ruth
1983, Atlanta, GA

SHABBAT SHALOM

The words come—sudden, unexpected. A greeting my heart offers when there is no one to reply. No one for me to say it *to*. Friday evenings, once a day of rest, a Sabbath, are now the most restless days of the week. My soul churns, *yearns* for rest, but there is no peace here tonight.

"Your ass is set!"

My husband Alfred's animated words thunder from the living room, shattering the small moment of quiet I found for myself by a steaming tub of water. It's our first time having anyone over since we moved. With the food out, our new neighbors all entertained, I used my baby's nighttime bath as an excuse to slip away. Despite my melancholy mood, Alfred's laughter and booming voice coax the corners of my mouth up in a smile.

"Sounds like Daddy's winning," I say, pressing my nose to my son's. He gurgles back, laughing and stretching his little starfish palm toward my face. He squirms as I lower him into the warm water. A grin squints the corners of eyes the same color as mine, a blue so deep it's almost purple. The contrast with his golden skin and cap of springy dark curls is striking. Some of me. Some of his father. Wholly himself.

Is he adopted?

The cashier had asked today, the syllables dragged into a molasses drawl, her wide eyes flicking between my son and me. It's not the first time I've been asked that since we moved to Georgia. Even in New York, this petite Jewish woman carrying *this* baby boy drew the occasional stare. But here? Every time I venture out, they can't seem to look away. Some are discreet, at least trying to hide their curiosity, but many don't even bother. From my experience so far, the famous Southern hospitality is, at least in our case, overruled by good old-fashioned nosiness. Sometimes outright rudeness.

I squeeze baby shampoo into my palm and rub it into his soft hair. "What have we done bringing you here, Ezra?"

I was so ready to get away from my family in New York, I didn't fully consider where we were *going*. My husband couldn't turn down a full ride to Emory University, and my mother and I were barely speaking by then.

"Alfred Stern," my mother had said, savoring the name. "And a business student at Columbia? What a catch, Ruth."

I could practically hear her thoughts. A nice Jewish boy with a nice Jewish name and a bright future. Well, she had the *bright future* part right, but I knew my atheist boyfriend, with his imposing height, smooth dark skin and stubbornly godless heart was not what Mother had in mind. I'd always assumed I'd marry someone from my own neighborhood. Certainly someone Jewish. Alfred walked into the bookstore where I worked and swept me off my feet without even trying.

"Lord above, they're gonna come to blows out there playing spades."

I look over my shoulder to find Janetta Allen, one of my new neighbors, whose husband is in law school with Al. She stands in the bathroom door, arms extended keeping her baby girl, Kimba, away from her body. Bright green peas and orange mashed carrots splatter Kimba's once-pristine romper.

"This girl eats like a tornado," Janetta says, nodding toward the counter. "Mind if I strip her down?"

"Oh, of course." I laugh at her squirming baby girl. "They don't stay clean for long, do they?"

"Oh, honey, I gave up on clean after baby number one." Janetta lays Kimba on the counter and peels the romper from her little body. "I'm happy to just keep 'em alive, rough as my kids are."

I glance at her slim curves a little enviously. I've had the hardest time bouncing back, but she doesn't look like she's had even one baby, much less plural.

"How many do you have?" I ask, rinsing the shampoo from Ezra's hair.

"Three." Janetta smiles, teeth white against her gorgeous brown complexion.

"The other two are with their cousins tonight. It took me the longest time to let them go anywhere without me. A few years ago, everyone here was on edge and keeping their kids close."

"You mean because of the child murders?" I ask, frowning.

The Atlanta Child Murders case, two years of more than twenty unsolved murders and disappearances, transfixed the whole country. My mother mentioned it as soon as she heard we were moving here.

"Yeah." Janetta sighs. "All little black boys and girls. I had to know where my kids were every second of every day. We even started sleeping in their rooms after one child was taken from their bed. Joseph in Keith's room and me in Kayla's. Well, that's behind us now, thank you, Jesus."

She glances at my necklace, onyx embedded into the Star of David charm. "Sorry. Forgot you were Jewish."

For some reason, we both find that comment hilarious, and laugh loud and long in that contagious way that makes you almost forget what was funny in the first place.

"Whoo. I needed that laugh," Janetta says, her lips still curved with leftover humor. "And thanks for having us over, by the way."

"Thanks for coming. We haven't had many visitors, believe it or not," I reply wryly.

Janetta pauses, her fingers resting on Kimba's bare belly. The look she offers holds sympathy and sees more than I probably want to show her. "You do know y'all have been the talk of the neighborhood, right?"

Her frankness draws a startled laugh from me.

"Can't say I'm surprised." I flick water into Ezra's eyes and he giggles, his face lighting up. "I take it there aren't many mixed marriages around here just yet, but it *is* the eighties."

Janetta shrugs, leaning a hip against the bathroom counter. "*Loving* was what? Just fifteen years ago? We're not that far removed from your marriage being considered criminal, and in the South, ignorance about race likes to linger as long as it possibly can."

The arguments I had with my parents and the snubs I suffered at synagogue in New York tell me the South hasn't cornered the market on intolerance.

"You seem familiar with law," I say instead. "You're a lawyer, too?"

"Oh, no, I leave that to my husband. I'm a teacher."

Kimba's small hand flies into Janetta's face, making us both laugh.

"She's beautiful." I nod toward the squirming baby girl. "How old?"

"Just turned nine months last week."

I pause, my hands going still in Ezra's curly hair. "When last week?"

"Last Thursday."

"The twentieth?"

"Yeah."

"They have the same birthday!"

"No way." Janetta looks at me with wide eyes and shakes her head. "What are the odds? We can have one big party if you want."

"That'd be really nice," I say, smiling because something *would* actually be really nice for the first time since we moved here.

Janetta rifles through her diaper bag. "I'm out of wipes and this child is so sticky."

"Why don't you just plop her in here?" I gesture toward the bathtub. "Plenty of room."

"You sure?" Janetta asks, hesitation in her expression as much as her words.

"Of course. Why not?"

Janetta smiles ruefully, walking Kimba over and settling her into the steamy water. "I guess I'm as bad as some of these busybodies around here. I assumed you'd be...I don't know. Stuck-up. Act funny."

"*Me* act funny?" I chuckle and frown. "Every time I leave my house people stare at me like I have two heads. At least once a week I'm asked if my son *belongs* to me. My husband is never home, and it feels like I'm in this whole state by myself. Of all things, I miss my mother, who rejected me for marrying a man who is not only *not* Jewish, but black. At this point, I'd kiss strangers to make friends."

The words tumble out in a rush of anxious air, like someone popped a balloon, forcing it into a frantic zigzag. How long have I stuffed it all, waiting for the pin to pop? I blink at tears that snuck up on my eyes and press a hand to my chest where the loneliness collects. It's quiet in the bathroom, with the sound of laughter and the boasting that comes with card games floating into the room in muted tones. I don't look up, afraid that if I do I'll cry and be unable to stop, but my fingers, buried in Ezra's hair, shake and my bottom lip trembles.

Janetta extends her open palm and nods to the bottle of baby shampoo behind me on the rim of the tub. "Can I get a squirt?"

I appreciate her not dwelling on my outburst. It gives me time to collect myself, and in the quiet, we wash our babies. I swallow the tears scalding my throat and cling to the love that brought me here, so far from my community and my family and my traditions and my faith.

"You know I don't have any Jewish friends," Janetta says. "You'll be the first."

Shabbat Shalom

I meet Janetta's eyes, dark, kind and curious.

"I'd like that." I smile and rinse soap from Ezra's little shoulders and back. "Though it's been months since I stepped foot in a synagogue."

"There's one a couple blocks over."

"Really? I was just thinking I want my son to grow up with the traditions I did. I don't want to cheat him of that. Some rabbis won't even acknowledge my marriage."

"Because Alfred's black?"

"Oh, no." I grimace. "Well, maybe some. Mostly because he's not Jewish. Some are more conservative than others. No one in my family ever married someone who wasn't Jewish, so…"

"Joe's family helped elect the first, the *only*, Jewish mayor of Atlanta," Janetta says, a note of pride in her voice. "Sam Massell. His vice mayor was Maynard Jackson. Four years later, Joe's people helped make *him* the first black mayor of Atlanta."

"Joe's family's into politics?" I pounce on the chance to talk about something other than my problems and pull Ezra from the bath, toweling him off, kissing his damp hair.

"Joe's family is into progress. Into change and making wrongs right. His father was a freedom rider. Marched. Sit-ins. Did it all. He's a legend here in the city. Streets and schools named after him. All of it."

"You're close to his family?" I ask wistfully.

"Close as I am to my own. Especially since my parents are gone. I was an only child, and Joe's family treats me like one of theirs."

"That must be nice." I choke out a humorless chuckle. "We got married at City Hall. My family wasn't there. Neither was his."

"You miss 'em? Your family, I mean?"

I nod. "I was just thinking about them, what they're doing on a Friday night. It's the Sabbath."

"I'm guessing they probably aren't playing cards and going through six-packs like there's no tomorrow?"

"No." I smile. "You can't even turn on the lights or cook or do much of anything on the Sabbath. When I was growing up, I thought it was the most boring day of the week. Now I realize it was the most peaceful."

"And your family turned their backs on you?"

"At first, yes. My mother actually started calling after Ezra was born."

"So things are getting better between you?"

"I haven't talked to her much. We both said some awful things when she first found out about Al. I've been so hurt and angry I just..." I blink at tears again, recalling the scent of challah bread and fish and chicken soup Mama would serve for the Friday evening meal.

"But you miss her?" Janetta asks.

I nod, swallow, and dry Ezra with a towel.

"Then, girl, call her back. Life's too short." Janetta pulls Kimba from the bath. "My mama passed last year. She never got to meet this grandbaby. If your mama's willing to put it behind you, give her a chance. Family is everything."

Laughter erupts from the living room, shouts, raucous voices. The heavy timbre of my husband, the lighter tones of others. I prick my ears to tease out a few phrases.

"Did they just say 'running a Boston'?" I ask, smiling and offering Janetta a towel for Kimba. "What's that?"

"In spades, it's when one team wins all the books."

"What kind of books?"

"You never played spades?" Janetta asks, surprise tipping the question up at the end.

"No. I didn't know Al played."

But as I think about it, in New York, Al was quieter. More reserved, to himself. I grew up there, and every corner felt like home. Al grew up in Chicago, and didn't have many friends when we first met on campus. I introduced him to my friends; none of them played spades. New York felt very much like my world. Atlanta? Even though Al didn't grow up here, this world already feels like his.

"If Al's running a Boston," Janetta says with a grin, "he not only plays spades, but he must be pretty good. What do you like to play?"

"You'll laugh," I say, self-conscious, but still managing to smile under the warmth of her encouragement.

"Probably, but is that so bad? Child, three babies, teaching badass kids, and struggling to keep my house halfway clean, I could use a laugh."

"I like playing mah-jongg."

"Mah who?"

We both laugh, me slipping a onesie onto Ezra and Janetta digging out a fresh T-shirt from her diaper bag for Kimba.

"My mother and Bubbe and—"

"Bubbe?"

"That's what I call my grandmother. They played mah-jongg with their friends when I was growing up. I called it an old Jewish woman game. Even though it's originally from China, we adopted it as our own. It's like bridge or gin rummy, I guess, but with these tiles. Anyway, I started playing with my mom's group one summer, and I got hooked."

For a moment, I can almost hear the clack of tiles and their calls of 'five crack,' 'six dot' and 'two bam' as close as the laughter in my living room. I can still see the tables laden with dark chocolate jelly rings, Bridge mix, pineapple and maraschino cherries pierced with toothpicks. Smell the pungent mix of their various perfumes, the scents socializing on a summer afternoon.

"You miss it, huh?" Janetta asks, resting a drowsy-eyed Kimba on her shoulder.

I've spent so much time hiding it from myself, and if I'm honest, from Al so he wouldn't think I regret marrying him, moving here, leaving home – that it's hard to admit. After a brief hesitation, I nod.

"Tell you what," Janetta says. "I'll teach you spades, and you teach me this Mao Tse Tung."

I chuckle at her deliberate mangling of the game's name. "It's mah-jongg, and you've got yourself a deal."

"Good." She turns to leave the bathroom, but pauses in the doorway to look at me over one shoulder. "And Ruth?"

"Yeah?"

Her smile is the kindest thing I've seen since we crossed the state line. "Call your mama."

CHAPTER TWO

Kimba
10 Years Old, Atlanta, GA

I PULL BACK THE CURTAIN AT OUR LIVING ROOM WINDOW AGAIN, like I've done a dozen times in the last hour.

"Get away from there." My mother taps my head when she walks past on her way to the kitchen. "They'll be over soon enough. Come set the table."

"Mrs. Stern holds Ezra hostage all weekend," I whine. "Going to synagogue and not getting to do stuff 'til Saturday evening."

"He's no more hostage on the Sabbath than you are on Sunday morning at Pine Grove Baptist for hours."

I follow Mama into the kitchen, already dreading sitting on hard pews in a stiff dress with bobby socks and ponytails tomorrow. From Friday sundown to Saturday evening, the Sterns observe the Sabbath. Well, Mrs. Stern does. Mr. Stern plays golf with my father, but Ezra and his mother go to synagogue on Fridays and Saturdays. Our two families always eat together Saturday nights, alternating houses. Sundays my family always eats with my grandparents.

"Here you go." Mama hands me a stack of plates. "I need to press your hair tonight after dinner."

"Do I have to?"

"Maynard Jackson is coming to the service tomorrow, so your

grandfather and daddy want everybody looking bright as new pennies."

"I hate getting my hair pressed." I pout, setting the plates in front of the empty seats.

"Push that lip in." Mama walks into the dining room carrying a covered Corningware dish. "Make yourself useful and bring in the chicken."

"Where's Kayla?" I mumble on my way back to the kitchen. "And Keith? Why am I the only one working?"

"'Cause you'll be the only one eating. I'm going out," my older sister says, seated at the kitchen table. She blows on freshly painted nails. "And I can't help set the table. My nails are still wet."

On my way to get the chicken from the stove, I swipe a hand over one of her nails.

"You little brat." Kayla glares at the dent in her manicure and tosses her emery board at me.

"Ow! Mama, Kayla's throwing things at me."

"You big baby," Kayla grumbles.

"I'm not a baby."

"Well, you sure sound like one," Mama says, walking back into the kitchen. "Whatever you would do if I wasn't standing right here, do that because I'm too tired to referee for the two of you."

"All I needed to hear," I mutter, grabbing a buttered roll from the basket of bread on the counter and throwing it at my sister.

"You better stop." Kayla deflects the roll, and it lands on the table in front of her. "If I didn't have a date, I'd deal with you now. If I were you, I'd sleep with one eye open."

"Date?" Mama stops on her way back to the dining room with another dish. "Who has a date?"

"Um…" Kayla glares at me like it's my fault. "I told you about him, Mama. You said it was okay if I went to the movies."

"You said you were missing dinner because you were going to the movies *with friends*." Mama continues into the dining room, but yells over her shoulder, "If your father hasn't met him, you know it's not happening."

"Keith is a year younger than me," Kayla shouts. "And you don't halfway know where he is most of the time. He's probably out with some girl right now."

Mama reappears at the kitchen door, both brows lifted in the face of Kayla's audacity.

"Who you yelling at?" She levels a stony look at my sister. "You lost your mind?"

"No, ma'am." Kayla sighs heavily, her lips tightening over some rebellion she probably thought better of. "I'm just saying."

"Just say it somewhere else," Mama says. "And Keith's a boy. It's different."

"Why is it different?" Kayla demands. "I'm *older*, but he has more freedom than I do. It's not fair."

"Oh, I think you have plenty of freedom, missy," Mama says. "You can take up 'fair' with your daddy. His meeting went late, but he's on his way home now. How 'bout that?"

The comment does exactly what Mama knew it would. Shuts Kayla down. Daddy doesn't have to rule our house with an iron fist. He's a stern man, but it's his heart that keeps us in line. He'd do anything for any one of us, and we know it. Disappointing him is punishment enough.

"Listen," Mama says. "When this boy of yours comes, just introduce him to your father and it'll be fine, Zee."

Mama always uses our middle names when she's being tender with us. All our first names begin with K. Kayla, Keith, Kimba, but our middle names are all for people our parents admired in history. Kayla Zora for Zora Neale Hurston. Keith Stokely for Stokely Carmichael. Kimba Truth for Sojourner Truth.

The doorbell rings and I shoot out of my seat, race to the living room and jerk open the door.

"Kimba," Mrs. Stern says with a smile, standing on the front porch holding a covered dish of her own. "Hi."

"Hey, Mrs. Stern."

She walks inside while Mr. Stern and Ezra cross the street from their house, both carrying dishes, too. In a line-up, you'd never know they were father and son. Ezra's much lighter skinned with blue eyes, and he's small for his age. Mr. Stern easily stands six feet six inches.

"Hey, Ez." I step back so they can enter. "Hey, Mr. Stern."

Mama and Mrs. Stern are already laughing in the kitchen. When they get together, there's no stopping them, whether it's Saturday evening dinners or the mah-jongg games they play with some of the ladies from Mrs. Stern's synagogue.

"Joseph late again?" Mrs. Stern asks, setting a basket of challah bread on the table beside the fish she usually brings.

"Girl, yes." Mama sighs and shrugs. "With the Olympics coming soon, Mayor Jackson is trying to get as much done as he can before his term is up. So that means Joseph's always late. He's on his way, though. Fifteen minutes tops."

"Mind if I watch the game while we wait?" Mr. Stern asks, nodding toward the living room. "Someone hasn't let me turn on the television all weekend."

Mrs. Stern's mouth tightens, but she and my mother both nod permission. Even though Mr. Stern doesn't believe in God, Ezra's mom draws the line at the Sabbath. Once the sun sets on Friday, she doesn't turn on the television or turn on lights or drive or anything until after the Saturday evening service.

"How was synagogue?" Mama asks, laying silverware by the plates.

"Good." Mrs. Stern sets a bottle of wine beside Mama's sweet tea. "Helen and Dina were there, the ones who came to mah-jongg last week."

"Oh, they were so nice. Couldn't play worth nothing, but nice." Mama glances at Ezra, her face softening. "How was Shabbat, Ezra?"

His skinny shoulders lift and fall, the shrug telling me all I need to know. His mop of dark, springy curls is helmeted from the little cap he probably took off a few minutes ago. The first time I saw Ezra wearing his yarmulke, I called it a Jewish Kangol.

Mrs. Stern didn't think that was funny.

"It's not dark out yet, Mama." I elbow Ezra. "Can we go ride our bikes for a little while?"

Mama and Mrs. Stern exchange a quick look and then nod.

"You can play twenty minutes, Tru," Mama says firmly. "Soon as that streetlight comes on, bring your narrow hips home."

I grab Ezra's hand and we head toward the living room. "Yes, m-m-ma'am."

I hate it when I stutter.

"Did I tell you Mrs. Downy called last week?" Mama asks, her voice lowered, but reaching us in the foyer as we're about to leave the house.

Mrs. Downy? My teacher?

I put my hand on Ezra's arm, stopping him so we can eavesdrop.

"No, what did she want?" Mrs. Stern asks.

"She wanted to talk about putting Tru in a remedial class."

"What? Because she stutters? Kimba's smart as a whip."

"I know." Outrage peppers Mama's voice. "She's having a hard year because a few of the kids started teasing her, but that's all it is."

Ezra and I stare at each other. He seems as focused on the conversation in the dining room as I am.

"I got to that school so fast," Mama says. "Drove over on my planning period and told her if she ever tried that again, she'd have to deal with me."

"Good for you, Janetta," Mrs. Stern says.

Shame fills my throat, makes me feel like I'm choking. I focus on the high shine of Mama's hardwood floor.

"Mrs. Downy's stupid," Ezra says, his first words since he came into the house.

I make myself look up and Ezra doesn't say anything else, but tips his head toward the door.

"You ready?" he asks.

I think every morning when Ezra wakes up, God gives him a tiny jar of words. He only gets so many, maybe a quarter of what the rest of us do. And he's so scared he'll run out, he uses as few of them as possible. Half his sentences are one word or a grunt. Weekends, he talks so little, I bet at the end of the day, he has leftovers.

Mama and Mrs. Stern have moved on, now talking about a sale at Dillard's. I nod and follow Ezra out the door. Outside, I grab my bike and Ezra runs over to his house to grab his. We meet in the middle of the street that separates our homes.

"Race?" he asks, his voice quiet.

Without answering, I hop on my bike and take off. Ezra sputters behind me. His kickstand clanks and his wheels whir as he speeds after me.

"Kimba, you can't just start," he yells from behind me. "We have to count off."

"Who says?" I shout back, shaking off the embarrassment of Mrs. Downy and laughing at the irritation in Ezra's voice. Getting a rise out of Ezra Stern is one of my favorite things.

"The rules say." His voice is closer now, his breaths little pants of exertion. "You always wanna break the rules."

He pulls up beside me, doing that standing pedal thing that gives him the edge in our races. Flashing a grin, he pulls ahead and rushes toward the merry-go-round that always serves as our finish line. To rub it in, he climbs off the bike, sets the kickstand down and sits on the merry-go-round to wait for me. At least he didn't do the *Rocky* dance like the last time he beat me.

"Cheaters never really win," he says, smiling and leaning back on his palms.

"Butthead." I set my bike and, ignoring him, walk over to the sliding board.

"And that was another come-from-behind victory, by the way," he says. "Since you like to cheat."

"I didn't cheat. A head start isn't cheating."

"Well, I didn't know you were gonna have a head start." He climbs up onto the monkey bars and hangs by his skinny arms. "You know what my daddy calls it when one person has a head start that the other person doesn't even know about?"

"What?"

"America." He laughs, and I grin even though I don't understand half of what Mr. Stern says most of the time.

"Did he hear anything about that job in Chicago?" I ask, facing him and hanging from the bars, too. I hold my breath while I wait for him to answer.

"He didn't get it."

Suspended from the bars, our bodies twisting, we face each other and give ear-to-ear grins. I've been worried Mr. Stern would get one of the many jobs he's always applying for up north.

"Why's your mom want to leave Atlanta so bad?" I ask, dropping to the ground, a dusty cloud puffing around my feet.

Ezra drops, too, and shrugs. "She says here, people still make a big deal out of me being mixed. She says in New York, folks won't stare or make dumb comments."

"What kind of dumb comments?" I ask, but I've heard some of them. I kinda know.

"Asking if I'm adopted," Ezra mumbles, his chin sinking into the collar of his T-shirt. "Asking what I am, or calling me Oreo or zebra, or whatever. Dad's applying in lots of places, but Mom's hoping for New York. She misses our family up there."

"You see them all the time, though." My insides are heavy like there's a roll of pennies at the bottom of my belly.

"Mama says holidays and a few weeks for summer's not enough. She wants to be closer to my bubbe."

Thinking about Ezra moving makes my stomach go all swimmy and my eyes burn and my throat tight. He's my best friend. We even have the same birthday. He can't leave.

"M-m-maybe your g-grandmother could m-m-move here." When I get nervous or upset, my tongue "skips," and I want to bite it clean in half. My speech therapist tells me to just take a deep breath and slow down before I talk. I forget sometimes, but Ezra never makes fun of me like some of the other kids do.

"Bubbe is never leaving New York," Ezra says. "She wants me to Bar Mitzvah."

I've learned a lot about Jewish traditions from the Sterns—enough to know that's a big deal.

"Are you gonna?" I ask, glad my tongue is cooperating again.

"I guess." Ezra shrugs. "I'd have to start going to Hebrew school every day after school."

"Crap." I relish the word my mother won't let me say. "What about chess? You just started competitions."

"I'll still play chess. It's a lot of time, but Mom says the busier I am, the less trouble I'll get into."

And the less time he'll have to play, to spend with me. I look around the park, empty now that the sun has set. The streetlight blinks to life, reminding us it's time to go home. Soon Mama will walk to the front porch and yell my name, telling the whole neighborhood I'll come home if I know what's good for me.

I take off running across the playground, willing to risk it to have a few more minutes with Ezra.

"L-l-let's swing!"

CHAPTER THREE

Ezra
12 Years Old

*B**E STRONG, BE VERY STRONG, AND WE WILL STRENGTHEN EACH* *other.*

> *Hazak, Hazak, Venithazek.*

The Hebrew words turn over in my head, sloshing with Outkast's lyrics pouring through the headphones fitted over my yarmulke as I walk home. This is my life—all the influences and interests colliding, conflicting, making sense and chaos. Bubbe wants me to become Bar Mitzvah, so I'm playing crazy catch-up, attending Hebrew school three days a week *after* school. I practice chess the other two.

Somehow, my grandmother, at only four feet eleven inches, casts a long shadow over me even from New York. I can't deny that little lady anything, and she knows it. A few months ago she was diagnosed with ovarian cancer, so when she begged me to have a Bar Mitzvah celebration, even though it basically requires me to be at synagogue all the time, cramming what the other kids have spent the last few *years* preparing for into less than two, I'll do it.

Grandma guilt.

Most of the kids at synagogue are cool, and I've made some new friends, but a few of them love finding ways to make me feel like I don't belong. Some laugh at me when they think I don't hear them, or maybe they don't care. When they have parties or go out together, I'm usually not invited. Mom says I imagine it because she doesn't want to believe anyone at the synagogue would treat me that way. My father says I'm definitely not imagining it, but to ignore it and keep my head down. Dad thinks it's all stupid anyway and asks at least once a week why I'm doing it. I tell him, and I guess I tell myself, it's for Bubbe. But there is a part of me that simply wants to understand as much as I possibly can about this part of myself—my Jewish heritage. Neither of my parents really know what it's like to live here as *me*. To look around and see no one who looks like you. To live with the stares and questions about "what I am." To feel like a puzzle, pieces hidden and scattered, and always trying to find and fit all my parts together. To see myself not as half this or bi-that, but *whole*.

The synagogue is only a couple of blocks from my house, and I'm almost home. Kimba and I don't go to the playground as much as we used to now that we're in middle school. She joined the band. Clarinet. She's good, but between my Hebrew classes and chess and her band practice, we don't see each other as much outside of school, which sucks. If I'm home before dark, we can get in a bike ride before dinner.

My house is just ahead when someone jerks my arm.

"What the…" When I look up, three boys from Hebrew school stand there, arms crossed, one smirking, one glaring and one frowning.

"We called you like six times," one of them, the glare-er, says. Robert. His name is Robert and he always sits slumped in the corner and struggles with the basics of the Torah though he's been studying for years.

"The music," I say, pointing to my headphones, which I slide down to rest at the back of my neck. "Sorry. I couldn't hear you."

I look between the three of them pointedly, lifting my eyebrows to ask what they want.

"We came to have a little talk," Paul, the smirker, says.

I fold my arms to match theirs. "So talk."

"Stay away from Hannah," Michael, the frowner, says.

"Who?" I turn the volume down on the portable CD player clipped to my belt.

"My sister Hannah," Robert says, still glaring.

Who even is she?

"I don't know who…"

Pale skin. A mass of freckles. Dark brown, tightly coiled ringlets. Looks away quickly every time I catch her looking at me.

"I barely know your sister," I say with a shrug. "But okay."

"Let's keep it that way, Fraction." Paul laughs.

Fraction. A new one, more inventive than Zebra or Oreo, but just as insulting. Lava percolates in my belly while Big Boi is reduced to a defiant murmur in my ears.

"Yeah, let's keep it that way." Robert thumps my forehead and snatches my yarmulke. "You don't need this messing up your 'fro, do you, Stern?"

"Stop playing." I reach for the cap, but Robert tosses it to Paul.

Paul's smirk spreads into a full-blown grin when he catches my yarmulke and twirls it on his finger. "Look, it's spinning like a basketball. You like basketball, right, Stern?"

All three of them are taller than I am, but I'm the one who would play basketball? I've never played in my life. I roll my eyes, but stretch for the yarmulke. Paul holds it over his head out of my reach and tosses it to Michael.

"Give it to me," I say, my words rattling against the cage of my gritted teeth.

"*Take* it from me," Michael counters, his frown lifted, but meanness still shadowing his eyes.

"That's the problem, right?" I ask, settling back onto my heels, no longer reaching for the yarmulke. "You think I'm going to take something from you?"

"What?" Michael's spiteful smile slips.

"Yeah," I say, stepping closer to him until only an inch separates our noses. "You hate that I speak Hebrew better than you do after months when you've been learning for years. And you hate that your sister likes me. Well, you can sleep at night because I don't like her back."

He pushes me hard enough that I almost fall, but I catch myself before I hit the ground. My hands slam into the concrete, palms scraping, but keeping me from landing on the sidewalk. My will and body overrule the wisdom of my mind, and I spring toward him without thinking, without weighing the odds. *Three against one.* I shove him back.

"This little shvartze pushed me," Michael spits, his glare reigniting.

Shvartze.

I've lost count of how many times Big Boi and Dre used the N word on the *Southernplayalisticadillacmuzik* album blaring through my headphones, and it slid right past my ears, a stingless barb never meant to harm. But hearing it wrapped in Yiddish from these boys who have everything and want me to have nothing? It's not the same. Coming from this boy, so proudly wearing his resentment and superiority, it's a knife hurled right through my insecurities. It's a slur that slices through every part of me, not just the black part.

Michael shoves me toward Robert, and Robert shoves me to Paul; they're tossing me between each other in a game of keep-away.

Keep your head down. Keep your head down. Keep your head down.

I try my best to grab hold of my father's warning, but my hands are raw and my ego is bruised and I'm tired of everything. Caution slips through fingers greased with rage. When Paul pushes me again, I slam my hand into Michael's face. Blood gushes from his nose.

"Shit!" Michael cups his face, blood running between his fingers. "You'll be sorry you did that. Hold him."

Robert grabs one of my elbows and Paul grabs the other.

"Hit me now, shvartze," Michael growls through the blood streaming over his lips. The first punch to my stomach steals all my breath, pain radiating from my middle. I slump for a second, giving the two boys holding me all my weight while I try to breathe. Another punch comes harder than the first, or at least more painful, and I wheeze, all the air trapped in my throat. When the third punch comes, I'm glad I can't breathe enough to speak because I'd beg him to stop.

He draws his fist back, ready to go at me again, but Robert drops my elbow and yelps. Paul drops the other, crying out in pain.

Michael looks over my shoulder, eyes widening. "What are you—"

Before he can finish that sentence, someone pushes past me. A clarinet case slams into his chest once, twice, three times.

"L-l-leave him alone!" Kimba screams, whirling, hitting the other two boys again with her clarinet case. Paul's face contorts with rage and he lunges for her, but on instinct, even through my breathless pain, I manage to step between him and her, bearing the brunt of his weight with a grunt. Kimba hoists the case high with both hands, poised to lower it like a hammer onto Michael's head.

"Tru, no!" I catch the case before it lands, pulling it out of her hands and letting it drop to the ground. I loop my arms around her small, wriggling body. She strains toward Michael's face, her fingers outstretched like claws, her face twisted in anger.

"What's going on down there?" Our neighbor Mrs. Washington, a few yards up toward our houses, stands on her front porch, hands on hips, wearing an apron with her frown.

"Let's get outta here," Paul hisses, grabbing Robert's arm and taking off.

Michael walks backward, keeping his eyes trained on me, and points one long finger. "This isn't over, Fraction! Stay away from Hannah."

He turns and sprints after the other two boys, rounding the corner and disappearing.

"Y'all all right?" Mrs. Washington yells.

"Yes, ma'am." I make my mouth smile and, letting Kimba go, I wave. From her expression, I can tell Mrs. Washington doesn't believe me, but with one last piercing look, she goes inside.

"Dammit," I say, trying out one of the curse words I use when my mother's nowhere around. "She's gonna tell my parents."

"I'm gonna tell them," Kimba says, her expression squished into a frown.

"Oh, that's just great. Yeah, tell them I got beaten up by some white guys from synagogue. As if my mom's not already just looking for an excuse to pack us up and move whether Dad has a new job or not. She'd send me to live with Bubbe in New York. Is that what you want?"

Kimba blinks at me, tears gathering to a shimmer over her dark eyes. "Y-y-you…"

She closes her eyes and presses her lips together, the frustration of not getting the words out clear on her face like I've seen it a hundred times before.

Take your time, Tru.

"You think she'd do that?" she asks more slowly after a moment, a tear streaking down one smooth brown cheek. "Take you away?"

I can't stand to see her cry.

"Don't… Don't cry. Nah. I'm just…no. Probably not. Let's just not tell her. Everyone's not like them. It's not a big deal, okay?"

"It *is* a big deal." She balls her small hands into fists at her side. "They punched you in the stomach."

She steps close, lifting my T-shirt. "Are you hurt? Did they—"

"Stop." I catch her hand, pushing it away from me, pushing her away. "I'm fine."

We're not babies anymore. Not little kids on the swings. Our parents sat us down last year and explained we're too old for sleepovers, and when Kimba tries to lift my shirt to make sure I'm okay, I know we're getting too old for a lot of things.

"They hurt you," she whispers, letting her hand drop. "Are you sure you're all right?"

She saw them hitting me. Saw me slumped like a wimp, short and small, while those bigger boys punched me. Shame curdles in my belly. Blood heats my cheeks. I'm white enough to blush, but too black to blend.

"I said I'm fine." The words leave my mouth sharp as needles, pricking us both.

"But, Ezra—"

"Kimba, just stop." I run my hands over my hair, my fingers tangling in the thick, tight curls.

My yarmulke lies on the sidewalk, marred by a dirty sneaker footprint. I bend to pick it up and twirl it like a basketball, watching it spin and spin on my finger in the silence that stretches thick as taffy between Kimba and me. A creaky, familiar song breaks the quiet, and both our heads turn toward the sound. The old ice cream truck comes into view, making its slow way up the street.

There are so many things I could say to Kimba. I want to explain how splintered I feel sometimes—how there's something always moving inside me, searching for a place to land, to fit, to *rest*. I want to tell her it's only ever still when I'm with her—that she's my best friend in the world, and I'd rather get punched in the stomach every day than move away and not have her anymore. But that's too many words that don't even come close to telling her what I feel.

"Ice cream?" I ask instead, keeping my gaze trained on the rickety neon-painted truck wobbling toward us.

I cross my fingers that she won't ask again if I'm okay because I don't think she'd know what do with the truth. *I* don't know what to do with the truth. I'm not okay sometimes. The familiar tune gets louder and closer.

Finally, she speaks. "Okay, Ezra. Ice cream."

CHAPTER FOUR

Kimba
13 Years Old

"P<small>SSSST!</small>"

The hiss comes as a piece of notebook-lined origami lands on my desk. I glance nervously from the little square of paper to the teacher at the front of our class. Mrs. Clay is the toughest teacher in the whole eighth grade. She doesn't play and I don't test her. Ezra and I were the only black kids in the gifted classes for the longest time, though I know most don't think of Ezra as black. They don't know quite what to make of his blue eyes and rough curls and tanned skin. To me, he's just my best friend.

At the beginning of this school year, another black girl showed up in class, Mona Greene. I didn't even know how much I needed that until she came. I always have Ezra, of course, but a girl who looks like me? Has hair like me? Understands this tightrope we walk between school and home, striking the right balance between being black enough and *just* enough black—I love having that. Mona busses in from a neighboring district through a program the city implemented. She's great, but she always *almost* gets me into trouble.

I run a finger over the paper on my desk and glance over my shoulder, catching Mona's wide eyes. She tilts her head, silently urging me to open the note. I jerk back around and eye Mrs. Clay cautiously.

When she turns to the chalkboard to write something about Charles Dickens, I slide one fingernail under a fold in the letter and ease it open as quietly as possible.

Kimba, I think you're so pretty and smart. Will you go with me to the dance?

Yes

No

Jeremy

The dance is in two weeks, celebrating the end of middle school and sending us off in style to summer and ninth grade. Mona, Ezra and I are all going, but none of us have dates.

I glance back over my shoulder at Mona, and a mischievous grin hangs between her cheeks like a hammock.

"Oh my God," I mouth to her, my eyes stretched.

"I know," she mouths back, nodding enthusiastically.

A long arm reaches across the aisle and snatches the note. I gasp, grabbing to take the paper back from Ezra, but he turns his lanky body slightly away from me, grinning and batting away my hands. Mrs. Clay suddenly turns around, probably alerted by the small noises I made. Ezra and I instantly go still and inconspicuous. Her narrowed eyes scan the class row by row, but after a few seconds, she turns back to the chalkboard and resumes the lesson.

Ezra's grin fades as he reads, melting away by centimeters. A frown squeezes between his brows. He places the paper back onto my desk, slumps in his chair and starts scribbling in the margins of his notebook. The words are in Hebrew so I have no idea what he's writing, but he presses so hard the pencil dents the paper.

"Ez." My voice comes out like a hissing cat, low and irritated. "Don't read my stuff."

"Since when?" he mumbles, not bothering to look up, his wide mouth sulky. His shoulders are parentheses, bowed, bracketing his body like they're holding him together. "We've never kept secrets from each other. I thought you and Mona were just playing around. I didn't know it was..."

He glares at the notebook and carves the Hebrew letters onto the paper, a torn black ribbon pinned to his T-shirt over his heart, a Jewish sign of mourning. It's been a hard month for him. Bubbe died two weeks before Ezra's Bar Mitzvah. The Sterns went up to New York right away for the funeral, even Ezra's father who has never really gotten along with Mrs. Stern's family. When they returned, we attended Ezra's

Bar Mitzvah at the synagogue, and the reception after. I didn't understand everything that happened, but I knew Ezra worked hard to learn Hebrew and prepare for the ceremony. He excelled, like he does in everything. I researched the best things to give, and found out gifts in increments of eighteen are kind of like good luck, so I gave him eighteen Pixie Stix. Mrs. Stern isn't usually strict about him keeping Kosher, but leading up to the Bar Mitzvah, he did. Pixie Stix are his favorite.

"Hey," I whisper. "I'm sorry."

He doesn't answer, but the muscle in his jaw knots.

"Ezra, I—"

"Miss Allen," Mrs. Clay cuts in, her voice like a snapping turtle. "Since you want to talk so much, you can read the passage."

What passage?

Crap.

I hate reading out loud. On paper, I can hold my own with any of the kids in our gifted classes, but when I read aloud, the words shuffle in my mouth and strangle my tongue.

"Um, n-n-no, ma'am." I clamp my lips together and swallow hard, closing my eyes and breathing deeply like my speech therapist suggested. "No, I don't want t-t-to t-t-talk. I'm sorry. I—"

"It was not a request, Miss Allen." She leans against the chalkboard, apparently uncaring that she's probably getting chalk dust all over her beige cardigan. "Read the passage."

"Um, o-okay." I gulp my fear down and study the board. "Which one exactly should I—"

"The one we've been discussing." Mrs. Clay huffs a long sigh. "The opening lines of the book, please."

I glance at the book on my desk, *A Tale of Two Cities*, and open it to the first page. Thirty pairs of eyes wait on me. The room is so quiet, I hear them breathing, hear my *own* shallow, panicky breaths. My dry lips will barely part to let the words out. I lick them and try.

"I-i-t was the best of times," I manage, my voice a croak. "It was the—"

"Louder so we can hear you. And please stand. You know the drill by now."

A drill I've avoided as much as possible the whole school year. I'm all sass and confidence in every other class and every other area of my life, but this one? Reading out loud? In front of everyone? Risking the disdain of the smartest kids in our school when my tongue lets me down? I'm terrified.

Picking up the book, I stand. "I-i-it was the best of times—"

Snickers break out behind me. I pause at my classmates' amusement, drawing a deep breath and starting again.

"I-it was the best of times—"

Whispers. Chuckles. Gasps from behind stop me again. I look around, glance over my shoulder and find Mona's eyes. They are wide, shocked. Her mouth hangs open and she covers it with one hand.

Before I can process the amused and surprised expressions all around me, Ezra stands and ties his windbreaker around my waist.

"What are you doing?" I ask him. "What's—"

He grabs my hand and fast-walks me down the row of desks and out the door without speaking. I look back, expecting Mrs. Clay's fury, but her face has softened. When her eyes meet mine, they're compassionate.

"All right, class," she says, her curt tone back in place. "That's enough. Let's get back to it. Darlene, would you read the passage?"

Ezra pulls me out the door and starts down the hall. I tug at my hand, trying to free it.

"What are you doing? Where are we going?"

He doesn't answer, but just keeps walking. I jerk my hand away and stop in the middle of the hall.

"Ezra, I know you've used your, like, twelve words for the day," I say, hands planted on my hips, "but you better tell me what's going on right now."

He stops, too, running a hand through his hair.

"Kimba, I…you…" He groans and closes his eyes.

"Just spit it out. What in the world? You tie this jacket around my…" I trail off, my brain finally catching up to wonder why he did that.

"There's a stain on the back of your pants," he mumbles, his eyes glued to the floor as he drags the words past his lips.

"A stain?"

Fire ignites beneath the surface of my cheeks. My fingertips go cold. My stomach lurches. I got my period for the first time two months ago. Kayla told me horror stories about this happening at school, and I've tried to be so careful. But today, I wore white shoes and white pants. I sit close to the front of Mrs. Clay's class, so all those students sitting behind me saw…

"Oh, God."

I take off running down the hall toward the bathroom, tightening the sleeves of Ezra's windbreaker around my waist. Ezra's footsteps behind me only urge me faster. I need to get away even from him.

"Tru!" he calls, but I keep moving. He catches up to me and takes my arm. "You okay?"

"Besides being dead from embarrassment?" I mumble, avoiding his eyes. "Yeah. Peachy."

"Those kids don't matter," he says, flicking his head in the direction of the class we just fled. "And you know you don't have to be embarrassed with me."

I look up to meet his eyes, and they're dark blue, almost violet. I love that color so much, but hate that it only comes when he's upset. "I'm okay, Ezra. Thank you for the jacket."

I start to untie it, but he places a hand over mine.

"Keep it until you don't need it," he says, his voice scratchy with discomfort. "I'll get it later. I know where you live."

We chuckle.

"Yup, right across the street." I smile, but squeeze his hand over mine. "Thanks, Ez. You always take care of me."

"We take care of each other," he says, his voice subdued when he looks up from our hands, his eyes intense. "Hazak, Hazak, Venithazek."

It sounds like Hebrew, but I have no idea what it means. "What'd you say?"

"Be strong, very strong." His fingers tighten on mine and he doesn't drop his gaze or slide a hand in his pocket, or any of the other Ezra things he does when he's unsure. "And we will strengthen each other."

The words are seeds sinking deep into my soul, into my heart. They take root and bloom. We've taken care of each other our whole lives. I don't know what to do with these feelings. What I feel for Ezra is as old as we are, and yet brand new. It's familiar, but blushing and breathless.

"Mr. Stern, Miss Allen," the vice principal calls from a few feet down the hall. "Shouldn't you be in class?"

"I have a female issue."

I've only had my period twice, but I've already discovered you only have to refer to it for men to start stumbling and looking uncomfortable.

"Well, yes." He tugs at his tie and clears his throat. "You, um, do what needs to be done."

He points to Ezra. "You don't have a, um, problem like that, Mr. Stern. Get to class."

"Yes, sir." Ezra looks at me, a small smile on his lips. "I'll see you later, okay?"

"Yeah, later."

With one final glance at the vice principal, I push through the restroom door. Thank God I'm the only one in here. I stumble into the very last stall.

Shoot!

I have no supplies. My bag is still in the classroom. I have no quarters to buy a tampon or pad from the machine. Mortification and helplessness bring tears to my eyes, but I swipe at them impatiently. The bathroom door swings open, and I stiffen, listen.

"Kimba?" It's Mona's voice. "You in here?"

"Last stall."

I open the door to find her standing there holding my backpack.

"Thought you might need this," she says with a tentative smile.

"Thanks."

I accept the backpack and close the door again, rifling through the bag to find a tampon and pad. Once the business is done, I come out to wash my hands. Mona's leaning against the counter.

"Everyone was laughing at me?" I ask, rubbing in soap under the water.

"Not really." Mona shrugs. "I think everyone was just surprised and kind of reacted at first, but then it just died down and we moved on when Mrs. Clay made other people start reading."

I hold my hands under the forced air to dry them.

"I'm not sure who was more traumatized," Mona continues. "You or Ezra."

Our eyes catch in the mirror. By some miracle, our lips start twitching simultaneously. And then the tension that's held my shoulders stiff and my back too straight for the last twenty minutes snaps, and I'm giggling. Mona giggles, too, hopping up onto the counter and leaning against the mirror.

"He hauled you out of there like he was the Secret Service or something," Mona says.

"I know, right?" I chuckle and shake my head. "That's Ezra."

The air dryer stops and I grab my backpack and head for the door.

The hall is empty, a stretch of muted voices behind closed doors.

"I saw him as he was coming back to class." Mona lets the bathroom door swing closed behind her. "Told him this was girl stuff and I got it."

"Bet that went over great," I say dryly.

"I know you guys have been friends a long time."

"Literally since we were babies," I say, smiling as memories over the years run through my mind. I've always had Ezra and he's always had me. I can't imagine it any other way.

"Yeah, well, he's a guy, and he's gonna have to get used to sharing you with friends who are girls. I mean, he's got Hannah now, and you don't have a problem with it, right?"

"Hannah?" My smile dims then fades to nothing. "Ezra barely knows her. They don't have any classes together or anything."

"Weren't they in that Bar Mitzvah thing, or whatever together at the synagogue a lot?" Mona nods even though I don't respond. "That's when it started. He didn't tell you?"

"Um, well, I'm not sure there's anything to tell."

"From what I heard," Mona says, looking around like the empty hall might be bugged before looking back to me, "her brother was mad about it."

Stay away from Hannah.

That's what the boy yelled that day they attacked Ezra.

"Ezra better be careful," Mona says. "He might be all 'Bar Mitzvah,' but this is still Georgia, and Hannah is still white and Ezra is still black."

Mona's grin tips to one side, and she leans against a locker. "Well, semi-black. Her daddy would say he's black, though I doubt she'll be taking him home to meet the parents."

"He's black when it's convenient for other people, and white when it's not," I say. "If Hannah can't introduce Ezra to her parents, then she doesn't deserve him."

She doesn't deserve Ezra, *period.*

"I'm gonna go." I shift the backpack on my shoulder and tug on the sleeve of Ezra's coat. "I need to call Mama and have her pick me up. These pants are ruined."

"Okay." Mona's mischievous smile returns with a vengeance. "What are you gonna tell Jeremy?"

An image of Hannah comes to mind, a memory from Ezra's Bar Mitzvah. Hannah dressed in pink, her face pretty and smooth and sprinkled with freckles. Her long, curly hair had been loose and hanging down her back. Is that what Ezra wants? Someone who looks more like his mother than like me? A lump burns in my throat like lit coal, and I have trouble swallowing past it.

"Yeah." I turn and head toward the office to call Mama. "I'll go to the dance with Jeremy. Whatever."

I call and leave a message at the elementary school front desk since Mama's teaching.

How long will she take?

In the hall, I lower my eyes every time a student walks by. Even seated and with the safety of Ezra's jacket, it feels like they can see my stain.

"Kimba," Mrs. Stern says from the office door. "You ready?"

I grab my backpack and tighten Ezra's windbreaker at my waist. She climbs behind the wheel of her green Camry and I take the passenger seat. Mrs. Stern pulls carefully out of the school parking lot like she's testing for her driver's permit.

"Your mom's in class, obviously," Mrs. Stern says. "So she asked me to come."

"Thanks," I mumble.

We ride in silence. It's not awkward exactly. More like the kind of quiet where you don't have to say anything and it's okay. Mrs. Stern often makes me feel that way. Maybe that's where Ezra gets it.

"So I heard you had a little accident," she says, shooting me a quick glance when we come to a stoplight. "You don't have to talk about it if you don't want, but if you do…"

I shake my head and fix my gaze out the window, staring at the trees dressed in their brightest colors, celebrating spring.

"Well, just know it happens to all us girls at some point," Mrs. Stern says. "Anyway, having just Ezra, I don't get to deal with the girl problems. I thought we'd have another, but we haven't been able to."

She doesn't sound sad exactly. I can see how Ezra would be enough for anybody.

"I do have a question," I say after another few seconds of silence.

"Oh, of course." Her voice is eager, and she flashes me an encouraging smile. "Anything."

"Why do you want to move so much?"

The smile slips and falls, and she presses her lips together like she'll only let so many words out at a time. "I miss my family, Kimba. I want to babysit my sister's children. I want to be in the synagogue where I grew up. I want meat from the deli around the corner and all the things that made New York not just a city, but my home. I want the little part of it where my faith and my community and the things that made me who I am all live."

She looks at me with sad eyes, with Ezra's eyes. "I was so glad to leave, to set off and do my own thing, go my own way, but my mother died and I wasn't with her. I want the wandering to be done."

I think about my grandfather, my parents, our huge family having dinners together every Sunday. Borrowing Kayla's things without asking. Cleaning the house together on Saturday mornings with my siblings, music blasting, and Mama singing Earth, Wind and Fire's "September" at the top of her lungs. Daddy's secret stash of cigars. The gazillion-piece puzzles Mama insists we do together sometimes when we've been going our own way and haven't been at the same table at the same time all week.

"I get that," I say. "But I don't want Ezra to go."

We pull into her driveway, and she stares at the garage door, the flowering bushes standing guard at the bottom of her porch steps, a hard little smile on her lips. "Don't worry, Kimba. I doubt we'll ever leave."

CHAPTER FIVE

Kimba

IT'S BEEN TWO WEEKS SINCE MY COUSIN CAME TO TOWN unannounced and showed out in Mrs. Clay's class right through my white pants. Ezra came over that night to get his windbreaker. There was a time when he would have barreled up the stairs and barely knocked before barging into my room. That night I faked cramps, asked Kayla to take his windbreaker down to him and say I'd see him later. She looked at me strangely. It was the first time Ezra had ever come over when I'd refused to see him. Maybe growing up means growing apart. And maybe it's other people meaning more to you than the ones who used to mean the most.

Like Hannah.

Jeremy is kind of taking me to the dance. Technically, Daddy isn't having it, so Kayla's driving me, Mona and Ezra to the dance, and I'll meet Jeremy there.

"Your hair looks good," I tell Mona in my bedroom while we get ready.

She peers into the mirror and pats her new asymmetrical haircut. "Ya think so?"

"Better than mine." I blow out a long breath, rustling the frizzy bangs hanging past my eyebrows. I should have waited to get it done. I got a fresh relaxer yesterday, and even slept with my head hanging off the bed to preserve the curls our hairdresser put in, but they're still kind of smushy. They have frizzed and retracted with the humidity.

"Maybe Kayla can help?" Mona asks, but doubt colors her voice. We both know Kayla can't be bothered half the time.

I wish Mama was here to do it, but she and Daddy are at an event with the mayor. As usual.

"Worth a shot," I say and hope Kayla's in a good mood.

I walk up the hall to Kayla's room. Anita Baker's "Sweet Love" floats through the door. Kayla still records the Quiet Storm from the radio to a cassette tape. She's probably listening to one of her mixes. I bang on the door.

"Who is it?" she asks over the music.

I roll my eyes. She knows who it is. Our parents aren't here and only the good Lord knows where Keith is. You can bet Friday's paycheck it involves some fast tail girls and a six-pack. He's got no business messing with either, which only makes them both more appealing.

"It's Whitney Houston. Who do you think it is? Can I come in, Zee?"

The door flies open unexpectedly and I stumble forward, head first.

"What do you want?" Kayla asks, arms folded under her breasts barely contained in a skimpy tank top. "Is it time to go already? I thought the dance doesn't start 'til seven."

"Yeah, that's right." I take my life into my hands and sidestep her, entering her inner sanctum. "I was hoping you could help me with my hair?"

She tilts her head, eyes narrowing in assessment. Anita Baker serenades us while I wait, tensed and ready for rejection, until she finally shrugs.

"Meet me in the bathroom."

Thirty minutes later, not only has she restored my curls to their former glory, but she's even applied a little makeup for Mona and me. Mama still doesn't like me wearing makeup yet, but one night won't hurt.

"This red looks good on you, Tru," Kayla says. She pops her lips at me. "Do like that."

I imitate her lip pop and glance in the mirror.

"Wow." My eyes, fringed with mascara-lengthened lashes and lined with black pencil, look bigger. Darker. Older.

"Right?" Kayla leans back, studying her handiwork. "You gonna kiss it all off tonight?"

Even though I know a blush wouldn't show through my skin, I'm still glad for the color she applied to my cheeks.

"Um, I dunno." I shrug. "Maybe."

"I bet Jeremy will want to," Mona sing-songs. "He's kissed a lot of girls in our class, and they all say he's great at it."

"You've kissed a guy before, right?" Kayla asks, staring at her reflection in the mirror and combing her eyebrows.

"Not exactly," I mumble, rubbing my lips together. The glossy color feels sticky now and I'd love to wipe it off.

"Shit." Kayla goes still, her hand pausing mid-air, her eyes shifting to me. "You never been kissed, Tru?"

"It's not a big deal," I say, defensive. "Lots of girls in eighth grade haven't."

"Have you, Mona?" Kayla asks.

"Yeah, last year." Mona slides an apologetic look my way and shrugs. "Sorry."

"So this Jeremy will want to kiss you," Kayla says. "Let me show you the basics."

My sister instructs me on French kissing using her hand, doing weird things with her tongue, moaning and closing her eyes in fake rapture. I just stare at her, confused and slightly alarmed and probably traumatized.

Fast tail.

The doorbell saves me from more fake French kisses.

"That's probably Ez," I say. "Lemme go put my dress on."

I leave the bathroom and dash to my bedroom.

"I always thought Ezra would be her first boyfriend," I hear Kayla telling Mona.

A scene plays in technicolor through my memory. Ezra and me in his backyard when we were six years old. He'd been to a wedding the week before and decided we should get married. Being Ezra, he had memorized all aspects of a Jewish wedding, and we reenacted them under his elm tree. When we got to the part where the groom could kiss the bride, he pecked me on the lips and we both giggled. My heart aches a little for that day. We're only thirteen and I know there is a lot more innocence to lose, but somehow, I, too, thought we'd save all our firsts for each other. I blink back hot tears thinking of him kissing Hannah tonight with her freckles and long, curly hair. I run a careful finger under my eyes so I won't mess up Kayla's hard work and head downstairs.

"Forget you, Ezra Stern."

CHAPTER SIX

Ezra

THIS IS THE WORST NIGHT OF MY LIFE.

I take that back. The night they called to say Bubbe died—that was the worst. We knew her time was near, and Mama wanted to go to New York right away, but Dad had a meeting and asked if we could wait one more day. Through the wall, I heard Mama crying, yelling it was his fault she didn't see Bubbe one last time. I know she was just lashing out, but I know it hurt Dad, and after a few minutes of her shouting at him, he started shouting back.

Yeah, that night was definitely worse, but this one's bad, too. Neon strobe lights illuminate the dark school gymnasium, and inflated rainbows dangle from the rafters. I guess there's a theme, but I wasn't exactly on the decorating committee so I have no idea what they were going for.

Tacky teenage?

Nailed it.

Chaperones and tables of punch line the edges of the room. I press my shoulders harder into the wall at my back, unable to tear my eyes away from the dance floor.

From them.

Mona settles on the wall beside me. "They look good together, right?"

Dragging my gaze from Jeremy dancing with Kimba, his hands

resting low on her hips, I shrug. Arms folded across my chest, I pull one knee up and dig my heel into the wall. I sat in the front seat with Kayla when she drove us here, and Mona sat in the back with Kimba. Maybe I'm wearing my invisibility cape over this stupid shirt and tie because they definitely forgot I was in the car. They coached Kimba the whole ride here on how to kiss Jeremy. I dropped my forehead to the cool car window and tried to block out phrases like "his tongue in your mouth" and "just suck on it."

I glance over at Mona and notice for the first time she's got one of those weird haircuts that's longer on one side than the other.

"Why are you looking at me like that?" she asks, a knitting between her pencil-darkened brows. Why do they always think layers of paint and stuff make them look better? I do have to admit Kimba looks really pretty tonight, though I like her lips without the red stuff. They're naturally this brownish-pink color. I stare at them all the time.

"I'm not looking at you any kind of way," I lie.

"I got lipstick on my teeth?" she asks, running her tongue over them.

"No."

I can't *not* look any longer, so I find Jeremy and Kimba on the dance floor again, still swaying back and forth. If I'm not mistaken, his hands are a little closer to her butt now.

"Ooooooh." Mona nudges me, her sharp little elbow punching my ribs. "Kyle is over there all by himself."

She pats the longer side of her hair and tugs at the hem of her short dress. "I'm going to ask him to dance."

I wish I could be that bold—could just walk out onto the dance floor and tell Jeremy to let Kimba go. I'd remind her that when we were six years old, she married me, and that it should count for something. Even though everything's different now, and we're about to enter high school, and our bodies are changing and I feel weird around her most of the time, some things should always remain the same.

"You gonna be all right by yourself, Jack?" Mona asks, squinting at me in the dim light.

She calls us the *Three's Company* crew. I'm Jack, she's Janet and Kimba's Chrissy. It took me a while to let Mona in. It's always been just Kimba and me. Sure, I resented that there were "girl" things Kimba told her that I don't know about, but Mona's good people. It seems like the way I feel about Kimba is scrawled all over my face, but Mona's never picked up on it, so I guess I'm better at hiding it than I think I am. Kimba certainly doesn't know.

"I'm all right, Janet," I say wryly.

"It's called a dance for a reason. You're supposed to...ya know, dance."

"I don't dance." I shudder at the thought of forcing my lanky limbs into some kind of rhythm. "No one wants to see that."

"Guess that's your momma's side, huh?" she teases.

I roll my eyes, grin and give her the finger.

"I gotta go before somebody snatches Kyle. You sure you'll be—"

"I'll be fine."

And I am fine through another song and a half. I'm not so much a wallflower as a potted plant, stuck and stiff, unmoving in a corner.

I'm considering walking the two miles home when someone steps in front of me. "Wanna dance?"

Hannah.

She's straightened her curls and her hair hangs to her waist. Her freckles hide behind a dusting of powder. Who told her to do that? The freckles are kinda cute. She looks me in the eyes, but there's something shy on her face, like she has to make herself do it.

"Where's your brother?" I ask. "Maybe you should check with him before we dance."

"I'm so sorry about that." Hannah covers her face with her hands for a second. "He told me what he did, but I was too embarrassed to talk to you about it before. It doesn't matter what he thinks. I don't care."

It's easy for her not to care what her brother or her father think about her liking me. She's not the one who got beat up on the way home from synagogue for nothing.

"So do you wanna dance?" Hannah asks again.

I glance back to the floor where the neon strobe lights bathe Kimba and Jeremy in an array of colors. She laughs at something he says and his hand slips down another inch.

"Sure." I push off the wall, knowing I can't dance for crap, but not caring. "Only a slow one, though. If a fast song comes on, I'm walking off the floor."

"Deal," she says, her pink, glossy lips pulled into a grin.

Hannah and I are usually about the same height, but she's wearing heels so she has a couple of inches on me tonight. I find a place for my hands to *be*, somewhere between her hips and her waist. I can still see over her shoulder, and when I glance up, my eyes meet Kimba's. She smiles, but I know every one of Kimba Allen's smiles by heart, and this one looks like the one she wore when her aunt gave her "bloomers" for Christmas. I frown back and tilt my head. There's nothing about the gesture that would mean much to anyone else, but Kimba and I have been working on our telepathy since stroller days, and she knows I'm asking what's wrong.

"Nothing," she mouths, that phony smile making a mockery of how sad her eyes are.

"Did you get a lot of money for Bar Mitzvah?" Hannah asks.

"Huh?" I drag my gaze back and an inch up to Hannah's. "Bar Mitzvah?"

"Yeah, Robert got a lot of money. I just wondered if you did."

"I guess." I shrug. "It went right into my college fund."

"You get any cool gifts?"

"Uh, yeah. Someone gave me eighteen Pixie Stix."

"Like the powdered sugar candy? How is that cool?"

It's cool because Kimba took the time to understand something about my heritage—took time to research the importance of chai, the significance of eighteen. Because she knows me well enough to figure keeping Kosher had been driving me crazy and my favorite candy was the perfect way to rebel.

My eyes drift back over Hannah's shoulder, but Kimba and Jeremy aren't there anymore. I search the dance floor, the whole gym in a frantic sweep, but there's no sign of them. Then I see *him* walking back into the gym wearing a frown. He goes right over to a girl named Clarissa and speaks to her, then leads her onto the floor. No sign of Kimba.

"Um, Hannah. I need to check on something."

"Now?" Hannah asks, the confusion on her face morphing into horror. "But this isn't a fast song. They're playing 'I'll Make Love to You.' You can't walk off the dance floor in the middle of Boyz II Men."

"Sorry." I shrug and turn to leave.

"Seriously?" Hannah yells at my back while the Boyz croon. "My friends were right. You *are* weird."

I can live with weird if it means Hannah leaves me alone. I walk up to Jeremy dancing with Clarissa now, his head dipped into her neck and his hands squarely on her butt. I'm surprised a chaperone hasn't run over and called him out for it.

"Hey." I tap his shoulder.

He looks up, a scowl distorting his even features. The girls love this guy. Star basketball player. Tall. Handsome. I can see why Kimba was here with him.

"What?" he snaps. "I'm a little busy, Elijah."

I don't even bother correcting him. "Where's Kimba?"

He rolls his eyes and lowers his head back to Clarissa's neck without answering.

I jab my finger into his arm. "Where is she?"

His head snaps up and there's fire in his glare. "What the hell is wrong with you? Can't you see I'm—"

"She was dancing with you. You disappeared. Now you're back and she isn't, so where is she?"

His scowl slides into a knowing smirk. "You into her, Stern?"

I don't respond, but the mocking gleam in his eye lights a fire under my collar.

"You're such a jerk, Jeremy," Clarissa says, turning her head to look at me. "She was in the girls' bathroom a few minutes ago."

"Thanks." I jog off the dance floor and out into the corridor toward the bathrooms. It's empty, with only an overhead fluorescent panel shining light. I stop in front of the girls' restroom.

"Is this really what you're about to do, Stern?" I mutter to the empty hallway.

Yes. Yes, it is.

I ease the door open just a crack.

"Tru," I shout-whisper. "You in here?"

The acoustics in the cavernous bathroom wrap my words in echo. This is stupid and some girl will walk out half-dressed any minute and report me to a chaperone.

"Kimba, are you—"

"Ezra, yes. Dang it. What do you want?"

My shoulders sag and the tight coil in my stomach loosens a little. I ease the door open a few more inches, poking my head in to see if anyone else is visible. It's empty and before I can talk myself out of it, I speed-walk in, zipping past all the stalls until I see Kimba's red flats. I tap on the door.

"You okay?"

"You can't be in here. It's the girls' bathroom. Geez. Get out."

"I know. I will. Just...are you okay?" I hesitate. "Did he...did Jeremy hurt you or something?"

Because if he did, I don't care if he's six feet taller than I am, I'll find a way to crush him.

"No. Um, no. He didn't hurt me." Her laugh drifts under the stall door. "I probably hurt him."

I lean against the door, wanting to be closer, even though I hear her just fine. "How?"

"He tried to kiss me and I bit his lip."

A huge grin stretches over my face. It's a relief that she isn't hurt, but also a relief that she didn't want to kiss him. Or maybe she did? I don't understand.

"Why'd you bite him?"

After a moment, the handicapped stall door opens. Kimba doesn't come out, but stays in place. She doesn't look hurt, or like her dress is ripped or any of the awful things I imagined. I hesitate, then step inside and lock the stall door behind me.

"You sure you're okay?" I ask. "When Jeremy came back by himself, I thought—"

"Told you I'm fine." She leans against the wall and looks down at the floor, shrugging. "I just realized I didn't want to kiss him."

I press my lips together to fight the smile that wants to break out all over my body. "Oh. Okay."

"Did you kiss Hannah?" she asks, her voice soft, her eyes still fixed on her shoes.

"Hannah? No. I didn't want to."

"You didn't? I thought...never mind."

"I don't know why her brother thinks I like her. And I don't know why she would think I did. I've never said anything to...never."

Her head still dips so I can't see all of her face, but a smile curls the corners of her mouth. "Have you ever kissed anyone, Ez?"

I don't speak, not sure how to tell her the truth without sounding like a total dweeb. There was a time when I told her everything, but things have been changing so much lately. The way we hang out, the things she tells Mona but doesn't tell me, the way I feel around her.

"No." My answer is so hushed I barely hear it leave my lips. "But I..."

"But what?" She takes a few steps toward me. "It's okay that you haven't kissed anybody yet. I haven't either."

"Maybe we could…" I clear my throat. "Maybe we should kiss each other."

When she doesn't respond right away, I rush on. "Just to get it over with, I mean. It's not a big deal. We don't have to—"

"Okay."

I look up sharply, connecting our stares in the quiet. "Okay."

In a few steps, I erase the small space left between us, standing close enough to smell her minty gum.

"Can I do something gross?" she asks, a smile pinching her eyes at the corners.

"With your tongue?" I ask half-apprehensively, half-jokingly.

"Ez." She laughs. "No. I mean…not yet."

She reaches into her mouth, pulls out a blob of gum and sticks it to the wall right under a poem scribbled in red ink that begins "Roses are dead."

"You r-r-ready?" she asks, her eyes are steady like she's in command, but I know what Kimba's actual confidence looks like, and she's as nervous as I am, which somehow makes me feel calm. I reach for one of her hands and link our fingers and I stroke my thumb along hers.

"Can I do something weird?" I whisper.

"With your tongue?" she whispers back, her smile as bright as the fluorescent lights out in the hall.

I chuckle and shake my head. "Not yet."

With my free hand, I reach up and swipe my thumb across her bottom lip, smearing her red lip gloss.

"What are you doing?" she asks, her mouth moving under my finger.

"Taking off this lipstick stuff."

"Why?" She's turned the volume of her voice down to *secret*.

"Because I like your lips the way they always are."

Her smile dwindles into a straight line, and the laughter drains from her eyes. I trace her top lip with my index finger, swiping until the red tint of gloss is mostly gone. Even after there's barely color left, I touch her mouth unnecessarily, so soft and pillowy. I should feel self-conscious or nervous or weird. It's my first kiss, after all, but I don't. It feels, instead, like I'm walking up to a moment that's been waiting on me all my life. Since we were both born on the same day in different cities. Since Mrs. Allen plopped Kimba into the tub with me before we could even talk.

I lean forward and press my mouth to hers, tentative in case she pulls away. Holding my breath because even the effort of breathing might detract from this place between our lips that deserves all my concentration. We're still for a second or two, my lips resting against hers, our eyes open.

"Aren't we supposed to close our eyes?" she whispers, the words cool across my lips.

"Yeah. On the count of three, we'll close."

She nods.

"One," I say, not looking away from her. "Two. Three."

Her lashes, dark and long with mascara, fall, but I cheat because I don't want to miss any of it.

Eyes still closed, she says, "Kayla said we're supposed to use our tongues."

I press my mouth to hers and slide my tongue across her bottom lip. Her eyes pop open.

"Did I do it wrong?" I ask quickly.

"I don't know, but I liked it."

She liked it.

I gently squeeze her fingers and lean in again, pressing our lips together. I don't know if she means to do it, or if it's a mistake, but her mouth opens and my tongue slips inside. Hesitantly, our tongues touch, stroke, and something sweet and sharp cuts down the center of my body. I wonder if she feels it, too. We both go still, looking into each other's eyes for a few seconds.

I don't know what I'm supposed to do, but I take her bottom lip between mine, and then she takes mine between hers, and I can taste her. Taste the red punch from the dance, taste her spearmint gum, taste her *trust*, which is the sweetest thing. And then I forget to think about it, forget to worry if I'm doing it right, or if I've messed up. Our heads bob and our mouths meld and we suck each other's tongues, and it's not weird at all. It's sloppy and wet, but in the best way. A new-to-me hunger rumbles inside, not for food, but for her. Every time I taste her, suck her lips, lick inside her mouth, the hunger grows. I reach up and cup her face, needing to be deeper and wanting the whole world outside this bathroom to go away. Wanting to make our own little planet in the last stall of the girls' bathroom and never stop kissing Kimba ever.

Mariah Carey's "Vision of Love" floats in muted tones to our stall.

Beyond these walls, back in the gym, they're at the dance, but in this corner on our last night of middle school, we have our own theme. Our own rainbows and lights and music and magic. We hold each other's breath and take each other's hands, crossing our hearts and guarding our innocence. We are on the cusp of *next*, but tonight, we have right now, and it's better than everything I've ever had and must be as good as anything to come.

"Ez," Kimba gasps into my mouth. "I need to breathe."

I don't. I'd hold my breath all night if it meant I could keep kissing her, but I pull back so she can. We're both panting, our eyes locked, our fingers entwined, my hand resting at the smooth curve of her neck.

It was perfect. A snow-globe moment where everything was shaken and all my particles are still drifting to the ground, resettling into a completely new person.

"Was that okay?" I ask.

Kimba's pretty lips, soft and fuller from our kisses, pull into a wide smile. "Let's do it again."

This is the best night of my life.

CHAPTER SEVEN

Kimba

"Y'ALL MIGHTY QUIET BACK THERE," KAYLA SAYS FROM THE front seat, catching my eyes in the rearview mirror. "Everything go okay tonight?"

"Oh, yeah. So much fun."

"For sure. It was great."

The replies rush out of us, piling on top of each other. Ezra and I watch each other from the corners of our eyes, secret smiles etched onto kiss-puffy lips. Mona's mother picked her up and took her home. Kayla came at ten o'clock on the dot to get us. We're in the back, separated by a decent distance, but our fingers twine on the seat between us.

"So what happened with Jeremy?" Kayla asks, her tone tilting up in that irritating way, like she's patting my head.

Ezra's smile wobbles. I squeeze his fingers until he looks at me. I roll my eyes and smile, waiting for a real grin to come back to his face.

"Did you do it like I told you?" Kayla asks.

"I didn't kiss Jeremy." I stretch my eyes at her in the mirror. "Just drop it, Zee."

"All right," she says, carefully maneuvering her pride and joy into our driveway. "You're starting high school in a few months. What are you waiting for?"

The perfect moment. The perfect person. That's what I had tonight.

"Hmmm." Kayla frowns at the garage door lifting to reveal my parents' Mercedes. "Mama and Daddy are already home."

The steel and chrome gleams in the overhead light of the garage. Kayla turns, propping one arm on the passenger seat and splitting a look between Ezra and me. "Out. The both of you. Tell them I'll be home by midnight."

"Where you going?" I ask, folding my arms across my chest and settling back like I'm not leaving until she talks.

"Nunya," she says, a wicked grin spreading her lips.

"Tommy." Exasperation makes me suck my teeth. "I thought you were done with him. You guys break up once a week."

"I decide when I'm done," she says. "Now get outta my ride."

Ezra climbs out immediately. I open my door and get out, but lean into the open window of the passenger side. "Don't do anything I wouldn't do."

"I'm not going to a convent, so I'm sure there will be plenty of things you wouldn't do."

"Whatever, Zee." I tap the roof of the car and watch her taillights when she pulls out and drives off.

Ezra stands in my driveway. He glances up the street and huffs a breath. Mrs. Washington stands on her porch watering the row of plants marching down her steps. Really? At this time of night? She uses those plants as an excuse to get the 411 when something's going down in the neighborhood.

Ezra takes my hand and leads me into the garage. He doesn't lower the door and doesn't let my hand go.

"Tonight...was..." He shakes his head and frowns.

Frowns? I thought it was perfect. I want to kiss him again right now. Did he not feel the same?

"Did I...did I do something wrong?" I ask. "Was it—"

"No." Ezra links our fingers and holds my gaze. "The opposite. It was exactly right. The best first kiss ever."

Relieved breath whooshes from my chest, and our smiles meet in the middle, between us.

"I was just thinking," he says. "You're my best friend." He looks up expectantly, leaving me space to respond.

"Yeah. Same. You're mine, too. My best friend, I mean. You know that."

"I was thinking about Tommy and Kayla. And all the people who break up and get back together and break up again. I don't want us to be like that."

"Are we…are we together? I know we kissed, but I wasn't sure if—"

"I like you, Tru," he says softly, his eyes lowered to the garage floor. "If you don't feel the same way then—"

"I do." I step closer and grab his other hand. "That's how I feel."

His smile comes on slowly, pinching at the corners like he's trying to contain it. "Okay. Good."

He sobers and glances up and pulls our hands between our chests. "I don't ever want something stupid to ruin our friendship. People break up all the time, and it freaks me out that something might…change, and then we wouldn't be friends."

"Yeah. I get that." I bite my lip and nod.

"So, pact."

"Pact?" I laugh. "Like the pacts we made when we were kids? Like we wouldn't ever summon the Candy Man? Or when we were seven, that I wouldn't tell anyone where you buried that candy pop ring?"

"You take that information to the grave, Kimba Allen," he says with false gravity. "You crossed your heart and everything."

"I'll never tell." My chuckle settles into a smile. "So what's this pact?"

His eyes trace my face, rest on my lips and send flutters through my belly. He holds his pinky finger out to me.

"Our pact is that we'll always be friends," he says, his voice quiet, sure. "That nothing will come between us, not even each other."

Not even each other.

I'm not completely sure what that means, but I hook my finger with his. "Pact."

"We should kiss on it," he says, tugging me closer by my pinky.

I'm breathless, waiting for our lips to touch and for that feeling I had in the bathroom to take over my whole body again.

"Damn you, Ruth!" Mr. Stern's angry voice travels from inside my house when our lips are separated by just a breath.

"Let me explain," Ezra's mother says, her words reaching us in the garage.

"*You can't explain this!*" he shouts back. "We're leaving, and that's final."

Leaving?

Our wide eyes connect, fear and panic rising inside me at the threat of Ezra's leaving. We hear the front door open so violently it slams against the house. Hurried footfalls pound down the steps. Leaving my house, Mr. Stern almost walks right past the open garage, but double-takes when he sees us inside. Fury twists his features.

"Come on, Ezra," he snaps. "We're going home."

"But, Dad, I—"

"Now, Ezra!" his father roars so loudly I'm sure Mrs. Washington got an earful while fake-watering her plants.

"Okay. Okay." Ezra drops my hand and leans forward to kiss me quickly. It's just a peck, but maybe he feels the little thrill like I do, because he lingers. He presses closer and slips his tongue inside. It feels good and right. I lift my hand to touch the thick curls at his nape.

"Ezra!" Mr. Stern yells from their porch across the street. "I'm not telling you again. Come. Now."

"Ezra," Mrs. Stern says, watching us through the open garage door. "Listen to your father. Come home."

"Okay." Ezra walks toward his mother, but turns at the last minute and glances at me over his shoulder, his eyes serious.

"I'll see you tomorrow," he says softly with his mother standing there waiting.

I nod, a strange feeling unfolding inside of me as my parents' raised voices reach me from inside the house.

"Okay. Tomorrow."

Mrs. Stern's face is tear-streaked and her hair is mussed, unusual because her appearance is always neat. Her mouth trembling, she looks at me for a long moment before speaking.

"Goodbye, Kimba," she says and touches Ezra's shoulder, urging him to walk away.

I close the garage and step cautiously through the kitchen door, being as quiet as I can in case I catch fragments of the argument.

"That's not fair, Joe," my mother says, tears in her voice. "How could you even…"

It goes quiet in the living room, a listening quiet.

"Tru?" she asks abruptly. "Is that you?"

I sigh and drag my feet from the kitchen to the base of the stairs in the foyer. My parents stand on opposite sides of the room, a gulf between them. My father's whiskey decanter sits on the coffee table, a rare sight since they don't drink much. Broken glass litters the bricks in front of the fireplace.

"What's happening?" I ask. "The Sterns—"

"Are not our friends," my father says harshly. "Stay away from them."

"No." It comes out before I even realize it, but I refuse to apologize. "Whatever you and the Sterns are fighting about, I don't care, but Ezra—"

"What did I say, Kimba?" my father growls, his face so distorted by rage that I don't even recognize him.

"But Daddy—"

"Go to your room," Mama says, her voice soft and firm and unyielding.

"Mama, I—"

"Go to your room!" she screams, tears leaking from beneath her closed eyelids. "For God's sake, can you for once just do what you're told and stay out of grown folks' business? Go to your damn room, Kimba!"

Mama never curses at me. I fight back my own tears and run up the steps. Their argument resumes downstairs, but muted, deliberately low-voiced and hiding. I run to their room and grab the phone on their bedside table. I could dial Ezra's number in my sleep. My fingers fly over the keypad without any thought, but the line is busy. I try again and again, but I can't get through. After a few minutes, I go to my room and flop onto my bed, not even bothering to wrap my hair or take off my dress.

It feels like I've lived a year in the span of a night. I don't know what's going on between our parents, but I do know what's going on between Ezra and me. We are *beginning*. I kissed my best friend and things will never be the same. Whatever happens between our folks, we have each other. And we'll always be friends.

In the morning, I wake up to sunlight pouring through my open window. My mouth is cottony, my dress is wrinkled, and I'm still wearing the shoes I thought all night were a little too tight. I kick them off, slide from the bed and find my flip flops. I don't even bother to change, but dash down the stairs and out the front door.

I come to a halt right on my porch. Mrs. Stern stands in their driveway loading suitcases into the trunk of their car. Ezra is tossing a duffle bag into the back seat when he sees me. He stops, glances at his mother and crosses the yard to meet me. My heart see-saws, happy to see him and scared to see him go.

"Ezra," Mrs. Stern says firmly. "We need to go."

He throws her an angry look, ignores her and comes up onto the porch. "Hey," he says, his voice subdued.

"Hey." I lick my lips and ask the obvious question. "W-w-where are you g-g-going?"

The harshness leaves his face and he reaches for my hand. "To New York."

"New York?" I ask, my chest tightening. "But camp's not for another t-t-two weeks."

Each summer, Ezra goes to Jewish summer camp near his bubbe. Even though she passed away, he was still planning to go this year.

"We're going early." A muscle in his jaw tightens. "Mama says we need to get away. My father's not coming with us."

"Why can't you stay here?" I ask, my voice plaintive, almost begging.

Ezra shrugs, a frown collapsing between his brows again. "They won't let me."

"But y-y-you'll be back, right?" I bite my tongue until tears prick my eyes. I hate how my words won't come out when I need them most—when it's most important.

"I'll be back." He glances around. His mother walks into their house, but leaves the car running. No one is out, not even Mrs. Washington. The neighborhood allows us a rare slice of privacy.

Ezra touches his forehead to mine and cups my neck.

The tears overflow, sliding down my cheeks and salting the corners of my mouth. I'm losing something. I'm losing him. I know it. Even though he says he'll be back. I just know...

"Don't go." It's a wet whisper that I can't hold back. "Ezra, I have a bad feeling. Like I won't ever see you again."

Even saying it, the words corkscrew right through my heart.

"It's only for the summer," he says, pulling back and lifting my chin, giving me a smile I know is forced. "I'll be back before school starts. You think I'd miss our freshman year in high school?"

I hesitate, but shake my head. "Ezra, kiss me."

He searches my face for a second, looks around, up the street that's never this quiet, this empty on a Saturday morning, and leans forward to press our lips together, slipping his tongue into my mouth. We're still tentative, barely sure we're doing it right, our lips and tongues clinging and wet and sweet. I thought it might have been the music or the decorations, the dance or the moment that made last night's kiss magical, but it's none of those things.

It's us.

That magic is still there when the only music is the distant buzz of someone cutting their lawn one street over. Still there when the mood lighting is nothing more than sunshine.

"Ezra," Mrs. Stern says.

We break our kiss and look up. She's at the car, elbows leaned on the roof on the driver's side. Her gaze flicks between us, her eyes sad and red-rimmed. "We have to go now, son."

The lump in my throat swells, hot and huge, and I refuse to release his hand for a second. I throw my arms around him and bury my face in his neck. His skinny arms tighten around me, and I feel his tears on my neck, too.

Don't go.

I want to make him stay, to beg him not to leave, to not ignore this awful feeling in the pit of my stomach, but Mrs. Stern honks the horn and climbs behind the steering wheel.

I love you, Ez.

It sounds ridiculous even in my own head, in my thoughts. We're thirteen. What do we know about love? The kiss, these feelings are so new, I can't make myself form the words, so I say the one word that will always mean the same thing to us no matter what.

"Pact," I whisper.

Ezra nods, sniffs and slowly lets me go, running his eyes over my face like maybe he thinks it's the last time, too. "Pact."

PART TWO

*"...It feels less like I am getting to know you
and more as though I am remembering who you are."*

— Lang Leav, *Soul Mates*

CHAPTER EIGHT

Kimba
Present Day

"WOULD YOU LIKE TO MAKE HISTORY, CONGRESSMAN?"

I've lost track of how many leaders I've asked that question. They always say yes, the thought of breaking ground intoxicating them into a knee-jerk response. It's usually the ones who answer fastest who don't even make a dent. The ones who take their time replying, who ponder it for a second, often have the best chance of changing the world. Phone pressed to my ear in the beats of silence while I wait for Mateo Ruiz, the Georgia congressman, to reply, I can practically hear him counting the cost, weighing his next words.

"Yes," he finally says. "And I look forward to your support."

"You'll have it." I press through my own hesitation to make the risky play. "I'd love to lead the charge for the first Hispanic governor of Georgia. My firm has a proven track record."

Understatement, since we just elected the sitting president.

"That you do," Mateo agrees. "I'm still figuring out the composition of our team, but I'll keep you in mind."

Keep me in mind? My phone hasn't stopped ringing since word got out that I turned down a cabinet position in the new administration. Every candidate on my side of the aisle worth their salt wants me running their campaign, yet the one candidate I actually want to

"Who else are you considering?" I ask, uninterested in beating around the bush.

"You're on a very short list, Kimba," he says dryly. "You know that."

"Me and...let me guess. Anthony Rodderick?"

His chuckle confirms I guessed right. "Anthony has a lot to offer, and he's a native son."

"I grew up in Atlanta. My family's one of the most influential in the city. You know that. I have a personal stake in seeing the first minority governor of my home state."

"I know you do, and of course I recognize the weight of the Allen name in Atlanta. You know Atlanta, but there's Atlanta and then the rest of the state, which we both know is a different demographic."

"Oh, I see. You think you need a good ol' boy to win the good ol' boys. Someone like me couldn't possibly understand anything beyond Atlanta city limits, even though I just elected a president for all *fifty* states."

"I need stability, and your company is in transition. I'm ecstatic to have our first Indigenous First Lady, but Lennix was half of Hunter, Allen & Associates. If we're honest, she was the face of it."

No one to blame but myself. I should have nothing to prove at this stage of my career, but I'm still being questioned. Still being tried. To some degree, I shot myself in the foot all those years ago making sure my business partner Lennix was the one on camera. My abhorrence for public speaking, always pushing her out there, led many to believe Lennix was running the show alone. Now that she's gone, some wonder if there's still a show.

Well there is, and I'm running it.

"With all due respect, Congressman, you won't need a face to win your election. You'll need a sharp political mind, experience and determination, all of which I have. While I understand your concerns about stability during this transition, I still have the most hungry, talented team in the business. None of our campaigns will suffer."

"Like I said, I'll keep you in mind."

I want to tell him he can keep this middle finger in mind, but then I remember how much I actually like him—that I agree with him on policy, on principle. That I honestly believe the things he wants to do might just transform the lives of the working poor and middle class in my home state. That means something to me. It's the bigger picture, and it's worth me setting my pride and ego aside long enough to wait for the answer I want.

Daddy used to say don't talk about it. *Be* about it. The fastest way to shut up someone who thinks you can't do something is to *do* something. Two years since he passed away, and his words continue to guide me every day.

"Yes, please keep me in mind, Congressman," I say, executing an internal *whoosah*. "I admire Anthony deeply and respect all he's done, but I think I'm the best person to lead you to victory in Georgia. I hope you'll come to agree."

He chuckles. "No one can ever say you lack confidence, Kimba."

"I'm a woman, a black woman at that, working in a male world. If I waited on other people to believe in me, I wouldn't get very far, and neither would my clients. And I take my clients far, Congressman." I let that sink in because we both know I just took one to Pennsylvania Avenue. "Get in touch when you're ready to talk."

He's one of the good ones. That rare politician who isn't a narcissist and who is actually in it for the people more than for himself. Because it's always a *little* for ourselves. While I wait for him to arrive at the right conclusion—that we should work together—I'll do a little work on my own. I'll search for things like tucked-away mistresses, hidden drug habits, brushed-under-the-rug convictions. Every closet has skeletons. I like to drag my candidates' dirty secrets out into the open before we even begin. If I can dig and find them, so can anyone else. I'm an *on the offensive* kinda girl, so I dig first and I dig deep.

"I'll be in touch," he says. "Either way."

Motion at the office door distracts me. My assistant, Carla, taps her watch and lifts her brows to disappear beneath purple-tinted bangs. My next appointment must be here. Considering who my next appointment is, I'm surprised she didn't just burst through the door. After all, this used to be her company, too.

"Congressman, I have to go." We disconnect and Carla smiles her satisfaction as she turns to leave.

My office door opens and a huge man walks in, speaking into a mic at his sleeve, his bulk shrinking the room.

"Excuse me?" I toss my cell phone onto the desk and lean my hip against the edge. "Did you just barge into my office?"

"I have to clear the space before the First Lady enters," he intones absently, walking around the room and checking I *suppose* for explosives.

"Uh-huh. I figured, but they *do* teach you to knock at the Secret Service, right?"

"Yes, ma'am," he says, a little color creeping into his cheeks. "Sorry about that."

"We all clear?" I ask with a teasing smile.

"All clear," he says into the mic, allowing a small smile of his own.

I quickly forget his rudeness when Lennix rushes in, arms extended.

"Kimba," she says, squeezing me like I'm a raft in rushing rapids. "Thank God."

I squeeze her back and then pry her arms from my neck after a few seconds. "Whoa, there, little koala."

"I'm sorry." She pulls away, grinning wryly. "I'm just glad to see a normal person."

She glances over her shoulder to where Secret Service man stands at the door like a centurion.

"Hal, thank you for checking the room," Lennix says. "You can wait outside."

Uncertainty skitters across his face for a moment, tightening the corners of his eyes and lips. He opens his mouth, probably poised to object, but Lennix holds up one hand and points to the door with the other.

"Thank you, Hal."

He turns to leave and closes the door behind himself.

"He's new," she says, rolling her eyes. "And zealous."

"Not one of the normal people, I gather." I cross the office to sit down on the couch and pat the cushion beside me. "Come tell Mama all the things."

When she walks over and sits, her dress pulls taut over her middle, revealing a little baby bump.

"Oh my God!" I touch the small mound, breaking pregnant lady etiquette because that's my godchild in there. "Look at our little peanut."

Her grin widens and her gray eyes light up. "I know. I've never been so happy about gaining weight."

"I bet Maxim is crazy protective and over the moon."

"All of the above and more. He's ecstatic. We both are." She rubs a hand over the little bump lovingly, her expression softening. "But it's happening when there's so much pressure, so much scrutiny, and people underfoot all the time. It feels like I'm rarely alone, much less alone with

Maxim."

She glances around the office, furnished with items we chose together when we first opened our political consulting firm. "I kinda miss normal life."

"Fuck normal. We are not normal chicks." I relax into the corner of the sofa and cross my legs. "We are in the League of Extraordinary Bitches. You hear me? You are the first Native American First Lady this country's ever had. Damn right it's pressure. Your agenda is the most ambitious we've ever seen from a First Lady, so yeah, it's hard, but you've got this."

When she first announced that her agenda was simply women, everyone asked her to elaborate. Just...women? Equal pay for women. Reforming maternity rights for women. Secondary education for women. She has assembled the Cabinet on Women's Empowerment, a body of experts who craft programs and solicit support from the corporate sector to partner with government initiatives.

"I'm so glad you're on the CWE," Lennix says, blowing out a breath. "I wish you'd reconsider the position Maxim offered you in *his* cabinet, though, so you'd be around the White House even more."

"As tempting as Chief of Staff is, it's like a desk job when I need to be in the field. This is where I belong. I want to be in the trenches and continuing the work we set out to do."

"I get it," Lennix says, almost wistfully. "You know how hard it was for me to walk away from our mission."

"You didn't walk away. You are *doing* our mission on a scale we never could have imagined." I waggle my eyebrows. "Speak to power? Honey, you *sleep* with power. When your baby's daddy is the leader of the free world, I'd call that on mission."

"I can't complain." Lennix laughs throatily, leaning back and resting her head on the couch. "Except it's you, and you're my best friend so you have to let me complain."

"Yup. Part of the job description." I wag a finger at her. "But so is telling you the truth. You are exactly where you belong and where you can do the most good right now. You have everything to be grateful for." I tip my head toward the closed door. "Other than Robocop out there acting like a bloodhound, sniffing for bombs under my Queen Anne desk. What's up with Mr. High Alert?"

"Like I said..." She smiles and shakes her head. "He's new. I do get tired of the constant Secret Service presence, but I get it. And they are so over the top now that the word is out I'm pregnant."

"We haven't had a baby in the White House since…" I frown, thinking back. "Wow. Since the Kennedys."

"Yeah, we're hoping for a better ending," she says dryly. "Thus all the hyper protection. There's like four more where Hal came from out in the lobby."

"Oh, I bet Carla is salivating. You know she loves a big man."

Right on cue, a knock comes and my assistant pokes her head around the door. There's a flush on her pale cheeks and her purple hair is slightly disheveled like she's run her fingers through it.

"Should I feed those men out there?" she whispers. "I could order lunch for everyone."

"That won't be necessary," Lennix says. "I'm not staying long, but thank you, Carla."

"Don't rush off," Carla says, her cheeks going pinker. "Really. It's no trouble."

"Don't get distracted by all those muscles," I warn playfully, "and miss my delivery."

"It just came." Carla's grin is abashed. "Should I bring it in?"

"Sure. Thanks, lady." I rub my hands together. "This is the dress I'm wearing to the awards ceremony in Atlanta. My family's foundation is honoring community leaders."

I always make sure our foundation has plenty of donations, but my limited hands-on involvement has been a sore point. My mother insisted I attend this event, and I'm actually looking forward to it.

Carla walks back through the door carrying a huge brown box. I gesture toward the work table on the other side of my office, thanking her as she leaves. Once the box is laid out, I tear through the packaging to find another box inside, this one white, emblazoned with the word *gLo,* and tied with a wide purple ribbon.

"I didn't know it was one of Lotus Ross' designs," Lennix breathes, touching the silk bow. "You guys know each other?"

"We met at the Image Awards not too long ago. She's a riot. You'd love her."

"I adore her stuff. That last line was fire."

"Are you kidding? She'll send you anything you want. A chance to dress the First Lady? What designer wouldn't jump at that opportunity?"

"I've been careful to make sure I'm wearing things by up-and-coming designers when possible, especially indigenous women. It's such a great way to draw attention to those who might get overlooked."

"I wouldn't exactly call Lotus overlooked," I say dryly, "since she just won the CFDA for womenswear designer of the year, but she's still pretty new to the game, so that kind of exposure could only help."

When I lift the lid of the white box and peel the fragile tissue paper away, Lennix and I both gasp.

"Holy crap," Lennix says, running her fingers lightly over the golden silk. "This will look fantastic on you."

"It was literally made for me." I lift the dress from the box, revealing the gilded fall of shimmering fabric. "Lo sketched it over drinks when I was in LA a couple months ago."

"You have to try it on." Lennix presses her palms together in a begging pose. "I wanna see."

"Okay! You lock the door. I'll get the windows."

While Lennix walks briskly to lock the door, I draw the drapes across the floor-to-ceiling windows overlooking the chaos of D.C. traffic and commerce. I rush back to the work table, anticipation humming through my every molecule. My girly reflex is fully activated. I'm already thinking about the Manolos I found to go with the dress, mentally accessorizing and wondering if I should wear my hair blown out or upswept and in its natural curls. Without self-consciousness, I strip off my slacks and blouse, standing in only panties and bra. Lennix and I are in that "over ourselves" stage of friendship you reach through time and trial. She, along with our friend Vivienne, were my extended family so far from home. I carefully slide the silk up to my thighs, frowning when it catches there.

"What the…" I mutter when the material only inches up incrementally, not quite clearing my hips. It pulls so tight that if I force it, the dress will probably rip.

"Oh." Lennix bites her bottom lip and tilts her head to the side. "Well, it…did she maybe send the wrong size?"

"I told you. She made it for me. One of these exists in the whole world, and Lo confirmed my measurements no more than ten days ago. I don't get it."

"I'm sorry, babe. Well, if we—" Her phone buzzes on the work table. She grabs it, still eyeing me with consternation. She glances down and grimaces. "Ugh. Dammit. I forgot we added a meeting to my schedule this morning. It's on possible legislation for improved maternity leave. Something with teeth. My secretary just reminded me."

"Go." I waddle over to her, careful not to make any sudden dress-ripping moves, and give her a quick squeeze. "Be the badass bitch First Lady I know you can be."

"And here I was looking for a motto when you had that up your sleeve this whole time," she says, the sarcasm thick, but still not eclipsing the concern when she pulls back from our hug. "Kimba, the dress—"

"It's fine." I force a smile. "I have a dozen dresses that should work."

If I can fit any of them.

"You get outta here. I don't want you to be late."

"Okay." She rushes to the office door and unlocks and opens it. Hal stands there, blocking our view of the lobby and Carla, who is probably on her fainting couch with all that broody testosterone in forced proximity.

"Love you," Lennix offers as a final parting and closes the door behind her.

"Love you, too," I mumble absently, staring down the length of my body with dismay. I've noticed a few lumps and rolls that stubbornly resisted four days a week of Orange Theory, but didn't realize it had gotten this out of control. I've been busy strategizing how I'll turn a swing state in an upcoming gubernatorial election. Lumps and rolls around my middle got back-burnered.

My cell rings and I grimace when Lotus pops up on FaceTime. I want to ignore it and call back audio only so she won't see me.

I answer, being careful to keep the phone aimed above my shoulders.

"Hey, Lo." I inject my voice with the enthusiasm the woman who has become a close friend would usually merit.

"Heyyyyyy." Her pretty face, surrounded by a huge, curly afro, lights up. "My assistant just told me we got a delivery notification on the dress. How is it?"

"It's..." I glance at the material pooled below my waist. "A little tight."

"Tight?" Lotus' sleek black brows snap into a frown. "It shouldn't be. We finalized measurements not long ago."

"It's not you," I rush to reassure her. "I've been gaining weight lately faster than I ever have in my life."

"Everything okay?"

"Yeah, but um..." I make sure the door is still closed. "I've also missed four periods."

The reaction is instant and comes with a boom.

"What the hell, Kimba?" Lotus' husky voice pops me on the head through the screen. "Did you take a pregnancy test?"

"Several." I groan and tilt my head back to contemplate the ceiling. "All negative."

"But *could* you be?"

I think back to my last hook-up. A unisex bathroom at the networking mixer off Fourteenth Street. It's a blur of hand-blown chandeliers, bottomless mojitos, blond hair, hazel eyes, a medium-sized dick and a DIY orgasm, but I *know* we used protection. And I have IUD insurance.

"It shouldn't be possible," I say on a long exhale. "I took all the precautions, but nothing's fail-proof, right?"

"Well, something must be up."

"I have an appointment with my doctor. They drew blood a few days ago and are running several tests. I go in to discuss the results tomorrow."

"Okay, we'll figure it out, but first things first." Lotus narrows dark eyes at me through the screen. "How much do we need to alter the dress so you can have it in time for the event?"

I reluctantly scroll the phone down my half-clothed figure to show her the poorly-fitting garment.

"Oh." Lotus pastes on a smile. "I can work with that."

"Lo, don't play me."

"No, I'm serious. Get Carla to take new measurements. Ship it to me next day. I'll make the alterations myself with a little wiggle room and send it back immediately. Sound good?"

I swallow a lump in my throat, put there partially by her kindness and partially by the problem I've tried to shove to the back of my mind for weeks. It has pushed its way front and center today.

I paste on a smile of my own. "Thanks, Lo. Sounds great."

CHAPTER NINE

Ezra

"**S**HOULD WE TRY TO MAKE LOVE?"

Aiko presses her naked body to my back. She wasn't nude when she came to bed last night, so I guess she stripped to enact this little scene. Her question feels clinical, premediated compared to how we first came together nearly a decade ago.

I was getting my Ed.D. at UCLA, and a classmate dragged me to a party in Sawtelle, where I had off-campus housing. Outside, Aiko was running some kind of makeshift photo booth from a gazebo. We were instantly attracted, and I made a rare departure from my usually cautious coupling protocol. Within hours, we were in her tiny bedroom screwing loudly and raucously, trying our best between giggles and orgasms not to wake her ornery roommate.

Should we try to make love?

That urgent, passionate night feels like a millennium ago beside her tentative question this morning. For a moment, I consider faking a snore, but it's that kind of avoidance behavior that has dragged this out for months.

Years?

Though Aiko and I never married, we've been together ten years, all Noah's life and nearly a quarter of mine.

"Ezra?" Aiko pokes her breasts into my bare back. "Did you hear me? Are you awake?"

"I'm up," I say, my voice sleep-scratched and reluctant.

"And?" She slides her hand around to my cock. "You want to? Should we try?"

Try? Does she even hear herself?

"It shouldn't be this hard, Ko." I shift so her hand slides to my hip.

She deliberately moves her hand back to my dick and squeezes. "Feels *hard* enough to me."

She squeezes my dick, I get hard. That's biology, but it's not a substitute for the healthy relationship we both deserve. We're in our thirties, not college students looking for a quick hook-up. I've given in to physical urges for years, hoping it would restore what we once had.

Intimacy. Passion.

But it hasn't and I'm no longer sure how to fix what is broken. Not between our bodies, but between our hearts.

She rolls away, the sheet snapping when she jerks it back with an angry flourish. Her feet hit the floor.

"I'm sorry," she says, drawing a deep breath. "It's just so frustrating. I don't know why this is happening to us."

I roll to sit up on my side of the bed and run weary hands through my hair. "We need to talk, Ko. Maybe it's time to…"

I glance over my shoulder and see her seated on the edge of the bed, faced away from me, her naked back bowed, her dark head bent. "God, Ezra. We have a son. We've been together so long. You're this quick to give up on us?"

"Quick?" My laugh emerges as scornful despite my best intentions. "We've been to couples' counseling. We've done date nights. Tried sex in public to fix this. Every damn thing Dr. Cairns recommended, we tried, and things aren't getting better." My words fall on us, a shower of pebbles that hurt when they land on us both. "Things have gotten worse, Ko."

"We haven't tried everything," Aiko says, her voice hesitant, hushed.

I stand, stretch and walk over to the window, pulling back the drapes to study Noah's garden out back. The sprinkler isn't on. I could have sworn I set the timer last night.

Aiko comes to stand in front of me, sandwiching her small body between my bare torso and the window. She's donned one of her colorful robes. With her long straight hair, dark eyes and golden skin, she's gorgeous. She's also a brilliant photographer and a remarkable mother to my son. It's easy to see why we began, but with our chemistry shriveled and dried and the arguments over nothing increasing—it's hard to see us making it much further.

"Ezra, we haven't tried everything Dr. Cairns suggested," she says again.

"What haven't we tried?" I ask, glancing over her head to inspect the tomatoes below, easy enough since barefoot she only reaches the middle of my chest.

"An open relationship."

My eyes jerk from a row of peas to her determined expression with her wide, tight mouth, set jaw and pleading eyes. "We didn't try it because it's a bad idea. You actually think me fucking someone else is the answer?"

"Maybe *me* fucking someone else is."

She probably says that to get a rise out of me, but we're past that. At least, I am. "Doesn't the fact that you want to sleep with another guy tell you something?"

"Maybe we just need a jolt, and experimenting a little could do that. Dr. Cairns' suggestion about an open relationship was to *save* what we have, not end it. You once asked me to marry you, Ezra."

"And you refused. You did us both a favor."

"You only asked because I was pregnant."

We'd only been dating five months when she realized she was pregnant. My mother had asked in horror if Aiko was planning to raise her grandson as *Hindu?* Hearing that most Vietnamese are Buddhist, not Hindu, didn't make Mama feel any better. I assured her my girlfriend didn't practice anything except photography. Aiko's profession is her religion, and she's practically evangelical in her zeal for it. She is about as much a practicing Buddhist as I am a Jew, despite my mother's efforts.

"You know I don't believe in marriage," Aiko says, "but we're as close as I'll ever come. You don't just discard that after so many years."

There are lots of ways I could pick this argument apart. One of the main reasons I haven't is still asleep down the hall.

Noah.

It's so simple with the three of us living under the same roof. I *cannot* see my son less. I want to read with him *every* night before he goes to bed. Breaking up with Aiko means breaking this arrangement, and things may have cooled between us sexually and emotionally, but we're still a family. We've raised an extraordinary little human so far, knock on wood, and we make a good team. I had no reason to disrupt that, but I'm afraid the disintegrating romance is now eroding everything else.

She loops her arms around my neck and lifts up to whisper in my ear. "Even if I fuck someone else, I'll always want to fuck you. I still want you, Ezra, and you still want me. Remember Taco Tuesday?"

Our whole neighborhood gathers for tacos every Tuesday, and one night a few weeks ago the patio bartender had a heavy hand. Wednesday morning, I had a hangover, hazy memories and regret to show for it. I'm not a monk. Every morning in the shower, my sexual frustration goes down the drain. I can't explain it other than we've been living like roommates for so long, practically platonically, that sex with Aiko just doesn't feel right anymore. Something can feel good, but not feel *right*. That night, we may have managed to feel good for a few moments, but I can't remember the last time we felt right together.

"It was the margaritas." I reach up to gently disentangle her hand from around my neck. Her arms flop to her side and she looks up at me, her expression earnest.

"It was beautiful. We slept together and it was beautiful again," Aiko says, though I don't know if she even believes that. I was too wasted to remember if it was beautiful or not. "I just want to get back to us."

"And this is your solution?" I shake my head. "Not interested. I don't want an open relationship. Or one that feels like..."

A prison.

I don't say it because I don't want to hurt her, but our life together, that bed when we're beside each other, feels like a cell. I still care about her deeply, admire her. But I want to be her friend again, not her inmate.

"Remember in counseling when we talked about what we saw growing up?" I ask, taking a different tack. "What we saw in our parents and how it affects us?"

"Yeah," she says, her eyes resigned because she knows my family history—probably knows what I'm going to say. She never met her father, a Japanese man who died before he could give her much more than her name.

"We've been struggling for a while, but I wanted to make this work for so many reasons. I wanted us to be a family for Noah. I wanted it to work because you're fantastic, and who wouldn't want to spend their life with you?" I sit on the edge of the window sill, looking out at our backyard, the garden Noah and I planted, the memories we've made here as a family.

"But you know what I've come to realize?" I ask, shifting my gaze back to Aiko. "I also tried to make it work because I grew up seeing *my* parents trying to make it work. Saw this huge gulf between them grow bigger and bigger, and the love that brought them together in the first place wasn't enough to fill it. They never gave up on the marriage, but somewhere along the way, they gave up on each other."

I take her hand and look into the familiar dark eyes swimming with bright tears. "I'd rather give up on this relationship than give up on you, Ko, and if we continue down this road, I'm afraid we'll keep going through the motions but end up resenting each other."

"You resent me?"

"No, but I think there's something you need that I'm not giving you and something I need that I'm not getting."

"Is it that piece of paper?" Her voice is dismissive, her tone bordering on derisive. "You're such a traditionalist. If we'd gotten married, would you be 'getting what you needed'?"

She's right. In a lot of ways I am traditional. I did always think I'd get married, even when I was young. In the midst of this thorny conversation, a memory sprouts, a fragile bud that opens, reminding me of my earliest ideas of marriage and family and what it meant to choose one person for the rest of your life.

When I was six years old, I got married on a spring day in my backyard. The bride wore a Paula Abdul T-shirt that declared *Straight Up* on the front. There was a tiny hole in the toe of her Keds, and her pink sock poked through it. Her hair was artfully arranged into two afro puffs. The groom wore a Superman cape and swimming trunks. Who knows why six-year-old Ezra was obsessed with swimming trunks, but there you have it. Mama had taken me to Aunt Rose's wedding in New York, and I knew as soon as I got back to Atlanta, my best friend and I should get married.

For once, Kimba let me have my way.

The low-hanging branches of the elm tree out back formed our chuppah. I couldn't remember any of the Sheva Brachot, so I made up my own seven blessings. I'm pretty sure they were things like all-you-can-eat pizza and Super Mario Brothers high scores. I grabbed two tabs from cans of Coke in the refrigerator for our rings. I can still feel the cold metal encircling my finger. I couldn't remember why they broke the glass at Aunt Rose's wedding, but we dropped one of Mama's mason jars on a rock, jumping back and laughing when it shattered everywhere.

And that was it. We were married. Kimba said we shouldn't tell the grown-ups because they wouldn't understand, and we should wait 'til we were older. She always seemed to know best, so I agreed.

"Ezra," Aiko prods. "Would marriage make a difference?"

I clear my throat, refocusing my attention to look her straight in the eye. "No, I don't think we should get married, but you keep bringing up this open relationship. Tell me the truth. Is there someone you want to sleep with?"

To her credit, she doesn't flinch, but I know her. That left eye twitches, which gives her away when she tries to lie or hide something from me. It's how I always beat her in poker.

"There's a guy I might..." She tightens the robe belt at her small waist. "Might be interested in. You know the photography safari I'm going on next week?"

"Yeah."

"He's, um, going, too," she says quickly, licking her lips.

Now it makes sense. She wants me to agree to this ridiculous open relationship so she and her fuck buddy can have at it for a month in the Serengeti.

"It's not just me," she says hastily. "An open relationship would mean expanding the parameters of fidelity for us both. I know you've been faithful. So have I, always, but isn't there someone you've...ya know, been attracted to?"

I swallow hard, not quite catching the memory I suppress on a regular basis before it rises up to torture me. Kimba Allen, all grown up and grieving at her father's funeral two years ago. So lush leaning into me. I wasn't prepared for the hug—hadn't expected to *feel* her. The elegant black dress had caressed her full, firm curves, and I'd curled my hand reflexively at her waist. I hadn't wanted to let go. As children we'd been close, but the thing I felt when I saw Kimba for the first time since the summer of ninth grade? It was more. Instantly more, and the kind of attraction a man feels for a woman. In just those few moments, it felt real and deep in a way I couldn't remember the last time I'd had. By then, Aiko and I were already in counseling and things weren't great. My strong response to Kimba warned it wouldn't be wise to maintain contact, but I'd still started the question.

"Should we..."

Exchange numbers? Stay in touch? Hold on tight?

I didn't ask, but she looked at me, *read me,* I think.

And answered the question with goodbye.

She saw my son. She saw Aiko. She may have even felt the instant connection that sprang fully born inside of me as soon as I laid eyes on her after twenty years, and she knew it was dangerous. So did I, but some reckless part of me wanted to say *fuck it. Message me. Talk to me. Sit on the phone with me for hours and I'll listen to you breathe.*

Just come back into my life, Tru. I want to keep feeling this.

But I didn't say any of that, and she said goodbye and I went home with my family.

And that was right.

But the suit I wore to that funeral carried her scent for weeks. I furtively sniffed the lapels, hungry to inhale what was left of her in the fibers.

"There's no one in particular," I lie. "But again, I'm not standing in your way."

"So you're fine with me and Chaz." She looks down at the silk belt she rubs between her fingers. "That's his name, Chaz. You're fine if we—"

"An open relationship isn't the answer." I lift her chin, coaxing her to meet my eyes. "I want to be with someone who only wants to be with me, and it would kill me if she was with someone else. You and I want different things."

"Isn't there a part of you that still wants me?" she asks, her voice husky, desperate.

I glance down at her slim loveliness. She's beautiful and some men would kill for what I have, but I don't feel that for Aiko anymore. I don't know when it stopped exactly, but I do know for weeks when I would open that closet and catch the slightest lingering trace of Kimba's scent, I'd go fully erect. I have a semi now just thinking about her. Guilt gnaws at my insides, and I step back from Aiko. I wish so many things were different, but if any one thing had changed, I might not have Noah, and he's the best thing to ever happen to me.

"I want you to be happy, Ko." I bend to kiss her forehead and squeeze her shoulder. "I'm not made for an open relationship, but I'm releasing you from this one."

"Ezra." She closes her eyes, and a tear slips over her cheek. "Oh, God. Is this really happening?"

So this is what the end feels like. Like rolling down a hill for years, wondering if you'll ever land in a ravine, and then stopping suddenly.

Crashing. Abrupt. Painful.

I thumb the wetness from her face. "There's a lot to sort out. Noah is my first concern. We never married, but to him, this will feel like a divorce."

"His birthday is coming up." She bites her lip, blinking damp lashes. "I already feel awful that I'll be away on this trip for it. Could we let him enjoy his party? I don't want this cloud hanging over it. He's so excited about his friends coming and—"

"I agree. We'll let him have his party." I kiss her forehead, pull her into a hug, swallowing against the painful burning of my throat. "We'll tell him when you get back."

CHAPTER TEN

Kimba

"**M**AMA, I'LL BE THERE."

I adjust my earbud and jog in heels the last few steps to my doctor's office building since some guy is holding the door open for me.

"Thanks," I say, flashing him a quick smile. He's staring at my ass. "Eyes up here, buddy."

His cheeks redden.

Awww. A blushing lecher. How cute.

He tugs at his collar like it just got tight. "Uh, sorry. I—"

"Dude, I'm just teasing you. It's fine."

He laughs, relief evident on his face before he ducks into one of the open office doors.

"Teasing me about what?" my mother asks. "Will you be home in time for the ceremony or not, Kimba?"

"I said yes." My home training nudges me. "Yes, ma'am."

"Good. There will be so many community leaders there, and you know we've named this new award for—"

"For Daddy, yes, Mama. You told me. It's amazing."

My family's legacy, especially in Atlanta, is long and impressive. I'm proud of my grandfather and my father, of all their accomplishments and all the good they did. Seeing how they lived their lives inspired me to do what I do—to live my life the way I have.

Younger Kimba didn't always have this perspective. Turning on to streets named after your father is great. Attending an elementary school named after your grandfather is great...until everyone starts expecting things from you. *All the things.* And the scrutiny can become so intense.

My grandfather was a Morehouse man. My daddy was a Morehouse man. My grandmother, mother, aunts, sister—all Spelmanites. When it came time for me to choose a college, it never occurred to anyone that I would detour from the prescribed path. My announcement that I'd won a full ride to Arizona State was met with shock and disapproval. I resented the suffocating expectations of everyone who knew my family. Atlanta felt like a city-wide trap. That scholarship sprang me free.

"And Kayla needs you to handle a few things for the ceremony," Mama says.

"What things?" I'm outside my doctor's office suite, but linger in the hall to finish my call. "What does she need me to do?"

"She...oh, Lord above. You tell her, Zee," Mama says impatiently.

"Tru?" Kayla's deep voice takes over the line. Even after all these years, my back straightens a little when my big sister enters the room. She manages everything from her children to our family's foundation like a five-star general.

"What do you need me to do at the reception, Kayla?"

"Well, hello to you, too, sis," she replies coolly.

I tap my foot and grit my teeth. I don't have time for this. I'm meeting Senator Billingsley from Michigan after this appointment. My schedule is basically a Jenga tower that Carla carefully constructs. I get behind on any part of it and the whole day collapses.

"Sorry," I say, forcefully scrubbing my voice of irritation. "Hello, Kayla. How are you?"

"Hmmmm. Don't do that polite shit with me."

"Zee, come on. I get straight to the point, and you call me out for being rude. I ask how you are and you accuse me of being *polite*?"

"I didn't say you were rude. You were impersonal. There's a difference."

"Can you please sister-splain the difference later and get to the damn point right now so I can continue with my day? I have a doctor's appointment like *now*."

"Doctor?" Concern shades her voice. "You okay?"

"Doctor?" my mother echoes from somewhere in the room. "Is she pregnant? Please, Jesus, don't let that child be pregnant."

"Ma, she's not pregnant." Kayla drops her voice. "Are you?"

"Don't have an abortion!" Mama screams from much closer. "We could give that baby a good home once we got past the shame of you having it out of wedlock."

I swallow a feral scream. I need something to strangle if I'm expected to endure this.

"I'm not pregnant." *Far as I know.* "Just some routine stuff. Now, what do you need me to do?"

"You sure?" Kayla asks.

I don't answer, letting my silence speak because I may snarl if I use words.

"Okay, okay," Kayla says. "So there will be about twenty community leaders recognized at the ceremony."

"Who are they?"

"Community leaders. I just said—"

"No, I mean do we know who these people are being honored in Daddy's name?"

"I've been really busy. You know. Protecting our family's legacy and all."

"The guilt I could do without, Zee. We're all aware you're the keeper of the flame for our entire lineage. Just say we don't know. It's fine. I was just wondering."

"We only recently notified them that they've been selected. Our associate director is contacting them to make sure they can all attend. She saw the list and vetted them, if that's what you're worried about."

"I'm not worried, I just wondered…never mind. What do you need me to do?"

"Present the awards. This was one of the final projects Daddy was working on before he passed. A few of these leaders he hand-picked. When he died, this fell by the wayside for a little while, but we have a committee who chose the leaders Daddy didn't get to."

She pauses and clears her throat. "He, um, actually left special instructions asking you to present the inaugural group."

"What?" I lean against the wall, weak and spent with missing my daddy for a moment. "He…he said that? He wanted that?"

"Yeah," Kayla says softly. "That's what he told the committee."

I pass a thumb under my eye to catch a surprise tear. Grief gives no warning sometimes. "Thank you for telling me, Zee. I'll do it, of course."

"Good. Now are you sure you're okay? You sound…off."

Kayla is such a mother. I mean, the woman *does* have five children, the last one still in diapers. Her fertility is actually quite disconcerting. No one person has had that many kids in our family since like… Reconstruction. But along comes Kayla, bringing *fruitful and multiply* back.

"I'm fine, Zee." The edge falls away from my tone, too. I think we actually enjoy sparring because it's hard to find anyone who can hold their own with either of us, but ultimately we love each other.

"You're in between campaigns, right?" she asks. "Why don't you consider staying in Atlanta for a few weeks? We miss you. Mama misses you."

"I do!" Mama yells. "Need to bring those hips home for a while."

I hear the affection behind the chiding. And that she misses me. Hidden beneath all the chaos of my life and demanding schedule, I miss them, too.

"Well there's always something popping off," I say. "We're gearing up for a few campaigns, but I'll see if I can stay a while. I hired some new staff to help now that Lennix is gone."

"Go, Lennix," Kayla says, and I can almost see her beaming. "That's my girl. You know we're proud of you doing big things up in D.C. Electing presidents and such. You sure about turning down President Cade's cabinet position?"

"Lennix asked me that just this morning. I'm sure."

"I saw she's pregnant. A baby in the White House. Ain't that something?"

"It is," I agree with a smile. "Okay. I'm gonna be late for my appointment if I don't go."

"See you next week."

"K. Bye." I disconnect and hurry through the office suite door and sign in. I flip through a magazine until they call my name and take me to my doctor's office.

"Do I need to undress or anything?" I ask the nurse.

"No. Sorry if the message wasn't clear. She just wants to discuss results."

"I'm not dying, right?" I joke.

"I don't know," the nurse replies with a straight face and walks out.

"Okay. She could use some interpersonal training," I mutter, settling into the seat across from the doctor's desk.

Dr. Granden strides in moments later, her salt and pepper hair pulled into a bun pierced with a pencil. She always gives a very harried impression, almost absent-minded, until it's time for her to actually talk to you about your health. Then you feel like she's in absolute control and you have her full, expert attention.

"Kimba, hi." She sits down and opens a file on her desk, a small frown bunching her brows when she looks up at me. She closes the file. "We got your bloodwork back."

Please don't let me be pregnant.

Please don't let me be pregnant.

Please don't let me be pregnant.

"I'm not pregnant, am I?" I ask, half-seriously, half-nervously. "Because I cannot afford that right now."

An odd look crosses Dr. Granden's face, almost like surprise. She adjusts her glasses and leans forward, elbows on the desk and steepled fingers at her lips.

"No, you're not pregnant, Kimba. I believe you're in perimenopause."

It takes a moment for her words to sink through the layers of my expectations. Never in a million years did I think she would say that. A startled laugh slips out.

"No. What?" I tilt my head, a puzzled smile crooking my lips. "I thought you said menopause, but you couldn't have—"

"Perimenopause."

"I'm only thirty-seven."

"Entering it early is not as rare as you might think." Her white-coated shoulders lift and fall. "Some women start at your age and stay in this pre-menopausal state for years. For some, it goes much faster. I have patients who started in their late twenties."

"What does this mean? W-what are you telling me?"

"How many periods have you missed?"

"Um…four. I…my periods have done that in times of stress before. Skipped. I just finished an election. I attributed it to that."

"Any hot flushes?"

"N-not that I've noticed, no."

But did I *not* notice? I've "felt hot" several times, but you feel hot sometimes. I would never have assumed feeling hotter than everyone else in the room or fanning on a day that wasn't especially warm meant *hot flashes*.

"Weight gain?" Dr. Granden probes.

I release a shaky breath. "Yeah. I do seem to be putting on a few pounds. Again, I assumed stress."

"What about insomnia? Mood swings? Vaginal dryness? Decreased sexual appetite?"

"Well, I'm a vampire, so I never sleep, but I guess? Maybe? As for mood swings, like I said, I'm coming off a campaign, so for a year and a half I basically fluctuate between Linda Blair and being a twelve-year-old rocking in the corner." I shrug. "We'd have to ask my assistant if I've been more of a bitch than usual."

Dr. Granden's lips quirk a little, but her eyes remain serious. "And the sexual appetite?"

"I think my appetite has been consistent. I may as well sleep with my vibrator under my pillow." I snort. "Satisfaction is another matter. Between you and me, doc, these fellas out here just ain't doing it right."

We chuckle, and I realize I needed that. Just something to lift this heavy weight from my chest. My whole adult life I've prided myself on the focus, the drive, the discipline required to reach my goals. The future was a plan I executed. Now the future, *my future*—at least one aspect of it—just spun out of focus.

Out of my control.

"Wait," I say, assembling the implications of what she's saying as the shock starts wearing off. "If I don't have a period, does that mean I can't have kids? Is that what you're saying?"

"Not necessarily, but the FSH level is significantly higher in your blood than typical."

"FSH?"

"Follicle-stimulating hormone. Your brain makes more of it as your ovaries produce fewer eggs."

"Follicle, huh?" I laugh humorlessly. "My ovaries have hair?"

She smiles, the tight line of her mouth easing some. "Not exactly. An increase in FSH alone wouldn't be enough, but coupled with the missed periods and other symptoms you report, and the tests we've done to eliminate what it *isn't*, the picture begins to become more clear."

Ovaries. Eggs. Hormones. Babies.

These are not the things that dominated my internal news cycle when I woke up this morning. Besides seeing Lennix and discussing a candidate's pro-life stance on a call before this meeting, I haven't given kids much thought today. Life, though, in its infinite wisdom, has shoved all of this front and center.

"Mind you," Dr. Granden says, "I'm general practice. I'm just telling you what all the signs indicate. Your test results are consistent with a woman in perimenopause, but I would like you to consult with a specialist, too."

"A sp-sp-specialist?" I ask, suppressing a groan of frustration that my damn stutter hits me as unexpectedly as my grief does sometimes. "This is going fast. What does this all mean?"

"If a woman is in perimenopause and wants to have kids naturally," Dr. Granden says, her voice softening into compassion, "she better move fast. You could have a year, maybe a little more if we're aggressive about re-starting your period. It's hard to say. There are things you can do. Hormone replacement therapy, which does have some risks, but you can talk those through with the specialist. Several of my patients have also had success with homeopathic remedies. Once we get your period back up and running, we can chart when you're most fertile and you can—"

"But I don't want a baby," I blurt. "I mean, I do someday, but not *now*. I'm not dating anyone. I'm not involved or interested. I have a gubernatorial campaign to run." *If the candidate chooses me.* "I...you're saying I have to have a baby *now*?"

"I'm saying if you don't get pregnant relatively soon, then odds are you never will."

I'm a rug Dr. Granden's beating, every word coming out of her mouth a *whack*, sending air and dust flying from me.

"I don't know what to say," I manage, though my tongue feels swollen in my mouth. "I'm not sure what to do. I—"

"If you want to keep even the possibility of children, of *a* child, then we should at least talk about trying to get your cycle back online. That's first."

"Uh, yeah. My cycle. Of course," I say automatically, trusting that the words coming from my mouth are the right ones. "Do you have water? I need some water."

Dr. Granden nods behind me. "There's a water cooler there. I can get it if—"

"No." I stand and turn toward the cooler. "I can."

I walk on shaky legs to the little stand at the back of her office. The colorful pattern of the carpet swims through a glaze of sudden tears, and the floor tilts beneath me. The whole world just slid to one side, and I'm holding on to an invisible beam, trying not to fall. My hands tremble around the little plastic cup as I fill it with cold water. Mere minutes ago, I was begging not to be pregnant, and now I may never be? My mother was just reassuring me she would still love her grandchild out of wedlock, and now I may never have one to give her…at all?

I gulp the water down along with these hard truths, immediately filling the cup again and draining it before making my way back to my seat.

"So you said restarting my period is the first thing. Can we do that for sure?"

The answer is scribbled across her face like one of her prescriptions, impossible to read. She confirms what I fear, though, with a shake of her head. "There are no guarantees. I'll leave it to the specialist to discuss likely outcomes, but I would think your chances are good. I'd prefer not to speculate, though."

My phone dings in my purse. I'm tempted to ignore it, but I don't have that kind of life. A ding could be a small fire, and if I delay responding, in no time it could be a conflagration, trending on Twitter and ticker taping on every major news outlet.

"Excuse me one second, Dr. Granden." I fish the phone from my bag to read the text message.

Carla: Hey. Just reminding you to leave the doctor's office soon or you'll miss your two o'clock with Senator Billingsley.

Me: Cancel Billingsley.

Dr. Granden places a plastic model on the desk between us. I vaguely note a vagina, uterus and fallopian tubes.

Me: Cancel everything.

CHAPTER ELEVEN

Ezra

"**S**ON, SLOW DOWN. YOUR FOOD'S NOT RUNNING FROM YOU. Stop chasing it."

Noah looks up, the expression on his small face abashed, but still eager, as if I spiked his oatmeal with Mexican jumping beans. He deliberately takes his time lifting the spoon from his bowl, opens his mouth exaggeratedly, and stretches his eyes really wide, sliding the spoon between his teeth in extra slow-mo.

Smart ass.

"And don't scrape that spoon over your teeth," I add, grinning and mussing the dark wavy hair that spills into his eyes. He begged us to let him grow it out after visiting his cousin Tao in LA, whose hair hangs past his shoulders in a pin-straight curtain. Noah's won't be quite that straight or silky, thanks to my genes. He'll grow up like I did, with hair finer than my father's and not quite as fine as my mom's.

"It's the first day of summer break," he reminds me unnecessarily and for maybe the tenth time since he woke up.

"I know." I take a few gulps of the strawberry smoothie I prepared for breakfast, sliding a small cup of it to him. "Drink up so we can take your mom to the airport."

"Yuck." He scrunches his face and turns up his nose.

"It doesn't taste bad, and it's good for you." I glance at my Apple watch to see if we're on schedule. The name *Joseph S. Allen* in the subject line of an email captures my attention.

I click the message open and lean against the counter to read from my wrist.

Reminder! The Joseph S. Allen Community Service Award for your outstanding leadership in education is coming up soon. Details below.

I was surprised when I received the email. Does Mrs. Allen know? Our parents were adamant about putting distance between the two families. Seeing Mr. Allen a few years ago when I first moved back to Atlanta was by chance, and I wasn't sure he'd recognize me, much less cross the street to shake my hand. He invited me to coffee and spent an hour listening to my plans to start a private school, Young Leaders Academy of Atlanta, serving low-income and at-risk middle school students. He was an important man. I'm sure he'd had better things to do than spend time with me, the kid of a family he had fallen out with.

He'd asked about my family, and I'd found creative ways to ask about Kimba without being too obvious or pathetic. When he died, I'd risked the censure of Mrs. Allen by going to the funeral, but I had to pay my respects.

And I'd hoped to see Kimba.

"I'm ready," Aiko says, rushing into the kitchen and grabbing a banana from the bowl on the counter.

Things have been weird between us. Not hostile, just uncertain in this limbo where we know our relationship is over, but Noah doesn't yet. I've been sleeping in the guest bedroom. After we decided to end it, it felt wrong to sleep in the same bed. Actually, it felt right *not* to, further confirmation that we're doing the right thing. Noah goes to sleep before we do and I'm up before he is, so he hasn't noticed the change.

"Mona promised to make sure you boys don't eat junk the whole time I'm gone," Aiko says, kissing Noah's forehead.

Mona and I reconnected by chance at a teacher's job fair. I was recruiting for YLA's first year. Once we got past the shock of seeing each other again, I realized she was exactly the kind of educator I wanted to build with.

Fast forward three years, and her backyard adjoins ours, separated only by a fence. She's not only the school director, but has become like a part of our family.

"Aunt Mona can cook vegetables from our garden," Noah says, oatmeal flying past his lips.

"Son," I chide. "That's disgusting. Don't talk with food in your mouth."

He rolls his eyes. I lift one brow. Shamefacedly, he mutters an apology. We have a system in this house, Noah and I, and there is never any doubt who is the boss of it.

"Vitamins." I point to the little dish of gels and gummies I laid out.

He eyes the pile of pills, mouth twisted up.

"Remember Pop?" Aiko asks. "How big he was? And see how big Daddy is? Take your vitamins, and you'll be big like them. Your dad used to be little, too."

"You were?" he asks.

"I was one of the smallest kids in my class." I raise my right hand. "Promise. Then around tenth grade, everything changed."

"And you got big like Pop?"

"Not quite," I say dryly. "Pop was six feet, six inches. Two inches taller than me, but I made up a lot of ground in a couple of years."

"And that was from taking vitamins?" he asks hopefully.

Honestly, no. That was just genetics. "Absolutely it was the vitamins."

In ten minutes, we're out the door and headed for the airport. When we arrive, I unload Aiko's small battalion of color-coordinated luggage.

"I'll miss you so much," Aiko says, holding Noah's face between her hands. "You'll be good for Daddy, right?"

"Yeah." He bites his lip, and I recognize his "I'm supposed to be a big boy and big boys don't cry" face. "A month is a long time, though."

"It'll fly by," she tells him, her voice falsely bright. They've never been apart this long before. None of us have. "And we'll FaceTime, okay?"

"Aiko!" a tall, sandy-haired man calls from the curb. "Perfect timing."

Surrounded by his own collection of bags, he eyes my ex-girlfriend like she's his favorite dessert.

"Um, yeah." She glances up at me, blinking fast and licking her lips. "Chaz, this is, um…he's…"

"Ezra," I say, stepping forward with an extended hand. "Nice to meet you, Chaz."

"Uh, hi." He shakes my hand, and his hazel eyes flick between Aiko, Noah and me.

Noah's taking in everything with his sharp eyes and quick mind. I don't give a damn if Aiko screws Chaz. We're done, but Noah doesn't understand that yet. In his mind, we're his parents. We live together. He doesn't see us any differently from his classmates' mommies and daddies who are married, and how we handle this transition into this next phase of life could affect him for years to come. It should be thoughtful and careful and measured and put his needs at the center, not our own.

I look to Chaz and Aiko, a hard set to my mouth, a warning in my eyes.

"Noah, Chaz works with Mommy," I say pointedly. "He's going on safari, too. Isn't that cool?"

"Wow," Noah says. "You'll take lots of pictures, right?"

"Of course," Chaz says, his smile uncertain. "So many pictures that we have to get started right away, buddy."

Noah hates being called "buddy." He thinks it's infantile. His word. Not mine. He looks up at me and scowls, and I give a subtle shake of my head, silently reminding him to be respectful. I grab a cart for all Aiko's bags, getting them loaded. Once that's done, it's time for Noah and me to go. There's such a mix of things in her expression.

Excitement. Hope. Anticipation.

Sadness. Guilt. Uncertainty.

"I won't," she says softly. "I mean... I don't have to if you don't want me on this trip. If you want to think about it, I can—"

"Ko." I squeeze her hand and look at her directly to emphasize my sincerity. "Enjoy your trip."

She searches my face, like she has to make sure she won't be damaging something irreparably if she takes this step with Chaz, but we've been broken a long time. We've held this relationship together with Gorilla Glue, masking tape and sheer force of will. But there are too many gaps and holes and tears. What we had will never be whole again, but we can be something new.

Noah and I watch his mother walk into the airport with another man, and I don't feel anything but hope that this can be the start.

I glance down at the watch on my wrist, at the email that might mean seeing Kimba again. There's a stirring in my chest at the thought, like hope shaking awake parts of me that have been asleep for years. I don't have time to think about it now, but take a second to reply that I'm honored to be recognized and looking forward to the banquet.

"Dad," Noah says, not patiently. "Can we please go now? It's the first day of summer break."

"I *did* hear that somewhere." I chuckle and muss his hair. "Let's go...*buddy.*"

CHAPTER TWELVE

Kimba

"SO I'LL BE IN ATLANTA FOR A FEW WEEKS," I SAY, LOOKING down the conference room table at my team. "I'm spending some time with my family between campaigns."

"Oh, I'm so glad, boss," Carla says. "We've all been worried about you."

"You've all been worried?" I narrow my eyes and stare at them one by one. "Been talking about me behind my back?"

They exchange furtive glances and start stuttering and stammering.

"I'm kidding!" I laugh, leaning back in my chair at the head of the long mahogany table and swiveling back and forth. "God, am I that bad?"

The newest team member, Felita, lifts both brows and casts a look to the side that says *weeeeeelllll*.

"I see you, Felita," I say, pointing to her with a grin.

She chuckles. "You've just seemed tired and a little..." She tips her head back and forth like she isn't sure of the right word, or rather, isn't sure she should *say* it.

"A little bit of a bitch?" I offer, laughing at them and at myself. "Yeah. I know."

If we weren't in mixed company, two of my team members being men, I might have told them my ovaries have rebelled and deployed weapons of mass hormones. A trip to the specialist confirmed that I am indeed in perimenopause, but I'll save that for a girls' chat. Men practically dissolve into puddles at the mere mention of a tampon, much less menopause. I don't have the emotional bandwidth or spare nerves for that today.

"This would be a good time for you all to consider a little time off, too, before we swing into high gear for the next round of campaigns." I nod toward Piers, who's been with the firm for years, one of our earliest hires. "You're doing some recon on Mateo Ruiz, right?"

"Yeah, but has he actually hired us yet?" Piers asks, his gray eyes sharp.

"He will." I keep my expression implacable. "We just had a great conversation. Only a matter of time. Now what'd you find?"

He runs a hand through his thinning brown hair. "So far he's clean as a whistle."

"Don't believe the hype," I say. "I wanna sniff his dirty laundry before we're out on the trail or in front of a camera. Everyone has skeletons, but I mean, are we talking *Bone Collector* shit?"

The team laughs, and so do I. I need this. I need work that I enjoy and that feels meaningful. This mission to put people in power who champion the marginalized—it's been the epicenter of my life since I graduated college to the neglect of everything else. With the very real possibility of never having my own children now, I feel the imbalance more than ever, but I can't say I would have changed a thing. Kayla carries out Daddy's legacy by overseeing our family's foundation. This is how I perpetuate the principles by which he lived. As for how our brother does it...who the hell knows?

My phone vibrates on the conference room table.

Keith.

Well, speak of the player and he shall appear.

"I need to take this call." I glance at the lunch we ordered spread out on the conference room table. "Go on and dig in. Carla, could you update everyone on our schedule for the next few days? I'll be right back."

I step into the hall and stride toward my office, phone pressed to my ear.

"Keith," I say, closing the door behind me. "To what do I owe this rare pleasure?"

"Can't a man just call to check on his little sister sometimes?" he asks, that liquid voice all the men of our family inherit pouring over the line. My grandfather and father put that compelling voice to use championing others' needs. Keith wastes his on simple charm.

"Yes, *a* man can, but *this* man usually doesn't." I chuckle to let him off the hook because he's that guy who makes everybody want to let him off. "I know you need something, but it's good to hear from you. What's up?"

"I heard you're coming home and might stay for a while."

"Maybe a couple of weeks." I perch on the edge of my desk. "We'll see."

"I'd love to talk to you about something while you're home."

Here we go.

"Oh?" I ask, keeping my voice only pleasantly curious instead of *I knew it.* "What about?"

"I'm thinking of running."

"From who?" I ask, laughing.

"Ha ha. Very funny. Running for office."

My smile disintegrates. "Which office?"

"Congress. I've been putting some feelers out, and there's real interest in me getting into politics."

"Of course there's interest. Your last name is on a dozen streets and schools and parks in that city. Name recognition alone means somebody wants to slap you onto a ballot. Doesn't mean you should."

"Wow. Tell me how you really feel, sis."

"Oh, I always will. You know that. Why do you want to run for office? You're making plenty of money practicing law."

"It's not about the money," he says, his tone stiffening like one of his heavily starched shirt collars.

"What is it about then? Tell me."

"It's about...the people."

"What about them?"

"I...well, I want to help them, of course."

"Help them *how*? Tell me their issues. Tell me their problems. What's the average income for people in that district? How are the working poor faring? Graduation rate? Voter suppression is rampant. What do you plan to do about it?"

"Whoa, whoa, whoa. Why are you attacking me?"

"Attacking you?" I suck my teeth. "Boy, please, you ain't ready. If you think this is an attack, try being in a debate, a hostile interview. I'm giving you the chance to show me you care about the people you would be representing. That you care enough to know how you can help *them*, not how this opportunity could help *you*."

"You put every client though this wringer before you take them on?"

Oh, he has no idea.

"You still stepping out on Delaney?" I ask, going for that weak spot he thinks I don't know about.

The silence between us is sticky and pulls like syrup.

"What?" he finally asks. "I don't know—"

"I *said* are you still cheating on your wife?"

I hear him swallow, but no answer.

"Get *your* house in order," I tell him, "before you think about running for mine."

"Your house?"

"Oh, yes, sir. I grew up in that district, Stoke, and I may not live there now, but I'll be damned if I'll send an ill-prepared, incompetent narcissist who can't keep his dick in his pants to the House of Representatives on their behalf. We have enough of those already. And I don't care if you're my brother. If you're not in it for the people, you could be my Siamese *twin* and I wouldn't stand with you."

"Damn, sis. It's like *that*?"

"It's like *that*. What do you think I do? You think I elected a *president* accepting bullshit answers to tough questions? *If* I work with you, and that's a big if because I'll tell you right now, I'm not impressed, I will not be played…*bruh*."

"You telling me the guys you help win elections don't cheat on their wives?"

"Of course, half of them do. Probably more, but they aren't carrying my last name into office." I pause for a second before going on. "Plus, it's trifling and your father raised you better than that."

He doesn't reply, but I hope he's thinking about it.

"Be better prepared when I come home next week," I finally say softly, "and we'll see."

"Thanks, Kimba."

"I said we'll see." I will the rod in my back to relax. "I love you."

"Love you, too."

"Kiss Delaney and the kids for me."

He hesitates. "I will."

I was hard on him, but he *does* have potential. And he comes from a long line of activists. I'll help him if he's in it for the right reasons. I'd help him because I know it would make Daddy proud—that there's nothing he'd like better than to see his only son having an impact in the city our family has given so much to.

"I got you, Daddy," I whisper, walking over to look at D.C. sprawled beneath my office window. "I got you."

CHAPTER THIRTEEN

Ezra

"**O**UR BEANS ARE BETTER," NOAH WHISPERS TO ME BEHIND his small hand.

I spear a green bean tucked beneath the stuffed chicken breast and pop it into my mouth. "You're right. Our garden is the bomb. We grow great veggies."

We execute an exploding fist bump.

"You know my favorite kind of vegetables?" Mona asks beside me, spooning up a portion of mashed potatoes. "Free."

The three of us laugh, as usual with Mona. The awards committee provided tickets for two guests. Noah was the obvious choice, and Mona since Aiko is out of town.

"Thanks for inviting me," Mona says.

"Thanks for coming."

"This is really an honor, Ezra. The whole staff is proud of you. Wait 'til your book comes out. You won't be able to shut us up."

I can't help but feel proud, too. I'm writing a book about the YLA journey, and someone actually wants to publish it.

"I heard Kimba's coming," Mona says.

My head snaps around. "What?"

"Yeah, I ran into Kayla in the bathroom and she mentioned it. I haven't seen them in years. We all kinda went our separate ways, huh?"

After Mom and I left, we spent the summer in New York with

family. I went to camp and assumed we'd head back to Atlanta. Mom didn't get to stay in New York for long. Before school started, my father accepted a job offer in Italy. Moving there was the best and worst thing for me. The best because even though I didn't speak the language and it was a foreign country, I *looked* like many of the people. I blended in. No one asked my mother if I was adopted or stared at us when I was with my parents. I could breathe in Italy in a way I hadn't felt free enough to do before, and it came just as I was becoming a young man—just when I needed it.

The worst was losing contact with Kimba. Her family moved, changed their phone number. This was before Facebook or Instagram. I had no idea how to get in touch with her, and with us in Europe, she had no way to get in touch with me. Mona told me later she didn't bus in for high school, but stayed in her district, so she didn't see Kimba anymore either.

"I wonder if she'll actually show." I sip my water and peruse the room slowly, searching each table and aisle for her. I've seen her on television a few times, but her partner, Lennix Hunter, now the First Lady, usually spoke on behalf of their clients. "It's almost time to give out the awards."

"Kayla said something about her flight out of D.C. being delayed." Mona shrugs. "I think she's taking a little time off and hanging here in Atlanta for a few weeks. Hopefully we can get together while she's in town."

I take another sip of water, disciplining my expression into impassivity. Inside, though, anticipation churns through my body. Kimba and I will be in the same state, maybe *around* each other, for the first time since we were thirteen years old.

"Whose flight is delayed?" Noah asks, taking a sip of the sweet tea.

"No more." I point to his glass. "Water for the rest of the night."

He crosses his eyes, which is his new thing he learned to do last week. "Okay, but whose flight?"

"Our friend Kimba," Mona says. "We haven't seen her in a long time."

"The one we met at her daddy's funeral?" Noah asks me.

"Yeah, that's the one," I reply, surprised he remembers. Though Noah has the memory of an elephant, so I shouldn't be.

"I hate I was out of town for the funeral," Mona says. "I would have loved to pay my respects and to see Kimba again. Funny how people you're so close to when you're kids, you don't even see for years and years. Decades even."

It doesn't feel funny to me. It feels tragic that the person I thought I'd know all my life is now a veritable stranger. Someone whose sentences I used to be able to finish. The few secrets I had at that age, Kimba kept. Now I don't know her at all.

"It's time." Mona nods toward the stage where Kayla stands behind the podium.

It's hard to reconcile this mature, almost staid woman and her closely cropped hair with the Kayla who used to show off her gold package Nissan Maxima all around our neighborhood.

"Good evening, everyone," Kayla says, spreading a warm smile across the crowd. "I'm Kayla Allen-Greggs, executive director of the Allen Foundation. I hope you've enjoyed the night so far."

"Not the beans," Noah mutters, pushing what's left of his food around his plate. "How much longer?"

"Not much longer. You've done great." I push his floppy hair off his forehead and chuckle. "We can grab ice cream at The Ice Box when we leave."

He fist pumps and I turn my attention back to Kayla, stuffing my disappointment since it looks like Kimba won't make it in time.

"This project acknowledging service excellence in our community was one of the last things my father worked on," Kayla says. "He wanted my sister, Kimba, to make these presentations. Come on out, sis."

Kimba walks swiftly from backstage to the podium, looking slightly harried.

And stunning.

Just like I remember from the funeral, but better, which I didn't think was possible. Rarely have I felt so completely focused on the smallest details of another person. The gold dress caresses her body, clinging to her curves, teasing me with tantalizing glimpses of glowing brown skin. Her textured curls are caught up high, leaving the graceful lines of her neck and shoulders bare.

"Good evening everyone," Kimba says, her husky voice shaping the words to roll over my nerve endings. "My flight was delayed and I wasn't sure I'd make it in time. I'm so glad I did."

She draws a deep breath and grips the edge of the podium before going on.

"My father always used to say whatever you do, be excellent," Kimba says. "Whatever you do, consider others. Big moves make big waves. Do big things. Make big waves. Tonight's amazing leaders were selected because of the waves they're making in our community. Sometimes we don't realize that the move we're making will be the one that changes everything, not just for us, but for someone else. Thank you for impacting your community as you follow your dreams."

"She's beautiful," Mona says beside me. "Can you believe that's our girl from middle school?"

"Hard to believe," I agree neutrally.

"For our first award," Kimba says, reading from the pages Kayla slid in front of her. "This doctor opened a clinic offering free mammograms to at-risk women with inadequate insurance coverage. Dr. Richard Clemmons."

Dr. Clemmons takes the stage with Kimba, she hands him his award, and they pose for a photo before she moves on to the next recipient on her list. I have no idea where I fall in the order. Does she know I'm here? Did her mother or Kayla know? Connect the dots between the Dr. Ezra Stern who opened the school and the kid who darkened their door basically every day from the time he could walk until his parents dragged him away?

"Next," Kimba says when she's about halfway through the recipients. "He founded and runs a private middle school serving low-income areas and at-risk students, ninety percent of whom are on scholarship. Students at the Young Leaders Academy of Atlanta have experienced, on average, an eighty percent improvement on test scores. This award in the area of educational excellence goes to…"

She falters, a frown gathering between her dark brows. She lifts her head abruptly, scanning the room and then doing a slower pass until she finds me in the corner.

"Ezra."

The room goes quiet for a second, the audience waiting for her to continue. She shakes her head. "Um, sorry. Dr. Ezra Stern."

Noah stands in his chair and claps and whistles and hoots. Mona hugs me, squeezing my shoulder. As soon as she lets go, she pulls the phone from her pocket and aims it at me.

"Video for everybody at school!" Mona says, laughing at what I'm sure is my exasperated expression when she thrusts the camera in my face.

I head toward the stage, smiling at the people standing and clapping as I pass. I have a vague impression of their faces, but I don't hear their applause over the clanging cymbal in my chest. Onstage, Kimba's smile flickers like candlelight. There's something uncertain on her face, in her eyes. I recognize it. I feel it, too. Ever since I read the email about this night, this moment loomed like a promise or a threat. The moment when I would see Kimba again.

When I reach the stage, she hands me the award, and we both turn for a photo.

"We have to stop meeting like this," she jokes, slanting a smile up at me.

"How would you like for us to meet?" I ask, trying to force a smile, but I can't. I mean it. It's not an idle question, and I can't make the moment as light as it should be. Seeing her only twice in more than twenty years feels wrong. It's never felt right to be apart from the person who once knew me better than anyone else—who knew me even as I was learning *myself*. When I saw her before at her father's funeral, what crackled between us felt like danger, the possibility of all that could go wrong. But now, I'm free. This time when our eyes meet, I can't help but wonder, if given the chance, what between us could go *right?*

CHAPTER FOURTEEN

Kimba

"**Y**OU'RE A DOCTOR?"

A dozen thoughts collide in my mind once we're off the stage and standing with all the recipients, awaiting a group photo, but that's the one I blurt out. I presented several other awards after Ezra's, but I couldn't tell you any of the recipients' names. I don't remember their faces. On autopilot, I presented the awards and smiled and posed, but all the while, I knew exactly where Ezra stood with the others behind me onstage. I could feel his stare—the heat and intensity of it tingling across the bare skin of my neck. As soon as all the awards were announced, I wasn't surprised when Ezra immediately appeared at my side.

"Of sorts," he replies to my question, shrugging. "Ed.D."

"Daddy!" The shout comes from the boy who is bigger and more like Ezra than the first time I saw him at the funeral. Noah throws his arms around his father, burying his face in his side. "You won."

"It wasn't a competition, son," Ezra says dryly, brushing a hand over his hair.

"I tried to explain," says an attractive woman around our age with dreadlocks pulled into a regal arrangement just behind Noah. "But he wasn't having it. You're a winner in his eyes."

I remember Ezra's wife vividly, a petite woman of Asian ancestry. This woman doesn't look anything like that, but she does look vaguely familiar.

"All that squinting," she says, turning laughing dark eyes on me. "And you still haven't figured out who I am?"

"We *have* met, right?" I ask, hating to admit I don't recognize someone, but too curious to pretend.

"He was Jack," she says, nodding to Ezra. "You were Chrissy, and I was—"

"Janet!" I shout, pulling her into a fierce hug. "Oh my God, Mona."

Tears prick my eyes, and I'm probably holding her too tight, but I'm overcome with how good it feels to see her again. When her parents decided she wouldn't bus into our district for high school, we kept in touch at first, but didn't maintain the friendship, caught up in new schools, new friends, and all the changes that came with growing up and inevitably growing apart. Eventually, with Ezra and Mona both gone, I found a new circle of friends, and so did she. I heard snatches of news about her until I left for college, and then nothing—until now.

"I'll let you off the hook because it's been so long since we saw each other," Mona says, pulling away to look me up and down. "Well, that and you gave us one of the best presidents this country has seen in recent memory. Congratulations, Kimba. When I saw you on CNN, I couldn't believe you were the same girl who hated reading out loud in class."

My cheeks go hot, which hasn't happened to me in years. Sometimes I'm shocked to hear my own voice, my words strong and clear and flowing. Who would believe the girl rattling off stats and details in front of a camera, for *millions* of viewers, used to hate reading in front of her classmates?

I look up to meet Ezra's stare, and I know he's remembering that day in Mrs. Clay's class. I'd forgotten this kind of telepathy we share, seemingly conducting thoughts between our minds with nothing more than a glance. There's a disconcerting intimacy to it that feels wrong when his mind isn't mine. Neither is his face, which settled into a roughly hewn beauty that I can barely tear my eyes from, or the big body standing like a tree offering shelter. I'm not his to shield. He's not mine to shelter. We're not each other's anymore.

I guess we never were.

"Wait," I say, looking between my old friends. "So you guys stayed in touch?"

"Not until we ran into each other a couple of years ago at a teacher's job fair," Mona says.

"I was staffing the school," Ezra says. "And there was Mona. She practically runs the place now."

"Now, we know that's a lie." Mona tsks. "This one's a control freak. It's bad enough I have to put up with him at school. Then we bought houses next door to each other. Aiko's a good neighbor, even if he isn't."

"Aiko's your wife?" I ask, looking from him to Ezra to Mona. "Where is she tonight?"

His expression freezes and his eyes widen. "Oh. Aiko's in Tanzania on safari," he says. "She's a photographer, but—"

"They're not married," Noah interjects. "Mommy says marriage is a social construct like gender and race."

A tiny startled silence is broken by us three adults laughing. Noah divides a puzzled look between us.

"It's not funny," he says, his little face earnest. "It's fact."

"Noah's right," Ezra says, turning to me. "Aiko and I aren't married."

Damn the breathlessness that seizes my lungs. I assumed they were married when I saw the three of them at the funeral and heard Noah call her Mommy. But it doesn't matter if he's married or not. He's *taken*.

"Just because they're not married," Mona says with a smile, "doesn't mean you aren't a family, right? Your parents have been together longer than a lot of married couples."

"I know." Noah grins, showing a missing tooth. "Mommy doesn't want Daddy to put a ring on it."

"And Beyoncé shall teach them the way that they should go." Mona laughs.

"I didn't realize you'd started a school," I say. "That's amazing, Ezra."

"Thank you." He shrugs, a gesture I remember from when we were kids to downplay praise and attention. "Like I said at the funeral, your father convinced me I should when I ran into him."

"Then it's only fitting you'd receive an award in his name." I twist the gold ring on my thumb Daddy gave me years ago. "It sounds incredible, what you're doing at the school."

"We're on summer break." Ezra hesitates, his glance fixed at some point on the floor, and then lifted to look me directly in the eye. "But you should come by sometime when you're in town. How long are you here?"

The question probably only feels loaded to me. Maybe the intensity of his stare, the heat generated by his nearness, is my imagination, but I can't look up when I answer, staring at my fresh manicure.

"Um, a couple of weeks," I say. "I'm taking some time between campaigns."

"We have to hang out," Mona says. "The *Three's Company* crew. Can't we get together for lunch or something?"

"Oh." I look up to find Ezra watching me closely, waiting. "Sure. That would be great."

"You used to love barbecue," she says. "You gotten all bougie on us, or you still okay with getting a little messy with your food?"

"It's been too long," I admit. "I'd love some good barbecue."

"You're thinking Tips?" Ezra asks Mona.

"Yeah. It's this new place near Ponce City Market," she says. "What do you have going on tomorrow?"

"This guy's got a play date." Ezra nods to Noah. "He's leaving me all day to go to Stone Mountain."

"Yup," Noah says, his smile wide. "You guys can keep my dad company."

"What do you ladies say?" Ezra asks us both, but looks at me. "You wanna keep me company?"

It's like that moment at the funeral when we could've exchanged numbers. It felt like a risk then. With this invisible live wire that seems to connect me to him, it still is.

Before I can reply, my mother walks up to join us.

"Ezra Stern," she says, a slight smile tugging at her lips. "Lord above, it is you. I hadn't looked at the final list so you could have knocked me over with a feather when I saw you and heard your name."

"It's me," Ezra says, his smile tentative. "How are you, Mrs. Allen?"

"Don't tell me you've gone and got stingy with your hugs," Mama says, resting her hands on her hips.

"No, ma'am." Ezra reaches down to squeeze my much shorter mother.

"Who would have thought?" Mama pats his back and then pulls away to peer up at him. "Tall as your daddy. It's good to see you."

It is? The last time she saw Ezra was the night of the argument. She did everything in her power to convince me I shouldn't look for him and seemed satisfied when my defiant efforts to find him proved fruitless.

"Good seeing you, too," Ezra says.

"How are your parents doing?" Mama asks, her tone polite and only mildly interested in the couple who used to be like family to us.

"My father passed away a few years ago." Sadness flits through Ezra's dark blue eyes, making them that near-purple color they'd become when he felt something deeply. Everything else about him may have changed, but at least that is the same. "Mom's doing well. She remarried last year."

"I'm so sorry about your father." Mama squeezes Ezra's hand. "Please give Ruth my best."

"I sure will." He turns to his son. "This is Noah, Mrs. Allen, the only grandchild and subsequently, spoiled rotten. Noah, this is Mrs. Allen, Kimba's mom."

"Hi." He glances up through long lashes at my mother. "My bubbe lives in New York."

"Ezra, you used to call your grandmother Bubbe, too. Ruth was so devastated when she passed." Compassion gathers in Mama's eyes. "Poor Ruth, losing so much."

"Mrs. Allen." A slim woman wearing glasses and a semi-anxious expression steps into our circle. "The board wants a few photos with you. You, too, Kimba."

"Thank you, Brenda," she says. "We better go. It was so good seeing you again, Ezra and Mona. Lovely meeting you, Noah."

"What about lunch tomorrow?" Mona says quickly, taking my arm. "We need to hang, girl. Catch up. It'll be fun."

Ezra doesn't speak, but the muscle in his jaw draws tight beneath his skin. He's looking down at the ground in that deliberate way he used to have. A casual posture that did little to hide his alertness. At least, not from me. Do I still know him?

"Kimba!" Mama says from a few feet away, already lining up for pictures. Something akin to anxiety marks her expression when her glance flicks between Ezra and me. "Come on."

I hear it again. Our parents' raised voices. The angry demands that separated me from my best friend. The desolation of watching from my porch as he left, knowing somehow, despite what he said, that it was for good.

"Say noon?" Mona asks. "Give me your number and I'll text you the address."

Ezra does glance at me then, and the look in his eyes wills me to say yes, even as Mama's expression urges me to pull away.

Not again.

"Noon?" I grab Mona's phone, punching in my number. "I can't wait."

CHAPTER FIFTEEN

Ezra

"MORE WATER, SIR?"

The server doesn't look much older than the girls at YLA, but if I'm not mistaken, she's checking me out. Mona and Aiko always say I'm bad at picking up on these things, but she's come to my table four times in five minutes offering water, and every time, the looks are bold enough that even I know what's up.

"Uh, no." I give her a polite smile. "I'll order something when my friends get here."

"Okay." She points to her chest...name tag. "Cherise. Just holla if you need me."

I give her another polite smile, this one a dismissal.

My phone rings and I know it's Mona before I even look at the screen.

"Let me guess," I say, already smiling. "You're running late."

"You don't know my life."

We both laugh because I very much do know her life, and she knows mine. Except I haven't told her about the breakup. Yet.

"Where are you?" I ask.

"Well, my cousin Alicia and I needed to run by this shop."

Flea market.

"And we were supposed to start early, but got behind," she says. "I'll be there fifteen minutes, tops. Kimba there yet?"

"Not yet." *But if she comes soon, I'll have fifteen minutes alone with her.*

"Some things never change," Mona says. "You were always early, I was always late, and Kimba was always—"

"Right on time," I say as Kimba walks into Tips and surveys the Saturday lunch crowd. "I'll see you when you get here."

"K, bye."

I wave to get Kimba's attention, smiling in a way I hope is normal. I don't feel normal. I feel...jittery, like my body resumed the adolescent state from when we were friends before. My palms are sweating. My heart is pounding. I'm this close to shoving my hands in my pockets even though I'm sitting down.

But she's so damn beautiful.

I'm not the only one who notices. A few men here with their girls cast discreet looks Kimba's way as she walks by, her stride confident, her generous curves shown off to perfection in the orange dress that stops a little above her knees. Curls riot around her face and brush her shoulders. Her makeup is light, but flawless. She looks...expensive. Even though she's dressed simply, sophistication clings to her as faithfully as the dress clings to her body. And when she gets close enough, her scent floats around me and makes me want to breathe so deep she's the only thing I can smell. It's lemony with something earthier beneath.

Cocoa butter.

She always wore it when we were kids. Her mother practically bathed them in it. Hell, more than once Mrs. Allen said *I* was ashy and randomly slathered it on me. Detecting the familiar scent beneath the light citrus makes me feel like somewhere under all this sophistication, she's still the girl I knew.

I stand when she reaches the table, opening my arms like it's natural, like I get to hold her every day, when it's actually been so long. Her hesitation is a millisecond before she smiles and steps into the hug.

She feels...womanly. Her breasts, soft and full, give against my chest, a seductive press. She's wearing flats and doesn't quite reach my chin, and her soft curls brush my jaw. Of their own accord, my hands slide down her back, trace the deep cinch of her waist and settle at the rounded curve of her hips. We both stiffen and our eyes hold, our breath seemingly suspended between us at the contact.

What the hell are my hands thinking?

I step back immediately, hands in the air. I never touch Mona or the other female teachers at YLA that way. I would never presume, but maybe it's our history, how close Kimba and I once were, how badly I want to know her again, that tricked me into a familiarity I haven't earned.

"I'm so sorry. I—"

"It's okay," she cuts in with a quick smile. "It's good to see you, too."

I laugh in a way that only mocks myself and gesture for her to sit down.

"Let me guess," she says, her smile wide and white against glowing coppery skin. "Mona's running late."

"Got it in one. She's on her way. She and Alicia hit every flea market within a ten-mile radius on Saturdays in search of their next great treasure."

"You can find some amazing stuff in flea markets."

"Somehow, I'm having trouble picturing you there," I say dryly.

"Don't be fooled. You can take the girl out of the A, but you can't take the A out of the girl. I could roll down to College Park right now and rip through a flea market."

"I'd like to see that."

"I said I *could*." She winks and takes a dainty sip of the water Cherise left on the table. "I'll leave the flea markets to Mona."

We laugh, and I turn my attention to Cherise, headed for us with her notepad.

"Y'all ready to order?" she drawls, much more businesslike, but still friendly, now that Kimba has joined me.

"We're waiting on one more," I tell her. "But do you still have those fried pickles? I didn't see them on the menu."

"Yep." She gives me a teasing grin. "You must be a regular."

"Regular enough. We bring our students here sometimes. The school isn't far."

"Which school?" She tilts her head and frowns.

"Young Leaders Academy of Atlanta."

"Oh my God!" Her face lights up. "My cousin Tribbie goes there."

"I know Tribbie. Seventh grade. She's in the chorus. Alto. Beautiful voice."

"And can't *pay* her to sing at church on Sundays." Cherise laughs. "My auntie says it's been so good for her. She also said you don't charge and it's a private school. How y'all manage that?"

"Fundraising." I shrug. "Generous donors from the community. Grants."

"Well, she loves it. Her grades are better and she—" Cherise shoots Kimba a self-conscious glance. "Oh. I'm sorry." She clears her throat and says, "I'll get those pickles right out. Did you want something other than water, ma'am?"

"Water's fine for now," Kimba replies with a smile, watching me speculatively when Cherise leaves. "Sounds like you're doing good work. Not that I doubted it. Daddy wouldn't have selected you if you weren't."

"Running into him was such a fluke, but sometimes what we call a fluke is fate, at least I like to think so."

"What'd you guys talk about? What'd he say?"

The hero worship for her father that so characterized her as a child is still in her eyes. I see that hunger for every detail of a loved one you didn't get nearly enough time with at the end. That was how I felt when my grandmother died, asking my mom dozens of questions she didn't want to answer, pouring over photo albums so I could see my bubbe at each stage of her life. Every detail was precious and made me feel closer to her.

"He said exactly what I needed to hear," I tell her because it's true. "I wasn't sure I should start the school—wasn't sure *where* to start, but he probed to figure out the things I was most passionate about." I laugh, the details of that fateful meeting coming back to me with a rush of fondness and respect for the man who was such a huge part of my life when I was a kid, and who was so notably absent after the night of the dance.

"He used to say your mission starts with people." Kimba brushes the gold ring on her thumb. "And your passions should fit on a napkin."

"Yup. He asked me about the kinds of students I wanted to help, and he jotted it down on a napkin while I talked."

"What'd you say?" she asks, her stare a welcome weight on my face. "What'd he write?"

I don't answer, but reach into my back pocket, pull out my wallet and extract the folded square I rarely take out, handling it like it's antique and fragile and worth preserving. When I spread it open on the table, she gasps, a smile blossoming on her mouth and her eyes shining with sudden unshed tears.

"It's been so long since I've seen his handwriting." She traces the loops and curves of the brusquely written words with one finger. The ink is faded, but the words are still legible.

Poor. Underserved. At risk. Bright. Ambitious. Capable. Hardworking.

And that's my kids. Those are the people, the families YLA is reaching, is helping. Even though I rarely take this little slip of vision out, it has guided me the last few years.

"What was on your napkin?" I ask, unable to look anywhere but at the woman seated in front of me. I was bowled over by her beauty when I saw her on television, even at the funeral and at the event the other night, but she was a symbol—almost untouchable. This woman, right now, at my table, sitting so close I can't escape her scent, impresses me with her heart. She's tough and smart and takes no shit. You only have to spend a few minutes with her to know that. But she's also real and soft and warm. I touched her with my hands, and as she discreetly swipes a tear from the corner of her eye, I see I've touched her heart.

"Um, let's see." She clears her throat, slants a smiling glance at me from beneath long lashes. "What did I write on my napkin? Disenfranchised. Marginalized. Forgotten. Left behind."

"And your mission?"

"To put leaders in power who care about the people I do; who'll work hard as hell to make life better for them. I could have done it a hundred other ways, but when I worked on my first campaign, politics chose me."

"It's a tough game."

"I'm a tough girl." She drains her glass of water. "Ask all the people who call me a bitch. They'll tell you."

"I see more than that."

"Maybe you see what you want to see."

"I want to see you."

The thread of awareness that has been slowly tugging me closer to her pulls taut. She looks up, her eyes widening and then narrowing at my words. I want to answer the questions in her eyes. She knows when someone is attracted to her. She knows about Aiko, about my family. Her unasked question hangs in the air between us. I want to reassure her that I'm no player and explain something to her I haven't even told Noah or Mona yet.

"So your napkin tells me what you're doing now," she says. "What have you been up to the last twenty years or so?" Her dark eyes soften. "After that night, where'd you go, Ezra Stern?"

"Jewish camp."

"I know *that*," she laughs. "And then? Like...everything kind of disintegrated. A few weeks after you and your mom left for New York, your dad left, too. Next thing I know, there's a For Sale sign in your front yard. You guys disappeared."

"I went to camp as planned for a few weeks, and then we moved to Italy."

"Italy? I didn't expect you to say that."

"I didn't expect it either. Dad got that job he'd been wanting, but it took us overseas."

"How was that?"

"It was hard at first. I missed…"

You.

That one unspoken word lands on the table between us, invisible but completely present. Kimba bites her lip and glances down at her menu.

"I missed everyone," I continue. "Missed home, but then I realized it was the best thing that could have happened."

"How so?"

"We moved into this neighborhood where several basketball players lived."

"Like, American basketball players?"

"Yeah. Guys who never made it to the NBA, used to be in the league, couldn't get a contract. Whatever. They ended up playing for an Italian team. And guess what?"

"What?"

"Half their kids were mixed like me. Literally white moms and black dads everywhere."

"Professional basketball players marrying white women? Shocking," she says with a laugh. "So you fit right in, huh?"

"Well, I was still *me*, so I'm not sure I'd ever 'fit right in' anywhere." We chuckle. Basically a case of *it's funny because it's true.* "But there were people who understood my in between-ness—who'd faced some of the same challenges living in America that I had. It was the perfect situation for me to be in at that time."

"How long were you there?"

"Four years. All of high school. My parents actually stayed a few years after I returned to the States for college."

"What school?"

"Howard for undergrad. UCLA for my master's and doctorate."

Her brows elevate. "An HBCU. Another thing I didn't expect."

"My mother made sure I understood my Jewish heritage, but when

I look back on my childhood, besides your family, I didn't have a lot of influences from that other part of me. I needed that, too, and Howard proved to be the perfect incubator to grow my confidence—my understanding of myself. The whole me."

"And then grad school in Cali?"

"Right."

"Is that where..." She glances down, runs a finger around the rim of her glass. "You met Aiko in California?"

"Yeah. I had just started my doctorate at UCLA. She was taking pictures at a party not far from campus."

"She's beautiful. I mean, I only saw her briefly at the funeral, but she was beautiful. There's a lot of her in Noah, too."

"She's an amazing mother."

Kimba runs her finger along the condensation of her glass. "So she doesn't believe in marriage?"

"No. I did ask when we found out she was pregnant, but she turned me down."

"I'm sorry."

"I'm not."

She gives me that look again, full of speculation and a tiny bit of censure. "Look, Kimba, there's something I want to tell you."

"Whoop! Whoop!" Mona says, plopping her oversized bag onto the table. "Hey, good people. Sorry I'm late. I had one nerve left, and Alicia worked it. Late ass. I love her, but she can't be on time to save her *life*."

"Must run in the family," I say dryly, forcing down disappointment that my fifteen minutes alone with Kimba are up.

"Watch it." Mona points a warning finger at me. "Sorry I'm late, Kimba. I promised you a good time and then stuck you with this guy."

Kimba breathes out a laugh, shrugging. "It wasn't so bad."

We look at each other, and it feels to me like the width of the table between us pulses. It pulls on my senses so strongly. Kimba lowers her lashes, sips her water and picks up her menu.

"Well I, for one," Mona says, "need a drink. Where's our server?"

I nod to Cherise, who is even now approaching, pad in hand and smile in place. "Here she comes, but you do realize it's only noon."

"I told you Alicia drained me," she sighs heavily and turns on a beatific smile for Cherise. "How's your margarita?"

Cherise snorts. "Strong."

Mona splits a smirk evenly between Kimba and me. "I'll have two."

CHAPTER SIXTEEN

Kimba

I'M IN HEAD-TO-KNEE POSE WHEN MY PHONE STARTS BUZZING.
Not now. I was just starting to get all centered, dammit.
It takes most people time to unplug. Me? You basically have to jerk the plug from the wall and toss it into a furnace before I can relax. It's the nature of what I do. It's how I'm made, but the homeopath Dr. Granden recommended suggested I try yoga to alleviate any mild hot flashes, mood swings and insomnia as a result of perimenopause. So each morning, I'm on the mat.

My phone buzzes again.

I thought I was being smart putting it out of reach. The hope was that if I couldn't reach it, I wouldn't answer it.

All the possible scenarios crowd out what little peace I was taking for myself. Could it be Congressman Ruiz? Maybe Piers with new information? Are Lennix and the baby okay? Mona?

Ezra?

Not Ezra.

Stop it with the Ezra.

The man is fine AF, yes, but he's *taken*. I'm not trying to walk on Aiko's grass, though to be clear, it is a *beautifully* maintained lawn. Yes, there is an attraction between us. I'd have to be a tree stump not to feel it, but that's perfectly natural. In addition to the bond of being best friends years ago, we're both healthy adults with typical needs.

Do not think about Ezra Stern's needs.

He *needs* to look at his wife the way he was looking at me over pulled pork yesterday. Wife...girlfriend...whatever someone is when they have your baby and live with you for ten years.

Her.

Resistance is futile. I hop up and rush across the small guest bedroom Mama converted into an exercise studio. Homegirl has a Peloton up in here. I snatch the phone from the granite counter where I left it and scan the text.

Kayla: What are you doing? It's hair wash day. Don't you want to come help your big sister?

Blessed assurance. Jesus is mine.

I shudder. Kayla has four girls and one boy. That's FOUR heads to wash with hair as thick and unruly as Kayla's when we were growing up.

Me: Couldn't I just give you a kidney? That sounds less painful and with a quicker recovery.

Kayla: Get your ass over here and help me. Besides they want to see their auntie. They don't know you're mean as a snake. I shield them from that truth. You're welcome.

Me: Then I won't tell them how their mother tortured me as a child either.

Kayla: You think I don't torture them? I would not be Janetta Allen's daughter if I wasn't torturing my children. I learned from the best.

Mama's speaking at one of her charity luncheons, so I *am* here at the house alone.

Me: Alright. Give me an hour.

Kayla: You have thirty minutes.

Ugh. Drill sergeant.

My Uber drops me off at Kayla's Brookhaven home approximately thirty minutes later. When I ring the doorbell, she answers with a child on one hip and another holding her hand.

"You're late," she says, turning and striding back through the marble tiled entrance with its soaring ceiling and dramatic staircase. I follow her slim figure back into the living room. It's a zoo, toys everywhere, children in various stages of undress, hair in disarray, and a collection of sippy cups congregating on the glass coffee table. In contrast, Kayla in her luxury loungewear and brightly colored silk head wrap looks completely serene and unbothered.

"I'm not late," I tell her, bending to hug my niece Triniti, who's working on a Rubix Cube. "Hey, Trin. I didn't know kids still played with things that don't require Wi-Fi."

Triniti looks up, her expression morphing from serious to less serious when she sees me. Ever since she was a baby, this girl has made you work for her smile. It makes them all the more beautiful and worth it. She flashes me a small one now, standing and wrapping her arms around my waist.

"Hey, Aunt Kimba," she says, her voice low and sweet.

A boy, the spitting image of Kayla's husband Lawrence, runs up to me. He's six now, if I'm keeping them all straight. I take inventory and make sure they each get a hug. In ascending order there's the oldest, Triniti, the twins Ida and Gwendolyn, the one boy Joseph, named after my father, and finally the youngest, still in diapers, Zaya.

"You hold Zaya," Kayla says, thrusting the baby at me. "I want to get Ida over with. She's tender-headed."

"I am not," Ida says, sitting on the floor between her mother's knees.

Kayla tugs the comb through one swathe of Ida's wild hair and the poor child screeches, catching the comb before it can go any farther.

Kayla gives me a *what'd I tell you* look, and moves Ida's hand.

"Tender-headed," she mutters.

I bounce Zaya on my lap. I didn't grow up thinking about how many children I would have. I don't remember Kayla doing that either, but she and Lawrence got right down to the business of making babies soon after they married and haven't stopped since.

"I have two sinks down here," Kayla says. "I can wash Ida if you can get Trin."

"Crazy thought," I say, "but ever considered taking them to a salon? They're all the rage these days."

"I do sometimes." Kayla shrugs. "It's not just about getting the hair done. It's about the *doing*. Don't you remember how we'd complain when Mama did our hair, but that was at least an hour where I had her undivided attention? She was always teaching, doing something with Daddy or out in the community. When she did my hair, though, she was all mine." She kisses Ida's forehead, the usual stern lines of her face softening. "I want my girls to have that sometimes."

Even though the lavishly decorated living room looks like a natural disaster struck, Kayla has this ecosystem, like every other thing in her life, under control. She probably doesn't even need my help.

She *doesn't* need my help but wanted me *here*. She doesn't just want me to bond with the kids. I could be wrong, but I think my sister wants to bond with me, too.

She's allergic to sentimentality, so I downplay my discovery.

"Cool, cool, cool," I say with a little grin that she returns after a pause.

"Lawrence always says he has no idea how we ended up having *your* baby," Kayla says wryly, smiling over Ida's volcano of hair.

"*My* baby? What do you mean?"

"Zaya. She looks just like you, Tru. You have to see that, right?"

I glance back to Zaya on my lap. Dark, curious eyes stare back at me. How did I never notice that Zaya has my eyes?

She reaches for one of the curls resting on my shoulder, pulls it and releases, letting it spring back into place with a bounce. She squees and does it again and again as if that is the funniest thing. She's the most beautiful little girl with her satiny brown skin and slobbery smile. How does Kayla not give her every single thing her heart desires every day? I would. I'd be *that* mom.

I'd be that mom?

Since when?

I'm not even sure I want kids, and my body is doing its best to take the choice away from me. I've been following the specialist's instructions. The yoga, the pills and herbal teas, but I've had no tangible image of what I was fighting for.

Until now.

This is why I'm doing those things. This bundle of exuberant unconditional love bouncing on my lap is why I'm making room in my already overflowing life for the things they say may give me a chance to have a baby. The crushing weight, the possibility that I'm too late, that I can't do it, that my body won't let me, falls on me.

"T-t-take her," I stutter, my tongue and lips tangling, my stomach roiling like I might be sick.

Kayla glances up from a stubborn tangle in Ida's hair. "What?"

"Take Zaya." I extend the baby to her, my arms trembling so badly I almost drop her. "I-I-I...just take her, Zee."

"Put her down on the floor," Kayla says, her frown deepening. "She can crawl, but what's wrong with *you?*"

"Nothing." I carefully set Zaya down by a pile of stuffed dice. "I just… God, it's hot in here. I need some air."

"Go to the patio." With her comb, Kayla points to a floor-to-ceiling wall of windows leading to a flagstone terrace.

I flee the house, the hot breath of anxiety panting down my neck. I step through the sliding door, close it hastily behind me and walk to the edge of their patio, stopping next to the aqua liquid glass of their pool. Humidity clogs the Georgia summer afternoon, and even when I draw in huge gulps of air, nothing cools me.

Is this a fucking hot flash?

A panic attack?

The warfare my body is waging, is it psychological, biological? Is hormonal warfare a thing?

I cannot breathe. Sweat sprouts at my hairline and on my top lip. I fan hot air into my face, pressing my lips tight against a scream scraping the inside of my throat. The sun is too bright and the sky isn't wide enough, the clouds seeming to drop and loom over me. I need to *run*, but I can't escape my own body. I'm tethered to this flesh and bone, and these ticking-time-bomb ovaries.

A chorus of laughter floats out to the patio on a song of childish joy, and it squeezes my heart until my lungs must be drowning in my own blood.

I don't need this shit.

The door opens behind me. I stiffen. Kayla is the last person I want to see me like this. She has a fundamental lack of tolerance for weakness, and I'm weak as a lamb inside right now. I hate it.

She walks up beside me but doesn't look my way, choosing to instead squint up at the sun.

"What the hell was that?" she asks, her voice a low, insistent shovel primed to dig.

"I don't want to talk about it."

"Did I ask if you want to talk about it?" Kayla is leader of the won't-let-up crew.

"Zee, could you just leave it alone?"

"I don't think I can."

She takes my hand in a strong grip. I jump, startled. She's holding my hand? I hazard a glance at her profile.

"What exactly are you doing?" I ask, a little laugh managing to squeeze past the rubber bands tight at my throat.

"We're having a moment, Tru."

"Did you schedule this? You know you can't just make moments happen, right?"

"Well, I am. It's happening." She turns to me, not letting my hand go, and when I glance over at her, the real concern in my sister's eyes dissolves my reservations.

"I'm sorry I freaked. I was...and then Zaya...and it just hit me. I haven't dealt with it, I guess."

"Please stop speaking to me in half-formed thoughts. I really can't bear it."

"I'm in perimenopause."

A shocked silence absorbs the sounds of laughing and screeching from the living room. I can't tell if there's any crying mixed in.

"Are they okay by themselves?" I ask, glancing back to the glass doors.

"Yes. Trin, Ida and Gwen can make sure Joe and Zaya survive me leaving the room for five minutes."

Five minutes? Jesus. I have to do this for that long? Could we have a shorter moment?

"Perimenopause." She says it slowly, turning the syllables like they're a foreign tongue and she's repeating them, having no idea what they actually mean. "You're not even forty. Isn't this early?"

"Yes, but it happens."

"I know it happens, but why is it happening to you? Are you sure? Who diagnosed you? Should you get a second opinion?"

"My GP diagnosed me initially but did refer me to a specialist who confirmed through additional testing."

"What do they recommend? Hormone replacement? I have friends going through this now, and there are some real risks with those treatments. Are you on medication? Will they harvest your eggs?"

"Zee." I squeeze her hand, laughing and pleased to find my breaths coming less laboriously now. "Please slow down."

"Slow down? *Do* we have time to slow down? What about kids?"

The girls are singing a verse of Beyoncé's "Halo" ...badly.

"What can I say?" Kayla shrugs. "I have one shortcoming, my awful voice, and they got it."

I snort and roll my eyes, but smile. "I haven't had a period in four months. So the first thing is to get it back. The homeopath is shipping a new detox treatment to see if that helps. I'm not doing hormone replacement for now. Trying alternative routes to manage the symptoms.

We'll see what happens."

"We should figure out if there's a family history." Kayla's brows gather together. I recognize that frown. It's mine whenever a candidate puts his dick in the wrong place or says something stupid into a live mic. Problem-solving mode.

"Look, you have five kids and the foundation and God knows what to take care of. I got this."

"See, that's your problem," she snaps, fire igniting in her dark eyes. "You always got something all by yourself. I'm your sister, Tru, even though you haven't been around for years, and we are every one of us damn proud of you." Her smooth throat moves with a hard swallow. "Daddy would be proud of you."

We stare down at our linked fingers and seem to hold the burden of grief in our two hands. And it does feel good not to carry it alone.

"Let me be there for you," she says. "I'm actually really good at it."

I nod, swiping at a renegade tear slipping from my eye despite my best efforts to stem them. "Okay, Zee."

The door wrenches open, and a wide-eyed Triniti stands in its frame. "Joseph threw up."

"Lord above," Kayla mutters. "I don't do vomit. Lawrence better be glad his ass is out of town."

"I have a strong stomach," I assure her with a chuckle. "You get back to hair and I'm on clean-up duty."

"Okay, but you know you're still washing at least one of those heads, right?"

Busted.

We're at the door when my phone buzzes in my pocket.

Mona: Cookout at my place this weekend. You're coming.

I did enjoy lunch with Mona and Ezra. It was like old times, but with a lot more innuendo and alcohol. And Ezra's fine ass. It's quite irritating how attractive he's become, and how my body seems to have this Jones for brilliant, nice Jewish boys with African violet eyes.

But I knew that already.

It feels good to actively be attracted to someone and not have to force myself to like him, to fuck him, to whatever. There's something delicious about the tension of the forbidden, how you dance around its edges, like caressing a trip wire. I shouldn't because it's obvious the attraction is so damn mutual. I don't think he'd ever act on it. He's a good man. Hell, I'm a good woman. We have a past. Shared our first kiss, for goodness' sake. It's probably just phantom crush pains. I'm strong enough to resist and Ezra's good enough to keep us safe.

The smell of whatever was in Joseph's little stomach hits us as soon as we enter the room, and Kayla waves her hand in front of her nose. "You sure you got it?"

I pull my phone out and type a quick reply.

Me: I'll be there!

"Yeah, I got it."

CHAPTER SEVENTEEN

Ezra

"YOU FIND ANY RIPE ONES, NOAH?"

My son waddles into view from behind a tomato vine, dragging a huge white bucket overflowing with tomatoes.

"All these!" Noah strains to lift the bucket, raising it approximately half an inch. "Are we taking them to Aunt Mona's cookout?"

"Some of them." I lift my bucket of cucumbers and relieve him of his burden, too, then head down a row of the garden toward the house. "But we're filthy. The Stern men need showers."

When Noah begged us to plant a garden, it was the last thing I had time for, but he's easily satisfied and doesn't ask for much. When other kids wanted expensive tennis shoes or the latest video game, he asked for a garden in our backyard. How could we deny him? My only condition was that he had to help dig it, plant the seeds and maintain it. At one of the busiest times of my life, as the school was taking off, the garden became a way for Noah and me to connect every day.

My cell phone is ringing on the kitchen counter when we walk into the mudroom and remove our dirty work boots.

"Maybe it's Mommy!" Noah yells, running inside ahead of me.

"Do not answer my phone until I know who it is." I bring the two buckets of vegetables into the kitchen and let the door slam behind me. If it is Aiko calling, I'll let Noah do all the talking. We spoke briefly a few days ago when she let us know she'd landed safely, and she said she would call back after they settled some. She and Chaz can have sex several times a day as far as I'm concerned, but it still feels weird talking to her and wondering if it's happening. When she returns, we have a new reality for Noah to acclimate to. I can't stand the thought of seeing him half the week while he's at another house with Aiko the rest of the time. But when she comes home, we'll figure it out.

"It's Bubbe," Noah says, looking up from my cell phone on the counter. "Can I answer?"

"Sure." I turn on the tap and rinse tomatoes and cucumbers in the sink.

"And Daddy won the award," Noah gushes a few minutes into his conversation with my mother. He hasn't stopped speaking since he picked up the phone. "And his friend gave it to him."

He finally draws a breath, pausing to listen to my mother. "The friend from TV. Kimba Allen."

He holds the phone to me. "Bubbe wants to speak to you."

I bet she does.

"Hey, Mom." I trap the phone between my ear and shoulder while I slice a cucumber.

"Why didn't you tell me you were receiving an award from the Allen Foundation?"

"Mom, it's not that big of a deal."

The silence fills with what she and I both know—it *is.* I never got the full story of what went so wrong in my parents' friendship with the Allens, but we moved and, as far as I know, they never had contact with them again. That volatile night cleaved our life into two distinct parts. In one of those parts, Kimba Allen was my best friend. In the other, she and her family didn't exist.

"Why would they…" Mom pauses, clears her throat. "Tell me how this happened."

"I received an email saying I was being honored for excellence in education. I went to the ceremony."

"And Kimba was there?"

"She was. She presented the awards. Kayla, Keith, Mrs. Allen—they were all there."

"How was Janetta?" Affection softens her tone, something that hasn't happened before on the rare occasions when we've referenced Kimba's family.

"She's good. She asked about you, too. She didn't know Dad had passed. She said to wish you well."

"Did she?" Mom chuckles. "I wouldn't have survived those first few years in Georgia without that woman."

"I know," I say, determined to step through the rare crack in the door. "So what happened back then? You were all so close, and then—"

"It was a long time ago," Mom cuts me off. "Kimba's made quite a name for herself. Not surprising. She was always the most like her father to me. How was she?"

I don't know how to answer that. She was twenty-four years older than the last time I kissed her. She's someone I used to know at a molecular level, but now I couldn't even tell you where she lives, or her favorite food.

"She's fine. Mona invited her to this cookout tonight."

The line goes quiet for a second. "Is Aiko still in Tanzania?" Mom asks, her tone careful and obvious.

"You know she is. Your point in asking at just this moment?"

"I'm not poking my head in your business, son. I just know how intense you used to be about Kimba. Seeing old...friends when we're having trouble with our partners can be dangerous."

My mother knows about the struggles Aiko and I have had. We've been open about it. I glance up to where Noah is playing a game on his iPad a few feet away. I would hate for him to overhear something prematurely. Aiko would be devastated not to be with me when he finds out. I'll tell my mom the truth later.

"Mom, don't worry so much." I stow the sliced vegetables in the refrigerator. "How's Stanley?"

"Ezra, I know you."

"Good. Then you know I would never hurt Aiko. How's Stanley?"

Cue heavy Jewish Mom sigh, laced with longsuffering.

"Okay, just remember what I said," she replies. "And Stanley's good. The doctor checked his stint."

My mom went from marrying an African-American atheist lawyer to the most Jewish man in New York City, Stanley Ebstein. He grew up attending the same synagogue as my mother and lived two blocks from her family's dry-cleaning business that dates back to the early 1900s. His family owns a chain of kosher delis.

"Put Noah back on the phone," Mom says after she catalogs all of Stanley's medications and their upcoming doctor's appointments. "I need to make sure he's ready for summer camp. You're flying him up next week, right?"

"Yeah." I walk over to Noah. "After his birthday party."

"Are you still staying for a week? It's been a while since you've seen everyone in the neighborhood."

My reflex response is to confirm I'll stay for a visit, but some traitorous imp reminds me that Kimba may stay in Atlanta for a few weeks.

"We'll see. Here's your grandson," I reply, handing Noah the phone before my mother can berate me.

I'm cleaning up the small mess I made preparing vegetables when Mona walks through the door that leads to the backyard.

"It's just me," she says, our standard greeting as we flow in and out of each other's homes.

"What's up?" I spare her a smile while I'm wiping down the counter.

"Answer your damn phone. I was catching up on *The Swamp People* and had to drag my ass from the comfort of my home to come over here. Are you happy now?"

"So sorry to have inconvenienced you. How can I help?"

"You got any Sriracha sauce? I'm out."

I nod toward the cabinet over the stove. "Up there, and Noah probably didn't answer if you tried to call. When he and my mom get on the phone, it's like a rerun of *The Golden Girls*."

"Don't I know it." Mona chuckles and goes on her tiptoes to reach the spicy sauce. "Folks will start arriving around seven."

"Need help setting up?"

"Nah. I'm keeping it basic. Just a few friends, some ribs, hot dogs, steaks, fried chicken, potato salad, watermelon, catfish—"

"Mona," I laugh, interrupting her long list of menu items. "That doesn't sound exactly basic. I'll bring wine and some fresh vegetables."

"Thanks, and Kimba confirmed she's coming." Mona's smooth skin crinkles at the corners of her eyes with an excited smile. "The *Three's Company* crew together again."

My ears prick and my muscles tighten at the news. I lean against the counter and fold my arms, going for casual and vaguely interested. "Oh, yeah? Cool."

"Right?" Mona hops up onto the countertop and leans back on her palms. "What do you think about Barry?"

"Barry? Barry like Barry Burrows, the math teacher from school?"

"Yeah. I was thinking about introducing him to Kimba."

"What?" I choke and cough. "Why?"

"Kimba's young and beautiful and successful. She may be too busy to stop and smell the testosterone. As her friend—"

"Who literally hasn't seen her in twenty-four years and has no idea what she wants in a guy...but go on."

"People don't change that much."

"Yeah, they actually do from age thirteen to thirty-seven."

"I think she and Barry could be cute together."

"Cute?" I grimace and shake my head. "Kimba's not cute, and any guy she would be *cute* with is all wrong."

"You're not saying that because he's white, are you? Barry is literally and figuratively invited to the cookout."

"Pretty sure I would be the last to disqualify someone based on them being a different race."

"Oh, yeah." Mona grins and grimaces. "True."

"And I'm aware of Barry's level of wokeness. I *did* hire the man."

"I bet Kimba likes her some woke white dick."

"Could you *not* do that thing where you forget I'm a grown man and say inappropriate things to me?"

Also avoid things that make me feel like the Hulk inside, like mentioning Kimba and someone else's dick in the same sentence.

The possessiveness is irrational. Kimba and I haven't been in each other's lives since *middle school.* I have no claim on her, but the feelings that never got the chance to fully develop are still there. I felt it Saturday.

Did Kimba feel it, too?

"Sorry." Mona laughs, obviously unrepentant. "Let me rephrase for your grown man sensibilities. What I meant to say is I think Kimba has had many, um...experiences, and would not be white boy averse."

What about biracial Jewish boys? Think she's into those?

"He doesn't seem like her type." I clear my throat. "Besides, she might already be in a relationship." *Okay, so I'm fishing.*

"She's not."

"How do you know?" *Now I'm probing.*

"I asked her on the phone."

"She called? You didn't say she called."

"Sorry, nosy. She texted me to say she was coming and I called her to scream about it. We got to talking. Turns out we're both in a drought."

"Drought?"

"Dick drought. She's running through batteries fast as I am."

"Dammit, Mona. I do not need to know how often you…" I glance over at Noah, who literally just said "oy vey" to my mother. "…do that."

And the mental image of Kimba masturbating will not be easy to shake.

Well, *fuck*.

Make that a *cold* shower for at least one of the Stern men.

"Well, she's doing that a lot, too." Mona laughs. "And even if she and Barry just hook up while she's here, it could—"

"No." The word storms from my mouth before I have time to think about it.

Mona tips her head, a frown puckering above puzzled eyes. "You're not like doing some weird, half-paternal, half-fraternal slut shaming thing, are you? Because Kimba will not appreciate that."

"Fraternal?" *Hardly.* "No, I just think…" I think what? That if Kimba's gonna fuck anyone on vacation it should be me?

"I hate we missed our formative sex years together," Mona says, tapping the heels of her Chucks against the counter. "The three of us, I mean. I can just see Kimba and me talking about our first time and you rolling your eyes and covering your ears."

Considering the huge crush I had on Kimba back then, I would have died inside. "Yeah, well, you hooking her up with Barry won't make up for it."

"You never know." She hops down from the countertop and grabs the sauce she came to borrow. "She went off to make that big name for herself, but the man for her could have been right here back home in Atlanta."

In a way, we both left this city to find ourselves. As much as I hated leaving Kimba, I found myself overseas. Kimba had to leave the city to carve out a space for herself, out from under the shadow of her family's name. Now we're both back where it all began. Where *we* began. I'm here to stay, but she's not. What are the odds of her coming back to town when Aiko and I just broke up? When I'm, for the first time in a decade, free to pursue her.

Like I said. Sometimes what we think is a fluke is really fate.

Whichever it is, I won't let it go to waste.

CHAPTER EIGHTEEN

Kimba

C OMING TO MONA'S COOKOUT WAS A BAD IDEA.
On so many levels.
Level one.

I could quite possibly eviscerate her guest bathroom. I've been either sitting on or kneeling before the porcelain throne for the last two days, digestively prolific from both ends, and I'm about damn tired of it. Between diarrhea and vomiting, I've been chained to my mother's house. There's a reason I put several states between us. We love each other, God knows we do, but after a day or so, two alpha females under one roof is a whole-ass mood.

Not a good one.

In addition to Mama's usual lecturing, advising and "guiding," she's also fussed over me, assuming I'm sick, a much more logical conclusion than the truth. The detox pills that may re-start my period arrived. The catch? They have run through my body like a typhoon.

Never thought I'd say this, but I *better* bleed.

Several of my homeopath's patients have not only restored their cycles through this remedy, but have gone on to have babies.

Do I even want to have a baby? I was hoping that wasn't a question I'd have to answer quite yet, but apparently, if I want to give birth naturally, the time is now...or at least within the next year or so...or never.

But first, my period has to come back. That's pretty much square one with reproduction.

Level two for why coming to this cookout is a bad idea?

Ezra Stern.

He's an old friend. A blast from the past. An all grown up, broody, brilliant, intense, tall and handsome blast from the past.

And he's taken.

Let that sink in, Tru.

I can't stop thinking about him, though. I keep seeing him, not just as he is now—handsome and towering and sex-on-a-magic-stick—but as he was *then*—kind, slyly witty, compassionate, and protective. He was my solace and my secret. No one else knew how amazing Ezra was back then, and I liked having him to myself. Now he belongs to someone else, and I have to respect that.

Our friendship always went deeper than connections I've had with other people. Aside from how I felt with Lennix and Vivienne, no one else came close. All my life I kept waiting to feel that kind of knowing with someone else. I mean, we were *thirteen*. But I never have. I thought, maybe hoped, we had outgrown that visceral bond, but it's still there. At least, I felt it immediately. It's the fiber of our friendship. You don't blame magnets for being drawn to each other. But if they're far enough apart, they can't stick. For the last two decades, Ezra and I were far enough apart not to stick, but now...

This is a bad idea.

I pull up to the address Mona texted me, surprised at the long line of cars crowding the street and wrapping around the block. If all these people are here for Mona's cookout, she would also call Coachella "a small gathering of friends." I park as close as I can and walk back toward her place. The Old Fourth Ward has changed a lot in twenty years. Now there are coffee shops, a yoga studio around the corner, and every other house is a newly-constructed three-story with a van or an SUV in the driveway.

Ah, gentrification. Atlanta is not immune.

I went through our old neighborhood to get here. Driving down the streets where Ezra and I used to ride our bikes, seeing the old park, now upgraded, the old rickety swings replaced with new ones, took me back to those days. Mrs. Washington's house, where she'd pretend to be watering plants so she could hear everyone's business, is still there, but there's a SOLD sign out front. Probably a close and doze. Our houses, mine and Ezra's, still stand facing each other and look almost the way they did before, just with fresh coats of paint.

I shove aside old memories. Considering the awareness between Ezra and me, revisiting the past won't serve me well.

I climb the steps to the wraparound porch, ringing the doorbell and taking in the swing, hanging plants and fairy lights while I wait. When the door opens, Mona greets me with hooping, hollering and hugs.

"Girl, get in here." She drags me farther into the house, which is wall-to-wall with people eating, drinking and talking.

"You found it okay?" she asks, steadily picking her way through the crowd.

"I did. Thanks for inviting me."

The last year has been dedicated to electing Maxim Cade president. There wasn't much time for cookouts or *hanging* out. I was on the road and on television a lot more than I wanted to be, but hey. That's the job, and God and Mateo Ruiz willing, I'll be starting up the next cycle in a few weeks. This is a reprieve and a chance for me to reconnect with my family, and this city that used to be my home.

And with old friends.

Noah runs up to me right away, his dark blue eyes lit and excited.

"Kimba!" he says. "You're here."

"I am." I've never been a kid person, but something about this one gets to me.

"Come play with me."

Play? I'm definitely not one of those "aunties" who gets down on the floor and crawls around with small humans on my back. Not even my own nieces and nephews, though cleaning up after Joseph was quite the baptism.

"Um...play?" I hope I don't have to crush his opinion of me as a "fun adult" this soon.

"Chess."

Chess? I should have known. This is Ezra's child after all.

He leads me to a chessboard set up on Mona's screened-in porch. I'm incredibly competitive, so I have to remind myself to go easy on him. He's just a kid.

"Checkmate," Noah says twenty minutes later, wearing a triumphant smile so wide it practically hangs off his face.

"But...wait." I review our last few plays. "How did you do that?"

"Strategy." He taps his temple and *winks* at me. "It's all up here."

"Well, you better bring it down here for a rematch," I say, reaching across the board to grab his king.

"No fair!" he squeals, running around to my side and reaching for the chess piece.

"She cheats, Noah," Ezra says from the porch door, muscular arms exposed by a short-sleeved T-shirt and folded across his broad chest. His hair is a sable cap shorn into ruthlessly restrained waves. His eyes, that navy color I remember when he's most relaxed, rest on his son in obvious affection and then turn on me, sending a jolt right down my middle.

"I do not!" I can't quite meet Ezra's intent gaze, so I focus on Noah. "That was beginner's luck."

"Who's a beginner?" Noah cocks one brow. "I've been playing since I was five."

"He's so much like you when you were this age," I tell Ezra. "And that may *not* be a compliment."

Father and son both laugh, and I find myself laughing, too, feeling lighter than I have in months.

"Son, go wash your hands," Ezra says, bending to kiss Noah's head. "Food's ready."

Noah runs inside. There are other people on the screened-in porch, some playing dominos or cards or just drinking, but the space seems to suddenly cave in on us, making it hard to breathe. It's the first wave of a Georgia summer, so it's already hot, but that doesn't account for how my breaths truncate, and I'm suddenly covered in a thin layer of simmering tension. It feels like this porch just became a tiny chessboard, and I'm awaiting Ezra's opening move.

"Don't feel too bad." Ezra plucks the king from my fingers and lays it on its side. "He almost beat me. Once."

"You created a monster in your image," I say, the laugh I force coming out breathier than it should.

"I like to think so. I taught him the most important thing to remember in chess."

"And what's that?"

He glances up from the board, his eyes tracing my face in that deliberate way of his. "The queen is the most powerful piece."

The bridge is out, and we stare at each other from opposite sides of it, each daring the other to leap. I break eye contact and clear my throat. "I think you held back some stuff when you taught me how to play."

He shakes his head, a rueful tilt at the corner of his mouth. "I never held anything back from you, Tru."

There's no innuendo in his comment. He's not flirting with me, even though you wouldn't know that by the fluttering wings beneath my ribcage. It's just the truth. We had that rare friendship with no limits other than the ones the world and our parents imposed.

"Remember when I explained that a black queen starting on a black square is called a queen getting her color?" he asks, grinning.

"I went around for days telling everyone I was getting my color." I chuckle and lean back in my seat, crossing my legs. I feel his eyes on me, following the length of my body. He lets himself look for a moment and then turns his head to stare through the screen out to Mona's backyard. I can't help but think of the man so blatantly staring at my ass a few weeks ago at my doctor's office. That did nothing for me, but a man *restraining* himself—Ezra trying his hardest *not* to look at me—stirs liquid heat in my belly. Even the stare he averts burns.

Mona walks in from the backyard.

"You guys ready to eat?" she asks. "Ezra, you're the only chef I know who abandons his masterpiece."

"You mean the hot dogs on the grill?" Ezra asks. "My work was done."

"And steak, and chicken," Mona says, looping her arm through his. "Noah will eat so much you have to roll him home."

"I have no idea where he puts it."

"You used to be the same way." I walk with them into Mona's backyard.

"All Ezra's food went to the future." Mona laughs, squeezing one of his well-defined arms. "And was just waiting for him to catch up when he got to high school."

"Very funny," Ezra says. "And do me a favor? Tell Noah it was the vitamins that made me grow so much bigger. It's the only way I can get him to take them."

"He's hilarious." Fondness is apparent in Mona's tone as we approach a table laden with too many dishes for me to even process.

Noah walks up and takes his place in front of his father in line. As we wait our turn, there's such an ease between the two of them. It's apparent Noah respects his father's authority, but they also seem to be friends. A lot of eight-year-olds would be squirmy with affection from their dads by now, but Noah leans into Ezra often, even grabbing his hand sometimes when he's making a point.

"I'm going to Jewish camp this summer," Noah tells me, his voice and face vibrant with excitement.

"Your dad used to go to camp in New York sometimes when we were growing up," I tell him, spearing a hot dog but skipping the bun. I'm hoping the homeopathic regimen will get my weight back to normal, but there's no need to tempt the goddess of cellulite with lots of carbs. My stomach has been surprisingly placid today. I hope the worst is over and I don't have to ruin Mona's bathroom. I keep envisioning that scene when Ben Stiller overflows the toilet in *Along Came Polly*. It could be that bad. Worse.

"I know." Noah frowns at the fruit Ezra dishes onto his plate, but doesn't voice the objection on his face. "I'm going to the same camp. Bubbe says it's a family tradition."

Ezra said something similar when he'd go up to New York for a few weeks each summer to the camp his bubbe preferred. He loved that woman so much. When I glance at him, his eyes are shadowed and his full mouth settles into a sober line. Some things you never quite get over, and somehow, I suspect Bubbe passing is one of those things for Ezra. I give his hand a compassionate squeeze.

"She was something else," I whisper to him while we wait for the steak.

"What?" He looks down at our hands and back up to my face. "Who?"

"Oh." I pull away hastily. "Sorry. I thought you might be thinking of your gran."

He stares at me for several seconds, and then his mouth tips at one corner. "Yeah, I was, actually. How'd you know that?"

It feels strange to know the path of his thoughts when it has been so long since we've seen each other—to still feel like some part of me is plugged into his emotions. To feel I might be able to know his mind as well as I know my own.

"Just guessing." I shrug, unprepared to go there with him, not the way my body lights up every time I catch him staring.

I turn my head and he's looking at me. I lose myself in his eyes, not in that dreamy, romance-y way, but in the mystery of them—of what lies behind the midnight-blue shade he pulls over his thoughts.

"Hey!" Mona snaps her fingers in the space that separates our faces. "You two are not doing that thing you used to do. I forbid it."

I blink several times, breaking the spell of ancient memories and new mysteries. "What are you talking about?"

"The two of you used to block everyone else out, get lost in some corner and only talk to each other," Mona says. "This is a social event."

"My favorite thing to escape from," Ezra says.

"Daddy's an introvert." Noah bites into a Hebrew National hot dog.

"Thanks, son," Ezra says, his mouth a wry curve. "I think they know that about me."

"He used to be a Kimba-vert," Mona says. "He was only social with her. Then I came along and he was at least sometime-y with me."

"Why?" Noah asks around a mouthful of hot dog.

"What have I told you about talking with food in your mouth?" Ezra asks softly. "And why what?"

"Why were you a Kimba-vert?"

Our gazes collide, and I look away first. I don't want to hear how he would answer that question, so I reply for him. "Your dad and I knew each other literally since we were babies," I tell him and take a sip of the freshly-squeezed lemonade Mona set out. "Longer than anyone else, so we were always really comfortable together."

"That's nice," Noah says. "I want a friend like that."

"You have Peter," Ezra says, taking a pull of his beer.

"But I'm not a Peter-vert," he says.

We all laugh, but once the humor fades, I find myself drawn to look at Ezra again. And dammit, he's looking back.

More people join us at the table, and soon everyone's laughing and telling stories. Most of them work with Mona and Ezra at YLA. It's obvious they respect Ezra a lot. And it's obvious to me that more than one of them, guys and girls, are crushing on him. If he weren't with Aiko, he could have his choice of office romances.

As the meal winds down, the bright colors of sunset fading into evening, I take my cue from Mona and start carrying empty dishes back into the house.

"So what'd you think of Barry?" Mona asks, opening the dishwasher and loading a few plates.

"Who?"

"You know. Barry." Mona straightens, puts her hands on her hips and offers a suggestive smile. "Dark hair, pretty brown eyes, wearing the Georgia Tech T-shirt."

"Oh, him. Am I supposed to think something about him in particular?"

"He asked if you were seeing anyone," she lilts.

"He did? Hmm. Not sure he's my type."

"Because he's not rich?" Mona asks, rolling her eyes.

"No, of course not. He's got a biker body."

"Biker body?"

"You know, that real lean look. Like he hasn't had a meal that wasn't an energy bar in a while and like he metabolizes every calorie before he even eats it. I'm not a little girl. I like a not-a-little man or I feel like I might crush him."

"You're not a big girl."

"Bigger than him." I laugh. "Does he or does he not bike?"

Mona blows out a short breath. "I hate you."

"I knew it." I point a serving spoon at her. "He's got that Lance Armstrong look."

"I can confirm he has both his balls."

I angle a WTF look at her.

"I mean, I don't *know know*, like firsthand," Mona says, laughing. "But one can assume."

"Well, this *one* doesn't need to know."

"Are you not in the market for a relationship? Or even a fling?"

"I don't know what I'm in the market for."

"Girl, same. And my mama is riding me hard about grandkids. I tried marriage and it wasn't for me. Lasted about two years and ended badly." A shadow crosses her face, and though I can see her try to shake it, she doesn't quite succeed.

"You think you'll try again?" I ask.

"Probably. Right person, yeah, sure. I love kids and might if only to have a baby and a partner I respect enough to raise it. How about you? You want kids?"

The question crashes into me unexpectedly, like a wrecking ball right to the chest. When people asked me that before, I played it off, or shrugged and said *someday*. Now my *someday* has an expiration date. I haven't allowed myself to process it, but standing alone in Mona's kitchen with an old friend, the first person I confided my "girl" stuff to, everything comes to the surface.

"I'm in perimenopause."

Mona frowns, then her eyes widen in realization. "You're in what?

Menopause?"

"Perimenopause, but yeah." I point to my midsection and pelvis area. "All of this is vacating the premises earlier than expected."

"But we're in our thirties."

"Exactly."

Mona stops loading dishes and gives me her full attention. "How do you feel? What does this mean for, like, kids? You want them?"

"I think I do, yeah, but not now. I didn't want them *right now*, and my doctor makes it seem like now or never. She thinks I may have a year and a half to two years, somewhere around there, if I want one naturally."

"Shit." Mona digs her hands into the front pockets of her denim cut-offs. "You already started treatments? My mother did hormone replacements." She winces. "Not that you're like my mom's age or anything. I didn't mean it to sound like—"

"Don't worry. I know what you mean. My mother's barely in menopause, much less me. And my doctor wanted me to try a homeopath first."

"How's it going?"

"Oh, it's going all right." I grimace. "I've been 'going' for two days straight. She gave me some detox pills and some other stuff to try to restart my cycle and address some of the other symptoms I have just a little of."

"Wait." Mona's eyes widen. "You don't have a period anymore?"

"Not in four months."

"And once your period comes back? Do you then start trying to have a baby?"

"Well I don't have anyone to *do that* with. Even if I can get pregnant, it's the worst time for that. I'm about to go back on the road for a campaign."

"Who?" Mona leans forward, her voice lowered.

"I hope Mateo Ruiz," I say, a bitter curve to my lips. "But he's not sure he wants me yet."

"You just elected the president," Mona says indignantly. "You don't have anything to prove."

"Yeah, that's how I thought about it at first, too, but each candidate has to feel comfortable with the person leading their campaign. He's right not to assume that just because I was the right person for Maxim that I'm right for him." I give a self-deprecating smile. "Besides, Daddy always used to say it was better to be accused of modesty than of being too big for your britches."

"He was such a great man. I know we haven't seen each other in a long time, but I would have come to the funeral if I'd been in town. Glad Ezra made it. I was surprised you two didn't keep in touch after seeing each other again."

"We were both really busy, I guess," I tell Mona, turning to place dishes in the sink because I don't know what my face would give away. "Lennix and I had just released our book. It hit the *New York Times*, which neither of us expected. Between the book tour and running a few campaigns, I didn't have much time for going down Memory Lane."

"What a fabulous life you're leading," Mona says, her smile pleased, proud. "And now, if Congressman Ruiz is smart, you might help Georgia elect its first Latino governor."

"It'll be quite the fight. If I get the job, it won't be the best time to be pregnant."

"Oh, yeah." Mona's expression falls. "You have a lot to think about."

"I'm hoping this time off here at home will help me figure out what I want, what's right for me."

"Well, while you figure it out," Mona says, tipping her head toward the window overlooking the backyard, "there's a fine biker dude who might take you on."

"I don't know about a summer fling. My life's too complicated right now for anyone to get the wrong idea about what I'm expecting."

"Maybe just a few dates."

"Nah. I don't really like to date. I just like to fuck."

Mona's eyes widen looking over my shoulder, and then squint as she laughs. "Oh my God! If you could see your face, Ezra."

I swing around and Ezra's standing at the door holding an empty tray. He doesn't look at me but walks past us to place the tray in the sink.

"Just like old times," he says. "Me walking in on some conversation I wish I could un-hear."

I wish I could *un-say* that last comment.

"Where's Noah?" I ask, changing the subject quickly.

"Beating another victim at chess." He doesn't look at me as he continues loading the dishwasher.

Is he judging me? I shouldn't feel self-conscious about what I said.

It's the truth. I *do* prefer just fucking. I don't like strings, to be tied to someone emotionally or socially simply because we had sex. By and large, sex has been physical with very few side effects on my heart. I'm fine with that, and Ezra doesn't get to judge me for it.

The silence that settles between us doesn't have the chance to grow awkward because laughter and shouts reach us through the window. I peer out to the backyard. Overhead lights strung in trees lend the scene a warm glow. Two lines form, people facing each other, and Marvin Gaye's "Got to Give It Up" drifts into the kitchen, the dance standard that no cookout is complete without.

"Oh, it's on!" Mona says, hips already swaying, fingers already snapping, arms already in the air. "*Soul Train* line! Come on."

"You guys go on ahead," Ezra says, giving Mona an indulgent smile. "I'll finish up in here."

"You sure?" I ask, meeting his eyes for the first time since my awkward comment. "I can help."

"Nah." He extends his smile to me, though it's less natural. "You know I never met a dance floor I liked, even if it is grass."

A memory takes shape. Me dancing with Jeremy, and Ezra swaying awkwardly with Hannah, our eyes meeting over their shoulders. Boyz II Men singing "I'll Make Love to You" before we even knew what it meant to make love. We had no idea our first kiss was right around the corner and down the hall. No idea it'd be with each other. Breathless innocence. The first taste of passion. My heart pounding through my training bra, and Ezra's hands so strangely certain even at that age of how to touch me. Not in bases, first or second or third, but in stages. Exploring, easing, caring.

"Girl, he hates dancing," Mona says, grabbing my hand and pulling me toward the door. "You know that."

I shoot one last look over my shoulder as we're heading out back, and he's watching me again. I don't have to wonder if he's remembering that night, that dance, that kiss.

That ending.

I know he is.

CHAPTER NINETEEN

Ezra

I'VE ALWAYS HAD TWO LEFT FEET.

My father tried teaching me to dance. He used to say my mother's genes took all my rhythm in the womb. I used to think black people just knew how to dance. It was something I missed out on. A stray piece of my puzzle I never found.

My parents were shocked when I decided after high school in Italy that I wanted to attend Howard University. My mother didn't know how to ask it, but she didn't have to. The *but why* was all over her face. I'd received acceptance letters from Cornell, UCLA, and Columbia, my father's alma mater. I didn't even have a scholarship to Howard, but I chose it; I wanted to immerse myself into the unique experience I could only have at an HBCU. I needed to explore that aspect of myself, that *black* part of myself, in a place where it was affirmed.

I've never regretted it. It solidified so many things about who I am. *All* the parts of who I am. My senior year, I did my student teaching in some of D.C.'s toughest schools and saw how the system had failed a lot of those kids. Saw how hamstrung many educators were by the very system that charged them to teach. That was when the vision for YLA first took root.

The kids at YLA love to dance, most of them executing the latest moves with an ease my body has never managed. Noah's still too young for YLA, but he's around a lot, and as soon as they turn on the music and start dancing spontaneously in the gym, the cafeteria, the courtyard, he's up and moving.

Like now. I'm sitting on this stacked stone wall encircling Mona's backyard, still the "potted plant" wallflower, while my son is dabbing, sliding and Fortnite flossing, his face lit up as he stands in one of the lines awaiting his turn in the spotlight. Mona powers down the open lane between the two lines, moonwalking, pop locking and freestyling with Marvin Gaye crooning encouragingly.

And then it's Kimba's turn.

That damn little dress she's wearing has tortured me ever since it walked through the door, swishing around her toned legs, hinting at an ass which, I remember from the times I've seen her in form-fitting clothes, is spectacular. The spaghetti straps slip off smooth brown shoulders as she shuffles down the open lane. She lifts her hands in the air, arms extended, worshiping the beat, twirling carelessly as the hem of her dress flies up, flashing the tops of her thighs.

I haven't been this hard in weeks. Months. Years.

Ever?

I don't remember having an erection around Kimba when we were growing up. We were kids. We were young. Even when we shared our first kiss, I wasn't afraid my body might betray me, confess to her the urges we weren't ready to act on. But now, watching her, wanting her as a man, not an untried kid, there's no hiding the effect she has on me. I'm sitting on the sidelines, not just because I'm apparently the only dude at the cookout who can't dance, but because if I stand, everyone will know my situation. Immediately.

There's no hiding this fully erect dick in my pants.

I've tried not to watch her, but I'm obsessed with the curve of her waist, the shadowy dip between her breasts, the elegant line of her neck, the way her hands dance in the air when she's animated. The intricate whorl of her ear when she pushes the curls away from her face. The regal profile and perennially-kissed pout of her lips. Hers is a boudoir body out in the open, a bold sketch of elongation and exaggerated curves.

I have to stop.

But I can't.

It's a compulsion. It's a high. After all these years, she's *here*. And I can't get my fill. All these people—I wish they'd disappear and I could have her to myself. I could excavate her mind and dig around in her soul and get close enough to hear her heartbeat. Beyond the desire to lay her down in the grass and plunge between those long legs, there's something I want even more. To know her the way I did before. No, *deeper* than I did before because now we're adults, re-formed by time and experiences.

I want to learn the new shape of her.

Unlike me, Noah is not an introvert. He inherited his openness, his "never meets a stranger-ness" from Aiko. He's only known Kimba for a short time, but he has no problem grabbing her hand and laughing, dancing with her. They look free and unfettered. Kimba kicks off her shoes, and her bare, pretty feet shuffle through the grass as easily as I've seen her walk red carpets on television. I didn't know what to call what I used to feel for Kimba—the desire to have her with me all the time; to know her better than everyone else did. It was an innocent possessiveness that she reflected back to me even then. She wanted that from me. It was earnest and pure. But the first time I saw her on CNN, talking easily, debating someone from the other side of the aisle, systematically picking apart his argument with surgical, intelligent precision, no sign of the stutter that plagued her before, I felt immeasurably proud.

But also jealous. Possessive. I'd discovered this beautiful butterfly when she was a caterpillar and she had been completely mine. Now the whole world marveled at the spread of her wings, basked in her vibrant color. Now everyone knew how fantastic she was and she'd never be just mine again.

"Dad!" Noah shouts over the music. "Get up!"

Still on beat, he dances over, dragging Kimba by the hand.

"You know better than that," I tell him with a laugh, flicking a glance at Kimba. She's glowing. It's not just the lights Mona strung through the trees, or even the fine sheen of perspiration misting her smooth skin. It's from inside.

She's home.

Somehow I knew she needed to come back. Does she realize how free she seems? I secretly worried about her from afar, watching her manage one of the most successful political campaigns in our nation's history. Watching her guide and ride Maxim Cade's presidential bid to political fame. It had to be exhausting. I wanted rest for her, and she seems to be getting it.

"Baaak baaak bak bak," Noah crows, doing his chicken dance. "Dad's scared to dance."

"Peer pressure," I deadpan. "Real original, son. And highly ineffective on someone like me. Know your opponent."

"Come on." Kimba joins Noah's cajoling, the two of them dancing in front of me as I sit stubbornly in place on the wall.

The classic Gaye tune finally ends, and something newer comes on. Something I hear the kids play at school. Cardi B.? Megan Thee Stallion? Some empowered, guns-blazing woman showing the boys how it's done. My students barely know the great hip-hop that tutored me in so much understanding of a culture I didn't have enough exposure to when I was young. Nas. Biggie. Pac. Those artists are *ideas* to them, icons whose music represents a distant greatness that doesn't actually shape them. Not the way they helped form me even when I lived in Italy.

"The song changed," I tell them with a shrug. "Oh, well. Maybe next time."

"If you're not gonna dance," Noah says, "I'm gonna go get dessert."

"One," I remind him. "One dessert. Choose wisely."

"Banana pudding," he tells me. "Want to come, Kimba?"

I reach out and take her wrist, pulling her closer to the wall. Everyone else has had her. I'm taking my time.

"Why don't you bring us something back," I say, tugging her to sit on the wall beside me. "Any red velvet cake? Is that still your favorite, Tru?"

She looks at me, bites her lip, and nods. "Yeah. If they have any. Thanks, Noah."

"Why do you call her Tru?" Noah asks.

Kimba and I look at each other, a smile growing between us. We lift our brows at the same time, a "you wanna tell him or should I" gesture.

"My middle name is Truth," she says. "So Tru for short, but only my family calls me that."

"But you're not her family, are you, Dad?" Noah asks.

"No, but we used to live across the street from each other, and we've known each other all our lives." I smile at him. "Some people feel closer than family sometimes."

"Like Aunt Mona?" His face brightens, his snaggle-toothed grin reappearing.

"Exactly," I say. "I think I saw German chocolate cake. Bring that back for your old man, okay?"

"Okay!" He dashes off and is swallowed by the still-not-thinning crowd squeezed into Mona's cozy backyard.

"He'll be back in about…oh, thirty minutes," I say. "He'll get stopped and pulled into a card game, a conversation, something, and forget all about us. That kid's like the mayor. I don't even know how he's mine."

Kimba shifts on the wall, crossing one long leg over the other. "I see a lot of you in him."

In the moonglow, her skin gleams like minted copper.

"Ya think?" I ask, discreetly inhaling that unique citrusy scent of hers and hunching to rest my elbows on my knees when my dick stiffens even more. This is so not good.

"For sure. He's curious, the way you were at that age. Sensitive, but still strong. You had a quiet boldness even then. Kind of this self-containedness. He has that, too." She lowers long lashes, shielding her dark eyes from me. "And his eyes. They're exactly like yours."

I can't resist touching her in even the smallest way, not a second longer. I tip up her chin, her heart-shaped face, until our eyes meet.

"We got interrupted the other day." The softness of my voice barely conceals my voracious hunger for every detail of what she's done while we were apart. "Tell me what's been up with you."

"A lot." She laughs, leaning back on her palms. "If I get started, we'll be here a very long time."

"I'd like to be here a long time. The longer the better."

I play that back in "Mona talk," and realize she would make it sound dirty. "I mean—"

"I know what you mean. We have a lot to catch up on."

I lean back on my palms, too, aligning our faces, our bodies seated on the wall. "I told you all about Aiko, Noah, my family, the school. Your turn."

"Well, I don't have those things," she says ruefully. "I've mostly just had work. In a way, I'm married to whatever candidate I'm managing at the time. They tend to take over my whole life."

"You want kids?"

"Honestly, I hadn't given it much thought until recently. Apparently my clock is ticking. Well, according to my gyno and my mother, at least."

"I hate it when we pressure women to reach certain benchmarks by certain times when we don't have those expectations of a man. Clooney was the man, a confirmed bachelor who could play the field, and we loved him for it. Same for Leo DiCaprio. Just taking his time, enjoying life."

"While a woman who wants to focus on her career," she says, "but have great sex with no commitments is slut shamed and pitied until she lands a man."

"No one could pity you."

"Oh, you'd be surprised." Her laugh is in a bitter code I'd love to crack. "Things look different from inside."

I used to be inside—used to know her from every angle. But that was the girl. This is very much a woman sitting beside me, a fascinating woman who tempts me.

"You obviously love your job very much," I say.

"I'm doing exactly what I was meant to do. I can't imagine anything else being more fulfilling."

"I get that. When I started YLA, it felt like I'd come face-to-face with myself. Found my path."

"The school, what you're doing, really is remarkable. I *may* have watched a few viral videos of your students on TikTok. They're amazing."

"They're my joy. Them and Noah, of course."

"You're a fantastic father." She tosses her head back, sending the hair dancing around her face. "I mean, it appears. You could be beating him at home for all I know."

"Only at chess," I say, chuckling. "Okay. You have to tell me. How'd you break with three generations of Spelmanites?"

"Very carefully." She shrugs, cupping her neck and tipping her head back to look up at the stars. "I didn't tell my parents I was applying to Arizona, but I needed options. The higher my father's profile rose here in the city, coupled with my grandfather's legacy, the more I felt the weight of it. I just wanted to be myself. To be seen for myself, and not through the filter of my last name. I couldn't find a place in this city, much less on Spelman's campus, where that could happen. I was suffocating."

She pauses, leveling her eyes on me briefly before looking away again. "Did you ever find out what caused such a huge rift between our parents?"

I have my theories, but I've always kept them to myself. What I think happened can only cause problems that should remain buried with my father and with hers. "No, never."

"My mom was adamant that we not have any contact. I defied her at first and searched for you. I mean, the internet wasn't anywhere near what it is now. There was no Facebook or Instagram, but I did try. Your bubbe had passed away, though, and she was the only relative of yours I knew."

"I wrote you several times. The letters came back return to sender. And when I called, your number had been disconnected."

"Daddy did a lot of work in the city that wasn't always popular," she says dryly. "When we moved, we got an unlisted number." Her laugh is husky, hollow. "Driving here today I passed through the old neighborhood. Our houses are still there. Mrs. Washington's house. The park, though it's been upgraded."

"You'd go there sometimes by yourself when you needed to clear your head."

"Like at that age I had *so* much that needed clearing." She laughs. "I was never there by myself long, though. You'd always come find me. Sit with me. Not talk, but just swing back and forth. You were such a quiet kid."

"Not with you."

"No." Our gazes lock, cling. "Not with me."

The silence deepens, but neither of us seem in a hurry to fill it. I soak in this moment, soak in her company, relishing it like the luxury time has proven it to be.

"You remember that old ice cream truck?" she asks after a few more seconds, a smile coming to life on her lips, in her eyes. When she smiles it's like a sunrise, spreading warmth as it ascends.

"That little song was so creepy now that I think about it." I chuckle.

"Oh my God, and the *driver* was creepy. We're lucky he never snatched us."

"He always had those orange Push-Ups you liked so much. Those were your favorites."

She tilts her head, smiling as she considers me. "How do you even remember that?"

"I remember everything, Tru."

The amusement in her eyes and the smile on her lips flicker, and she goes silent. I shouldn't have said that, not like *that* in a way that reveals just how much those times meant to me. Still mean to me.

"What was mine?" I ask. "My favorite ice cream?"

I just don't know when to stop. What would it even prove if she remembers?

Her protracted silence tells me she doesn't.

"Never mind. I wouldn't expect you to—"

"Nutty Buddy."

My eyes meet hers in the dimming light, and I'm transported to the night of our first kiss when we promised to always be friends no matter what.

"I should have tried harder to find you." I shake my head. "I was so caught up in—"

"Moving to an entirely new country?" she interrupts, touching my hand. "I was still here in this one, and high school was rough. Just surviving took all my focus. It's natural for people to lose touch with friends they knew that young as they start new phases with new people."

I flip my hand to link our fingers. "Not for us it wasn't. We should have always been in each other's lives somehow."

She hooks our pinkies. "Pact," she whispers.

"Pact." I nod, holding her stare and her hand. The air between us thrums like a heartbeat. Her lips part on a breath, and it takes all of my restraint not to lean forward, wipe away the lip gloss and kiss her again like I did once before.

"Here you two are." Mona's words dent the tension building between us, but nothing could shatter it. "I told you not to monopolize each other, and what do you do as soon as my back is turned?"

Her good-natured smile slips when she sees us holding hands. Her glance bounces between our fingers and our faces. She and Aiko are friends, but I know Ko didn't talk to her about the break-up before she left. Mona thinks it's wrong for me to hold Kimba's hand. By the way Kimba jerks away and the guilty expression on her face, so does she.

Before Mona can voice the question and the disapproval her expression clearly conveys, Noah walks up, balancing three small plates.

"I got 'em!" he says triumphantly. "Red velvet for you, Kimba." He passes a plate to her and then another to me. "German chocolate for you, Dad."

"Thank you, son."

"Yeah, thanks, Noah," Kimba says, slicing into her huge wedge of cake.

"Is Daddy being a Kimba-vert?" Noah asks, his grin widening even as Mona's frown deepens.

"He was," Mona says, her tone firm, a warning. "But I'm here to break that up. Come on, Kimba. There's some *other* people I want you to meet."

Kimba stands from the wall, her skirt floating around her legs. "Sure. Why not?"

When I saw her at the funeral, I knew it would be like this for me— that I would crave her. That I would want to know her this way again. She knew it, too, and she shut it down. I wasn't free to do anything about it, to cultivate it when I saw her two years ago. Now I can.

Isn't there someone you've been attracted to?

When Aiko asked me that question a few weeks ago, I didn't see a path to do anything about my response to Kimba, but now she's *here*. I should have tried harder to keep her in my life before. I was a boy then, but now I'm a man.

And there's a napkin in my head with Kimba's name scribbled all over it.

CHAPTER TWENTY

Kimba

"SO THIS MIGHT BE BOLD," BARRY SAYS, "BUT COULD I HAVE your number? Maybe we could get together while you're in town?"

I should.

For one, I haven't had sex in a very long time, and I'm tired of doing all the heavy lifting to keep myself satisfied. Also, if I do decide to have a baby in the next year and a half, I haven't exactly been out there fostering relationships. I'm infamous for the no-strings, hot-and-dirty package. Last but not least, why not? I'm here a few weeks and some companionship wouldn't be awful. He does have that really lean biker body that I'm afraid if I straddle, I might break, but he's attractive in a very *kale greens* kind of way. He's smart and funny. Seems kind. Focusing on a date with an available man makes more sense than fixating on someone who is *taken* and has a family. It doesn't matter that I felt more alive, more *seen* talking with Ezra than I have in years. I can't let it matter. I need to do the right thing, and avoiding time alone with Ezra is the right thing.

"Kimba?" Barry frowns, his voice uncertain. I've left him hanging.

"Oh, sure. Sorry." I fish my phone from the pocket of my skirt and we exchange numbers.

"I gotta go." He grins. "But I'll call you this week."

"Great," I force myself to reply with a smile.

He isn't gone for two seconds before Mona takes his place by my side, grinning hard. "Did I see you and Barry with phones out?"

"You're worse than Facebook. I *just* clicked on him, and you're already flooding my timeline with ads for wedding dresses."

"I know. I know." She giggles and pulls her locs back from her face, knotting them at the crown of her head. "I'm just excited to see you connecting with someone." Her smile falters and she licks her lips. "Someone available, I mean."

"All right. Now you're vague-booking me." I give her a wry look. "You weren't this passive-aggressive in eighth grade. Say what you have to say, Janet."

She glances around the living room where some people are still talking, but most are packing up and making their way to the door. She tips her head to the kitchen. "Come help me for a sec."

We walk into the kitchen, which is miraculously empty. She starts putting away covered dishes.

"I know you and Ezra used to have a very special friendship," she says after a few moments. She leans against the counter and gives me a level look. "But you have to be careful."

"Careful?" I ask, propping my hip on her island. "How so?"

"You know how so, Kimba. Ezra grew up to be pretty impressive."

He always impressed me.

"I mean," she continues, "fine as hell now, obviously. Tall, handsome. The whole thing, and smart as all get-out. And he has a huge heart. Lots of people at school get caught up in how kind he is to them, and I tell them what I'm about to tell you."

"Which is?"

"He's not available," she says flatly, firmly. "Aiko is my friend, and I know they love each other very much. They have a son together. Please be careful. You don't want to destroy that."

"It's been a long time since you and I knew each other, Mona, but I assure you, I didn't grow up to be a homewrecker."

"I know," she says, her eyes wide. "But he has a wife—"

"They're not married." I have no idea what prompted me to say that, but I instantly know I shouldn't have.

Mona's expression hardens, her glace sharpens. "They may as well be. They've been together nearly a decade. Noah's the center of Ezra's world. You shouldn't jeopardize that and you for damn sure should not be holding his hand."

She's right. You rarely see a car wreck coming. It happens suddenly, unexpectedly, before you can avoid it.

She's telling me if I continue down this road, I'll crash. She's telling me to slow down. To pull off to the shoulder and let the storm pass.

I could lie to myself and pretend it's just me, that I'm the only one wrestling with this temptation, but that's a lie. Ezra has been watching me all night. I feel his eyes on me every time he's near, and I just want to look back. If I'm not careful, I'll set us on a collision course that could ruin everything.

I'm here for a few weeks and then onto the next mayor, governor, congressman. I could destroy his relationship, damage his family and be back on the campaign trail, leaving him to deal with the fallout.

"Kimba!" Noah bounds into the kitchen. There's a small stain on his T-shirt that looks suspiciously like banana pudding. "You're still here. I thought you'd already left."

Ezra enters behind him. He leans against the counter and pulls out his phone, fixing his attention there instead of on what's happening in here. Instead of on me.

"I'm still here," I say, unable to stop the smile that plays on my lips when this kid is around.

"Good," Noah says. "I wanted to invite you to my birthday party on Sunday."

Ezra's head swings around and I feel his eyes on my profile. I also sense Mona holding her breath, willing me *not* to accept.

"Oh, Noah. Happy birthday," I say. "Thank you for inviting me. That's so sweet."

"Will you come?" Noah presses his palms together, pleading dramatically. "I'll be nine. You're only nine once."

Mona and I laugh. The unyielding line of Ezra's full lips pulls into a smile. His eyes soften on his son.

"I don't know, Noah." I lick my lips and push my hair back. "I—"

"My mom's not here," he says, lowering his head, his smile disappearing. "She's on safari, but at least I could have all my friends around. That might make up for it some."

This kid's good.

I glance at Mona's neutral expression, which somehow still manages to appear disapproving. I look over at Ezra, and his eyes are that near-violet color that deepens with his most intense emotions. I feel him *willing* me to accept.

"Please." Noah looks up at me, his eyes identical to his father's.

"Okay. I'll come."

Noah breaks out into some dance that causes him to wobble his legs and point his fingers in the air. I'm sure I've seen it when football players make touchdowns. I can't help but laugh, as do Mona and Ezra.

"You know you just got played, right?" Ezra asks, but his smile is pleased.

"I'm aware, yeah."

Our eyes hold despite Mona's watchful stare. Did I get played, or did I get exactly what I wanted?

CHAPTER TWENTY-ONE

Kimba

IN THE ALLEN HOUSE, SATURDAY MORNINGS ARE FOR CLEANING.

At least, they used to be. Mama would be up by seven cooking breakfast. Pancakes and sausages. As soon as the meal was done, she'd assign Kayla, Keith and me chores, and we couldn't go out and play or do anything until the house sparkled. We griped, but once the music was blasting and we were singing and dancing, we had that house clean in no time. My rendition of Whitney Houston's "Dance With Somebody" into a dust mop microphone? Classic.

Saturday morning in my mother's house is much different now. It's not the starter home my parents purchased to be close to Emory while Daddy was in law school. The Sterns don't live across the street, subdued until sunset on the weekends, observing Shabbat.

Daddy's gone, God rest his soul.

Kayla's married with her husband and five kids, God *bless* her soul.

Keith is a father and husband, too. *Hmm-hmm.*

When I come home, it's just Mama and me. A sweet woman named Esmerelda hums as she cleans the house, top to bottom. Our family home is now at an elite Buckhead address, tucked among some of Atlanta's most expensive properties. It's eleven o'clock and Mama still hasn't stirred.

In the breakfast nook, I sip the herbal tea the homeopath recommended to help with hormonal balance and to possibly alleviate some of the weight gain. I squint against the bright sunlight, angling my phone to eliminate the glare. A text message from Piers.

Piers: Got a second?

I don't bother to reply but dial him right away.

"Talk to me," I say, taking a bite of the cantaloupe I sliced for breakfast.

"Good morning," Piers says. "Hope I'm not disturbing time with your family."

I glance around the empty room and listen to Esmerelda's vacuum running in the living room. "You're fine. Tell me what you got."

"It's interesting doing opposition research for a candidate who hasn't hired us yet on a man who hasn't even declared that he's running against our not-client."

"Ah. But I don't just read the tea leaves," I say, laughing and leaning back in my seat. "I *grow* them. Some of us wait for the future to unfold, and others bend it to our will. Knowing our probable opposition's dirt at this stage may prove useful in securing the position itself. So Burton Colson. Dirt in the streets? Dirt in the sheets? What ya got?"

"Definitely in the sheets."

"Balance sheets or bedsheets?"

"Both."

"Send me a full report, including pics if you have them. And dirt in the streets? What'd you find?"

"Some business practices that, while not illegal, wouldn't make him look good to certain key voting demographics."

I rub my hands together, cantaloupe abandoned in favor of dirt. "Ooooh, my favorite. What is it?"

"Let me dig a little more to see what I can find and then I'll share."

"Okay. I'm gonna trust you, but next week, reveal all."

"Promise."

"Oh, and Piers?"

"Yeah, boss?"

"Take some time off. I highly recommend it."

We hang up just as Madame Mother enters the room clad in a simple silk robe with her hair brushed into curls. Mama's still relaxing her hair, and probably will kneel at the chemical altar until the day she dies. She's never had work done on her face. Why would she? Her skin is nearly as smooth and taut as it was when I was a kid.

"Morning, Mama." I sip my tea. "You look lovely."

"Thank you." She sets her coffee on the table along with a plate of eggs and toast. "What is it the kids say? Black don't crack? That black girl magic?"

Hearing her parrot things "the kids" say makes my lips twitch.

"Who was that on the phone?" she asks.

"Piers, one of my staff. We're gearing up for the gubernatorial race."

"Which one?" She pauses in buttering a slice of toast.

"Georgia." I wink and flash her a smile. "I'm hoping Congressman Ruiz will hire us."

"Did Keith talk to you about *his* campaign?"

My smile slips. "Briefly."

"And?" Mama cocks an imperious brow.

"We'll see."

"We'll *see*?" Mama drops her toast and any pretense of casual interest. "Kimba Truth Allen, are you telling me you'll get that white boy elected president, make this Mateo man a governor, but can't be bothered to help your own brother?"

My chin auto-lifts, defiant before I have time to catch it. "I'm *telling* you I'm not sure Keith should be running at all."

"And who made you the expert?"

"I did, Mama. I literally made myself the expert by doing this and doing it well the last fifteen years of my life."

"Don't forget what your father used to say." Mama resumes buttering her toast. "Family is most important. Don't get too big for your britches."

"My britches are sized just right, thank you very much," I say, caressing the gold ring on my thumb. "Daddy also said never take on a problem that has no solution. If Keith isn't cut out for this, he'll spend his entire political career going from one fire to the next frying pan. I, for one, will not babysit his ass through that, and I won't mislead the people of this district into that disappointment."

"If you won't help him, we'll find someone who will."

"You are completely missing the point," I say, dropping my volume to mutter. "As usual."

"What'd you say? Don't be talking under your breath to me, young lady. Say what you have to say if you're gonna say it."

"I *said,* you're missing the point. This isn't about me not wanting to help Keith. This is a question of him being fit for office and ready to serve. I pressed on some very basic issues, and he wasn't prepared to discuss them. He's got a long way to go before he's ready to run." I set down my tea and look her in the eyes. "And do you know he cheats on Delaney?"

She doesn't reply, but bites into her toast and smiles over my shoulder. "Esmerelda, all done?"

"Yes," the soft reply comes from behind me.

"Thank you. Then let me grab my checkbook." Mama stands and shoots me a look loaded with reproach and warning. "I'll be back."

When I was growing up, that look paired with that tone would have me stewing in dread and trepidation. Instead, I can't wait until she comes back. I'm *right* and I want this fight.

"As I was saying," Mama starts when she sits down again.

"Actually, *I* was asking if you know your son cheats on his wife, and I was waiting for your answer."

"I'm aware they've had some challenges, yes, as all young couples do. That doesn't make him unfit for office. Surely many of your candidates had those kinds of...challenges."

"Of course, but they wouldn't be dragging the Allen name through the mud with their weak character and incompetence. Daddy's legacy is attached to Keith, and—"

"Ha!" Her scoffing laugh cuts over my point.

"Excuse me? But did *you* have something to say? If so, say it, Mama."

"Your father's legacy," she says, rolling her eyes. "Girl, is that tea or Kool-Aid you're drinking? Your daddy wasn't perfect."

"He was a great man," I fire back, ice stiffening my spine.

"I'm not saying he wasn't. Of course he was, but the women married to great men know they fart in their sleep and leave the toilet seat up. They are *human*. Your brother is human, imperfect, the same way your father was imperfect."

"My father was no cheat."

"How do you know what goes on between a man and a woman behind closed doors?"

"Are you saying—"

"I'm saying Keith and Delaney's problems shouldn't keep him from serving this state. You hold him to an impossible standard, which is your father. He always did spoil you."

"Spoiled? Me? Keith is the one you *both* spoiled, allowing him privileges neither Kayla or I ever had simply because he was a boy. Letting him run wild so now he's an entitled, underachieving, underperforming brat who assumes he can ride my father's name and legacy into office. Well, not on my watch and not until I'm satisfied he will serve the people of this district well."

Mama sighs with a despairing shake of her head. "You're just like your father."

"Thank you."

Mama whips a glance at me, rolls her eyes and relinquishes a tiny smile. Against my will and better judgment, my lips quirk, too. Our clashes of will usually end in mutual respect.

"Look," Mama says, "I know Keith has some growing to do, but no one's perfect. Your daddy certainly wasn't when we first got married."

"I repeat. Are you saying Daddy cheated on you?"

Mama's expression closes. She pulls her lashes down and tightens her lips at the corners. "Your father was faithful our entire marriage, as far as I know, and he was the kind of man who couldn't have lived with that lie. So...no, he didn't cheat."

Relief releases the breath I was holding. "I don't expect Keith to be perfect, but I do expect him to do better and to be prepared."

"His heart is in the right place. He's not corrupt like some of these folks running for office. If you'll be in Georgia anyway, helping Congressman Ruiz run for governor, it'll be easier to advise Keith, too."

My shoulders, held battle-tense, relax a bit. "We'll see. Ruiz has to choose me first. There are a few firms he's considering."

"Considering?" Mamas brows snap together. "Did he not see what you did for Maxim Cade?"

"Well, Maxim is a once-in-a-lifetime candidate. Charlie Brown probably could have managed that campaign and won."

"Don't do that, Tru," Mama says, eyes narrowed, voice dropped. "They diminish us enough without you making yourself small. You descend from queens. And I'm not talking about going all the way back to Africa. I'm talking about your grandmother who put her life on the line as a freedom rider. Your aunt who was a pastor when they said women couldn't be and led one of the largest congregations in the South. Your great-great grandmother, who, with a sixth-grade education, opened her own restaurant and became one of the wealthiest women in this city."

"I know, Mama." I chuckle at her shaking the branches of the family tree to make her point. "You've told us a million times."

"Well don't you forget it. Congressman Ruiz would be lucky to have you manage his campaign, and better hope you're still available and interested by the time he realizes it."

"That part," I agree, feeling some of my usual confidence surfacing. I reach across and touch her hand. "Thank you, Mama."

She squeezes my hand briefly before pulling away to eat her breakfast.

"And I'll see what I can do for Keith," I say grudgingly. "At least sit down with him and hear where his head is at."

Mama nods. "Thank you. I'm the first to admit he's not always...responsible, but he has potential. If your father were still around..."

She's right. Daddy would have whipped Keith into campaign shape by now and had him on someone else's ballot years ago with his own run as the end game. I should have seen that. Should have done that. Kayla runs our family foundation, but I inherited Daddy's strategic mind. Who will I have to pass it on to?

"Um, Mama," I venture, poking the remnants of my cantaloupe with a fork. "Can I ask you something?"

Mama nods, not looking up from her newspaper that is still delivered to our front door every morning. It's been so long since I saw the news in ink on paper, it feels like she's holding an artifact.

"Do you know if we have a history, on either side, of early menopause?"

Mama's brows bend and dip. She shakes her head. "Not that I know of. Why do you..." She drops her paper to the table and her wide eyes snap to mine. "The doctor. Is that why you were seeing the doctor that day?"

Way to connect the dots.

"I'm in perimenopause, yeah."

"But you...you're not even forty." Mama slams a hand on the table. "Pesticides."

"Um...huh?"

"It's those pesticides and those GMAs and—"

"I think you mean GMOs."

"Yes." Mama points her fork at me. "Them. And steroids. All in our food, in our water."

"You're not wrong, but are you sure there's no family history?"

"No one I remember. Girl, my mother still had pads under the sink at sixty."

Between a grandmother still menstruating into her twilight years and a sister who has birthed five children from her actual body, I'm feeling reproductively inadequate to say the least.

"So what does this mean for children?" Mama asks, frowning. "You can still have them, right? You're so young."

"I haven't had a period in four months. Without one of those, no kids. So I'm working with a homeopath to at least get that back, and then I can decide."

"Decide? Well, how much time do you have to decide?"

"Year and a half. Maybe two." My shrug is more careless than I am. "I can't just reproduce on demand. If and when I can get my period on track, I need someone to reproduce *with*, and I have no prospects. And I'm not sure I want to drop everything to have kids right now. If this window closes and I want kids later, lots of babies are up for adoption and need homes. I don't need a sperm donor for that."

"I know you've never felt pressure to have kids," Mama says. "Or to get married, for that matter, but I think you'd make a wonderful mother, if it means anything to you."

"That does mean something, and thank you, Mama."

"You keep doing what the doctor says and we'll get through this."

The weight that's been heavy on my shoulders since Dr. Granden first uttered the word "perimenopause" feels that much lighter with every person I share it with.

First Kayla. Then Mona. Now Mama.

I'm beginning to think I should have come home a long time ago.

CHAPTER TWENTY-TWO

Ezra

"I LOVE THEM!" NOAH SAYS, GRINNING AT THE TICKETS AIKO left for him.

"You do, honey?" she asks, her expression concerned on the Skype screen. "They're passes we can use whenever. We've been to the aquarium so often, I thought a trip to Nashville for the planetarium might be fun. And I know you're really into the stars right now."

"It's great," he assures her. "And the other things were awesome, too."

Aiko asked me to take a bag full of birthday gifts she'd left to his bedroom first thing this morning.

"I wish I was there." She blinks hard, and I can tell she's trying not to cry. She doesn't want Noah to know. "But so many people are coming to your party today."

"Yeah, and we'll jump on the trampoline," Noah says. "You should see it, Mom. It's the kind with a net."

"Your mom actually helped pick it out," I interject. "She wanted to make sure she saw it before she had to leave."

"You did?" Noah asks.

"Yup." Aiko shoots me a grateful look. "Sure did. I wanted this to be the best birthday ever even though I'm not there."

"And four of the guys from school are sleeping over," Noah rolls on. "Dad says he'll make stuffed French toast for breakfast." He looks at me like I may have forgotten.

"Sure." I nod. "Tomorrow's breakfast will be lit."

"Dad," Noah groans, obviously embarrassed by my hipness. "Don't say lit, okay?"

"Got it."

My phone buzzes on the kitchen counter by the laptop. It's my mother calling through FaceTime.

"Bubbe!" Noah squeaks. He glances at Aiko uncertainly.

"Oh, baby, answer," Aiko tells him. "I've kept you long enough. Go talk to your grandmother. I love you."

"Love you, Mom. See you when you get back." He grabs my phone. "Dad, can I take it outside to show her my trampoline?"

"Sure, but bring it back to me before you hang up," I tell him. "I need to talk to her about you flying up there for camp."

He runs off and out the door to the backyard.

"I should be there," Aiko says despairingly. "I'm missing his birthday, and he's going off to camp for weeks. What if he—"

"You're exactly where you should be," I interrupt before she can spiral. "And you're an incredible mom. You've sacrificed a lot for him, for me, for this family. Delayed things in your career, put off some of your dreams. This trip is just for you, and you deserve it. He'll have a great birthday today and see you when you get back."

"You sure?"

"Am I sure that he won't be emotionally scarred because you missed this one birthday party? Yes. Besides, the trampoline and the sleepover cover many transgressions."

"You always know what I need to hear."

"You have nothing to feel guilty about."

"Oh, God, but I do." Affection and torment and tears flood her eyes. "I slept with Chaz."

I allow her words to sink in, waiting to see if I'm angry or hurt or jealous, but I'm not. "You didn't do anything wrong," I tell her, glancing out to the backyard to make sure Noah is still there. "We're not together anymore."

"I know." Fresh tears fall over her cheeks. "He wasn't you, Ezra, and I haven't been with anyone else for ten years. I felt like I was cheating on you."

"You're not, and if you're worried about my feelings, I'm fine."

She hesitates and then releases her next words in a rush. "I know you said before there wasn't any one in particular you were attracted to," she says, barreling ahead before I can amend that statement. "But I want you to promise me something."

"What?" I ask warily.

"When you…" She swallows and closes her eyes. "If you sleep with someone else, I want you to tell me."

I'm already shaking my head. "Ko, you know how you get. You've got a jealous streak a mile wide. How would that even be helpful *or* healthy?"

"I'm not that bad."

"Jill Schaffer."

"That bitch," Aiko spits. "She was after you from the moment we met her at parent-teacher conference."

"No, she was just being friendly. You *thought* she was after me, and made that poor woman's school year a nightmare."

"She should not be teaching children if she's going to lust after their fathers."

"My point," I say, pausing to let it sink in, "is that me telling you if I sleep with someone else won't go as well as our conversation about Chaz did, and you know it."

With perfect timing, or bad timing, depending on how you look at it, Chaz walks into the hotel room wearing a pair of neon board shorts.

"Babe, you ready for that swim?" he asks.

When he's fully in the room and realizes she's on Skype, red crawls under his skin. "Dude, I'm sorry. I didn't realize you were—"

"It's fine." I give him a very civilized smile. "I gotta go prepare for this party anyway."

"Take lots of pictures," Aiko says, blinking at tears again. "And video, Ezra. You always forget the video. I'll text Mona."

"Good idea. Have a great swim." I flick a glance between her and her new lover. "Goodbye, Ko."

Once I'm done Skyping with her, and then talking with my mother about Noah's upcoming trip to New York, it's almost time for everyone to start arriving. I barely have time to shower and change.

"This is not the eighth-grade dance," I tell myself while contemplating what I should wear. "Just throw on something, man."

My options are basically cargo shorts…or other cargo shorts. I always look neat at school, usually wearing a suit since the kids are required to wear uniforms, but out of school? I'm not exactly concerned about what I'm wearing.

"It's just me!" Mona yells from downstairs. "You here?"

"Uh, yeah!" I pull a YLA T-shirt over my head and grab cargo shorts option number one. "Coming."

From there, it's a blur of balloons, cake, ice cream, a random piñata Noah insisted on, and lots of people. So many people. His entire class, but also everyone on our street and several YLA students. Barry is here. Mona made sure to announce it when he arrived, lest I forget her genius plan to hook Kimba up with the math teacher.

"You think Kimba's still coming?" Noah asks.

"I don't know, son. She's a really busy lady. Something may have come up that she had to take care of."

His face falls a bit. "I really like her."

"Yeah, I do, too."

I'm in the kitchen lighting candles when she arrives. From the other room, the low, seductive roll of her voice mingles with Mona's. I freeze, the lighter suspended over the cake for a second. My damn palms start sweating.

"Not eighth grade," I remind myself grimly.

I walk the lit cake out to the backyard, and Mona starts the birthday song. We cut the cake, and I still haven't actually seen Kimba, but I know she's here somewhere.

"Dr. Stern."

I turn to find one of the seventh-grade girls from YLA standing there. "Hey, Karinne. Thanks for coming."

"It's a great party. The step team prepared something for Noah's birthday. Is it okay to do it?"

"Are you kidding?" Noah will freak out over this. He loves their impromptu step shows. They're about to start competing nationally. "Thank you. He'll love it."

"Okay." Karinne's face lights up. "I'll get the team together then."

She's such a bright kid. Her mom got her master's and opened her own business in downtown Decatur, one of the coolest parts of Atlanta's changing landscape. Karinne's father isn't in her life, so I, and a lot of the other men on staff, make sure we're providing her good male role models where we can.

As I knew he would, Noah nearly comes out of his skin when the step team does their birthday routine for him. Mona's recording it and will probably post it to Instagram and TikTok, or whatever they call it, later. We've had several videos go viral, thanks in no small part to her. She's on top of our socials.

"Wow. They're fantastic."

I turn and Kimba's standing beside me, eyes fixed on the step team leaping and clapping and shouting in rhythm like I could never make my body do.

"Yeah, they are." I clear my throat. "I wasn't sure you were gonna make it."

"I almost didn't come." Her laugh is reluctant, reserved. "I probably shouldn't have."

"I'm glad you did." I brush her fingers with mine and turn my head to look directly into her eyes. "Really glad."

"Ez." She pulls her fingers away, lowering her head so her hair falls forward to partially obscure her profile. "Don't."

"We need to talk." I reset my attention on the step team, on Noah sitting on the edge of his new trampoline wearing wonder all over his face. "Don't leave, okay?"

Her chest heaves with the weight of her sigh. She's wearing skinny jeans and one of those stretchy, tube top-y kind of strapless shirts. It outlines the fullness of her breasts and the dramatic dip of her waist and ass.

"I don't know." She shakes her head. "Mona was right. She—"

"Mona doesn't know what I need to tell you. Not yet. Stay. I want to talk to you after everyone leaves."

She hesitates, but she finally nods.

"Thank you," I say.

"Kimba!" Noah runs up. "You came!"

"I told you I would." She smiles down at him. "Dude, your party is amazing."

"Thank you." He bounces on the tips of his toes. "We're about to open gifts."

"My favorite part!" Kimba says. "I hope you like mine."

"You got me a present?" Noah's eyes stretch and his mouth falls open.

"Of course I did."

"Let's go over to the gift table and check out your birthday haul," I tell him.

It's quite a lot. I don't even remember getting this many gifts at my Bar Mitzvah. I think of the eighteen Pixie Stix Kimba gave me and can't help but look over at her and smile. She's standing a few feet away with Mona and lifts one brow.

"What?" she mouths.

I shake my head and mouth back. *"Later."*

Her gift is one of Noah's favorites, and one of mine, too.

"Ezra's Big Shabbat Question." Noah reads the title of the book once he's torn off the wrapping paper. The book isn't that large, but my name leaps out at me immediately, of course. There's a brown boy on the cover wearing a yarmulke. I go completely still and don't think I'm even breathing. What a book like this would have meant to me thirty years ago when no one at my synagogue resembled me. A book like this would have reflected me when the only place I saw myself was in a mirror. That she found this book and shared it with my son? It means everything.

"Wow." Noah's small face sobers. "This is...it's great, Kimba. Thank you so much."

I think he knows this book really means something. For him, maybe for me. His blackness hides deeper in his pores than mine, diluted even further by Aiko's Asian heritage, but I make sure he knows my history, my father's history, and his father before him. I make sure he knows about *all* the influences, cultures and ethnicities that came together to make him who he is. It's a rich, varied heritage, and I wouldn't shortchange any part of it.

"I'm glad you like it." Kimba shrugs, smiles. "I saw it in the bookstore and just thought..."

"It's perfect," I say.

She drags her eyes from Noah's face to mine, and if I could kiss her right now I would. She looks away and chews at the corner of her mouth.

"Noah!" one of his classmates calls. "Trampoline."

"You go on," I tell him, taking the book from him. "I'll hold on to this."

He runs off, leaving Kimba and me in an electric storm of silence.

"Kimba," Mona calls from the other side of the yard, looking between us. "Can you come help me with that thing in the kitchen?"

"What thing?" I murmur for Kimba's ears only.

"That thing that will put me somewhere other than standing beside you."

"Hey." I grasp her elbow and bend my head to whisper in her ear.

"Don't forget to stick around."

"Ezra."

"Just give me a chance, Tru."

"A chance for what?" She looks up at me, her smooth face crinkled into a frown. "I don't think—"

"Hear me out for old time's sake? If our pact ever meant anything to you, give me a chance to explain."

"That's not fair."

"I know, but this is just like chess. You are the most powerful piece on this board. All the power is in your hands."

"I don't feel like I have all the power."

"How do you feel?"

"Honestly—" She breathes out a short laugh. "A little helpless."

I know what she means. The pull between us is alive, is burning beneath my fingertips on her skin. Even surrounded by friends and colleagues who know I've been with Aiko for a decade, who know I would never cheat on her, who *don't* know we aren't together anymore and would judge me...even knowing the necessity of discretion, I can barely keep my hands off Kimba.

"Can I tell you something and you believe me?" I ask.

"Yes."

"I've never cheated on Aiko, and I never would." I dip my head to catch her eyes with mine. "Please trust me."

She searches my face for several heartbeats and then gives a slow nod. "Okay. I trust you."

"Kimba!" Mona's tone is just shy of strident. "Please."

"I better go," Kimba says, starting off. She pauses and looks at me over her shoulder. "I'll wait around, but only for a few minutes, Ezra. I don't...I can't..."

She shakes her head and walks away.

CHAPTER TWENTY-THREE

Kimba

"I F THIS WAS NOAH'S PARTY AT NINE," MONA SAYS, "CAN YOU imagine this kid's sweet sixteen?"

I laugh and scoop the last of the candy debris from Noah's piñata out of the grass. "We'll be that kid's entourage by the time he's sixteen."

Mona glances around Ezra's backyard and heaves a long sigh. "All done. Food's put away. Place is clean. Everyone's gone home. Ezra's making sure four third-graders don't kill each other and go to sleep."

"Ezra's lucky to have you." I sit on the edge of the trampoline. "You're like part of the family."

Mona gives me a measured look before sitting beside me, the net enclosure at our backs. "Aiko, too. They're all like family to me."

"Well then, they're *all* lucky to have you."

Mona tips her head toward the fence that separates her backyard from this one. "Why don't you come over for a glass...or bottle...of wine?"

"Raincheck?"

"You're about to leave?" Mona probes.

"In a little bit, yeah."

Her gaze drifts back toward the house. "This won't end well, Kimba. It can't."

As much as she may be right, I hold on to Ezra's frankness from earlier tonight. "You know him, Mona. Have you ever even suspected him of being unfaithful?"

"No, but you were never around."

"That wouldn't have made a difference."

"I would have said that, too, before I saw him with you. Kimba, I know how a man looks at someone who is just a friend, and that is not how Ezra looks at you. I just hope no one else noticed. He's a pillar of this community. A hero for these kids. I don't want him throwing that away because he's curious about what might have been."

"I don't want that either, and it won't happen. We're just talking, Mo. We haven't seen each other in a very long time. We were best friends from the cradle. Just trust us, okay?"

"Okay." Her one word lilts with notes of doubt and warning, but she turns toward the fence, unlatches the door and walks through to her side.

Once she returns to her house, it's so quiet. Not even an hour ago, this yard was teeming with activity and music and food and partygoers. After Mona leaves, I only hear the lonely chirp of crickets.

"What are you doing here, Tru?" I ask aloud.

Ezra's assurances, Mona's warnings—none of them weigh more than the knowledge that lines the secret crevices of my own heart.

I want him.

But I would hate to hurt Noah, or tempt Ezra to cheat on Aiko. I don't want to compromise my own convictions. So why the hell am I still here? He said I could trust him, but that's not what I'm worried about.

I can't trust myself.

I fall back through the split in the net enclosure, flopping onto the trampoline. The surface answers with a little bounce. That tiny hiccup of buoyancy lifts the heaviness, the doubt inside of *me*. With no audience but an empty backyard, I kick off my flats, stand on the trampoline and attempt one tentative hop. And then another. A bigger one that propels me higher and higher still. So high my arms fly over my head. My feet and legs absorb the shock, the energy of each bounce, and I'm soaring and landing and springing and laughing. For just a few moments, I don't want to think about my ovaries betraying me, or that I'm never done proving myself, no matter how much I succeed. Someone still needs to see more from me before they give me a chance. I want to forget that the boy who used to feel like mine is now a man I can't have. I leave all my problems on the ground and just jump.

I catch sight of Ezra watching me, one shoulder leaned into the back doorjamb, an old affection on his new face. In some ways, I'm still reconciling this adult "fine ass" Ezra with the boy who took up much less space in the world, but who was even then, my *whole* world. I lose my focus mid-jump and fall on my butt. The trampoline, bouncily forgiving, throws me back up and springing to my feet. My forced breaths come loud in the quiet night as our stares tangle. We've snared each other with a look and I can't wiggle free. Ezra's smile dwindles and he takes a few steps forward until he's at the lip of the trampoline.

"Can you imagine if we'd had one of these growing up?" he asks.

"We would never have gone to school."

He nods to the surface where my feet still lift a few inches reflexively. "May I?"

"It's your trampoline," I say, as breathless from his proximity as I am from exertion.

He steps through the net and onto the taut surface, taking my hand. A kaleidoscope of butterflies instantly migrates from my belly to my throat. I should object even to this contact, but I don't. I simply look from our joined hands to the smile on his face.

"Let's jump," he says.

And then we're bouncing, facing each other, looking into each other's eyes as the trampoline tosses us into the air. It hits him first, the laughter. A smothered chuckle when he releases my hand to bounce on his butt, then to his feet, and then springing higher into the air. And then I'm in its clutches, the mirth, the giggle spilling out of me like an overturned bin of pixie dust. It suffuses the air around us, the joy. We're kids again, without cares or responsibilities. There are no ceilings on our dreams or walls on what could be. We could jump all night and laugh until dawn. Except after a few minutes, we stop bouncing to land on our butts and lie on our backs and look up. There's a silver scythe moon slicing through the black velvet sky.

"The stars are a blessing tonight," Ezra says, his voice hushed like if he speaks too loudly, he'll scare them off. "Living in the city, you don't always see them like this. These are special occasion stars."

I smile at the whimsy of the boy that survived in the man. "And what's the occasion?" I turn my head to study the rugged beauty of his profile.

He turns his head, too, and his smile evaporates like cotton candy on your tongue, a sweet vanishing. "Us," he says. "We're the special occasion."

Who moves first, I'm not sure. Later my pride will say he did, but that could be a lie to exonerate myself. Regardless, his hand is cupping my face and my fingers burrow into the shorn curls at his neck. His thumb brushes my mouth, an echo of our first innocent kiss, but this kiss isn't tentative or shy. He tugs my chin until my mouth opens and he licks into me, hungry and reckless. I lick back, I suck back, I *groan* back. This kiss flies into the sun, melting my iron will and burning my reservations to ashes. I fight my way through the lust fog and search for reason, a mirage in the distance, something flickering in and out of sight between hot fantasy and cold, hard reality.

"You said I could trust you," I pant between kisses. "I don't cheat, Ezra."

He stills, opens his eyes, rests his forehead against mine, his harshly drawn breaths fanning over my lips both wet and burning. "Neither do I."

He rolls away onto his back and runs a hand through his hair. The motion flexes his bicep, and I allow my eyes to wander over him, so big and fit and finely made. The wide chest beneath his T-shirt heaves like he's been running. I am, too. Running from this, from him, from the traitorous desires that threaten to flatten my convictions to nothing. Just below the taut line of his stomach, his pants are tented with an erection.

Shit.

"I need to go." I sit up, but he takes my wrist gently and pulls me back down. His scent, the heat emanating from his body intoxicate me, and I draw deep breaths of him. Fill my lungs with stunted possibilities and forbidden desires.

"Don't go yet," he says. "Let me explain."

I feel his eyes on my face, but refuse to turn my head, to get caught in the violet-hued trap of his eyes. "You'll explain why you say you don't cheat, but then you kissed me?"

We both know I kissed him back.

He's the one to sit up this time, drawing his knees to his chest and looping muscle-corded arms around his long legs. The T-shirt strains across the width of his back.

"Aiko and I have been having trouble for a long time."

"Oh, Ezra, don't be that cliché. What else? She just doesn't understand you? Do you also have some etchings inside you'd like to show me?"

"She actually understands me very well," he replies, his voice unamused but not annoyed. "It was one of the things that first drew me to her—how we got each other. I hadn't really had that with another girl since you." His laugh comes short and self-deprecating. "I mean, that and the fact that she was gorgeous. That didn't hurt either."

Jealousy I have no right to burns a hole in my belly.

"I don't know if…" He grips the back of his neck. "I've never said this out loud, but I don't know that we would have lasted very long if she hadn't gotten pregnant. Had it not been for Noah."

He glances over his shoulder, and his eyes are sad. "We tried, Kimba. *I've* tried. We've been in counseling the last couple of years. It hasn't gotten much better. She even wanted to try an open relationship, which I shot down."

"Oh, wow." I've never been a possessive chick, but I know I couldn't share Ezra. "You're still with her, though, right? It's still cheating for us to…it's still not right."

"She's in Tanzania sleeping with someone else as we speak, with my blessing."

"I don't…" I frown and press my palm to my forehead. "I don't understand."

"We broke up before she left, but didn't want to ruin Noah's birthday, especially with her leaving so soon. We both need to be here to help him process it once we tell him."

I want to look away, to break the contact between our eyes, but this moment is quicksand, holding me immobile and pulling me under. "What do you want?"

"You know what I want."

My body comes to life at his words, under the intensity of his stare and the promise of satisfaction for us both. He doesn't say any more for a moment and then clears his throat, goes on. "Mona's trying to hook you up with Barry."

"And?" I ask, watching to see if his impassive expression tells me more than he has.

"Don't."

Just one word. Downright polite, but when he lifts his lashes, his eyes are black-blue, midnight swimming in the deepest ocean.

"I overheard you tell Mona you like to fuck," he says, trapping the fullness of his bottom lip between his teeth. "So do I. If you're in the market for someone, I'd like it to be me."

The seductive offer, the dark rasp of his voice caressing the word "fuck" snatches my breath. I'm not sure which is more dangerous. Ezra *taken* or Ezra *for the taking*. Rarely have any of my sexual relationships been complicated. It was a release, a transaction of pleasure between two consenting adults who were free to transact with whomever they pleased.

I already know Ezra would be a different story.

"Ez—"

"I don't want to see you with him."

"I know you've been off the market," I say dryly. "But that's not exactly how a man talks when all he wants to do is to fuck."

"What do you want me to say? That I don't feel anything for you? You know that's a lie. Whatever was between us when we were young never got the chance to become...more. But it's still there, and it could never be nothing."

The words resonate with truth, and all I can do is agree. I felt it at the funeral. I felt it as soon as I saw him again. God knows I felt it when he kissed me.

"You don't have to worry. I was gonna let Barry down easy when he calls."

"Good," he says, satisfaction in his narrowed eyes. "Do that."

I look down at my hands. "I don't want Barry."

"Do you want me?"

It's a bold question. Everything about this conversation is bold, unabashed, bare.

"Yes." I shake my head before he can pounce on my admission. "But I'm not sure this is the best thing right now for either of us."

"Let me decide what's best for me."

"You're just getting out of a long-term relationship. I'm starting a new campaign." *Fingers crossed.*

Not to mention all I'm going through with my health. I *won't* mention it, but it's yet another reason why I don't want emotional attachments right now. And he's right. Between Ezra and me, it could never *not* be emotional.

I scoot to the edge of the trampoline, still inside the net, but with my legs hanging over the side. I'm poised to leave but can't make myself go. He tenses and doesn't speak.

"The attraction between us..." I scrub my hands over my face.

"Well, I'd be lying if I said it wasn't strong."

He angles a look at me that is at once heated and sly. "You must admit we both kiss a lot better than we did at thirteen."

I lean into him and drop my head to his shoulder like I did so often when we were growing up. "Oh, I don't know. For a first kiss, I thought it was pretty perfect."

He links our fingers together on his leg. "It was. I had high hopes for us after that kiss."

"What did you hope?" I ask, my voice soft, hesitant, a careful tread.

"I hoped it was just the beginning. I hoped that I'd come back from camp for high school and we'd be..." He turns his head to look at me, and the intensity, the tenderness there is familiar because it's always been there. I've seen it a million times and never fully knew what it was. How could I have then? "I hoped we'd be together."

I don't know what to say. It was a long time ago and we were so young, but I wanted him then as much as my fledgling heart knew how to want someone.

"Look, I don't want to lose you again." His fingers tightening around mine underscore his words. "If you decide you can't...don't want to...I want you in my life, Tru, even if it's only as a friend. Just don't leave me again."

I'm not sure what to say to that, so I glance down at our linked hands and find a distraction sketched into his skin. "You have a tattoo."

He turns his wrist over so I can see the Hebrew characters better.

עולם תיקון

"What is it?"

"Tikkun Olam. Basically, 'repair the world.' I started thinking about this concept when I had to do my Bar Mitzvah project. I went through that for Bubbe, but it actually did shape a lot about me as a man. I started YLA because I saw it as my contribution to make the world, at least one part of it, better."

"I'm really proud of you, Ez. I knew you would be amazing, but what you've done for those kids, for those families? It's life-changing."

"You're proud of *me*? I was in the airport waiting for a flight, and you came on one of those televisions in the gate waiting area, commentating for MSNBC or something. Some candidate. I almost missed my flight. They were shutting the doors, but I couldn't move. It was my first time seeing you grown up. I was transfixed. I knew you'd be beautiful, but..." He shakes his head wonderingly. "And you were so fluent. So confident. Not a stutter in sight."

"That took years to get rid of. And it comes back if I get really nervous. I still hate public speaking. I always made Lennix do that stuff as much as possible."

"Something changed for me after that. I had known you were out there somewhere, but to *see* you? I couldn't stop thinking about you."

"When you showed up at Daddy's funeral, I couldn't believe it." I chuckle. "I'm pretty sure I flung myself at you."

"I was glad. I wanted to hug you, but it had been so long since we'd known each other, I wasn't sure if there was protocol. And I imagine a lot of people you grew up with try to insinuate themselves into your life knowing you're close to such important people."

"You could never be a lot of people, Ez. There's everyone else, and then there's you."

The look on his face is something hot and needy, ardent, mirroring what's building inside of me. My heart swells in my chest, scraping against my rib cage, barely contained. This time, I don't have to wonder who moves first.

It's me.

I lean closer and press our lips together, eyes open and looking right into his. His glance, his frown, asks if I'm sure.

I'm not. How could I be?

But I close my eyes and deepen the kiss, a foolhardy fall I may pay for later. It's not even all the rationalizations that spur me to kiss him again. I could tell myself they broke up and that Aiko moved on first, but none of that actually runs through my mind when our tongues wrap around each other and our sighs entwine. My mind, consumed with the taste and feel of him, shouts one word over and over, an insistent refrain.

Finally. Finally. Finally.

He lays me down back onto the trampoline, and in the dark, the netting makes a world of mesh and magic, population: us. Our kisses turn desperate. What was gentle grows urgent, and he's clutching me, squeezing my leg, my arms, my ass. Exploring my body like a blind man seeing with his hands. The pressure is just right and too much and not nearly enough. I tear my mouth away, kiss his jaw, drag my lips down his neck. He sucks my earlobe, finding a direct lust line to my pussy. I squirm and whimper.

"You like that?" he breathes into the tiny cove between my neck and ear.

I nod, tightening my hands at his lean waist when he does it again, taking time with my ears and ghosting kisses down my neck and over my shoulders. When his lips meet the barrier of my strapless top, he pauses, hovering over my breast.

"I want to touch you here so badly my hands are shaking," he says, his voice a husky rumble. "Can I?"

I can't even breathe to get the "yes" out. Anticipation thieves my breath and beads my nipples. I barely manage to nod before he's cupping my breast through the shirt, dusting kisses along my collarbone. All the while, he pinches my nipples, squeezes my breast.

Oh my God. Please suck it.

I press deeper into his palm, willing him to pull the top down so he can see how hard my nipples are. How much I want his mouth on me. He just keeps raining infuriating, drugging kisses everywhere but *there*, churning a frenzy inside of me. I close my eyes, willing myself not to beg, and then I feel the wet heat of his mouth through the thin fabric.

"Ez," I moan. "Yes, please."

Hallelujah, he tugs the shirt down, slowly sliding it until the night air mists my nipples into proud peaks. I open my eyes and he's staring at my chest like it's Christmas morning. His breath is hot at the underside of my breast, blowing steam through my body. He takes my nipple into his mouth with an insistent, starving suction of his lips and tongue. It's not gentle, but it is a long, hard draw, transporting me through a tiny tunnel of pain to pleasure that explodes between my legs. A hundred words, a thousand ways to tell him that feels *soooooo* good flood my mind, and my mouth falls open, but no sound escapes. Ezra alternates, laving and sucking and biting one breast, pinching and plucking and kneading the other. I think I could come from just this, but he recruits other parts of my body in this sensual attack. He presses lightly at the juncture of my thighs, asking not with words, but with his touch.

I already know my voice will fail me, so I simply nod. He unsnaps my jeans, slides the zipper down, his fingers deft, eager. There's no fumbling or searching. He skates under the lacy rim of my panties, finding my clit unerringly quickly and passing the pad of one finger over the cluster of heat and nerves.

"Jesus," I gasp. "Lord."

"Open your legs."

I widen for him, and he rewards my obedience with the most

delicious intrusion of one huge finger plunging inside. He adds another, stretching me, plundering me. His hands, lips, tongue, conspire to drive me over the edge. He sucks my breast, rubs my clit, and fingers me with relentless tenderness and pounding urgency.

"Shit, shit, shit." My back arches and my head tips back and my body surrenders every molecule, splintering into a million writhing particles. I dig my heels into the trampoline as the orgasm washes over, tears through me. A jaw-rattling scream scrambles up my throat, but I bite my bottom lip, trapping the sound inside. I grind down onto his hand, shameless, careless of my obvious greedy need. I'm chasing this to the very end. I allow myself a few tiny whimpers as the last of it coats my whole body, twisting through my limbs and tingling my toes.

Ezra's hands slow. His kisses gentle, but he doesn't stop until I'm completely still, ragged breaths my only outward motion. I'm moving inside, though.

I'm a filthy feather floating back down to earth.

CHAPTER TWENTY-FOUR

Ezra

I STEAL A LOOK AT KIMBA'S FACE, DIMLY LIT BY THE MOON AND shadowed by the netting of the trampoline. We're lying down, facing each other, our bodies like confidants, huddled close. My hand rests just inside her panties, the unzipped waistband of her jeans gaping open. Her top is pulled down, the fabric scrunched at her waist. Her breasts are bare, the coppery skin glimmering, her nipples wet and plump from my kisses.

I didn't think we'd get this far tonight, but I'm damn happy about it.

"Oh my God," she says, her voice stripped, husky. "Are you kidding me?"

Her throaty laughter is a chime filling my backyard like music.

"What?" I ask warily. This could go many ways. Sideways.

"That was incredible." Splayed out beside me on the trampoline, she looks spent. Her facial muscles slacken except for the tiniest satisfied curve to her lips. "You're really good at that, Dr. Stern."

I chuckle and tip my head to the side until it touches hers. "If I hadn't moved to Italy, that probably would have happened in the back seat of some car or under bleachers when we were in the tenth grade."

"I doubt very seriously you would have been able to do *that* in the tenth grade." She sighs, sounding both content and impressed. "From my experience, teenage boys aren't quite that considerate."

She glances down the length of our bodies to the erection poking through my shorts.

"Speaking of considerate," she says, her hand drifting to my belt. She gives me a questioning glance, like she has to ask permission.

"I hope you don't think I'm gonna turn down whatever you're thinking." My shoulders shake from the laugh rumbling in my chest. "Because I won't. I'm down for whatever."

"Good," she purrs, sitting up, rising over me with her breasts out and mischief on her pretty, kiss-swollen lips. "Because I—"

"Dad!"

We both freeze. Kimba takes her hands from my belt and the entire lower half of my body violently objects.

"No." I shake my head, denial preserving my erection. "He's fine. He—"

"Dad!" Noah screams again, his voice carrying from his bedroom through the upstairs window.

"Shit." I swipe both hands over my face and haul myself to a sitting position on the trampoline beside Kimba. "I better—"

"Yeah." I could weep when she pulls her shirt back into place. "Sounds like you're needed."

"If I don't want him to maim his classmates," I say, pulling the net back and standing, "I better not ignore that."

She scoots to the edge and starts to climb out. I take her hand to help her down, more out of desire to touch her again than necessity. When she's on her feet, I pull her into me. Barefoot, she's much shorter than I am. I can't help but remember our first kiss when our faces aligned almost perfectly because we were the same height.

"It really was a perfect first kiss," I murmur, smiling.

"It was." She glances down at our joined hands. "Ezra, I don't mean to send you mixed signals, but just because we…"

Her gaze drifts back to the trampoline, a steamy reminder of what took place.

"Like I said." She sinks her teeth into her bottom lip and focuses her stare on the ground between our feet. "I need time to think about this."

Disappointment deflates the hope in my chest. I take her face between my palms gently. "I have to fly Noah to my mom for camp, but

I'll be back in a few days. Let's talk then?"

Reluctance and desire war in her eyes, and she finally nods. "Okay. When you get back we'll talk."

"That's mine!" Noah's near-hysterical voice from upstairs interrupts us again.

This kid.

"Sounds like a battle royale. You better go." She chuckles and drops my hand. "I'll see you when you get back."

CHAPTER TWENTY-FIVE

Ezra

"**H**E LOOKS JUST LIKE YOU THE FIRST TIME YOU WENT OFF to summer camp," my mother says tearfully, watching Noah get in line for check-in. "I hope he'll be okay."

I study my son objectively. There are some physical similarities, but Noah is a lot more self-assured than I was at that age.

"I bet he'll be just fine," I say wryly. "He usually is."

"Like you in that way then, too," she says, casting one last look Noah's way before starting with me back toward the car. "You were so confident."

That startles a snort out of me. "*I* was confident? Which kid were you raising, Mom?"

"You were small for your age, and not sure where you fit in," she says, a defensive note on my behalf in her voice. "But you had a strong sense of yourself, though you may not have realized it at the time."

"Kimba called it self-contained," I tell her, sliding into the driver's seat.

My mom shoots me a sharp look that I ignore while I adjust the mirrors. We drove Stanley's Cadillac, a huge boat of a car. I can't imagine why he keeps it, living in the heart of New York City.

"I know you said Kimba's on TV sometimes," Mom says carefully, "but I haven't seen her. You know I avoid politics whenever possible. How is she?"

How is she?

So pretty it makes my heart hurt to think of everything I've missed. Every questionable fashion choice, bad haircut, and acne breakout through high school. All the contouring and shaping and discipline it took to form her into who she has become.

How is she?

Powerful. Vulnerable. Brilliant. Kind. Ruthless.

"She's great."

"Well, that's nice," Mom says, an unspoken "don't ruin your life" woven into her statement.

The memory of Kimba panting and writhing under my hands on the trampoline rushes back in a wave. The sounds she made, the scent and wetness of her on my fingers, the texture of her skin—velvety and sugar-scrub sweet. The sensory recollection lands on my chest and heads immediately south. I shift because I'm in the car with my *mother*. This would only be more awkward if she could read my mind.

"What are you thinking about?" she asks.

I turn my head and meet her narrow-eyed stare. I'm convinced women are imbued with extra senses upon giving birth.

"Nothing," I mutter, turning my attention back to the road ahead. "Why?"

"You had a pinched look."

"I just dropped off my son at summer camp for the first time," I say, trying to sound concerned even though I know Noah will end up holding the conch if things were to go all *Lord of the Flies* at Jewish camp. "Any parent would have reservations."

"You just said yourself that he'll be fine," Mom says, shooting me an arch look. "Maybe you should spend less time worrying about Kimba and more time making things right with your girlfriend. Remember her? Noah's mother?"

"Mom, there's something I need to tell you."

"What is it?" she asks, anxiety already weaving through her words. "Are you—"

"Nothing bad. It's just… Aiko and I broke up."

"And that's not bad? I was hoping you'd get married someday."

"It's been ten years, Mom. Aiko didn't believe in marriage when she got pregnant with Noah, and she still doesn't."

"Is that why you're breaking up?"

"No. We're breaking up because we shouldn't be together, and staying for Noah is actually a disservice to us all."

It's quiet in the car, and I can't help but wonder if she's thinking about her own marriage. Over the years, my parents drifted so far apart that by the time Dad died, they were practically living separate lives. My mom completely re-immersed herself into her community, her family, her synagogue when they moved back to New York. My father dug his heels deeper into the notion that it was all nonsense. He worked more, was away from home more. I wouldn't be surprised if he eventually found someone else that he kept on the side. I suspected, but I'm glad I never knew for sure.

After a few moments of quiet, Mom looks out the window and clutches the purse in her lap. "Well, it sounds like you know what's best."

Considering that Aiko is already sleeping with Chaz and I'm potentially getting my chance with Kimba, I think I do.

CHAPTER TWENTY-SIX

Kimba

"LOOKS LIKE YOUR TIP WAS RIGHT," I TELL FELITA ON THE phone. "The future governor of Georgia is here tonight."

I find Burton Colson, Mateo Ruiz's probable opposition, on one side of the ballroom at the charity gala, and Congressman Ruiz on the other.

"Whomever that will be," I say. "They're both here."

"Good," Felita says. There's a muffled conversation in the background.

"You out?" I ask her.

"No, watching *West Wing*, season three."

"That's the best season."

"Wrong. Season two is better, but three *is* great. So what's your game plan?"

"Work this room," I say, scanning the luxurious ballroom. "See what I can find and get out of here. I'm supposed to be on vacation, you know."

"I know that." She laughs. "I just thought you forgot. Make sure you do something good for yourself while you're in Atlanta."

I've done enough *good for myself* the last few years. After what Ezra did for me on that trampoline, I've caught myself wishing he could handle all *my good* in the coming future. He's still in New York, which is a good thing because when I woke up horny last night *in my mama's house*,

I might have been banging on Ezra's door if he was in town.

"If I want to get out of here as fast as possible," I tell Felita, "I better go. Enjoy season three."

"K. Bye."

I search the room until I find Burton Colson again. The billionaire CEO ran for mayor of the town where he grew up, winning easily. Rumors of his probable gubernatorial bid have been circulating for the last two years. He put an end to the speculation last week when he officially announced his candidacy. I could predict everything about this man—where he'd have gone to college, the woman he'd marry, the causes he'd choose to lobby. I even got his mistress right. His wife's a brunette. I called him for a redheaded sidepiece. Pictures from her early life show mousy brown, but a bottle turned her red, so I win on a technicality.

What can I say? That Allen gut. I got it.

But there are things I couldn't possibly know about him. That's the dirty laundry Piers is sorting through now. These days, a mistress isn't enough to derail a campaign. The public is too jaded to allow something as minor as a mistress to keep otherwise good leaders out of office. And generally, I agree. When the world's on fire, give me a competent leader who knows what the hell she's doing over the chick who never cheated on her partner, but couldn't lead me out of a paper bag. Character does count for something, though, and as Colson's opposition, it's my job to expose...possibly exploit...his weaknesses. I doubt there's anything that could completely disqualify him, but there's certainly something that could turn votes our way.

Or Mateo's way, rather, since he still hasn't hired me.

But he will.

Unless the man *sitting with him* right now, a few tables over, has anything to say about it. Anthony Rodderick and I grew up in this business together. We graduated around the same time. Started working in politics right out of college. Did the same grunt work to pay our dues. Now we both run political firms and vie for some of the same big fish candidates.

I drift from conversation to conversation, working my way closer to Congressman Ruiz's table. Anthony never leaves his side. I should not be angling to see Mateo Ruiz. He knows what I can do. My resume speaks for itself, or at least it should. He's worried that Lennix is gone and I can't manage on my own? I've been doubted at every turn, and I always pull through. I just elected a president. If he'll give me the chance, I'll deliver this state to him. Skulking around ballrooms, positioning myself for his consideration, hoping I can "accidentally" run into him—this is not a good look. And if this was a game of chess, this would not be my move.

I politely end the conversation I'm in and head into the women's restroom. The bathroom is done in richly patterned silk wallpaper. Benches with plump cushions line the walls. Egyptian cotton hand towels, costly soaps and fragrant lotions are stacked neatly on the marble sink counter, but the greatest luxury this room offers me right now is solitude.

I set my clutch onto the counter and face my reflection in the large gilt-framed mirror. Kayla's stylist did my makeup for the gala. She employed a heavier hand than I usually like, but I must admit she did a great job. Long-lashed dark eyes stare back at me, a palate of peacock colors brushed across my lids. I never wear fuchsia, but the matte color pops purply-pink against my skin, painted over a mouth that looks even wider and fuller than usual. My hair, pressed straight, falls around shoulders left bare by Lotus' creation. It's a masterpiece of jewel tones—blues, greens, and purples subtly reflecting the colors decorating my face. The dress is a fairy tale, a strapless tulle bodice, nipped waistline, and flared skirt that bells out in layers of iridescent wings ending just above my knees. My only jewelry are the round emeralds glimmering in my earlobes and the gold ring Daddy gave me that rarely leaves my thumb. I take it off and read the inscription inside.

To thyself be Tru. Love, Daddy.

He gave me this ring when I settled on Arizona State. The whole family accused me of believing the schools that shaped our family for generations weren't good enough for me. That wasn't it. I just needed to get away from it all. From *them* all and make my own way.

Daddy got it. He always did.

Losing Daddy remains and may always be the most devastating moment of my life. When he died, that unconditional love and acceptance died with him and left behind such a void. The last few years, I've kept busy enough to fill that void with work and ambition and, yes, power. I've acquired power for myself and for others by staying in constant motion. But with the problems crowding in on me—the possibility of never having children, and maybe never getting this shot to make history for the state of Georgia because the congressman is "keeping me in mind," I can't be still.

Not to mention I'm still not sure what I should do about Ezra. Oh, I know exactly what I *want* to do, but can I afford the emotional attachment it could easily become with him? Can I afford that now? And should we get involved when things are so uncertain with Aiko and Noah? Family shit gets *messy*, and I have enough mess of my own.

I stride from the bathroom and come face-to-face with Anthony Rodderick, my sometime-nemesis. Yale educated. His family are Augusta National board members who yield power across the entire state. He holds a guaranteed spot on Sunday morning's political news circuit that I usually eschew. He's your typical entitled male, but a liberal, so in some ways he's even blinder to his own privilege because wanting to save the world assuages his guilt for getting all he wants from it.

"Kimba," he says, his deep voice modulated by an expensive education, years of breeding, and just the right twinge of a Southern drawl to keep him approachable. "So good to see you again."

"Good to see you, too, Tony," I say, deliberately using the sobriquet I know he hates.

His expression twitches almost imperceptibly if you don't know what you're looking for. But, of course, I do.

"I think the last time I saw you," Anthony says, "was at the Inaugural Ball."

He leans against the wall and slides his left hand into his pants pocket, but not before I notice the lighter band of skin where his wedding ring used to be. Relationships—marriages, families, friendships—are the greatest liabilities of any campaign. I know that firsthand.

"It was very gracious of President Cade to invite his rivals to his big night,"

Anthony continues, grudging admiration and some envy evident in his voice.

"The president is a gracious man," I reply neutrally.

"And his wife, too. You'd know that better than most considering she was your business partner and best friend. Must be nice when your connections land you the plum jobs."

"You'd probably know more about that than I would."

His scoffing laughter slithers under my skin. "Seriously? My family may be rich, but there are no schools, parks, bridges or streets named after us." His expression goes granite. "And that kind of thing means nothing to Mateo Ruiz. He's more interested in winning over people in this state who would resist his bid. People like my family and the guys I grew up with. I *know* how to reach them."

"I know how to reach them, too. *Being* like your enemy is not a battle strategy. Thinking like them is. I could outthink you with a concussion." I step close enough to whisper in his ear. "And you know it."

He chuckles, his eyes roaming over my face and body with undisguised admiration. He'd fuck me if he could, but that won't ever happen. I turned him down when he was drunk enough to actually ask, which only makes him more determined to beat me.

"Maybe," he whispers back. "Maybe I know it, but Mateo doesn't, and he's *this* close to hiring me to run his campaign. You could always come work for me, Kimba. I'd take real good care of you." Innuendo sours his voice.

"Tony, you wouldn't know how to 'take care of me' with step-by-step instructions, but I'll consider...no guarantees now...hiring you to work for *me* on Mateo's campaign. I'm sure I could find something for you to do. If I remember correctly, you make a great cup of coffee."

"We'll see about that," he says as I turn and head for the exit. I'm not sure what it will take to persuade Congressman Ruiz, but this wasn't it. I'll know my move when it's time to make it, and it will have Congressman Ruiz coming to *me*.

I pull my phone out to call for an Uber and see a text message from Mona.

Mona: Wanna get faded? I have wine and edibles. Gummies, to be exact.

These men who think I should bow and scrape to them have me feeling tight and close to my feelings. I could use some loosening.

I hit send on my message back to Mona.

Me: Girl, on my way.

CHAPTER TWENTY-SEVEN

Kimba

AT LEAST I'M NOT AS DRUNK AS MONA.

This occurs to me, though, whilst my legs are straight up in the air, the hem of my dress is scrunched at my waist, and my head hangs off the arm of the couch. I may not be drunk exactly, but maybe a little looser than I planned? And I only had half a gummy.

"I'm deadass serious when I ask this question," Mona says, her words only slurring the slightest bit.

"What's the question?"

"Are you ready for the question?"

"I just said...dammit, I'm ready. What's your question, Mo?"

"Where are all the brothers who eat booty like groceries?"

It's completely silent for several seconds and then we both start giggling uncontrollably. My head, hanging upside down, bobs against the back of the couch. Mona, stretched out on the floor, staring up at the ceiling fan, cackles and grips her midsection.

"Is this keeping you up at night?" I ask. "Not is the overall temperature of our planet rising at an unsustainable rate? Not how will we address the problem of mass incarceration? Or equal pay for women? But your existential question centers around men who eat ass?"

"I need a man who's not afraid to put in that work. I mean, girls can do it for ourselves, but we can't do *that*. And I get sick of getting myself off. I wanna share the burden."

I snort. "Ain't that the truth."

"My BOB gets the job done, yeah, but it's not…intimate. Ya know what I mean?" The amusement fades from Mona's expression. "There's nothing like being touched."

Like the urgent squeeze of Ezra's hands on me, the caress of his breath. The gentle touch of something as simple as being helped down to the ground. The desperate need in how tightly he clutched me. It had been affirming.

Mona's right. There's nothing like the touch of someone who wants you as much as you want them.

"I miss being fucked," Mona says. She sits up and reaches for her wine, shunning the glass and taking the bottle straight to her lips. "Feeling a man inside me, hitting that spot over and over, that makes me lose my mind. Clawing and scratching because the shit is so good. I miss being kissed and held."

She lies back down. "Hell, I miss waking up with somebody *beside* me. That morning wood poking you from behind." Her laugh is bittersweet. "My ex liked to fuck first thing. Said there was nothing better to start off his day than…" She shakes her head, leaving the thought incomplete.

"You miss him?" I ask softly.

"He cheated on me." She bites her bottom lip and takes another swig of wine. "Yeah, I miss his trifling ass."

"I'm sorry, Mo. How'd you find out?"

"Oh, he was decent enough to tell me himself because he wanted out. Sat me down and said he'd met someone at work. She was younger, skinnier and lighter than me, but, *of course*, none of those things mattered to *him*. Their minds had met on an intellectual plane."

She shoots me an icily ironic look. "Bitch *did* graduate from Penn. Made me sick. Miss I Got Everything And Your Man. He better *not* be eating her ass. He never ate booty or did any freaky, adventurous shit with me."

Mona's funny as hell even when she's hurting, so an involuntary smile quirks my lips. One she ruefully returns.

She sits up again, cross-legged, and flings her long dreadlocks over one shoulder. "I could have cheated. Think I didn't have offers?

Opportunities? I did, but I would never do that to another person."

I sit up, leaving my legs in the air resting against the back of the couch, but propping my elbows on the edge. "I kissed Ezra."

As soon as the confession hits the air, I want to take it back. Damn wine, loosening my lips and lowering my guard.

"Kimba," Mona groans, dropping her head to her hands. "You said you had this under control. That you were just friends. Just gonna talk."

"Yeah, but that was before he told me—"

"I don't care what he told you." Mona stands a little unsteadily, the fog clearing from her eyes. "That's somebody else's man. A good woman. A *friend* of mine. The mother of his child."

"But Mo—"

"Don't *but Mo* me. They've been together almost ten years. You can't just waltz into their lives from on high for a month and tear that family apart."

"I'm not tearing anything apart. I—"

"How could you, Kimba?"

"She's fucking someone else," I blurt. Were I completely sober, I doubt I would have said that.

"She's *what?*" Mona's eyes widen and her mouth hangs open. "Aiko?"

"I shouldn't have said anything." I groan, not drunk enough for a hangover, but just drunk enough to make a fool of myself and put everyone's business in the streets.

"But ya did, so go on. Explain."

"You and Ezra are friends. He'll tell you when the time is right."

"The time is *right now*, honey. You opened this can of worms. Don't try to go shoving them back in now."

I sigh and pluck at the frothy, shimmery layers of my skirt. "She asked for an open relationship. Ezra didn't want it, said things weren't getting better, and they've decided to break it off."

"Aiko asked for an open relationship?" Mona's face is skeptical. "Homegirl gets jealous, green as a butter bean over Ezra. I can't imagine her being okay with him...are you sure?"

"Well, that's what he told me. He says he wanted to make a clean break because they've been having trouble for a while."

I sit up enough to glance at her over my shoulder. "Is that true?"

"I mean, I know they were seeing a counselor, but I assumed it was just them being smart, proactive. Keeping the lines of communication open."

"Oh, they're open all right," I say dryly. "According to him, they're over."

"So Ezra told you this and you two kissed?"

I clear my throat. "Twice."

"And did you do more than kiss?"

I love Mona, but I'm not getting into the details of Ezra's fingers inside me, his mouth hot and suckling at my breast. In my mind's eye, there's an aerial shot of Ezra and me on that trampoline, breathing hard, turned into each other, unable to look away in the moonlight, intimacy curling deliciously between our bodies.

"Just kissed, but he wants more." I meet her eyes across the room. "So do I."

"Look, I'm not that chick who tells a grown-ass woman where to get the dick or how to run her life," she says, "but I wouldn't be your friend if I didn't say this. They are a family. Aiko is not just some girl he found on Tinder and then decided it's quits. He hasn't been with anyone but her for ten years, and they have a son together. Things happened fast and things just happened. It ain't over 'til it's over, and if anyone gets hurt when things go south, it'll be you."

And I cannot afford to be hurt, not with everything already on my plate.

The kitchen door opens and heavy footsteps approach the living room. I'm on high alert, but Mona looks pretty calm about it.

"Well, here we go," she says resignedly.

"It's just me," Ezra yells from the doorway.

The sight of him standing at the entrance to Mona's living room sends shock spearing through me. He looks *goooooood*. His broad shoulders fill the doorway, and the dark jeans and YLA T-shirt show off the lean muscles in his arms and legs. His hair has grown just a little, long enough to curl the slightest bit, and my fingers pulse with the need to scrape across his scalp and burrow into the soft pelt of it. A little scruff shadows his sharply drawn jawline. He's sun-bronzed, contrasting with the white flash of his smile.

A smile that evaporates when he sees me.

"Tru, I didn't know you were here." He clears his throat. "Sorry to barge in, Mo."

"Like you don't bust up in here every damn day unannounced," she says. "One day, you gonna get an eyeful."

She walks over and gives him a hug. He watches me over her shoulder, his eyes running along my bare legs, still flung over the couch. My instinct is to sit up, cover myself, preserve some modesty.

But I don't.

My *other* instinct is to make him want me the way I want him. The heat of his stare is addictive. His eyes caress my bare shoulders and legs, and despite the warm summer night, my body is covered in goose bumps.

"You're back early." My voice comes out husky, breathless.

"Uh, yeah." He makes no move to come farther into the room. "I wanted to get back."

When he looks at me, *I missed you* is in his eyes.

I'll wait is in the hands he shoves into his pockets.

Without saying a word, his body tells me with eloquence how he feels, what he wants. I want it, too, but Mona's warnings ring in my ears.

If anyone gets hurt when things go south, it'll be you.

"I got edibles and wine," Mona tells him, walking back to her bottle on the floor. "Join us."

"You know I don't do weed," he says wryly. "I can't spare that many brain cells."

He focuses on her while he talks, but his gaze keeps drifting back to my legs. I bend my knee and run my fingers along my thigh.

Just to see what happens.

He lowers his head. His Adam's apple bobs with a deep swallow. The muscle in his jaw flexes.

"Noah got to camp okay?" Mona asks, flicking a look between the two of us.

Ezra nods. "He walked in like he owned the place, of course."

"He probably will by the time it's over." Mona laughs. "You've gotta play Monopoly with this kid, Kimba. Ruthless kingpin."

Her comment falls into the vat of silence accumulating between Ezra and me. We watch each other warily, furtively.

"So, no gummies," Mona says, grabbing an unopened bottle of wine from the coffee table. "Wine? Join the party."

"I think I'll go actually," he says, his voice deep and graveled. "I just wanted to let you know I was home early in case you needed anything."

"Like a good neighbor," Mona says. "Oooooh, what if I lived next door to the State Farm guy? He's so fine on those commercials. I'd be borrowing sugar every day."

"Yeah, well," he says, his words clipped, controlled. "I'm gonna go."

When he leaves, Mona looks at me and shakes her head. "Be careful, girl. If I were you, I wouldn't."

But she's not me, and looking at the empty place where Ezra just stood, I already know I probably will.

CHAPTER TWENTY-EIGHT

Ezra

"**D**AMN SPRINKLERS."

I crush the dried leaves of Noah's tomatoes in my fist. The system has been unreliable for weeks. The timer's been temperamental. It looks like the garden wasn't watered at all while I was in New York.

"I need to get someone out here to check it," I mutter, walking to the collard greens in the rear of the garden.

I *do* realize midnight is an odd time to perform such a thorough inspection of our vegetables, but it seems like as good a way as any to distract from the fact that Kimba is next door in Mona's living room.

Her legs were flung carelessly over the side of the couch. Long and toned and the color of burnt honey. The bodice of her strapless dress barely contained her breasts. She probably didn't realize the top of one nipple, like a drop of chocolate, was barely visible from just the right angle.

I stood at just the right angle.

Hell.

I drop to my haunches and check the soil the sprinklers would only reach when they oscillate. Looks like it hasn't seen a drop of water.

A noise brings me to my feet. Kimba stands at the fence dividing my yard from Mona's. She aims a tentative smile over a row of corn stalks. "Can I come in?"

I nod, but don't otherwise move. I stand still because I'm afraid if I get much closer, I'll grab her and won't be able to let go. She's obviously been out based on her attire. I've seen her on television dressed like this. Awards shows. Events. Political functions. Polished and pulled together in a way that probably requires a third party. A *stylist*. That confection of a dress forms a shimmering bell from her waist to her knees. Her shoes look like they cost about as much as monthly tuition at YLA. Her hair, which I'd gotten used to seeing in its natural texture, falls pressed, straight and shiny around her bare shoulders.

"You look pretty," I say unnecessarily. I'm sure several men, any number of them with eyes in their heads, told her that tonight.

"Thanks." She carefully makes her way toward me through the string beans.

"Date?" I keep my voice casual, neutral, the exact opposite of how the thought of her on a date with someone else actually makes me feel.

"What?" She frowns and tilts her head.

"Were you on a date?" I ask with excruciating pronunciation.

"Oh, no." She smiles, slants a knowing glance up at me. "Would you care if I was?"

I don't reply, but just stare at her, unblinking, letting her *feel* my answer instead of wasting words.

"I wasn't on a date. It was a charity event." She grimaces. "A work thing. I wasn't expecting you back from New York for a few days."

I pluck idly at a dead leaf on a tomato vine. "Yeah. I wanted to get back."

To see you.

I wanted her answer. I know I have a lot of baggage. Having a kid is one thing. Living with his mom for the last decade? Being in the midst of negotiating what is practically a divorce—it's complicated. I'm not exactly a safe bet. I get it, but I can't *not* ask Kimba to take this risk with me. As irrational as it may seem, since we were only thirteen when I left, this feels like our second chance, and I'll do just about anything to have it. She picks her way down the row of vegetables, her stilettos sinking into the soil. Her ankle turns, bringing a grimace to her lips.

Her pretty, painted lips.

I like your lips the way they always are.

Thirteen-year-old Ezra was on to something. As beautiful as Kimba looks with the artistry of her makeup, I still prefer her lips bare.

I haven't moved, and she keeps walking toward me. My hands

twitch with the compulsion to hold her, so I stuff them in my pockets, an old tell she can still probably easily read. I make a deal with myself. Until she says *yes*, until she says she's willing to give us a chance, I won't touch her.

The chemistry between us is electricity over an open flame. It destroys reason, and I want her as clear-eyed and level-headed as possible if and when she agrees to try with me. As clear-eyed and level-headed as you can be after a bottle of Mona's wine and an undisclosed number of edibles.

Kimba looks steady and sober enough when she stops in front of me on the row of collards.

"So, Noah was good?" she asks.

"Yeah." For once, I don't want to talk about my son.

"And your mother? She was okay?"

I for damn sure don't want to discuss my mother when I'm sporting a semi in front of the literal girl of my dreams. "She's good," I reply tersely. "Did you need something, Kimba?"

Like me? Do you need me? Because I need you, and if you keep standing here in my garden looking like this, smelling like summer and seduction, I'll take you, so get on with it.

"Oh." She glances down at her expensive shoes, covered in dirt. She clutches her clutch, pressing the little purse to her waist. "Yeah, well...I've been thinking about what you said."

"What I said?" Endangering my good intentions, my legs carry me a step closer to her. "What I said about what?"

She huffs an exasperated breath and slides a glance to the side, over to the squash. "About us...giving this a try. Since I'm here in the city and you're..." She glances up at me and then quickly back down. The fairy lights we strung around the garden streak shadows with her eyelashes on the tops of her cheeks. "...available."

"Available?" I risk a step closer, not wanting to hope, but liking where this is going. "Yeah, I'm available."

I pause, holding my breath and balling my fists in the pockets of my jeans.

"Well, since you're available and so am I..." She gives me a level look and draws in a bust-lifting breath. "I'm saying yes."

That magic word sets me into immediate motion. I reach for her, scooping her close and wrapping my arms around her waist. I bend my knees so I can bury my nose in the silky sweep of skin from her shoulder, up her neck and behind her ear. Her fingers in my hair are the most delicious kind of torture.

I pull back to brush my thumb across the vibrant coat of lipstick, smearing it. Her lips are soft as petals under my finger. I do it again and again until nothing but the natural pinkish-brown of her mouth remains. Her breaths come harder every time I touch her lips, and she's panting, her eyes never leaving my face. I cup the back of her head and bend, giving her one last moment to think better of it—to pull away. But instead she leans in, meeting me halfway, her mouth open and her sweet tongue seeking mine. I groan into the kiss, searching the silky interior of her mouth, my hands roaming down her back and squeezing her ass through the shimmering layers of fabric.

Just when I think I'll combust, cold water sprays my face and back and arms.

"What the...?" I look up to the sky, expecting rain.

"It's your sprinklers," Kimba says, sounding horrified and wriggling to get out of my arms.

The hell I'm letting her go. The water dances over us, a shocking shower soaking me through. She squirms in my unbreakable hold. "Ezra! My hair!"

The silky, straight strands are wet and clinging to her neck. The perky layers of her dress now droop with the weight of water. I laugh and pull her even closer.

"Ezra Stern," she grits out. "If you don't—"

It only makes me laugh harder because if she could see herself, she'd laugh, too, but she can't so I'm laughing for both of us. She turns in my arms, poised to run, but her high heel gets stuck and her foot sinks into the mud.

"Dammit." She pushes the wet hair from her face and bats at my arm around her waist. "Let me go."

"No way I'm letting you go," I whisper in her ear through a clump of damp hair that's already starting to curl. "You said yes."

She goes still. Stops squirming and looks up at me over her shoulder, her lipstick smeared, her mascara streaked. The annoyance slowly dissolves from her expression, and a smile, the kind I haven't seen since we were kids, high on anticipation and down for whatever, breaks out on her face. I spread my hand over her stomach and pull her back into my chest, angling my head so I can reach her mouth, and I kiss her.

It's the kind of perfect kiss that has nothing to do with technique or experience. Nothing even to do with ardor, though that's evident in the way we clutch, we cling. It's perfect because it's her and it's me and it's about time and it's overdue. And we kiss like there's no tomorrow because there have already been too many yesterdays, too many years we were apart. Centuries separated us, but now here we are and here's our chance. It's not ideal and it has its complications, but it's ours. And we're taking it.

Also, I was wrong. This sprinkler system? *Perfect timing.*

CHAPTER TWENTY-NINE

Kimba

I'M WET AND PAST CARING ABOUT IT.

Ezra's sprinkler continues its assault on my blow-out and my Jimmy Choos, but I can't stop this kiss. He holds me from behind, his arm wrapped possessively around my waist. I reach up, clenching my fingers in his soaked hair and pressing his mouth deeper into mine. His lips are soft and starving, stirring all my senses to life. He moves his hand up from my waist and squeezes my breast. I turn into him, pressing my curves into the hard plane of his chest. He tugs at the bodice of my dress and runs a thumb roughly over my nipple.

"Inside," he mutters, raining kisses down my neck. He grabs my hand and turns to run through the garden. My heels keep getting stuck in the mud and I turn my ankle every other step.

"My shoes." I stop and bend to take them off, but he dips under my midsection and hoists me over his shoulder.

"Ezra Stern!" I squeal, bouncing against his back, the rows of vegetables a blur as he dashes through mud and squash and tomatoes. "If you drop me…"

When we reach the back door, he opens it and steps into the mudroom, my body still slung over his shoulder. He slides me down his front and carefully sets me on my feet.

"We're a mess." I laugh.

Lotus' gorgeous creation may be unsalvageable, the vibrant wings limp and flopping around my hips and legs. My high heels squish as soon as they hit the hardwood floor. Ezra's jeans and shoes are sloshed with mud. Water beads his face and hair, crystalline droplets suspended from his long lashes. His YLA T-shirt is transparent, plastered to the heavy muscles of his chest and tapering to his ribs and narrow waist. He reaches back and wrenches the sodden shirt over his head.

My laughter evaporates along with all the oxygen in the mudroom when I come face-to-pectoral with his broad, wet, naked chest. His body is something beyond the basics of human anatomy, overreaching into divine engineering. With trembling fingers, I trace his abs, his chest and broad shoulders, strength and sinew draped tightly over bones. I touch his mouth, the well-drawn bow of his top lip, the alluring fullness of the bottom one. Ocean and midnight sky, desire and tenderness swirl in his eyes. A voluptuous silence swells and curves between us, thickening by the second.

"Tru." He brushes his knuckles across my cheek and pushes the wet hair away from my face. "Let me see you."

I jerk down the shade at his door and find the zipper at my back, tugging until the bodice gapes, liberating my breasts, proud and heavy, tipped up at the ends with large brown nipples.

"Shit." He runs reverent fingers over them. My breath hitches. "You're…"

He swallows and cups my neck, bends to run his tongue along my collarbone, lapping up the beads of water on my skin. He wanders to one breast, pulling on it with his mouth so softly, with such care, my knees literally go weak. He licks the halo surrounding my nipple over and over. The drag of his tongue provokes a shudder through my whole body. He takes my hand, linking our fingers, and gently pushes me, urging me to sit on the mudroom bench. Dropping to his knees, he removes my ruined heels and pulls my legs over his shoulders. His head disappears under the iridescent layers of my skirt and he strokes along the bare skin of my thighs, lifting my knees higher, wider. When his finger probes the edge of my panties between my legs, I instinctively tighten my knees. His head bobs beneath the skirt, lips tugging on my clit through the silk underwear.

"Oh." I press my palm to the wall beside me. "Ez."

He does it again, a teasing, tantalizing bite and suck, his mouth hot and wet through my panties.

I groan, shifting my hips, spreading myself wider, silently begging him to take it with nothing between us. His fingers are at my hips, slipping beneath the scrap of silk, tugging until the panties skim my flesh in a slow ride down my thighs, over my knees, calves and feet.

Off.

He reverses, kissing up my calf. He sucks behind my knee, disappearing again under the dress, dragging his tongue over the sensitive skin of my inner thigh. The blunt tips of his fingers pry me apart, hold me open. His breath caresses my clit, and my heels reflexively dig into his back. I press my palm harder into the wall, shaking with anticipation.

Before I'm reduced to begging, he licks me, whisper-soft and barely there. His groan vibrates against my thigh. Spreading me wider, he opens his mouth over me, running the flat of his tongue from my opening to the tight cluster of nerves at the top of my pussy. His thumb brushes my clit while his tongue plunges inside me, setting a steady, fucking pace. With his other hand, he cups my breast, squeezes, pinches, twists my nipple.

"Oh, God, oh, God, oh, God," I chant, the words melting in my mouth, slurring drunkenly.

Mindlessly, I rock my hips in time with his mouth. I can't stop my fist from banging the wall. I can't stop my knees from tightening around his head. A moan climbs from my belly and wails out of me at the apogee of my pleasure. It feels so good, my mouth falls open on a silent sob. I'm rocking and writhing and *his*. I'm so completely his right now. He's eating me out, but he has me eating from the palm of his hand. No one has ever taken care of me this way, this thoroughly, with such selfless abandon and dedication to my pleasure.

Even after I come, liquid bliss spilling from my body and I'm slumped against the wall, he doesn't stop nibbling, tasting, squeezing my legs, dragging me closer like a bowl he has to lick clean.

"Tru." Passion and layers of expensive fabric muffle his voice. With tingling hands, I push the skirt away so I can see his face. His mouth and chin glisten and his eyes are glazed. I rub my thumb across his bottom lip.

"I want to fuck you," he says.

I want that. Even though I just came *hard* and *long*, an emptiness swallows me from the inside out. Need burgeons from that void—the need to feel him pistoning in and out, to know the intimate slide of our bodies. I stand on wobbly legs, pull his hand, pushing his shoulder until he takes my place on the bench. He runs his knuckle between my breasts and over my belly until he reaches the band of my skirt where the bodice hangs useless. I reach back and undo the button at the base of my spine. The dress falls to the floor in a vivid cascade, fanning around my ankles. I'm naked and barefoot in his mudroom. I haven't shed all of the extra weight that comes with this damn condition, but I'm not self-conscious. Not ashamed. He's looking at me like I'm the sunrise and he's grateful for a brand new day. He runs his palms up and down my thighs, over my hips. He squeezes my ass, brushes my nipples. I sway under a fresh wave of pleasure but help slide his boxers and jeans off.

"Come here," he whispers, curling his fingers around my leg and urging me toward him. I lift my knees on either side of his hips, straddling him. He grips my ass, lining our bodies up.

"Shit." He presses his forehead to mine. "Condom."

I reach down to grab my discarded clutch and quickly pull out the little sleeve containing credit cards, my license and, in a hidden compartment, a condom.

Taking him in my hand, I rub my thumb over his leaking tip, squeezing the slightest bit. His head falls back, exposing the corded strength of his throat. I stroke up and down, gently at first, learning the hot slide of silk over steel. And then faster, firmer until his hips jerk and the muscles of his thighs flex beneath mine. He mumbles something incoherent. I don't let up, pumping his dick and bending to suck his nipples.

"In," he rasps.

"What?" I mutter at his neck, drowning in the earthy scent of him, fascinated by all his male textures—rough, smooth, hard, velvet, silk, stone.

"In," he says abruptly, clearly, gripping my hips and sliding me forward. "Let me fuck you."

I slide the condom over the hard, hot length of him, and then slowly interlock us. The first time Ezra enters my body, the world cracks open. Tectonic. Like two plates of earth shifted, melded to make an entirely new plane. We go still in unison for just a second, the newness of a completely unique dimension comprised of his body and mine settling into place. And then we move, a slow, sensuous give and take of soul and flesh that makes us pant and moan and grind and groan. Our mouths open, gasping. He fills me completely. I press my temple to his and rock my hips over him. He maps my back, my ass, my thighs. I'm territory he claims with his hands and lips and the covetous heat of his eyes. And I take possession of him. Squatter's rights, a field Aiko abandoned that, whether she knows it or not, is now *mine*.

He reaches between us, rubbing his thumb over my slick clit. The pace quickens; the need is feral. My breasts bounce as I ride him hard, one palm slammed into the wall over his shoulder and one hand squeezing my own breast with just the right pressure to send me spiraling. Another climax jerks my body forward until we're heart to heart. He pounds up into me, squeezing, spreading my ass open and stiffening, the hard muscles of his stomach contracting. A moan wrenches from him as he empties himself. I grab his chin, tugging his mouth open, and lick into him with long, languid kisses that bob our heads and twist our bodies and wall out the world. The years fall away like a torn veil separating him from me, then from now. It hasn't been years. There has only been one long day for us on which the sun has never set. We were never lost, and this place has always been waiting for our wandering hearts, for our prodigal souls to finally, together rest.

CHAPTER THIRTY

Ezra

"TELL ME ABOUT YOUR FIRST TIME."

Kimba asks the question in the middle of the night. After we dragged our limp bodies from the mudroom and up the stairs, we stumbled into the guest bedroom and made love again, this time a slow, savoring union, commemorating what was the best sex of my life. I spoon her under the covers, pushing the damp hair, half straight, half coiled, away from her neck and ghost kisses over her soft skin. She presses her naked back into my chest.

"My first time?" I tighten my arms around her middle and spread my hand over her stomach. "It should have been with you."

"Obviously." She reaches back, scraping her nails through my hair. "But who was the little wench?"

I chuckle and push my knee into hers from behind. "Francesca Aldi. I was fifteen. She was sixteen. My first time. Not hers."

"Where was it?"

"Rome. Her house. Her parents were away. She didn't know it was my first time. I was too embarrassed to tell her."

"Oh, Ezra." Kimba turns to face me and rubs a thumb over my eyebrow and down my cheekbone. "I bet you were so dear."

"I hope not." I choke out a laugh. "'Dear' is not what a guy wants to be his first time having sex."

"How was it?"

"I remember feeling deflated. Disappointed, like everyone had played a trick on me—convinced me sex was this amazing thing I wouldn't be able to get enough of. Don't get me wrong. It did feel great. Better than my hand and a fistful of lotion."

She snickers and pulls the comforter higher over our naked shoulders.

"But I always thought my first time would be fireworks." I hesitate and then tell her the truth. "I guess I always thought my first time would be with you. I don't think anyone could have lived up to that."

She nods. "Same."

"What about you? Who was it? Where? Was it good?"

I want to know everything all at once so I can stop thinking of her with anyone else.

"Terrell Anderson." She chuckles. "It was a total cliché. Prom night my junior year. He was a senior and got us a room. I had to lie to my parents to stay out. Kayla covered for me and made sure I had condoms."

"And was it good?"

She laughs, but it's laced with regret. "I guess for him. Not for me. I was disappointed, too. Even more for how he acted after it was over."

"What'd he do when it was over?"

"Another cliché." She rolls onto her back and studies the ceiling. "He told all his friends he'd fucked Joseph Allen's daughter."

"Bastard," I mutter, wishing I could find the piece of shit and tear him apart.

"Very much so. When I found out he'd told people, I confronted him and dumped his ass. He didn't like that. I was a junior who should have been happy he'd deigned to take me to the prom, much less pay for a hotel room and dispose of my virginity."

"What'd he do?" Because I can already tell he did something I'll hate him even more for.

"He told me if I didn't let him fuck me again *and* suck his dick this time, he'd post pictures of me in the cafeteria. Pictures he took while I was asleep. He even threatened to send them to my father."

"Motherfucker. What'd you do?"

"What I always did with my problems." She smiles sadly. "Went to my father."

"You told him—"

"I told him everything. I always could." Her naked shoulders gleam in the moonlight when she shrugs. "He told me not to worry. Said he would take care of it, and he did. I don't know exactly how, but there were no photos and Terrell couldn't even look me in the eye to the day he graduated."

"I hope your dad did something incredibly painful that ruined his future."

Kimba slants an amused glance to me. "He might have. Daddy did have his ruthless streak."

I shake her playfully under the covers. "That's where you get yours from."

"Damn right." She laughs but sobers after a moment. "Terrell ended up going to Morehouse. If I hadn't known before that I didn't want to go to Spelman, I knew then. I didn't want to be that close, to run into him."

"Did that idiot affect your decision not to go to Spelman?"

"Not just that, but it did kind of push me over the cliff I was already standing at the edge of. My family name, reputation here in this city, started feeling like an albatross. I wanted to set it aside for a little while and have a clean slate in a new place. Arizona gave me that."

"That's where you met Lennix Hunter?"

"Yes." A wide, open smile touches her lips. "We were two peas in a pod from day one and have been best friends ever since."

"Is it silly that I still get a little jealous hearing you call someone else your best friend?"

"Yeah, that's really silly." She throws her leg over mine and pulls me close until her breasts are crushed between our chests. "Because you should know by now that no one could take your particular place."

I search under the covers for her hand, link our fingers. "I didn't even know how much I missed you until I got you back."

"I felt it at the funeral." She breathes out a shaky laugh. "As soon as I saw you again, I knew it would be like this."

"Is that why you shut me down?"

She gnaws at the corner of her lip. "When I saw Noah and Aiko, realized you had a family, knowing the pull I felt between us right away, I knew it would be too dangerous to stay in touch."

"We'd been having problems even before that, and we'd gone to counseling, but I wonder if some part of me gave up after I saw you, hoping our lives might intersect again."

I hate to even say that out loud. I hear how it sounds. It was a subconscious thought I'd never given voice to.

She's quiet, running her fingers through my hair, soothing the turmoil that idea causes.

"Does it make you feel guilty?" she asks after a few quiet seconds.

I press my forehead to hers. "I don't know what I feel, but it's nothing related to regret. I *did* try, had been trying, but after that funeral... I knew why you didn't give me your number. I felt it, too, that pull. I can't even reduce it to just attraction. It feels like we were this one thing that was severed in half, and our parts *want* to be rejoined."

Wow. That sounded intense.

"I mean—"

"Yes. That is how it feels," she says.

We've only been back in each other's lives for two weeks. We just made love. It's too soon to say what I know is true. What has always, on some level, at least for me, been true.

I love her.

She might not call it that yet, and I won't say it aloud, but I know it. We were born on the same day. I'm not overly religious, and I'm not sure what I believe about other lives, other worlds, and other dimensions. I do know if soul mates are real, Kimba is mine. I believe that if people are "created," we were made together. She was there for my scaffolding—there when my flesh was knit over my bones. And if love is not just an emotion, but a type of eternity, an infinity that lives in our hearts, then we have always been in love. It's an ageless thing that isn't about puberty or chronology, or even if we get to live our lives together.

But when we are apart, I ache.

I can disguise it with friends, mute it with other women, distract myself with goals and dreams, but the truth remains. If I don't have Kimba, there is a part of me missing. And as much as I tried with Aiko, as much as we've done together, built together, despite the beautiful boy we *made* together—she is not my soul mate. How could she be when there was Kimba?

"What if she'd said yes?" Kimba asks. "When you asked Aiko to marry you? What if you'd been married when we met again?"

"I would have been faithful to her," I say without hesitation, with absolute conviction. "I wouldn't have betrayed my vows or done anything to hurt Noah and Ko, but *I* would have hurt. Probably for the rest of my life, a part of me would always hurt wondering if I could have had you."

Barely visible in the moonlight, on the cusp of dawn, she glances up at me through a fan of long lashes. "Who says you have me now?" she asks, her voice teasing, but I see the contentment in her eyes.

"I say I do." I caress her hip, her back, her finely boned face. "And you have me if you want me."

"You know I want you." She reaches up to brush her fingers over my face, too. "I always have."

CHAPTER THIRTY-ONE

Kimba

"Y OU'RE FUCKING BRILLIANT."

"Huh?" Ezra asks absentmindedly, paying more attention to the flame under his pan than to my compliment. "What'd you say?"

"I said you're brilliant." I hold up the iPad I'm using to read his manuscript. "Your book, the YLA story, is incredible, Ez."

"Oh. Thanks." He flashes me a smile and then goes back to his French toast. "The key to getting this right is the milk-to-bread ratio."

I hop off the counter and walk over to stand beside him at the stove. "Would you forget about your French toast for a minute and listen to me?"

"But it's *stuffed* French toast." He takes the pan off the burner and pulls me into his arms. "And I could listen to you all day. What were you saying? Something about me being a handsome, sexy genius?"

"Um…those weren't my exact words." I laugh up at him.

"I could have sworn that's what you said, and I'm never wrong." He slides his hands over my ass in a pair of his boxer shorts. "Some even say I'm fucking brilliant."

"They probably just like your big dick," I whisper and blink up at him as innocently as I can manage.

"I get that a lot." He drops a kiss on my head and turns back to his French toast. I lean down to rest an elbow on the counter and watch him work.

"A lot?" I ask teasingly. "Have there been *a lot?*"

He pauses mid-toast-flip and slants me a glance. "Are you asking how many people I've had sex with?"

"I mean, it's none of my business. If you don't want to—"

"Eight."

Eight?

Lord above, only eight?!

"Oh." I straighten and rest my hip against the counter. "What a, um, single-digit number that is."

"Well, I've been with one person for ten years so...what about you?"

What about me? I'm tabulating years of hook-ups, one-night stands, fuck bois and carrying the one.

"If you don't want to," he says, cracking an egg into a bowl, "it's fine. I don't care how many people—"

"I don't know."

He glances up from whisking eggs, a small frown puckering his dark brows. "You don't know what?"

"My number. I don't know how many people I've been with."

He resumes whisking, his frown clearing. "Oh."

The whisking eggs and whirring refrigerator are the only sounds in the kitchen. I've never been embarrassed by my choices. I enjoy sex. I've had it with a lot of people. People I really liked...or tolerated...but didn't want to commit to. I've always been safe and never mean about it. I was upfront, and when someone wanted more, I let them know "more" wasn't an option.

"I just never..." I cross my arms over my stomach, fold one bare foot over the other. "I haven't been interested in committed relationships. There hasn't been anyone I wanted that with."

"Tru." He stops whisking and gives me the full impact of his undivided attention. His eyes are placid blue. No shadows or undercurrents. "I don't care." Ezra pushes the bowl aside and faces me. "But there is something I feel like we should be clear on regarding how you've handled sex in the past."

Here we go.

"You've never wanted to commit before," he says.

"Right. I've never wanted any strings attached."

"I know I said we could be just sex, no emotional attachments." He shoves his hands in his pockets. "But I feel like I have to be honest with you. Having you back in my life has been...it's been exactly what I need, and what I felt last night... I've never felt that way before."

I'm not even sure my heart is beating, but it also feels like there's a tumult in my chest. "What are you saying, Ez?"

His mouth flattens into a hard line and his jaw hardens to stone. "I want strings."

"Y-you do?"

"I want strings." He links our fingers, strokes his thumb across my palm. "Ropes, if necessary. I want anything that keeps you with me and me with you and tells everyone else don't even think about it."

I'm stunned and incredibly turned on, but that doesn't take much where Ezra's concerned.

"You...you do?" I ask faintly...again.

"I wouldn't do well sharing you."

The thought of sharing him pours acid into a deep cut, a completely unfamiliar feeling, but I can't deny it's there. "I agree," I tell him.

"Look. We're already redefining the relationship," he says. "Strings attached?"

"I can't believe I'm saying this." I step closer, tipping up on my toes to kiss him. "But yes, I want all the strings."

If I wasn't really into Ezra before, after I had his stuffed French toast, I would have been.

"Wow." I pat my full belly. "Now I get it."

"It's Noah's favorite," he says, taking his empty plate and mine to the sink. "Wait'll you see what we're having for lunch."

"First of all, I can't even think about more food right now." I walk over and loop my arms around his waist, press my front to his broad back. "Second of all, I need to go home."

He tenses under my cheek. "Already?"

"I could let you see me later today," I say, smiling and huddling deeper into the taut muscles of his back.

He turns, cups my face in both hands and dots kisses along my jawline. "How very gracious of you."

"I do have to get home, though. My mom…let's just say I'm already due an earful. My dress should be dry by now. I can catch an Uber."

"No way." A frown settles on his face. "I'll take you home."

"Ezra—"

"I said I'll take you home."

Before I can protest further, his cell rings. He leans over to inspect the screen and sighs. "Aiko's mom. She probably wants an update on Aiko and Noah. I can call her back."

"No. Talk to her." I slip out of his hold. "I'll get dressed and be ready by the time you're done."

"You sure?"

"Absolutely."

He nods and reaches for the phone. "Chào mà."

I do a double take at the base of the stairs. Ezra speaks Vietnamese? He leans against the counter, continuing in words I don't understand, crossing one arm across his chest while he's on the phone. There's a familiarity, affection in the exchange with Aiko's mother. Noah's grandmother. They've known each other ten years, so it makes sense.

Hearing him actually speak Vietnamese with such ease underlines how tangled his life is with Aiko's. Even if they aren't romantically involved anymore, they're inextricably linked through Noah and so many other things I can't even begin to anticipate.

Upstairs, I go to the laundry room where Ezra hung my dress. It's slotted on a metal bar between a tiny red robe with bright flowers and a blouse I couldn't fit one boob into.

"Wow, she's petite," I mutter, tossing Ezra's boxers and T-shirt into the hamper. I slip the dress over my head, slide my feet into my mud-splashed, misshapen Jimmy Choos and walk back to Ezra's bedroom. Actually, it's the guest bedroom where he told me he's been sleeping. I venture down the hall to a door that opens to the master.

Their bedroom.

It was dark and we were mad with lust last night when we came upstairs, but I consider the room in the glare of daylight. A pair of pink silk bedroom slippers peek from beneath the edge of the bed. Photos of all sizes fit together like a jigsaw puzzle on one entire wall. Different seasons of life chronicling their little family's journey together. There's pictures of them—at the Eiffel Tower, Disney World, the Grand Canyon, dressed up for Halloween.

In the hospital, the day Noah was born.

There's such joy on their faces. Ezra and Aiko both look young and proud and overwhelmed. She's holding Noah and Ezra has an arm around her. He's beaming.

"You okay?" Ezra asks from the doorway.

I jump guiltily and step away from the wall.

"I'm sorry. I wasn't trying to be nosy. The door was open and I was..."

Ezra lifts both brows and smiles a bit. "Curious?"

"Yeah, I guess." I look back to the wall, running a finger over a photo of the three of them at the Space Needle in Seattle. "Noah's been all over, huh?"

"He loves to travel." Ezra walks up beside me, studying the photos. "Next year, he wants to go to Israel. Shocking."

"I love how interested he is in his Jewish heritage."

Ezra breathes out a laugh and shakes his head. "A lot more interested than I am. He asked me if I'll start taking him to synagogue. I am *not* that Jew. I was a lot more involved when I was younger, but mostly because of my mom and Bubbe. As I got older, there were some things I wanted to keep, and some that just didn't matter as much to me."

"We all have to figure that stuff out for ourselves." I slip my arm through the crook of his. "I still am half the time."

"Mom is determined to get her a good Jewish boy even if she has to skip a generation. Remember how miserable we were on the weekends when we couldn't play because of Shabbat?"

"Our mothers got sick of us, but we always complained when we couldn't be together."

"We always wanted to be together as kids." He kisses my temple, pulling me in closer to his side. "Seems like not much has changed, huh? How do you think they'll react to us?"

"I guess we'll find out after it's actually broken off with Aiko once and for all."

There's a loaded, stiffening silence. He pulls back and looks down at me.

"It already is broken off. It's just a matter of telling Noah," he says. "You know that, right? I'm not some guy trying to fool a side chick into being with me. I just have to do what's best for Noah."

"I believe you. I guess being up here in your room, in her space and seeing her *life* with you—I just realize you've been together a long time."

"We have been and half that time it wasn't working. We've put this off much longer than we should have. It was going to happen regardless of us, Tru. I promise you that."

I see the truth in his eyes, but I also see the truth on these walls. It twists my insides to think I might have any part in breaking up a family.

"I better get going." I make my smile extra bright, but he isn't fooled.

"Kimba—"

"No, I just need to get home."

He nods, obviously reluctant to let the subject go. Neither of us says much as we walk down the stairs and to the garage. I try to push aside the guilt... Is it guilt I'm feeling over Aiko? Why should I feel guilty? She's screwing some guy in Tanzania. Ezra said this imminent break-up would have happened with or without me back in his life. I tell myself all those things, but when Ezra opens the door for me, and I climb into his Land Rover, I—

"Wait. You pushing a Rover?" I ask, surprise and amusement effectively squelching my conflicted inner monologue. "Well, look at you."

He rolls his eyes and backs out of the garage, but a tiny tilt at the corner of his mouth is enough to encourage me to continue.

"Being a brilliant educator must pay well."

"Not as well as electing presidents, I'm sure."

"I do all right, but the book deal was quite lucrative. Who's your agent? What kind of deal did they offer? I'm telling you, Ezra, your book is fantastic and once it's published, your whole life will change."

"I like my life as it is." He turns his attention away from the street long enough to spare me a quick smile. "When I was approached about writing the book, someone had seen one of the videos on our Instagram account and thought we had a story to tell."

"They were right. Reading about your early days frustrated as a teacher, how you've built something for families who might otherwise have had to settle for an inferior education—it's inspiring."

"I want more people to know about our students and our story," he says. "More donors and investors so we can continue helping students who can't afford private school and live in places where, frankly, their schools suck. Your zip code shouldn't determine the quality of your education."

His passion, his dedication to his students deepens my understanding of the man he is now. Reading that manuscript filled in some of the gaps the years created.

"I don't remember you wanting to be a teacher when we were growing up," I say.

"I don't think I did. I wanted to do well in school, of course, but I entered college unsure what I should do with my life."

Something niggles my memory and breaks through. "Bubbe was a teacher!"

"She was before she retired; you're right." He angles an impressed smile at me. "Great memory. She was the reason I first decided to at least give teaching a chance, and I fell in love with it."

"What do you like most about it?"

"The part I don't get to do anymore," he says ruefully. "Actually teaching. Seeing a mind expanding before your very eyes. Seeing things kids learn literally change the way they see the world and see themselves, reimagining what they're capable of."

He chuckles and shakes his head, one hand on the steering wheel. "Now it's fundraising and administration and conferences and speaking engagements, though I do as few of those as possible."

"Well, plan on speaking more. I make my living knowing things and I know this book is gonna be a huge success. You'll be on morning shows and doing book tours before you know it."

"You think so?" One brow dipped in skepticism lifts. "It's not even a huge publisher."

"It doesn't have to be. Your story, what you've built and are doing," I say in a rush. "It's huge." I gesture in the air like a wand waving over his imposing figure behind the wheel. "And all that won't hurt."

His lips pinch at the corners and he snorts. "All that? Why, Ms. Allen, to what are you referring?"

"You know how you look, Ezra. Don't play the modest card with me. I dealt this hand."

"When you kissed that scrawny thirteen-year-old in the girls' bathroom, you had no idea he'd grow another foot and a half, huh?"

That precious memory overtakes the present, and we're not in the subdued luxury of his Rover, just minutes from my mama's house. We're back in that stall, both unsure if we're doing it right, but completely sure we want to do it wrong together. His father's genes may have kicked in, lengthening and broadening his body, but reading that manuscript, I know the shape of Ezra's heart never changed.

We pull up in front of my parents' house and he parks. As soon as the car is still, he reaches for my hand, studying our fingers twined together. "I was thinking the other day that I wish I'd gotten to see you grow up. Maybe you can dig out some pictures for me."

"Maybe. I did love seeing you through all the years I missed."

Years she had with him.

"Kimba, I know seeing the pictures in the bedroom upset you a little—"

"No, they didn't upset me. They just reminded me that even though the sex is amazing and it feels like we've been together since the beginning of time, we haven't. You have other people in your life and so do I. I know you want this to be easy, Ezra, however you and Aiko dissolve this relationship, but I have a feeling it won't be."

He leans in to cup my face with one big hand, his palm rough, his touch gentle against my skin. "I don't think it will be easy, Tru. I just know it will be worth it."

He closes the last few inches between our lips, rubbing his thumb across mine and then kissing me in that deep, drugging way that makes every thought flee my head. There's no room for anything else but this sensation, this man.

"Dammit, Tru," he whispers into the kiss. "I want you again right now."

He pulls my hand down to his lap so I can feel the hard truth between his legs. I take him in my hand through his pants and squeeze, roll up and down slowly, torturously.

"Shit," he hisses at my temple. "Making out in my car and getting a hand job in front of your mom's place certainly feels like something we missed in high school."

I laugh and trail my lips over to his ear.

Tap! Tap! Tap!

The loud rapping on the passenger-side window startles us apart. Keith stands beside the car, arms folded, smirking. He gestures for me to roll the window down. With a frustrated sigh, I do.

"Hey, Tru," he drawls. "It's kind of tacky doing this shit in broad daylight in front of Mama's house."

"What do you want?" I growl at him, my eyes narrowed to slits.

"What kind of brother would I be if I didn't intervene when I saw my sister doing something wrong?"

"Wrong?" I shake my head. "Have you been drinking? I'm not doing anything wrong."

"Oh, I'm sorry." He leans forward just enough to catch Ezra's stony eyes. "I thought I saw you at Daddy's funeral with a wife and a kid, Stern. And from what I'm hearing, you're a rising star in the community."

"Ezra, goodbye," I say, reaching for the door handle.

"Kimba," Ezra says, frowning. "I can—"

"He's just pushing my buttons. I'm gonna go, Ez," I tell him softly. "We'll talk later."

He stares at Keith through the window, his eyes hard and cold as glass.

"Keith, go," I say, not turning to make sure he complied but reaching past Ezra to roll up the window.

"We weren't doing anything wrong," Ezra says immediately, cupping my face again. "You know that."

"Yeah, but no one else does." I shake my head and sigh. "Until this is all sorted and in the open, we can't be seen together like this. Anyone who knows you will assume you're cheating on Aiko. I don't want to tarnish your reputation that way, or for it to get back to Noah somehow."

He nods, but a heavy frown mars the smooth line of his brow. "Yeah, I know. You're right, but I'm not giving you up for the little time we have before you go back on the trail."

"*If* I'm going on the trail. Ruiz may not even hire me. He has someone else he's considering."

"Then he's a fool."

"You might be the slightest bit biased, Dr. Stern."

"If you mean infatuated," he says, laying a quick kiss on my lips, "enthralled, blinded by your beauty, then yes."

"Beauty, huh?" I flip down his visor mirror.

My hair is a snarly nest of curls, pressed straight in some spots. I splashed my face, but the color of the lipstick Ezra smeared from my lips is still faintly visible around my mouth.

"Oh, yeah," I say, sarcasm dripping from my words. "My beauty is blinding."

He takes my face between his hands, his eyes sober. "I could look at this face forever."

Forever.

At six years old, it was nothing to slip a ring, still cold from the fridge, onto my finger and say the words that would bind me to that boy all my days. The simplicity of it contrasts starkly with the twisting road that lies ahead of us as adults.

"I better go."

With one finger, he tips my face back around and then kisses me. He tastes like French toast and possibilities, and I'm ravenous. In seconds, my hand is back on his dick and his fingers are under my skirt, begging entrance at the edge of my panties. He slips one finger under, inside.

"Fuck," he breathes against my mouth. "How are you this wet already?"

Vaginal dryness, my ass.

I shift my hips just enough to create friction, ease the ache. He thumbs my clit and my mouth falls open. My thighs spread. My nipples harden in the bodice of my gown.

"Lord above," I gasp, pulling his zipper down and slipping my hand inside his pants.

"Shit." He presses his forehead to mine.

A car rushes by, shattering any illusion of privacy. We sit in the front seat, panting, reaching for some form of composure. His finger is still inside me, and he'll have to remove it because for the life of me I cannot bring myself to ask him to. It feels too good.

"I should go," I say for the millionth time, but make no move to do anything that would actually dislodge him from my body.

"Yeah." He nods and huffs a laugh. "You said Lord above."

"What? When?"

"When I was…" He pushes his finger in a little deeper, making me moan. He slowly withdraws. "When I was doing that, you said Lord above like your mother used to say."

"Yeah, I do that sometimes."

"Can I see you tonight?" he presses. "Will you stay?"

"Ez, maybe I shouldn't until we—"

"We'll be discreet. I can come pick you up."

"That is not discreet." I pause, biting my lip. "I'll take an Uber."

"Okay. I'll cook dinner." He moves forward to kiss me again, but I lean back, glancing around the empty street. "Tonight."

It seems to require a Herculean effort for me to get out of his car. The pull, the temptation to stay there with him for as long as I can, is strong. After so many years apart, when we're together, it feels like I'm exactly where I'm supposed to be. All my molecules, every atom, is at peace, but stingingly alive. It's like when your foot falls asleep, and the needles of sensation come with sudden movement. For so long he wasn't in my life, and suddenly he is. And beneath the layers of pleasure and delight, there is a sick feeling that just as suddenly as I found him, I'll lose him again.

"Tonight," I say, smiling through the window and turning to walk up Mama's long driveway.

He doesn't pull off until I'm inside, and I immediately wish he was here. Mama and Keith are both in the front room waiting for me.

"Well, well, well," Keith says from the white couch in Mama's sitting room. "Look who's home."

Mama always had a "front room" when we were growing up, which we would use under threat of severe punishment. Now we're adult enough to sit on the white furniture, but it seems Keith still wants to play childish games.

"Keith," Mama says, her tone much milder than the curiosity in her eyes. "Leave your sister alone. If she wants to cavort with a married man in front of the entire neighborhood, what business is it of ours?"

"I was not cavorting," I say, running a weary hand over my bushy hair. "And Ezra's not married."

"The way you look," Keith says with obvious relish, "you can't tell me you haven't been doing some cavorting, and I've seen the woman he lives with and his son. I just hope you don't...how did you put it...tarnish our father's legacy too badly."

"You don't know what you're talking about," I say, but with less heat than I would if he didn't have *some* ground to stand on. Guilt twinges my conscience as I remember those little pink slippers under the bed. I glance down at my owned ruined stilettos. If the Choo fits...

"I'm not judging you, Kimba," he says, the spiteful amusement leaving his expression. "I'm just asking you not to judge me, especially for something I've dealt with. Delaney and me, we're working on it."

Working on it.

That's what Ezra said he and Aiko did, but that's over. He's done 'working on it,' and he admitted he may have started giving up after we met again.

"Monday." I pull one desecrated Jimmy Choo off and then the other, standing barefoot and holding them by the heels. "I'll meet you at your office Monday morning. Nine o'clock. You better have a plan. The people of this district deserve real solutions, and if you can't prove to me you have some, I promise both of you…" I pause to include Mama in my warning glance. "There's not enough sibling goodwill or guilt in this world to make me help your ass."

"Fair enough, sis," Keith says, his smile wide and genuine. "And sorry for cock blocking."

"It was not cock blocking," I say indignantly.

He raises knowing brows, and I remember Ezra's prominent erection. Okay. Maybe there was some cock.

"I'm going to shower," I settle on saying, turning toward the stairs.

My phone rings when I reach my bedroom and I pull it from the clutch.

Piers.

"Hey, what's up?" I ask, walking into the room decorated in shades of ivory and gold.

"I have something that could be big," he says. "On Colson."

He sounds like a cop who's been on a stakeout all night and has finally gotten some movement. The excitement in his voice has me coming to a halt, my toes digging into the thick carpet.

"Go on."

"I found several female executives who'd been fired or departed abruptly from one of Colson's companies or another for suspicious reasons."

"Okay. And?"

"And I started digging. They cited a toxic workplace culture."

"Toxic how? Piers, roll it out faster."

"They were all black women who claimed to have been fired or left his companies because they'd been asked to change their hair."

"Their *hair*? Change it how?"

"They were told their hairstyle was 'too black' and asked to find a style more appropriate for the corporate culture. Some of them complied and spoke out after they found new positions. Some didn't and found themselves with low scores at their next performance evaluation, and eventually pushed out altogether."

Outrage on behalf of those women bubbles up inside of me. Outrage and understanding. I know what that's like. Working in politics in DC, I know what it's like to feel like the token and expected to speak on behalf of an entire community. I also know what it's like to press and perm myself into the form most likely to succeed.

"I figure if Ruiz hires us," Piers says, "we can use this against Colson in the general."

"Oh, no, my friend. This is how we convince Ruiz he should hire us *now*. Our contact over in the CNN newsroom—we still have her?"

"We have several," he says dryly. "We *did* elect the sitting president."

I swallow the nerves that always threaten to rear when I have to speak in public. It used to be that I could shove Lennix out front and avoid the spotlight, but now it's just me. Congressman Ruiz and the rest of the world seem to doubt that I can stand on my own. But this is no time to doubt *myself*.

Like Mama says, I descend from queens.

"Feed her this story," I tell him, walking over to my closet to see if I have a particular jumpsuit from Lotus' summer collection. "Then tell her I want to come on."

"You do?" Piers' astonishment is clear. Everyone knows how much I hate the camera.

"I do. Make it happen."

I hang up without waiting for a response and immediately dial Kayla.

"'Bout time you called," she says by way of greeting. "This is what you always do. You disappear."

"Can we fight and make up later? I need your help."

Those are magic words. The mother in her can't resist desperation. "What's up?"

"You still have that great stylist? The one who specializes in natural hair?"

"Lorette, yeah. Why? You need her?"

I touch my tangled cloud of hair. "Yeah. Bad."

CHAPTER THIRTY-TWO

Ezra

"UH, MAYBE ANOTHER TWO WEEKS." I RUN A WEARY HAND over my face and adjust my wireless headphones. "I can have the final draft to you then."

"Oh, good." Sienna, my editor, sounds relieved. "We're so excited about this book, Ezra. The sooner we can get early copies out, the better."

"I'm excited, too." I close my laptop and lean back in my seat.

"No, like, we're *really* excited. We're talking Oprah's Book Club level excited. We can't wait to get this to her team. To Reese. All the libraries."

"Whoa. Okay. I didn't realize there would be such a...a push."

"Are you kidding? Disadvantaged kids. Philanthropy. Quality education. This is *Lean On Me* stuff."

"I'm no Morgan Freeman and there are no baseball bats in my book." I chuckle. "But I'm glad you feel good about it."

"Not to mention you."

"Me? What about me?"

"Your own story is fascinating. Biracial. Jewish. Grew up here in Atlanta then off to Europe. Howard. UCLA for your doctorate. Returning to your roots to do good. Perfect set up."

"We'll see."

"I already know," Sienna says. "Let's check in next week. Loved what you showed me so far and can't wait to read the rest."

"Great."

When we hang up, I glance around my home office and just absorb all the good in my life. A book I wrote is being published. I wouldn't have imagined that. My dream of serving families struggling to access quality education has more than come true. It's *thriving*. I pick up one of the pictures on my desk of Aiko, Noah and me. I have a remarkable son for whom I'd do anything. And Aiko…

I'm almost there. Almost completely free and clear to start a new chapter with Kimba. Nothing will stop that. Not this time.

"It's just me!"

The door to the backyard slams and Mona's footsteps pound through the mudroom.

And stop.

I leave the office and head toward the kitchen. Mona's standing in the mudroom, holding one of the shimmery wings from the dress Kimba wore last night.

"Guess she didn't go straight home," Mona says. "When Janet's away, Jack and Chrissy will play."

"It's not like that," I say, walking into the kitchen and leaning against the counter.

"Oh, so you didn't fuck her?" Mona and I stare at each other, stewing in the silence left behind by her intrusive question.

"That's none of your business, Mo," I say softly, trying to keep my voice even, even though her comment annoys me.

"Since when?" she demands, an answering irritation in her voice. "You and Aiko are my friends. Noah is practically my godson. I love you all. I love Kimba. I don't want to see any of you get hurt."

"There are things you don't know." I draw a deep breath and then plunge ahead. "Aiko and I broke up."

"I heard."

"You heard? Where?"

"From Kimba after a bottle of wine. I'm sure she didn't mean to tell me. Blame it on the alcohol and half an edible."

"Oh." I hate awkward shit like this. "Well then, you know that whatever happens between Kimba and me, which is our business and not yours, is not cheating."

"Whatever," she says, rolling her eyes and hopping up onto the counter. "Good luck with this throuple thing you're doing with Ko and

Kimba."

"Throuple?"

"Yeah, it's like the three of you as a couple."

I bark out a laugh. "We are not a throuple."

"A threesome?" She waggles her eyebrows. "The only threesome I've ever been in is me, Ben and Jerry, but I'm wide open."

"Definitely not a threesome." My smile disintegrates. "I only want Kimba."

She closes her eyes and pulls her locs over one shoulder, the move I've come to realize means she's about to lay something on the line. "I hope you know what you're doing, my brother. Your son doesn't even know you and his mother are breaking up, and you're already sleeping with Kimba."

"And Aiko was already sleeping with Chaz."

"Chaz?" Mona's whole expression perks up. "The cutie who went with her on the trip? That's who she's hitting? Nice."

I give her the most longsuffering look I can muster.

"I mean, sorry." She covers her mouth, but I still see the grin peeking through.

"This isn't funny, Mo."

"You're right. It's not." Her expression sobers. "Isn't this all happening really fast? I mean, you just saw Kimba again two weeks ago."

"I saw her at her father's funeral." I shove my fingers through my hair and drag them over my face. "I knew then."

"Knew what then?" Mona's eyes narrow and she frowns.

"That what was between us before—"

"When you were *children*, Ezra. You hadn't seen Kimba since you were thirteen years old. Come on."

"It doesn't matter. I know it sounds crazy to you, but until I left Atlanta, I was closer to her than to anyone else. When we couldn't find each other, yeah, we moved on. That happens when people grow up. They grow apart, but that closeness didn't die. It was just…waiting for us to find each other again."

"And you think she feels it, too?"

"I know she does. We didn't exchange numbers at the funeral because she saw Noah and Aiko, and she knew if we stayed in touch…" I don't finish that sentence. I don't have to. The strip of Kimba's dress in her hand completes that thought.

"Kimba would never cheat," I say. "Neither would I."

"I just want to go on record saying I still don't think it's wise." Mona hops off the counter. "I think you should have given it a little more time. At least until Aiko's back and Noah knows."

"Kimba will be going back to D.C. by then. I didn't want to wait. Aiko didn't wait." I give her the look that I hope shuts this conversation down. "I shouldn't have to, either."

CHAPTER THIRTY-THREE

Kimba

“HOW DO I LOOK?”

Kayla studies me, running critical eyes over my hair and makeup, taking her time inspecting another of Lotus' creations, a dark blue jumpsuit with wide legs and fitted, quarter-length sleeves.

“Can we make the hair a little bigger, Lorette?” she asks.

“Bigger?” Lorette, Kayla's hair stylist, and I ask in shocked unison.

“If this hair gets any bigger,” I say, patting my natural curls Lorette volumized considerably, “I'll float right back to the eighties.”

The three of us laugh in the small dressing room as I wait for the producer to come get me.

“If you're going on national television defending our right to wear our hair however the hell we want,” Kayla says, “I say go big.”

“I think this is big enough.” I glance in the mirror. It's hard to believe that's my hair dusting my shoulders. “Remember when I did the big chop?”

“Oh my God.” Kayla cackles. “Mama is still not over you cutting all your hair off. She called you Florida Evans for months.”

“I remember.” I roll my eyes. “But I was tired of putting chemicals in my hair. It's taken years to grow back, but I've never regretted it.”

“It took me a few years to get up the nerve.” Kayla pats her short cap of natural hair. “But I can't see myself going back either.”

"And you shouldn't have to," I say. "And if someone wants to perm their hair, they shouldn't be condemned for that either. That's what tonight is about. Being able to be our authentic selves and not be punished for it."

"And about calling out Congressman Ruiz's future opponent, right?" Kayla grins knowingly.

"Oh, yes. That, too. It's a risky move, but I think it will pay off. We'll see if I'm right."

My phone buzzes on the dressing room counter. Ezra's name flashes up.

"Oh." Kayla purses her lips. "A little birdie told me something about you and Ezra Stern."

"Lemme guess. That little birdie was our brother? Keith doesn't know what he's talking about." I pick up the phone, and I step out into the hall to gain the tiniest measure of privacy.

"Hey, Ez."

"Tru, hey."

By some silent, mutual agreement, we both fall quiet. I'm remembering our kisses in his car this morning. Urgent and hungry. I'm remembering last night, how we couldn't get to each other fast enough. How my desire for him was fathoms deep. How I couldn't reach the bottom of it.

"I can't wait to see you," I tell him, hush-voiced, making sure no one is around.

"You have no idea. I miss you already. What time are you coming for dinner?"

"I, um, let me call you when I'm on my way. I'm kind of in the middle of something and I'm not sure how long it will take." I squeeze my eyes shut tight. "I'm going on CNN."

"That's great. What are you talking about?"

I give him the abbreviated version of what Piers found and how it's been reported.

"And by commenting on this," he says at the end of my explanation, "you kill two birds with one stone? Exposing Colson's discriminatory practices and—"

"And taking Ruiz's probable greatest threat down a peg or two, while giving us a sore spot to return to for black and brown female voters when the election rolls around. He thinks he needs the good ol' boys to win this state. I want him to realize we can take this state with a broader coalition than that. This is one step in that strategy."

"It's a queen move."

I chuckle, liking the sound of it, but not fully understanding. "What do you mean?"

"In chess—"

"Why am I not surprised?"

"As I was *saying*—" He pauses meaningfully, a smile in his voice. "In chess, when you run an attack on your opponent, you need the queen's strength. It's easier to capture a king using the queen than any other piece on the board. *You* are running offense on Ruiz's behalf."

"Ain't that the truth. Never send a man to do woman's job. You're right. It *is* a queen move. Thank you."

"Just the truth," he says. "Now you'll text me when you're on your way?"

"I will."

"And you'll spend the night?" he presses, the timbre of his voice going a few shades deeper and darker.

"Gladly, Dr. Stern."

"Ms. Allen!" a young lady with a clipboard calls from the end of the hall. "Five minutes."

I nod and smile. "I gotta go."

"Are you nervous?"

"You know I am." I touch my forehead. My fingers are trembling. "Every time I have to do this, I'm scared I'll stutter or somehow—"

"You've got this. I've seen you enough times to know how poised you are. I'm so proud of you."

The door at my back opens and Kayla pokes her head out. "Did I hear someone say five minutes?"

"Yes, bat ears," I say with a grin. "You did."

"Well, hang up with lover boy, and let's do this."

"Did she just call me lover boy?" Ezra asks.

"You don't have to sound so *chest out* about it." I laugh. "I'll call you later."

"You'll be fantastic. You always are."

"Thanks, Ez," I whisper, catching sight of the producer. "I gotta go."

"You know I'mma need this full story later, right?" Kayla asks.

I roll my eyes, shake my head and hand her my phone to keep during the interview. "I do know that, yes."

Kayla walks with me as far as she can but has to wait in the wings. No matter how much support and encouragement you get from the sidelines, when that red light on the camera flashes, it's just you. The anchor, Chelle, begins the segment by setting up the story, so I have a few moments of reprieve before I'm on camera.

"Some disturbing news today about Georgia gubernatorial hopeful billionaire businessman-turned mayor Burton Colson," Chelle says, looking steadily into the camera with enviable poise. "Accusations of discriminatory practices in the workplace based on hairstyles. Not a new problem, but one several female executives formerly employed by Colson's corporation hope they can bring to light."

A video package runs interviewing several of the women, all shades of black and brown and gold, wearing a range of natural hairstyles and head coverings from 'locs to braids to hijabs to natural curls like mine in varying textures. A pattern emerges from each of their individual stories—one of a toxic corporate environment that required complete compliance with an anglicized standard, and if they didn't, penalized them.

"We have on-set with us Kimba Allen," Chelle says once the video package ends, "well-known political advisor and the campaign manager for President Cade's successful run. Kimba, thanks for joining us."

"Th-th-anks for having me."

Dammit. Not now. Don't you dare.

I draw a deep breath and relax the muscles under my tongue, willing myself to calm down and not get overwhelmed.

"What do you have to say about these accusations, Kimba?" Chelle asks.

"I'm disappointed." I slow my words deliberately and concentrate on steadying my breathing, slowing my heart rate. "But can't say I'm surprised. This is the kind of thing I and women like me have dealt with all our lives. We've been held to a false standard of beauty, one that's impossible to maintain. I grew up, like so many, believing I had to press, perm, weave—do whatever it took to make my hair what those who wanted me to assimilate said I should."

"Is that something you've faced working in politics?"

"Oh, certainly. I'm used to being one of the only in many of the circles where I've served the last two decades. And the microaggressions are many and never stop. The awkward questions about my hair, people touching it without my permission. Those things are unacceptable, but practices like these cited by the women who worked for Mr. Colson? Those affect our pocketbooks and how far we can go, not based on our performance, but based on something as superficial as our hair."

"Several of the women indicated managers told them their hairstyle was 'too black,'" Chelle says. "What do you say to that?"

"I think comments like those, expectations like those, are the reason we need legislation like the CROWN Act."

"And for those who may not know, what's the CROWN Act?"

"It's legislation designed to combat discrimination against people of color for wearing natural or protective hairstyles. This is a form of racial injustice with measurable economic consequences. CROWN stands for Create a Respectful and Open Workplace for Natural Hair."

"California was the first state to pass it, right?"

"Yes, and other states have followed. Hopefully, at some point, we'll have federal legislation. Too many of us are working in environments where just being who we are goes against some written or unwritten company policy. Simply being myself is an act of resistance." I tsk. "But I must say it is discouraging to hear that someone running for *governor* perpetuated these practices. We need leaders who represent *all* people and respect the traditions and customs of *all* their voters, not just those who look like them."

I stare into the camera and hope Colson, Ruiz, and that damn Anthony are all watching.

"For black and brown girls, the world is full of sharp edges, and with every step forward, we risk being cut," I say. "We have enough to worry about. Our *hair* shouldn't be a hazard. Our *hair* shouldn't be an impediment to success. We need candidates who understand that. Who understand us. I hope the state of Georgia has other candidates to choose from. Someone besides Mr. Colson."

CHAPTER THIRTY-FOUR

Ezra

I'M COVERING A STEAMING POT OF PHO WHEN THE DOORBELL rings. Probably Kimba. She texted from the Uber fifteen minutes ago. When I open the door, I can barely restrain myself from kissing her right on the porch. She's still wearing the blue jumpsuit from the CNN spot. Her hair is huge, coiling all around her beautiful face in a careful chaos. Her makeup is flawless, and that is the first thing I want to change. Getting her out of her clothes is the second.

I tug her in, close the door and cage her against it right away.

"What took you so long?" I ask, bending to kiss her lightly on the lips. "Like it's hard being gorgeous on CNN while speaking truth to power."

She giggles and reaches up to plunge her fingers into my hair. "You watched?"

"You were fantastic. I knew you would be."

"I stuttered in the beginning."

"I didn't even notice."

She searches my face and grins. "Liar."

"It didn't matter and it didn't detract one bit from how powerful you were. Knowing how you struggled with that in the past, seeing it growing up, and then seeing you now, I'm amazed. Do you even realize how incredible it is that you fight those fears off to follow your dreams? The fact that you do things like that, put yourself in situations you know make you uncomfortable and shine that way makes you more of a badass than if it came easily to you."

She blinks up at me, her eyes sobering. "I hadn't thought of it that way."

"That's why you should keep me around," I whisper, dusting kisses along the tops of her breasts exposed by the jumpsuit's low neckline. "That and I promise to do this every chance I get."

I slip a finger inside the jumpsuit and coax one nipple out of hiding. The erotic sight of her plump breast makes my mouth water instantly. I take it between my lips, groaning at the soft texture, the stiff button against my tongue. I suckle gently at first, my dick going hard at the moans that slip out of her. Then my hands slide down to palm her full ass, and I suck so hard my cheeks hollow.

"Ezra." She bangs one hand against the door. "Keep doing that. I love it when you suck my tits."

She reaches between us, finding my dick and grabbing it, stroking me through my jeans. I choke, pulling my mouth away from her breast to draw a deep breath. I run frantic hands over her back and sides, hungry to see all of her.

"Dammit," I growl, close to coming just from her touch. "How the hell do I get this thing off you?"

Shit. My dick is a slab of concrete and my balls feel heavy.

"Help me get this *damn* thing off you, Tru." I trace the curve of her waist, the plane of her back searching for a zipper, a button, a peephole, *some* way in and off. "How do you pee wearing this thing?"

Panting, laughing, she slides one shoulder out of the jumpsuit, exposing a lacy bra barely containing her breast. I take her tit into my mouth, sucking through the cup of silk and lace. She wiggles until the other sleeve slides down her arm, the top flopping over. I plunge my hand down the waistband and cup her pussy through her panties. She's soaked and my hand is wet between her thighs. I drop my head so our temples kiss, and I turn my nose into a cloud of fragrant curls.

"I want to taste your pussy again, but I also want to fuck you immediately. It's a conundrum."

She pushes at the gathered waist of the jumpsuit, forcing it over the exaggerated flare of her hips and ass.

"Door number two," she laughs huskily. "I promise you can eat me out later."

The dark blue silk slithers down her long legs. She steps out of the jumpsuit, standing in her panties and bra and heels. She doesn't wait for me but shimmies out of her underwear.

"Bra, too," I order, my voice gruff with desire, my mouth slack with awe.

Her body is made with a reckless disregard for resistance. Full, firm, heavy breasts tipped with chocolate kisses. There's a decadent fullness to her hips and thighs and ass. Aiko is extremely petite, and I've never compared the women I've been with. But by my response to Kimba's body, I could tell myself I just never realized I'm a breast man. I'm an ass man. A leg man. All the things Kimba has in abundant beauty, but that would be a lie. Kimba could be smaller. Bigger. Less toned and less smooth. My preferences aren't defined by what a woman has, but by who *this* woman *is*.

I'm a Kimba man, and I think she's ruined me for anyone else.

I don't *want* anyone else.

She strips off the bra and reaches for the heels.

"Keep them." I catch her hand, linking our fingers by her head against the door. "Let's fuck."

"I have one request," she says breathlessly.

"What?"

Her eyes drop between us and she licks her lips. "Can I suck your dick just a little bit first?"

Somewhere in my youth or childhood, I must have done something good. I look up to the heavens and offer a silent alleluia.

"You may," I manage to grit out.

Our gazes tangle, and she pulls her hand free of mine, opens my belt, slides down my zipper, and pulls my pants and boxers down until my dick appears.

"Oh." She sighs, holding me with one hand and caressing my balls with the other. "This is good. This is very good."

The tip is already leaking and engorged. I've always been a man of few words and she's talking too much. I push on the elegant curve of her shoulder, pressing her to the floor, to her knees. She takes me into the warm, wet world of her mouth, sucking me, licking up and down my shaft like I'm one of the ice cream push-ups she used to love.

The sight of this powerful woman on her knees, naked except for her costly shoes, devouring my cock, just about undoes me. Saliva spills from the sides of her mouth as she takes me so deep her throat closes around me. Sounds strangle in my throat. I close my eyes in brief, beautiful agony, but open them again because the sight of her doing this is too riveting. Her nipples brush against my legs. I imagine my tongue dragging from the top of her pussy and between the firm, naked globes of her ass. I want to spread her and eat until my tongue aches. When I see her hand moving between her legs, that's it. I can't take another second.

"Up. Now, Tru. Shit." I groan, fitting my hands under her armpits and pulling her to her feet.

I push her fingers, wet with her juices, into my mouth. It's ambrosial and I lick every trace of it away and bring her fingers to my nose.

"Fuck, you smell good." I drop her hand abruptly and grip under her thighs, hoisting her up, aligning our bodies. "Dammit, condoms."

"I'm…" She licks her lips and lowers her lashes. "I'm, um, protected, and clean."

"Me, too. Can we?" When she looks up, a shadow in her eyes gives me pause. "What is it?"

"Nothing." Her smile chases the shadow away and she links her ankles at the base of my spine, rests her back against the wall and grips my neck. "You don't need a condom. We're good. Let's do it now."

Now.

Forever. Always. Never end.

I plunge inside and it's a rhythm in my head echoing the rigor of our bodies. Her pussy contracts, squeezing my dick, and my reason, my thoughts scatter. The house could burn down around us as long as this door and the two of us were still standing and fucking against it.

My hands clench under her thighs, holding her in place while we grind together, crushing the desire between our bodies. I reach the end of her with a rough thrust. Her breath catches and her eyelashes flutter. I hit that spot again and again until her eyes roll back in her head and her arms fall away from my shoulders and she's limp against the door, me supporting all of her weight while my thrusts grow more frantic, out of control. She bites her lip and tears roll down her face.

"Jesus, Ez," she whispers, her lashes dampening on her wet cheeks.

The rush of her climax washes over me. I'm as deep as I can physically go and my body keeps searching for a hidden passage to get closer to her, to inhabit her the way, with every kiss and every thrust, she inhabits me.

"Kimba." I shift so one arm holds under her butt and her back is supported by the door. With the other hand I lift her chin. "Look at me."

She opens glazed eyes.

"Your number," I rasp. "I don't care about it. I don't give a damn who you've been with. How many. Baby, I don't give a fuck."

Some of the haze clears, her gaze sharpens, focuses on me.

"But I want to be the last," I tell her, letting her search my eyes, my face so she'll see the truth I can't hide from her anymore. "I couldn't be the first, but I want to be the last. No one else. You understand what I'm saying?"

Another tear slides from the corner of one eye and down the sleek curve of her jaw. "I understand."

And like a million times during our childhood, she hears the things I don't say aloud. She reads between lines of invisible ink when no one else even knows I'm writing. It feels too soon to give it voice, but every part of me, body, soul, heart and spirit quakes with the inescapable truth I know she saw even though I didn't say.

Our first time together was stolen from us, and I don't hold against her any who have come since. But the truth was carved into ancient tablets of stone and etched into our hearts.

I love her.

And from here on out, I want to be her last.

CHAPTER THIRTY-FIVE

Kimba

"THIS IS DELICIOUS." I TRY NOT TO SLURP A SPOONFUL OF THE savory pho too loudly. "You *made* this?"

"Please don't be too impressed." Ezra smiles through the glow of the candles on the dining room table. "You've had my stuffed French toast and my pho. That's the extent of my culinary talents unless it's in a box and says, 'add water.'"

"Well, you're very talented." I roll a lascivious look over him seated across from me. "In the most delightful ways. I love the way you fuck."

The boy Ezra would have blushed and shoved his hands in his pockets, shuffled his feet had I said something like that to him. Not that I would have in the eighth grade, but even when our classmates made dirty jokes back then, red would crawl up Ezra's neck and over his cheeks.

The man Ezra returns my look with interest, his eyes caressing my nipples pebbled through his T-shirt.

"What you said." I tip my head toward the foyer. "Out there."

"What about it?" He doesn't hedge or pretend he doesn't know which part I mean.

"You said you wanted to be my last."

"I do."

We stare at each other through steam and candlelight, seeing clearly.

"I'm not asking you to put a name to it or formalize it yet, Tru, but

I already know I only want you."

For an anoxic second, I can't breathe. Those words take my breath, steal my reasons for never wanting strings. What if *he* is the reason I never wanted strings? For the first time with anyone, I want to put a name to it.

Us.

Mine.

His.

Love.

I sort through the new emotions he has inspired. Are they new? Or just *renewed* from our childhood? *Reborn* into this age, this new epoch of our lives?

The back door opens to the kitchen.

"It's just me!"

Ezra's lips tighten and exasperation crinkles a frown on his face. I touch his hand on the table.

"We'll talk more later," I say, keeping my voice low. "Promise."

"Pho!" Mona yells from the kitchen. "I thought I smelled it wafting all across the backyard through my window."

Ezra rolls his eyes and silently mouths *"wafting."* I cover my mouth to suppress the giggle that threatens to come out. He gives me a wry grin and drops his head back to stare at the ceiling when we hear Mona in the cabinet getting a bowl, rummaging through the drawer for a spoon.

She walks into the dining room wearing a huge smile and a T-shirt declaring I AM MY ANCESTORS' WILDEST DREAMS.

"Damn." She frowns, taking in the dimly lit room. "Y'all got it all dark in here."

She turns on the overhead light, simultaneously dispelling the darkness and the romance. She plops down beside me with her bowl and a glass of water.

"You're outta beer, Jack. You know I like beer with my pho." She points her spoon at him. "Ya slippin'."

"I would have stocked up," Ezra says, his words clipped and sarcastic, "if I'd known you were coming."

"I always come for pho, silly rabbit," she says. "Kimba, you were so good on CNN tonight, by the way. Your hair looked fabulous."

"Thanks, Mo." I pull a knee up to my chest, propping my heel on the seat.

"That jumpsuit you had on." She executes a chef's kiss. "Perfection.

I need it."

"A Lotus Ross design."

"Ooooh, I like her and that husband of hers—um, the ex-NBA dude."

"Kenan?"

"Yasssss. Fine ass."

She casts a glance over my attire, several steps down from what I wore earlier on the show. She looks at Ezra, whose shirt is inside out.

"Did I interrupt?" she asks with a straight face, but her lips twitch. "Y'all been in here fucking?"

The three of us break the silence with laughter.

"You're forgiven," Ezra drawls, standing with his empty bowl. "Want more, Tru?"

"No, I'm good."

He stops beside me and drops a kiss in my hair before striding back to the kitchen for seconds. The silence between Mona and me grows heavy with the weight of her concern.

"You sure you know what you doing?" she finally asks, her voice subdued.

"I do, yeah, Mo."

Ezra walks back in and sets a beer in front of Mona. "One was hiding in the back. Don't say I never gave you anything."

"Thanks, boss."

I'd almost forgotten she works at the school.

"You off for the summer?" I ask her, taking another spoonful of pho.

"Yeah," she says. "We have limited summer programming."

"Thank you again for managing so much, letting me focus on finishing the book," Ezra says.

"You know I got you, Jack." She tosses a napkin that bounces off his face. When we were in school, I was the thing they had in common, but now they obviously have their own relationship and she truly is part of his family.

She slurps a big spoonful of pho. "Mama Tran's recipe?"

"Mama Tran?" I ask.

"Aiko's mother," Mona answers. "She makes the best pho I've ever tasted. By now, Ezra's is a close second."

The rich flavors all of a sudden rot in my mouth. The woman he was speaking Vietnamese with. She's practically his mother-in-law.

When I glance up, Ezra is watching. He knows me too well. I try to force a smile, but at every turn I'm reminded how deep his ties with Aiko go and how disruptive pursuing a relationship with me so soon may be.

I stand and pick up my bowl, only half the soup eaten, and walk into the kitchen. Dumping the rest down the garbage disposal, I lean against the counter and look around. Photos of the three of them are pinned to the refrigerator. Reminders are written on the chalkboard for Noah, half in English, half in Vietnamese. A decorative mug on a shelf reads "Best Mom Ever."

I look up and Ezra's standing there.

"You okay?" he asks, his voice low, private.

I'm captivated by the concern, by the emotion on his handsome face. Forget Mona. Who cares about Mama Tran's pho recipe, and fuck that mug. Ezra's mine. I'm his, and no one's going to make me feel bad about it. I tip up onto my toes, weave my fingers into his hair and bring his head down for a kiss.

"Oh, good grief," Mona says from behind us. "Am I gonna have to deal with this every time I enter a room from now on?"

"Yes," Ezra says against my lips. "If I have my way."

"It's my way, too," I whisper to him.

"All this smooching," Mona says, rinsing out her bowl and loading it into the dishwasher. "You've come a long way since Jeremy. Wasn't that the guy who was your first kiss at our middle school dance?"

"I was her first kiss," Ezra says, pride in the smile he aims at our friend. "Shows how much you know."

Mona's mouth drops open. "You two turds!"

We all laugh, and my phone rings. *Piers.*

"I need to take that," I say, wiggling out of Ezra's grip. "Hey, Piers. Thank you again for all you did today. I won't forget it."

"Oh, yeah." He clears his throat. "That. Just doing my job. There's some, uh, new developments."

I frown. "It was good intel, right? Colson's company—"

"Oh, yeah. The intel was accurate. I actually have more on him where that came from we can use when the time is right. No, there's something else I need to discuss with you."

I glance over at Ezra, who I can tell is barely listening to Mona. He keeps looking over at me, every glance a simmering flame I can't wait to turn up all the way once Mona leaves.

"Maybe we can talk about it Monday," I say, my eyes locking with Ezra's in an unspoken, but absolutely clear message. "I think I'm busy tonight."

Ezra nods in decisive agreement.

"Okay," Piers says. "But I think you'll want to hear what else I've learned."

I force myself to focus, dragging my gaze from Ezra's tall frame. "More dirt?"

"Uh, yeah. You could say that. It's…well, it's dirt, yes."

"You can give me all you got on Colson on Monday, Piers."

"It's not dirt on Colson."

"Then who's the dirt on?"

"Your father," Piers says, drawing an audible breath. "The dirt's on your dad."

CHAPTER THIRTY-SIX

Ezra

"YOU STILL MAD AT ME?"

I force myself to focus on Mona. Through my kitchen window, I can see Kimba sitting on the trampoline in the backyard. She's been on the phone for twenty minutes, and based on her expression, it's not good news.

"Huh?" I ask. "Mad at you for what?"

"Busting up in here when you obviously wanted some time alone with Kimba."

"I always want to be alone with her," I say absently. "I've had to get used to sharing, though I'm still not very good at it."

"I don't mean to beat a dying horse," Mona says, sipping the last of her beer, "but this won't be as easy as you think. You'll be asking Noah to adjust to not only the fact that you're no longer with his mother, but that you're now with someone else."

"We don't have to roll everything out at once. If Noah's mature enough to understand why we never married, he's certainly mature enough to understand that we never will. We'll still be a family. It'll just look different."

"And you hope Kimba will be part of this new family you're dreaming of?" Mona snorts. "Based on what I've seen of Kimba, a white picket fence might feel like a cage. She's gunning for the nation's next hottest campaign, and she's coming off the last one. Take what you can get, but don't expect everything from her, okay?"

I'm still turning her words over in my head, figuring out what's true and what I can "settle" for from Kimba, when Mona yawns.

"Busting up your little love nest has worn me out," she says, heading for the back door. "I'm going home."

I walk with her into the yard. She waves to Kimba, who still sits on the edge of the trampoline and waves back with a small smile, her attention obviously on the phone call. I check the garden, a cover for the fact that I want to be nearby when Kimba finishes her call.

"Okay, Piers," she finally says. "Keep me posted, and thanks."

I cut through the squash and string beans to reach the trampoline. She extends her hand, a worried look on her face. I walk over, climb up onto the trampoline and pull her inside the net covering with me. I lay us both down and tuck her into my side, pushing the hair away from her face.

"Everything okay?" I ask after a few silent seconds.

She shakes her head and wraps an arm around my waist, squeezing tight. Angling my head down to see the frown on her face, I lift her chin with my index finger. "What is it? What's wrong?"

"Piers, a guy from my team who always has his ear to the ground for me, heard something...disturbing."

"What'd he hear?"

"He found out someone's written an unauthorized biography about my father."

"He was a great man. Lots of public figures have biographies written about them. Is there something bad in it? Lies?"

"Definitely lies." She pulls away and slants a searching look up at me. "This author alleges my father had an affair."

"What? Who do they say he had an affair with?"

"Your mother," Kimba says, her voice quiet and questioning. "That's ridiculous, right? My dad would never...your mom...it makes no sense."

I don't respond. When the rift happened, I didn't understand anything except we were moving away and I didn't get to see Kimba anymore. That was all I cared about. When I was older, I replayed that night over and over in my head and started assembling the fragments into something that, though horrific, made some kind of sense. Our parents had an affair. I had no idea who cheated with whom, or even if my speculation was right. But hearing Kimba say it aloud, I realize it may have been.

"It's not true." Kimba pushes up to sit and look down at me. "You know my father. He'd never…it's a lie, Ezra. We have to prove it's a lie. We have to talk to your mom so she knows they're telling these lies about her. That they're planning to publish these lies about my father."

"Yeah." I sit up and put my arm around her shoulder, kissing the top of her head. "We will."

"Why don't you sound shocked?" She pulls away, peers into my face in the moonlight. "You don't believe this, do you?"

I stare back, wishing I had learned to lie to her, but I never did. "I don't know what to believe."

"Believe *me*." She scrambles off the trampoline and walks swiftly back into the house. I heave a sigh and follow. She's already up the stairs and in the guest bedroom by the time I join her. She jerks my T-shirt and boxers off, tossing them onto the bed and walking over to the chair where she draped her jumpsuit. She pulls it on and slides her feet into the high heels.

"Where are you going?" I ask, as if I don't know.

"Home. I have to warn my family." She stops and closes her eyes. "My mother. What am I going to tell her?"

"What did Piers say exactly?"

"He says there's an early copy going around. Several people have read it, but it hasn't been published yet. It paints my father as some kind of hypocrite for posturing himself as a civil rights activist and pillar of the community, *which he was*, while having an affair with your mother, which he wouldn't do. I know in my bones they didn't, Ez."

Considering how evasive my mother has always been, I honestly don't know what to believe. A tear slips down Kimba's cheek, which she brushes away impatiently.

"I need to get home, tell my family, figure out a battle plan, including an injunction to shut this shit down before it hits bookstores." She grabs her bag from the bench at the foot of the bed, pausing to look at me. "Can you talk to your mom and find out why anyone would lie about this? Help me get to the bottom of it?"

I nod wordlessly and follow her down the stairs, reaching for my keys from the dish on the foyer table. "I'll take you home."

"No." She looks from my keys to my face and bites her lip. "I already called for an Uber."

I frown and glance at the front door where, not two hours ago, we shared our bodies with each other, peeled our souls back for each other. Will it only take a rumor for us to lose that again so quickly?

Her expression is implacable, and maybe I could persuade her, but it's obvious she wants to be alone.

"Will you please call me when you know more?" she asks. "After you talk to your mom?"

"Will *you* promise that we won't allow our parents' drama, whatever this is, to come between us? Because I'm not losing you over some stupid shit, Kimba. Not again."

"I just don't know what to believe." She looks at me, uncertainty in her eyes. "I don't want to lose you either. I do know that."

It's a small comfort, but I take a few steps forward and press her soft body into the door. I bend to brush her bottom lip with my thumb, and then kiss her, gently at first, and then with increasing heat and intensity. The visceral attraction, the thing that magnetizes us, that has always drawn us together, doesn't fail me now, and she's pliant and kissing me with unchecked hunger within seconds. Her phone dings with an alert, and she pulls back, checks her cell, and grimaces. "My Uber's here."

I open the door for her and she rushes down the steps toward the waiting car. Before she gets in, she turns to me one last time. "Call your mom."

So many times I probed this issue with my mother, seeking confirmation of my suspicions and hoping I was wrong, but she always managed to shut it down, play it off or freeze out my attempts. I watch the taillights of Kimba's Uber die, swallowed by the night.

"Not this time, Mom," I say. "This time there's too much at stake."

CHAPTER THIRTY-SEVEN

Kimba

"**T**HIS IS RIDICULOUS," KAYLA SAYS FROM HER SEAT AT THE kitchen table the next morning. "Daddy? Your source must be mistaken."

I look at each of them, Mama, Kayla and Keith, and wish like hell I could spare them this ordeal. Mostly Mama, who has been largely silent since I broke the news to them at the emergency family meeting I called. She's probably in shock.

"I wish he was wrong." I thank Esmerelda for the toast and herbal tea she's become so adept at preparing.

"I mean, Ruth Stern?" Keith asks, his face twisted disparagingly. "I don't believe it. If Daddy was gonna cheat, it would be with somebody finer than Ruth Stern."

All three women at the table swivel our heads to him as if on a string and glare.

"Daddy wouldn't cheat ever," I snap.

"You *would* comment on the way she looks." Kayla sits back in her seat and folds her arms across her chest. "Typical."

"Ruth is a good woman and was once one of my best friends," Mama says, her voice low but sharp. "Keep her name out of your mouth, Keith."

A heavy silence follows her words, and my siblings and I exchange a meaningful look.

"Mama," I say, my voice careful. "Can you think of why someone would start a rumor like this and if there might be some granule of...?" I look to Kayla for help.

"Truth," Kayla finishes. "If there might be something that *did* happen that someone is twisting into a lie?"

"Your father never cheated on me," Mama says, standing. "Not one day. I know it, and I'll make sure the world knows that, too, if this trash makes it to publication."

"It won't," I vow. "We'll get it straightened out before that happens."

She nods and walks out.

"Keith." I kick him under the table and find some small satisfaction in his tiny yelp. "You're the family lawyer. I have a call scheduled with the publisher first thing tomorrow morning. I need you to put the fear of God in them that if they publish this crap they'll have a slander trial on their hands that will bankrupt them."

"Will do." He stands and grabs one of the delicious croissants Esmerelda put out for breakfast. "But I have to get home. Delaney will kill me if I miss Sunday dinner."

"Sounds good," I say. "And, Keith?"

"Yeah?" He turns at the door, handsome and looking more like Daddy every day.

"After we deal with the publisher, let's talk about your campaign."

"All riiiight." He drags the word out like he's giving me time to change my mind about helping him.

"You have a lot to do if you want to run."

He flashes a smile, gives me a salute and heads out the door.

"That was nice of you," Kayla murmurs, standing and gathering the Hermès bag her husband gifted her after baby number five.

"I *am* nice."

"You don't get as far as you've gotten in politics being *nice*. Also, in case I didn't mention it, you did a great job last night. Your nieces and nephew loved seeing you on TV."

"Well, thanks for making sure my hair looked great." I laugh, pulling out my phone to check my email.

"Anything would have been an improvement on that *just got fucked* hair you were sporting when Lorette got ahold of you."

"You ain't slick," I say, not lifting my gaze from the phone screen. "No comment. I'm not talking to you about it."

"So you *are* sleeping with Ezra Stern?"

"Zee." I spare her a look long enough for her to know I'm serious. "I don't want to talk about it."

"And what's up with that common-law wife of his?"

"She's…they're not married." I give up, setting my phone on the table. "Since you're not taking no for an answer, like you never do, what do you want to know?"

"I already asked you what I want to know. Number one. Are you fucking him? And number two, what about the woman he lives and has a child with?"

"Number one, yes," I say defiantly. "I'm fucking the hell out of him. And number two, she let him go and she doesn't get him back. Satisfied?"

Kayla's lips twitch. "I think the question is are *you* satisfied? He putting it down?"

Flashes of Ezra pounding into me against the front door have me shifting in my seat, suppressing whimpers.

"I'm satisfied," I understate.

"Then let's head this fiasco with his mom off at the pass so you can focus on *staying* satisfied." She smiles and gives me a rare squeeze. "And happy. I'd like to see you happy."

I think about all the things I have to wade through before I can get to happy. This biography. The situation with Aiko. My damn ovaries.

I want to be your last.

The memory of Ezra's words soften all the tense, tight parts of me. The road to happy looks long and rough right now, but he makes me want to try.

CHAPTER THIRTY-EIGHT

Ezra

"MOM, WE NEED TO TALK."

"Ezra, hi. How are you?"

"I'm fine. Did you get my message last night?"

"Message? Where'd you leave it?"

"On the home phone. Your cell voicemail is full."

"Oh, you know I never check either of those, honey."

"That might explain why it's full. My message said we need to speak urgently."

"Is everything okay with Noah?" Concern spikes her voice an octave. "I checked in on him yesterday and—"

"The point of Noah gaining more independence at camp is to *not* check on him every day, Mom. I hope you haven't been long-distance smothering."

Because I've experienced that firsthand.

"Me? Smother? Of course not. He did happen to mention on one of our *few* calls that you don't have any mezuzahs in the house."

This turn of conversation has nothing to do with why I called or anything I've even considered. Ever. "Mezuzahs?"

"You grew up with them in our house, Ezra."

"Of course I did, but—"

"And yet when I asked Noah if he had one hanging on *his* door, he said no."

"Mom, how about you bring some with you when you bring Noah back and hang them on any door you see fit. Sound good?"

"Well, it's your house, of course. It's up to you."

Is extreme patience a sport?

"Can we get back to the reason I called? It's important."

"Oh, yes. Sorry. What do you need?"

"The truth."

"Ezra, don't be mysterious. The truth about what?"

"Did you have an affair with Joseph Allen?"

Shock reverberates in the silence that falls between us over the miles.

"Because that's what some biographer has written in a book that's publishing soon. Is it true?"

"It absolutely is not true," she replies, her voice curt.

"So you deny it?"

"Do I deny having an affair of any kind with Joseph Allen? I unequivocally do."

"Then what happened between the four of you the night of that argument?"

"That is none of your business. You are my only son, and I've sacrificed a lot for you. I've done all I could to ease your way in this world, as any mother should, but I do have a private life, and you have no right to it."

"Mom—"

"You asked for the truth and I gave it to you. It's a lie. When is the book coming out?"

"If Kimba gets her way, which she often does, it won't come out at all, but it has been written and it's due to publish soon."

"Well, she has to stop it," Mom says, anxiety tightening her words. "They'll ruin that man's reputation. And, oh God. Poor Janetta."

"Are you worried she'll believe it?"

There's a long pause from the other end before my mother answers. "No. If anyone knows that's a lie, it's Janetta."

"You two used to be so close, but after that night, everything changed."

"People change." There's a shrug in her voice, but I don't buy it. "We moved away and made new friends, new neighbors. Life goes on."

"Are you telling me that what happened that night has nothing to do with this rumor? If there's anything you can share that will clear your names, you have to tell me."

"I've told you what you need to know, what you asked me. No, I didn't have an affair with Kimba's father."

"Okay. Then we'll figure out how to make this go away."

CHAPTER THIRTY-NINE

Kimba

"THIS IS ACTUALLY PRETTY GOOD," KEITH SAYS, FLIPPING through the manuscript Piers managed to procure so we'd have it first thing Monday morning.

"Stoke!" Kayla slaps her copy onto Mama's dining room table. "It's a lie."

"I don't mean the part about Daddy having an affair with Mrs. Stern," Keith says. "But they got all the other stuff about his life right. His work in civil rights, all he's done for the city, his record as a prosecutor in those early days right out of Emory. It's well written and makes him look great."

"You mean except for the whole cheating-on-his-wife part?" I ask, tossing my copy onto the table alongside Kayla's. "Yeah, well if I put a drop of ink in a glass of water, will you still drink it?"

"Depends on how thirsty I am." He laughs. "And based on our conversation with the publisher, they're pretty thirsty."

"He did sound like he will take this all the way," I mutter, biting the inside of my cheek. "We need to find out who this biographer's source is for the affair. He doesn't make it clear in the text."

"It's such a small part of the book overall," Kayla adds. "If they'd just remove that one *lie*, I'd be fine with it."

"They're counting on that lie to sell a lot of books," I say.

"We can't let that happen," Mama says from the door, her copy tucked under her arm. She decided to read hers upstairs in her bedroom while my siblings and I have camped out downstairs all day reading it over wine and snacks from the pantry.

"It's a lie," she continues. "Joseph was never unfaithful, and for them to tarnish his reputation, his legacy this way…they can't."

"We won't let them," I promise, even though my back's against the wall and I'm not sure how to stop them without drawing it out into a long court battle, and probably sensationalizing it even more.

"I'll keep working the legal angle," Keith says, standing and stretching. "Well, it's been real, fam, but I've given my whole day to this. Didn't make it to the office, but I gotta make it home."

"Same." Kayla stands. "My kids are on their way home from camp. I need to go get dinner ready."

Kayla looks down at her phone when it buzzes. "Ugh. What'd I tell you? My kids. It'll take me forever to get rid of them all. I want an empty nest so bad."

"And you'll be an emotional wreck when they leave. Believe me," Mama says, laughing. "Send them over here next weekend. You and Lawrence get some time to yourselves."

Kayla's usually haughty expression softens, and she kisses Mama's cheek. "I'm gonna take you up on it and leave before you change your mind." She heads for the door and waves over her shoulder.

"I'm out, too," Keith says. He bends to drop a kiss on Mama's head and then mine. Mama walks him to the door and I hear my phone ringing in the distance. I race upstairs where it was charging.

Ezra.

"Hey," I say.

"You said you'd answer your phone."

"I know. I'm sorry. Phone died. Did you talk to your mom?"

"Yeah. She denies it."

"Well, of course she does," I say easily enough despite the deep relief that pours through me. "It's not true."

"Do you have any more to do there?"

"No. I've done all I can do for today, I think. We'll start again tomorrow."

"Come spend the night," he says, sending shivers along my skin.

"With you?" I ask teasingly.

"That was the idea, yes," he says, a smile evident in his voice.

"Could we…?" I hesitate, not sure I want to bring this up now. "I don't want to stay at your house tonight."

"Noah's not due back yet. We—"

"It's Aiko's house, Ez. Her photos, her slippers and robe and clothes and Mommy mug. She's everywhere, and I would like a night with you where every time I turn around I'm not confronted by your life with her."

"I'm sorry, Tru," he says after a loaded pause. "I should have realized that, but a hotel feels...seedy. I understand discretion, but I don't want you to feel in any way that we're sneaking around or doing something wrong."

"I don't feel that way, but we don't have to go to a hotel. I know just the place."

CHAPTER FORTY

Ezra

"I DIDN'T GET TO COME HERE WHEN WE WERE GROWING UP," I tell Kimba. "It's beautiful."

Lake Lanier's surface shines like volcanic glass under the moonlight, black and bright.

"My grandfather bought the lake house right before you guys moved." She sets down a plate of cold cuts and the fresh-baked bread we bought on our way here. "Things picked up significantly for Daddy—not just the money he was making, but all the work he was doing. It became a good place for us to get away from the city."

The Allens' lake house is modest, but comfortable. Its best feature is the private dock that leads to the lake. We're having dinner under a small covered structure set at the end of the dock.

"The glamorous life, huh?" Kimba jokes, proffering a sandwich. "I really go all out for my man."

I grab her by the waist and pull her onto my lap, inhaling the unique mix of lemons and cocoa, which shouldn't work, but is intoxicating on her skin.

"Say that last part again," I say into the cove behind her ear.

She turns to me, kisses my jaw. "Which part, baby?"

I make a note that I also want her to call me baby later. "Don't tease me, Tru. You know. Say it again."

"My man." She hooks her arms behind my neck. "You like hearing that you're my man, Ezra?"

"Very much." I cup her breast, brushing a thumb over her nipple and smiling against her throat when her breath hitches. "Your man is hungry."

"So is your woman," she says, slanting her mouth over mine, kissing me possessively with ardor that matches mine.

"Are you gonna feed me, or what?" I mumble into the kiss as it slows. She smiles against my lips and turns back to the table to grab the sandwich, offering it to me for a bite. I tighten my hands at her waist and pull her closer to my chest.

"Today was exhausting," she says, biting our sandwich and offering it to me again. "That book has taken over our lives."

"You guys read it?" I sip from the glass of wine she brings to my lips.

"Yeah." She rolls her eyes. "It's actually really good, dammit. Gripping and makes Daddy look like a giant, besides accusing him of philandering with your mother, of course."

"I wonder if taking that approach might work better. Meaning, you see all that's great about the book. Negotiate with the publisher that if the author removes that one aspect, the Allen family will help promote it."

"Hmmm." Her dark brows knit and she nods. "That could work, but I still want to disprove that lie about Daddy. It's too incendiary. Poses too much of a threat to his memory, to his legacy and what he means to this city. I need to speak to the author, find out the source and prove it false."

"If anyone can do it, you can." I open my mouth and look at her expectantly. "Food, please."

She chuckles, leans in and offers me another bite. We eat one sandwich together, exchanging bites and kisses, alternating with sips of wine from one glass. In this moment by the water in moonlight, we share everything.

"I'm sick of talking about this damn book," she grumbles when we're done eating. "Have you heard from Noah?"

"Briefly." I gather our plates and trash and toss them into a bag. "He's fine. Wondering if he can stay an extra week."

"Will you let him?"

"No." I chuckle and take her hand as we walk up the dock and back toward the little house. "I miss him too much."

Her rich laughter rolls out over the lake and she lifts my knuckle for a kiss. "You're such an incredible father."

"Thank you. I love kids," I say, opening the door and letting her into the house ahead of me. "I wish I had more."

Her first step into the living room falters for just a second and her smile slips. I hear what I just said. Shit. Does she think I'm saying I wish Aiko and I had more kids? Or that I'm imposing any expectations on her?

I follow her into the bedroom. "Kimba, I didn't mean—"

"I know what you meant," she says, sitting on the edge of the bed. "You've poured your whole heart into YLA, and I saw you with the kids at Noah's party. It's apparent how much they love you and why. You're just as much a dad to some of them as you are to Noah."

I'm quiet for a moment, thinking of all the kids in our school who don't have dads, who come to me for advice, look to me for guidance.

"I did want more." I sit beside her, take her hand, and the soft mattress gives beneath my additional weight. "We didn't intend to get pregnant with Noah. Hell, it was the worst timing. I was a poor doctoral student barely able to take care of myself, but later, after Aiko and I had been together for years and things stabilized, I wanted another baby."

"And?" she asks, her voice quiet, yet alert with something I'm not sure of yet.

"And Ko didn't. She'd sacrificed a lot. Delayed some opportunities when she had Noah, moved to Atlanta because I wanted to set the school up here. The last thing I wanted to do was make her feel pressure."

"How'd that make you feel?" Kimba asks.

"I didn't resent it at all."

Kimba breathes out a little laugh, looks down at our hands in her lap. "In some ways I envy her."

"No." I angle until I can see her face, look into her eyes. "You have nothing to be jealous of. You know that, right?"

"She had all those years with you. She's had a life with you." She dips her chin to her chest. "A child with you. I wouldn't trade the path I've chosen for anyone else's. I love the choices I've made. I stand by them, but choosing one thing often means not choosing something else. I look at my sister. She complains, but her kids are the joy of her life."

"I'm sure you had offers," I force myself to say, not wanting to hear about the men she could have had and kept. I'm just glad she didn't tie herself permanently to any of them so I can have her now.

"Daddy used to say don't waste time on things that don't set you on fire inside, and I haven't. Every campaign, every election, each candidate—I've believed in. I believed that putting that person in power advanced one of my convictions."

She bites her bottom lip. "I felt the same about people. I didn't want to waste time on anyone who didn't set me on fire inside. And there have been people I liked, people I enjoyed sex with, but no one I wanted to build a *life* with. That's why I never committed. No one ever set me on fire inside."

She looks over at me, her eyes telling me before her words do. "Until now. You set me on fire inside, Ezra Stern."

I can't breathe. I can't swallow. I can't move. My composure teeters on the head of a needle, but I at least have enough presence of mind to know exactly what I should say right now. "I love you, Tru."

It feels like the words have been waiting on my tongue for years, for the moment when I was old enough, free enough to feel them, to say them. The look on her face says she's waited that long to hear them from me. She slides her fingers into my hair and touches her soft lips to mine.

"I love you, too," she says. "So much."

I kiss her so deeply, I struggle to breathe, but I can't make myself stop. She's my air and her heartbeat a talking drum, telling our story through the walls of our chests. I want us to be one, to be joined and hooked and sealed together. Breaking the kiss, she sits on the bed and lies back, her lips wet and full. She watches me with a sultry expectation. Keeping her eyes on me, she undoes the line of buttons holding her sundress together. The panels fall away, revealing plump breasts cupped in gold satin and lace. She sits up, shrugs out of the dress and reaches behind her back to unclasp the bra. Her breasts spill free, and I reach out a hand to touch her, but she shakes her head, her eyes dark and molten.

"Watch me," she whispers.

She lifts, pulling the dress from under her, tossing it aside. She does the same with the gold panties, sliding them off and tossing them away, leaving her naked on the bed. She lies back in a cloud of curls. I swallow hard when she lifts her knees and spreads her legs, honoring me with this beautiful, bare intimacy.

"Are you watching?" she asks, her voice husky and hot.

I manage to nod and try not to drool.

She slides slim fingers down the plane of her belly and between the fat lips of her pussy, squeezing her clit.

"Shit, Tru," I hiss, moving forward.

"Watch."

She palms herself, an aggressive move that flattens the lips and the tight bud of nerves. Her fingers go to work, brushing against her clit at first slowly, then with more speed, more pressure. Her back arches and she moans, her eyes squeezed tightly shut. I can't resist. I sit beside her, hoping to catch her scent. I know how she smells, how she tastes, and my mouth waters for it, but she's so clearly in charge of her own pleasure I don't even want to intrude.

"My breasts," she gasps. "Suck my breasts."

Thank God.

With permission to be part of the hottest thing I've ever witnessed, I take her nipple between my lips. Her hips are bucking and she slaps her pussy, so I know she doesn't want gentle. I bite down, and she moans, her fingers going faster.

"Yes, Ez." She dips between her legs, gathering her essence, fingering herself with one hand but she offers me the other, wet and shiny. I take her fingers into my mouth, lick the webbing between, drag my lips over her palm, searching out every trace of her. I knead one breast and suck hard on the other.

"Oh my God, that's it." She screams, her hips bowing off the bed, her body stiffening with the tempest of her pleasure. She rides her hand and bites her lip and pulls her knee back, opening herself wider to her plundering fingers. I keep kneading her breasts but pull back enough to watch her because I know this is just as much for me as it is for her. She knew what this would do to me. There's already a wet spot on my shorts from seeing her come. She moans with the sensations and after several seconds, stills.

"Stand up," she commands hoarsely, her eyes dark, possessive slits. "Undress for me. I want to see you."

I do, my gaze latched on to hers. I peel the T-shirt over my head, relishing the hungry crawl of her eyes over my chest and abs. I undo the belt, pulling it through the loops and tossing it to the floor. My cargo shorts and boxers follow, falling around my feet. She licks her lips, her eyes zeroed in on my dick. I take it in my fist and pump, slowly, rubbing my thumb over the wet tip. In seconds, I'm lengthening, thickening. I widen my legs, plant my feet to brace for the torrent.

"I'm gonna come if I don't stop," I gasp.

"Then stop." She spreads her legs. "Give that to me."

I kneel on the bed between her thighs and line our bodies up. Supporting myself on one elbow, I push the hair from her eyes.

"Whose are you?" I've never asked another woman for this, never needed it. But at the core of who I am, I know I belong to Kimba. I want to hear that she feels the same.

"I belong to myself," she says, a spark of defiance in her eyes. "And to the boy who married me when I was six years old."

I pull back and stare down into her eyes, alive with love and peace and fire. "You remember."

"I remember everything. You owe me a lifetime."

The distance between us is a physical ache when she's saying the things I've dreamed of hearing, reflecting the words that have been locked away in my heart for years. Treasures I thought would rot, would fade with age, but never have. Our love is as bright and real as the day we were made together. I plunge into her body, and she wraps herself tightly around me, arms and legs clutching me to her. I brace one hand on the headboard, curl my arm under her knee and push in deeper, finding no resistance, only a warm, wet, tight welcome.

I surrender to every primal urge I've checked. I fall through the trap door to my basest desires, biting her neck, her breasts. Slamming into her with such force that the headboard bangs the wall and the bed slides.

"Oh my God, Ez." She drops her arms behind her, over her head, giving her body to me completely. "As hard as you want. As long as you want. Just keep fucking me like that."

I seize the fullness of her ass in one hand, squeezing, pushing in deeper, urging our bodies beyond the limits of flesh and bone. That place where we're joined is a gateway to what I want more than anything. I'm desperate to reach her heart, her soul.

We claw and bite and sigh and snarl until her body trembles beneath me with sobs and shudders. Even after she comes, I go on, needing to release, but not wanting this to end in case it's all a dream. When I come, it's with a primal roar that ricochets through my marrow and tears at my throat.

We lie there in the dark, our bellies pressed together, a tangle of sweat-slicked limbs and hurried heartbeats. I can't imagine leaving her body right now, so I don't. Our skin cools and our breathing evens into a quiet that doesn't need breaking. We rest in our own thoughts and in each other's arms.

"I need to tell you something," she finally says.

"Okay." I find her hand, link our fingers. "What is it?"

"I'm in..." Her fingers tighten on mine and I hear her swallow. "I'm in perimenopause, Ez."

I don't know what *peri* in the front of it means, but I do recognize *menopause.*

I reach over to turn on the light, but she stops me. "Don't."

Reluctantly, I pull out and lie down to face her, making out the shape of her face in the moonlight slanting in through the window

"You're too young for that, right?"

"It is early, but it happens for different women at different times. This is when it's happening for me."

"So what does this mean?"

She hesitates. An uncharacteristic uncertainty hangs around her. She's always sure, but right now, even in the dark, I see that she is not.

"I haven't had a period in four months, almost five now. I may have a year, eighteen months to have a baby naturally. It's hard to know, but there is a definite, shrinking window. There's an expiration date in the near future."

I'm not the sharpest tool in the shed sometimes. It takes me a few moments to realize the uncertainty, at least in part, might be because of me.

"You don't think it makes a difference to *me*, do you? I know this is a big deal, and I'll support you whenever it gets hard, but I'll love you no matter what. You know that, right?"

"You're a great father," she says, somewhat haltingly. "Earlier you admitted to wanting more kids. I don't want to be presumptuous, but I think we have some kind of future together."

"That's not presumptuous at all. I know you're in D.C. and are on the road a lot, and I'm here in Atlanta. We'll work it out but make no mistake. You are my future, Kimba."

"I feel the same way, which is why I wanted you to know that it's possible I won't ever have kids naturally. I'm still deciding what I want to do."

"What's the decision? What are you considering?"

"I want to elect Georgia's first Latino governor."

"And you will."

She smiles, cups my face and strokes my jaw. "Only a man in love would be that confident that I can. It's gonna be hard as hell."

"Hard as hell is your default setting, Tru. It's not my love for you that tells me that. It's your track record. It's who you've always been." I pull her into me, stroke down her back and kiss her temple.

"I wasn't thinking about having a baby right now," she says, laying her head on my chest. "I'm not sure I want to focus on that if I need to focus on Ruiz's campaign."

"Can you do both?"

"I don't know. I can take the things the doctor has recommended to restart my period."

"They can do that?"

"Sometimes. If they can, there's a chance I can have a baby, but I don't know that I want to just because someone says it has to be now. I could adopt later."

We could adopt later.

That's what I hear. Noah doesn't even know Aiko and I have broken up. There is a lot of transition ahead and we have to handle it carefully, but there's no doubt in my mind I want to spend my life with Kimba.

"It just felt wrong not to tell you," she says. "I didn't want you to think I was keeping it from you or hiding anything."

"I'm glad you did." I pull her closer, wishing I could shield her from every threat to her happiness, her peace of mind. "We'll face this together."

She feels small nestled against me. The humanity of naked skin and shallow breaths reminds me the woman the world sees as so powerful is also vulnerable. The privilege of intimacy has shown me that, and I fall asleep dreaming of ways to keep her safe.

CHAPTER FORTY-ONE

Kimba

I'M STILL IN BED WHEN MY PHONE RINGS ON THE NIGHTSTAND THE next morning. Ezra's humming in the bathroom. He's such an early bird and is already up. I've been receiving notifications ever since the CNN spot from friends and colleagues congratulating me, but the number flashing across my screen is the only person I actually hoped to hear from.

"Congressman Ruiz," I say, sitting up in bed, heart in my throat and phone to my ear. "Good morning."

"Good morning, Kimba," he says. "Hope I'm not calling too early."

"There is no too early in this game. You know that, sir."

"Good. Well, I wanted to call and tell you that was a brilliant audition the other night."

I grin, but keep my voice even. "I'm sorry? Audition?"

"You were trying to prove what a valuable asset you'd be in the fight against Colson come November."

"Is that what you think?" I ask, unable to keep the smile from my voice.

"That's exactly what I think," he chuckles. "It worked."

I leap out of bed and allow myself a fist pump and a quick body roll before replying. "What exactly are you saying, sir?"

"I'm saying, let's meet this week to talk about what it'll take to win this great state of Georgia. You ready for that?"

"Oh, I stay ready."

"That's what I hear. Good work on Colson. Looking forward to winning with you and your team."

Ezra walks in from the bathroom as I'm hanging up. "Everything okay?"

I practically skip across the room and throw my arms around his neck. "Ruiz just hired me."

"Tru, that's amazing." His strong arms tighten around me, the perfect hold. "I'm so happy for you. Proud of you. You did it."

"I haven't done anything yet." I pull back, laughing up into his face. "Colson won't roll over and play dead."

"Of course there's a long road ahead, but we have to celebrate this. You saw the chance and you made the move." He takes my face between his hands, looking at me intently, so much love in his dark blue eyes.

"I know this is the first campaign without Lennix and you feel like you have something to prove, but you don't. Mateo Ruiz just made the best decision of his life. He chose *you*. Not your father or your family name or your partner. *You* seized that opportunity. *You* set aside your own fears and insecurities to go on that show. *You* spoke truth to power and called Colson out on his shit. In front of millions." He squeezes my waist and drops his forehead to rest on mine. "And I'm so incredibly proud."

There have always been hard-to-reach places in me that only Ezra could find, could touch. Even when we were kids, when I barely understood myself, in a deserted park on a pair of swings, he would ask the right questions or he'd leave me the quiet to figure things out myself. All the times we were there for each other rush back to me on a loop.

And we will strengthen each other.

If only I had known this was possible for us. I would have torn the world apart searching for Ezra Stern.

"I've missed you so much," I whisper, tears burning my throat. "I'm so glad you're in my life again."

"I'm glad, too," he says, his voice husky with the emotions darkening his eyes. "And you're not getting rid of me."

"I have no desire to."

He seems to hesitate for a moment and then continues. "Last night you trusted me with something hard." He tilts my chin up, searches my eyes. "I don't just want you when you're strong. I want you when you're vulnerable, when you're lost, when you're not sure. I see the armor you have to put on to make it in your world. I just want you to know here, with me, you can take the armor off."

All my life, I've had to be the strongest one in every room. It was expected of Joseph Allen's daughter. It was required in the shark pond of politics. No one wanted to make room for me, so I had to make room for *myself*.

Fine.

That's what you do. You put in that work if you want the rewards. And I've accepted that I have to work harder than everyone else sometimes just to get the same results. That's the reality girls like me learn to live with. We use it to make us stronger. I kick those doors down, whether it's in work boots or Jimmy Choos. Looking down at the floor, my feet are bare. Here with Ezra, my *soul* is bare, and at his words, I slump against him and for a few moments, I rest. It's a sigh of the soul and his arms tighten around me. He kisses my temple and strokes my back. It feels so good to let someone love me, to let him cherish me, to share my burdens with his strong shoulders.

"You okay?" he asks.

I look up at him, trace the strong line of his jaw and the dark silk of his brows. He doesn't like it when I say he's "dear," but that's exactly what he is. Dear and rare and precious and *mine*.

"I am now."

"You sure you're okay if we swing by my house first?" Ezra asks after we've showered.

"Sure." I tug the fitted sheet from the bed. "You need to change for your meeting, right?"

"Right." He grabs his standard YLA T-shirt from the bench at the end of the bed and slips it on. "I can't believe I forgot I'm supposed to meet the publisher downtown at noon or I would have brought the right clothes with me. I had it in my calendar for tomorrow. Glad my editor reminded me. I'll just change at home. I can drop you off at your place and make it there in time."

"Sounds good." I gather the bedding and pad around to kiss his jaw.

He pats my butt, kisses my cheek and steps away. "I'll load the car."

"I'm just gonna put these in the laundry room. There's a service that comes to clean. They'll change the bed."

We just added this laundry room. We'd planned some upgrades and renovations for a while, but then Daddy died and no one seemed to care until recently. The lake house hasn't been used much lately, but my family had some good times here. Now that Congressman Ruiz has tapped me to run his campaign, I'll make sure this house gets use while I'm here, even if it's just for Ezra and me to get away.

The laundry room is small and neat and has a shiny new washer and dryer.

"Nice," I mutter, stuffing the bedding into a hamper in the corner. The early morning sunlight shining through the window catches a glint of gold. I glance down and see the tiny tip of something in a far corner. It's actually lodged in the crack between the wall and the floor, and I would have missed it if the sun hadn't wanted me to find it. I squat and coax it out with a fingernail until it's fully revealed on the floor.

The star of David.

And at the center, an onyx stone.

My breath catches. I've seen this charm before. Ruth Stern wore it all the time when we were growing up.

I pick up the charm and run outside. Ezra's stashing my overnight bag and slamming the trunk.

"Ez," I say, my heart racing with the possible implications of what I've found. "You said you never came here before, right?"

"Right." He leans against the car and studies me. "What's up?"

I hold out my hand, palm up, with the Star of David charm, a little tarnished, but still gleaming. He stiffens and then lifts it from my hand.

"This looks like my mom's, but I haven't seen it in years. She lost it." He looks from the charm back to my face, his expression reflecting the same speculations.

"If you never came with your family, then how would that be here?" I ask. "We just knocked out some walls when we added a laundry room. Maybe the charm got dislodged or shuffled around in the commotion. I found it in the laundry room. Your family never came here, so why would your mother's charm be in this house?"

Everything I believed about my father goes out of focus, blurred through a sheen of tears. "Do you think... Ez, do you think they came here together? *How* would it be here unless she was?"

"I have no idea." Ezra's fist closes over the charm. "But I will find out. I promise you that."

The silence between us on the ride back to the city throbs with our unspoken thoughts. My heart is too heavy for words. Disappointment in my father. Hurt on my mother's behalf. I'm disillusioned that the man who guided me more than anyone else at one point may have lost his way. I know he was human. Despite what Mama thinks, I wasn't deceived that Daddy was perfect, but this?

While Ezra drives, my phone starts ringing, wresting me from the chaos of my own thoughts and plunging me into chaos of another kind. One I know how to manage.

Work.

I texted Carla and Piers with the news about Ruiz, and my phone has been pinging ever since. Carla's already projecting what it will take to make Georgia our base for the foreseeable future. In addition to celebrating, Piers wants to discuss new findings about the author of the biography. I tell him to get me a number so I can confront this person myself. Even if the charm does raise the possibility of my father's infidelity, I don't want a sensationalized book and the inevitable media circus that will come with it—the reexamination of all the good my father did through the lens of one mistake. If I can protect my mother and my family's legacy from that scandal, I will.

We pull into Ezra's driveway, and I'm on the phone with Carla when he lets us into the house.

"My clothes are still in the master," he whispers.

I nod, half-listening to Carla, and follow him up the stairs.

"Yeah, I need that info," I tell her, sitting down on the bed and glancing around the room again. The photos of him, Aiko and Noah prick the smallest drop of jealous blood in my heart. He has a past. He has a family. I already love Noah and can see how being his father helped shape Ezra into the man he is today. Aiko? I hope she and I can be friends and things can be amicable in the transition ahead.

I'm momentarily distracted by Ezra's chest, abs, and ass as he changes clothes. His muscles contract and flex with the simple movements. He's so *big* now. I never would have forecast that Ezra would be as physically imposing as his father, but he is. And he's oblivious to how horny it makes me—not that it takes much where he's concerned.

"Did you hear me, Kimba?" Carla asks.

"Huh?" I sit on the edge of Ezra's bed, devouring every inch of sleek, naked skin before he covers it up. "What was that, Carla?"

"I said when will you come back to the city?"

"Soon." I know I'll have to at least once before we set up shop here, but I'm reluctant to leave Atlanta.

For years I only came home for rare visits and holidays, but this trip has reminded me of all the things I love about the city and given me new things to embrace. I'm glad to make Georgia my base for a while. For the first time in years, I want to be close to home.

I disconnect the call and walk up to Ezra, kissing the granite line of his jaw. He dips, angles so he can catch my lips. The kiss catches fire and he sits on the edge of the bed, pulling me down to his lap. This is happiness. Passion. Contentment in a way I've never known it before. Even the shock of what we found at the lake house, the problems that still lie ahead, can't diminish that.

"What the actual fuck, Ezra?"

I nearly fall out of Ezra's lap at the angry question but catch myself and land on the bed beside him.

"Who the hell are you?" Aiko demands, glaring at me and walking fully into the room.

I've only seen her in real life once, at my father's funeral, and that was from a distance. The photos on the bedroom walls didn't tell the full story of her beauty. Her face is a pale oval, her lips red as cherries, and her hair swings in a dark curtain to her waist. The expression on her face belies her fragile petiteness. She's delicate and steely, a lovely weed in my garden.

"You have two seconds," she says, venom dripping from her words, "to get this bitch out of my house."

Bitch?

Hold up.

"What are you doing here?" Ezra stands, his expression strangely calm in the face of her obvious rage. "You aren't due back until next week."

"What am *I* doing here?" She steps closer to him, only coming to the middle of his chest, and points a slim finger at me. "This is my *home.* What's this bitch doing in our bedroom, Ezra?"

That's two. You got one more strike, Aiko.

I'm losing patience with this one fast. Ezra knows. He glances between the two of us like he's caught between two she-bears.

"Don't call her that," he snaps, the words clipped, a frown marring the harmony of his features. "Her name is Kimba, and you won't disrespect her."

"Disrespect *her*?" Aiko's voice breaks, and she takes her trembling bottom lip between her teeth. "What's she doing here, Ezra? In our *bedroom*? Really?"

He scrubs his hands over his face and releases a heavy sigh. "Look, I know it's disconcerting to come home and find someone else here like this, but this isn't *our* bedroom anymore. I was just changing clothes because my stuff is still here." His voice, his expression gentles. "You know I wasn't sleeping here even before you left, Ko."

"Yes, but I didn't think..." She lowers her eyes to the floor. "So soon?"

"Babe!" a voice calls from downstairs. "Everything okay?"

"Chaz, I'm fine," she yells down, her eyes never leaving Ezra's face. "You can leave the bags at the door."

A silence booms following her words, those few seconds after a bomb drops before you can hear again.

Ezra looks back to her, brows skyward. "Your new lover is downstairs *in our house* and you want to talk to me about soon? I can say for sure that you found someone new before I did. You found someone new before you even *left*, so don't come in here calling Kimba a bitch and trying to make me feel guilty. You don't have grounds for that."

He has to sort this out and my presence isn't going to help. Besides, I'm tired of being both the center of and the bystander in this drama. And if Aiko calls me a bitch one more time, I can't be held responsible.

"Ezra," I say, standing and focusing on him, not Aiko's malevolent gaze burning through my clothes. "I should go."

"Yeah, you should," she snaps. "We have family business to discuss."

She should be glad I have enough control left to ignore her. Ezra shoots her an exasperated glance and then turns his heated gaze, midnight blue, blazing, to me. "I'll walk you out."

We start toward the bedroom door, but Aiko steps in front of me, running her eyes over my sundress and flats, my hair and face. "I know you."

I'm not famous. My candidates are. The average Joe wouldn't recognize a political analyst on the street from a few television appearances, so I'm not sure that's where she thinks she knows me from.

"The funeral," she whispers, turning an accusing look on Ezra. "We went to her father's funeral. I remember because it was the day my grandmother had her heart attack."

I remember, too. Seeing her on the phone, pacing in the grass, distress etched onto her pretty face.

"You said she used to be your best friend." Aiko sputters, shakes her head. "Did I really find someone else first, Ezra? How long has this been going on? Oh my God."

"No." Ezra closes his eyes, and I can see the discipline it takes for him to remain calm in the face of her rising hysteria. "You're right. We did attend Mr. Allen's funeral, but Kimba and I hadn't seen each other since. That award I received, the event Mona and Noah attended with me—Kimba's family foundation sponsored it and we saw each other there."

She draws a deep breath and releases it in an indignant puff. "I'd only been gone a few days."

"And nothing happened right away," Ezra says, his gaze drifting to me and softening with something so much more than affection. There's no way Aiko will mistake it for anything other than what it is.

"You *care* about her," she whispers, horrified. "Do you think you're in love with her? Already?"

There's a part of me that doesn't want him to tell her, doesn't want to hurt her any more than she obviously is already. But the alpha part of me that feels like he's always been mine since the day we were born wants to pin her to the wall and growl that he was on loan, but he's *mine* again and she will back the fuck down.

But it's Ezra's call.

"I knew it would be hard for you," Ezra says, not addressing her question directly. "But we need to be civil and adult about this. How we handle the transition will affect how Noah adjusts. We'll work out the details. You can have the house. I can stay nearby so Noah can—"

"You have it all figured out, huh?" Aiko interrupts.

"We have a child together," Ezra says. "It would be irresponsible for me not to have considered how this will affect—"

"Two," Aiko says, her smile dropping, her eyes hard and flat, a pane of glass over her emotions.

"Two?" Ezra frowns. "Two what?"

"You said we have a child together," Aiko says. "But we have two."

She turns to me, challenge and pain mixing in her expression. "I came home early because I'm pregnant."

CHAPTER FORTY-TWO

Ezra

"Y OU'RE *WHAT?*"
        I've been careful with my words, disciplined in my
emotions since Aiko walked in, but her ridiculous
statement pulls the pin on my control.

"Pregnant." Aiko looks at me, hope rising in her eyes and lifting the
corners of her mouth. "A baby, Ezra. You always wanted another one."

Kimba flinches, and I see her face again last night, uncertain in the
moonlight, hear her voice shaking as she told me she may never have a
child.

"Years ago," I remind Aiko. "I wanted another baby years ago. You
didn't. It was fine. It's not something we've discussed in a long time and
you know it. And if you're pregnant, it's not mine. We've barely had sex
all year. Chaz would be—"

"Barely is not never," Aiko says softly. "Once is enough. And you
fucked me once."

"No, I..."

Taco Tuesday. Margaritas.

I gulp back the bile of regret and force myself to meet Kimba's
questioning gaze. She knows before I say it, grabbing her purse from the
bed and leaving the room. I bite off a growl, toss a frustrated glance at
Aiko and start after her.

"Wait here," I clip out.

"It's my *home*," she yells back. "Where else would I go?"

I take the stairs so fast I almost fall down the last two. Chaz is staked out by the door with Aiko's bags. A muscle tics in his jaw and his hands are clenched into fists at his side.

Me, too, man. Me, too.

This is about as awkward as a situation could possibly be. There is no greeting that would be appropriate, so I blow past and leave him for Aiko to deal with. Through the screen door, I see Kimba already outside on the porch, head bent over her phone.

Pulling the door closed behind me, I put my hand over hers. She snatches it back, shaking her head.

"Ezra, do not." Her voice is steady, but her hand trembles around the phone, despite her death grip.

"Look at me."

She doesn't, training her eyes to the porch floor. I cup her face, locking my hands gently around the high cheekbones, feeling the tense muscles at her jawline.

"Please talk to me, Tru."

I hear the begging in my own voice and don't care. Nothing means anything if she leaves this porch without hearing me out, without giving me a chance. She pulls free of my hands and steps away.

"You have, let's see." She looks at her phone. "Three minutes before Lamont, my Uber driver, arrives. Talk."

"You can't let this come between us."

She whirls around at that, her sundress flaring out and re-settling around her long legs. "Let this come between us?" She barks out a disbelieving laugh. "If Aiko is pregnant with your baby, there *is* no us, Ezra."

"The hell there's no us. You can't say that."

"What the *fuck* do you expect me to say? That I'm fine with it? I'm not. Don't ask me to be. I can't..." She presses her lips together and blinks rapidly. For a moment, I wish I didn't know her as well as I know my own hands, my own heart. There's so much hurt under her fury and I know her too well not to see it.

"I'm just hearing all of this for the first time," I say. "Just like you. I don't know what the hell is going on. Don't know what's true or—"

"But it could be true. You did sleep with her, right?"

"Once. One time in months, and we've lived together for ten years. You can't actually be angry that I slept with my ex-girlfriend once weeks ago before you and I even started."

"Not so ex." She laughs, the sound void of amusement. "This is her home, that's her bedroom, possibly your baby she's carrying. Not so fast with the ex."

"Chaz is literally standing at the door." I take her hands, holding on when she tries to pull away. "If Aiko *is* pregnant, it could just as easily be his."

"This is some Jerry Springer shit," she says, her breath coming hard. "I don't need this. If I were a client of mine, I would advise them to walk away and not look back."

"Is that what you want to do?" I ask, my voice solemn, my heart cracking. "Walk away from me?"

She squeezes her eyes shut, blocks me out. "I don't know. I don't know anything right now."

"You know this."

I clasp her neck and drag her close, pressing our lips together. She withdraws, but I pursue, needing the tinder of our passion to catch fire, to remind her. It only takes a second. As soon as our lips meet, I hunt for the taste and texture of her tongue and the sweet, slick lining of her mouth. She softens, moans, leans into me, clenching her fingers in my hair, gripping my jaw, prying my mouth open wider. I let her take as much as she wants, touch me how she wants. I run my hands in a tight wave down her back and clutch the swell of her ass.

She feels so good.

She was made for me. She can't forget that. No matter how bad this cluster fuck with Aiko looks right now, Kimba cannot lose sight of us. With subtle thrusts of my hips into her, I remind her how instantly hard the feel, the scent of her makes me.

The seeking movement is a faint echo of what we shared just hours ago at the lake house. She was mine. I was inside of her where I belonged, and if it wasn't broad daylight on my front porch, I'd turn her dress up and be there again.

"Shit." She groans, reaching between us to palm my dick. My teeth clench. I want to lose myself in this, desperately wish I could let her take me out, fall to her knees and suck me off. But Chaz is inside just feet away and my neighbor two houses down just came outside to mow his lawn.

"Baby," I mumble against her lips. "Come back inside so we can figure this out."

My words shatter the spell our bodies always work on each other and reality filters back into the haze we made. Bob's lawnmower fires up. Two moms chatter at the stop sign, pushing strollers. An alert sounds from Kimba's phone.

She glances down, licking lips swollen and wet from my kisses.

"Lamont's here." She stomps down the steps toward the Prius idling in front of my house. "I have to go."

CHAPTER FORTY-THREE

Kimba

"SO THE PUBLISHER IS SOFTENING SOME ON THE LEGAL END," Keith says. "But exerting your *wrath of Kimba Allen pressure* would probably help. Are you calling them today?"

I blink a few times, dispelling the mental image of Aiko yesterday standing in their bedroom crowing about having Ezra's baby.

"What?" I clear my throat and focus on my brother's frowning face. "Yeah. I'll do it."

I look around the office at our family foundation's headquarters, like it will give me a clue of my next step. "What am I doing?"

"Where is your head?" Kayla demands from behind her desk. "Everything I've said to you this morning I've had to repeat."

"I'm sorry." I lean back in my seat and release a long breath. "Just a lot going on. Yeah. I'll call the publisher. Piers found the real name of the author. She's writing the biography under a pseudonym."

"What's the name?" Kayla asks.

"Um, lemme see." I glance at my phone, flicking past Ezra's name and all the messages he's sent that have gone unanswered and find Piers' last message. "Serena Washington."

Keith frowns and sits on the edge of Kayla's desk. "I knew a Serena Washington."

"For real?" I ask. "Who?"

"Remember Mrs. Washington?" Keith asks.

"Our old nosy neighbor?" Kayla's face lights with recognition. "That old lady caught me in so many compromising positions."

"All of *high school* was a compromising position for you, Zee." I laugh, ducking when she throws a paper clip at me. "You know it's true. Mama didn't call you fast tail for nothing."

"So fast," Mama says from the door. "Thought your daddy would lose his mind from all those boys coming to the house."

"I was not that bad," Kayla says, trying to fake outrage because she knows she was.

"You were," Keith, Mama and I say in harmony.

The four of us laugh, and it reminds me of all the good times we had growing up. Feels like the Saturday mornings when the work was done and we'd stop for lunch in the kitchen. Laughter, macaroni and cheese, and chicken nuggets while I waited for the sun to go down, for Shabbat to end so Ezra and I could play.

Ezra.

I pull my phone out, not surprised to see two new messages from him. I haven't responded, but he won't stop if I don't.

Me: Give me some space.

Ezra: Call me.

Me: Have you asked your mom about the charm?

Ezra: Not yet. Just a few things going on here, as I'm sure you remember.

Ezra: I miss you.

Damn heart. Skipping beats and shit.

Me: It's only been a day.

Ezra: A day of you ignoring my messages.

Me: After this meeting, I'll call you.

Ezra: If you don't call, I'll come to your mother's house.

That is a scene I want to avoid at all costs. I heave a sigh and slip the phone back into my purse. The preternatural quiet from my typically boisterous family makes me realize they're all staring at me.

"What?" I ask, giving them each a piece of my frown. "What are you looking at?"

"Who you texting?" Kayla aims her chin at my phone.

"Is it that Stern boy?" Mama asks with a smile. "Nose been wide open for you since he was old enough to know."

"What does that even mean, Mama?" I ask. "Old enough to know what?"

"What girls are for," Keith drawls.

"Focus, fam," I say, trying to keep my voice light when my heart is Titanic in my chest, overburdened and sinking. "Less talk about my love life and more about this damn biography. Piers got me a number for the author, this Serena Washington, so I'll try to find her today."

"Yeah, like I was saying," Keith interjects. "I knew a Serena Washington. She was Mrs. Washington's niece. Lived across town, but bussed in one year. She was in my class."

"That would be quite a coincidence," Kayla says. "Though Washington isn't exactly a unique name."

"If there's a connection," I say, standing and grabbing my purse, "I'll find it."

I stride to the door, but Mama stops me there with a hand on my arm.

"Tru," she says. "I love you, and I'm glad to have you home."

I'm taken aback for a moment and look from her hand on my arm to the sincerity in her eyes.

"Yeah, I forgot how good it is to have you around," Keith says, his cocky grin softened around the edges into a sweet smile.

We all look to Kayla, silent and watching us.

"What?" She smirks. "Tru's been a pain in the ass all my *life*."

The obvious humor behind her insult spurs us all to laugh again, and I realize how much I needed things to be right with them with so much going wrong.

"Love you guys." I split a grateful smile between them all. "Zee, is there an office I can use to make some calls?"

"Yeah," she says. "Empty office at the end of the hall."

I walk down the corridor and close the office door behind me with a decisive click, leaning against it, almost afraid to call Ezra. Number one, what's happening under his roof will affect the rest of my life, and I have no control over it. Having no control makes me feel like one of those blow-up wavy, flailing things you see advertising tires and used cars. Number two, the only thing I hate more than feeling out of control is feeling weak. And Ezra is my weakness.

There's no way I'm moving forward if that baby is his. The worst thing for my state of mind embarking on one of the most important campaigns of my life would be battling menopause…while someone else is pregnant with my boyfriend's baby. When I'm away from him, when I don't see him or hear his voice, or *feel* him, I know that's what's best.

But he makes me weak. Will he make me stupid, too? Will wanting him mean accepting something I know for *me* is wholly unacceptable?

I dial.

"Tru," Ezra answers on the first ring, his voice even, but with a thin line of anxiety strung through it. "Hey."

"Hey." The line goes quiet, but there's no telling what he'll say so I fill the silence first. "Any word on the charm?"

His pause tells me that isn't where he wanted to start this conversation.

"I left my mom a voicemail," he says. "She's not great about checking those, but I'll try her again. I spoke to Noah, though, and asked him to have her call me back. She sneaks in a call with him every day, though she denies it."

I allow myself to smile, thinking of Noah's quick, eager grin and his eyes, exactly the shade of Ezra's, always bright with questions, sharp with intelligence. "He's a pretty great kid."

"Yeah, he is." Ezra clears his throat. "Aiko has no idea how far along she is."

That levels my smile into a straight line. "Oh, yeah?"

"She and Chaz have been sleeping together for three weeks. It's early, but it could very well be his."

"And when did you last sleep with her?"

"Seven weeks ago." I don't have to tell him it's more likely that it's his. He knows that. "She's trying to schedule an appointment with her doctor so we can know for sure."

"You'll go with her?"

"Of course." I hear the frown in his voice, hear the tension of wanting to detach from this *for me*, but being too good of a man to send her alone. I resent him and fall deeper in love with him in the same breath.

"That's good. You should go."

"Kimba, I need to know what you're thinking."

"You know what I'm thinking. I'm thinking…" I swallow the hot tears crowding my throat, give myself a moment to steady my voice before continuing. "I think if this is your baby, you should be there for your family."

"Aiko is Noah's mother and my friend. I'll be there for her whether this is my baby or not, but that's not what I'm asking you. What are you thinking about *us*?"

"Ezra, there's a lot of balls in the air right now." I skirt around the question, not because I don't know the answer, but because I'm afraid with a word if I let him, with one touch if I see him, he could change my mind. "I have a lead on the biographer. Keith thinks she might be related to Mrs. Washington."

"Nosy Mrs. Washington? From the old neighborhood? No way."

"Maybe. Could be just a coincidence. I'll try to find her, talk to her and see."

"That's one ball in the air," he says wryly. "Can we talk about our ball?"

"Let's see what happens at the appointment before we have this conversation."

"I don't need to know if the baby is mine to know I want you," he says in a rush, like he's afraid I'll hang up. "If I'm the father, I'll be a good one. You know that."

"You're a fantastic father. I would expect nothing less."

"But my mind hasn't changed about Aiko. Our relationship is over and has been, and my heart hasn't changed about *you*. I still want to be your last."

"Ez." I push the pain out in a long breath. "Don't."

"Tru, don't let this ruin us."

"I need to go."

"If you could—"

I hang up. I have to.

I dial Piers immediately to stop myself from calling Ezra back.

"Hey, boss lady," he says. "What can I do you for?"

"You got that address yet?" I ask, forcing the conversation, the turmoil with Ezra out of my mind. "For this Serena chick? I think I'll pay her a surprise visit. Best she doesn't see me coming."

"Sneak attack. I like it. I should have the address soon. I'm working on it. Oh! I thought of something that might prove useful in your quest."

"What's that?"

"So that publisher has a parent company," Piers says. "And you'll never guess who it is."

"Who?"

"The Rafferty Group."

"Come again?" I sit on the edge of the desk, not sure I heard him right.

"Yup. Rafferty."

"As in James Rafferty, the man we helped elect governor two years ago?"

"The same. He obviously isn't involved in the day-to-day right now, governing and all, but it's his family's business. He still has pull."

"Then so do we."

"He owes you," Piers says. "Not only did we get him elected, but we covered up that—"

"Piers," I cut him off. "I'm the girl who buries the bodies then forgets where they lay. Yeah?"

"Yeah. Sorry."

"It's okay. The fine governor knows that we know. That's all that matters. He'll want to do us any favor he can. I'm about to shut Serena Washington down. Great work, Piers. *This* I won't forget."

"You need Carla to set up a call with the governor?"

"Nope. I'll call him myself."

CHAPTER FORTY-FOUR

Ezra

"THAT WAS HER ON THE PHONE, WASN'T IT?"

Aiko stands at the door to the guest bedroom where I've been sleeping. I sit on the edge of the bed, phone still in my hand. Kimba hung up long ago, but I still hear her voice, the resignation in it. If this is my baby, I'm going to lose her, and it's like a shoal of piranha trapped in my belly, a feeding frenzy of anxiety and dread.

I don't answer Aiko's question, but stand and cross the room to leave. She doesn't move, but blocks my exit, a tiny wall keeping me inside.

"Ko," I say, hearing the impatience in my own voice. "I need to get by."

"Ezra." She runs her hands up my chest.

I slip past her, striding out into the hall and heading down the stairs. I settle in at my desk, open my laptop and try to distract myself with all the other things that require my attention. There's an email to re-schedule the publisher's meeting I missed because of Aiko's bombshell announcement. I need to finish this book. Another email from the YLA finance director regarding next year's budget and a grant we're applying for. I need to look at her projections.

I need to settle the issue of this pregnancy.

I need Kimba.

My head drops into my hands. It's futile trying to concentrate when my future hangs in the balance. I give up, let myself feel the weight of possibly losing her...again. Not as a boy who had no idea what a magnificent woman she would become, what we could be together, but as a man who's known her body and glimpsed her soul, been consumed by the fire that burns inside.

You set me on fire inside, Ezra Stern.

"We need to talk," Aiko says from the door.

"Talk to Chaz." I lift my head, refocus my attention on the laptop and try again.

"Chaz is not the father of this baby."

I do look at her then. "Oh, so you didn't fuck him the last three weeks? Was I mistaken about that?"

Color floods her pale cheeks and she drops her gaze to the floor. "Are you going to condemn me for something we agreed on?"

"Absolutely not." I shut my laptop and give her a level look. "But you can't condemn me either. You want to have your cake and eat it, too."

"I want you, Ezra," she says, swallowing hard. "I didn't want to end our relationship. I wanted an open one."

"Again, cake. You know me, Ko. What would ever make you think I'd want that? I don't care that you slept with Chaz."

"Maybe that's what hurts most because it's killing me that you slept with Kimba as soon as my back was turned."

"Your back wasn't turned. You left," I say, slicing a hand through the air. "With *him*. We broke up and agreed to tell Noah when you returned. Don't try to re-write history because the truth is suddenly not as convenient."

"History is re-writing itself, Ezra." She walks deeper into the office, one hand on her stomach. "And there's nothing convenient about an unplanned pregnancy at nearly forty on the cusp of the biggest opportunity of my career. I didn't ask for this either. You were there that night. I didn't fuck myself."

"I know that." I expel as much of the frustration as I can on a long breath. "If this is my baby, you know I'll support you, but we won't be together." I look at her directly so she can see the finality on my face. "Not again. And not just because of Kimba. I hadn't even seen Kimba when we broke up. You and I ending things was the right thing to do, for all of us. It still is."

"But it *hasn't* happened." She crosses the room, presses her palms to the desk and leans forward. "It hasn't happened because Noah doesn't know. Our families, our friends don't know. When Noah comes home, we tell him he's going to have a little brother or sister and he'll be ecstatic. Things go back to normal."

"I don't want normal. I want Kimba."

Hurt shows in her sharply drawn breath, in the tears that fill her eyes right away.

"Ko," I say, deliberately gentling my tone. "I told you before you left that I wanted one person I could love for the rest of my life. That person is Kimba, and I know it seems soon to you, but I've known her since we were babies. Even when we were separated, I never stopped knowing her."

"If I ask you a question, will you answer honestly?"

"Always."

"Did I ever even really have a chance?"

I give the question the consideration it deserves and force myself to be honest with her while still being as kind as I can. "Probably the best chance anyone has ever had. If you'd said yes when I asked to marry you, I would have found a way to keep my distance from Kimba when our paths crossed again."

"You couldn't have just been friends?"

I glance past her toward the kitchen, the mudroom, and flash back to that night when Kimba and I first made love. The wild sounds we made. The desperate craving that hung in the air. That absolute long-sought rightness of being inside her for the first time.

"No, I don't think I could have been just her friend, even though I fooled myself that I could have."

"When did you fall in love with her?"

I feel the cold metal around my finger again. Smell the freshly cut grass in my back yard. Hear the glass breaking on the rocks.

"I was six years old." I chuckle humorlessly and touch my empty ring finger. "And again when I was seven. Eight. Nine and ten. I think I fell in love with her every day for the first thirteen years of my life, and as soon as I saw her again, my heart just remembered."

She watches me, her face pinched, but some semblance of acceptance finally entering her eyes. My cell phone buzzes on the desk, breaking the poignant, painful mood.

"My appointment is tomorrow," Aiko says, turning to leave. "First thing."

I check the screen and answer right away. "Mom, hey."

"Hey! You said you needed to speak with me urgently. Is everything okay?"

"Yes, it's quite urgent. If you ever checked your messages, you'd know when your son needs you. Noah told you to call?"

"When would I have talked to Noah?" she hedges.

"Okay. Never mind. I'll deal with that later. I have a question for you."

"All right." Even though she says it, I hear the caution in her voice.

"Did you ever visit the Allens' lake house?"

The question drops into a pool of silence so deep I almost lose track of it.

"Mom? Did you hear—"

"I heard you. I…why would you ask me that?" Caution becomes evasion.

"I don't remember us ever going with them up there. Kimba's grandfather bought it not too long before we left."

"Yes, so why would you—"

"Your charm was there, Mom," I cut in before she can find a way to lie to me without telling me anything at all. "The star of David you lost that summer? Kimba and I went to the lake house and she found it in the laundry room."

"What laundry room?" she asks and then gasps.

"Yeah," I say, drawing out the word. "They just completed renovations that knocked out some walls and shuffled some things. The laundry room wouldn't have been there…when you were."

She releases a long, tired sigh on the other end of the line.

"Nothing's ever as it seems, Ezra," she says, her words weary and cryptic.

"I'm not interested in how things seem. I'm interested in how they were. How they are."

"Your father and I were having problems," she says, her voice shrinking. "I wanted to leave Atlanta—needed my family around me."

"I remember."

"And you know how badly I wanted to get you out of the South. Your father and I both wanted to expose you to broader experiences. Even I didn't dream of going overseas, but it turned out to be good for you, didn't it?"

"Yes, it was great for me, besides the fact that it meant I lost Kimba."

"Yes, I'm sorry for that now. At the time, it seemed like the best thing to do."

"What was the best thing to do? Move? Why? What happened?" I pause and then ask the question again, the one she denied before. "Were you unfaithful to Dad?"

I can practically hear her courage gathering and taking shape before she says the word.

"Yes."

I nod and expel a sigh. Finally, the truth. "I don't condemn you, Mom."

"Good. Because you have no right to," she says, defiance coming across clearly.

"Of course not. I just meant I would never judge. Can you tell me what happened?"

"We swore, the four of us, that we would never tell. We went our separate ways, and agreed we'd take it to the grave."

"Well, two of you are already in the grave, and the truth is coming out if Kimba can't stop this book from being published."

"No, honey. It's like I said before. Nothing's as it seems. That's not the truth."

I frown, resting my elbows on the desk and touching my head, trying to piece her words into something that makes sense. "I don't understand. Start from the beginning."

"It began, like most affairs do, with loneliness. I was so lonely." A breath catches in her throat. "We both were."

CHAPTER FORTY-FIVE

Kimba

"WE'LL BE IN TOUCH."

The next day on Serena Washington's porch, I turn to face the woman who has caused all this trouble. She looked so much like her aunt that when she answered the door, I couldn't stop staring. I wanted to snap a picture and text it to Ezra so he could marvel, too. The woman who was always on her front porch sweeping, stealthily snooping on our entire neighborhood, has a doppelgänger niece, and she's as worrisome as her aunt.

"You really think you can get me a book tour?" she asks as I'm leaving after hours of hashing out terms and getting things settled.

"I can, but of course we have some editing to do before the book can be released. Fortunately, the publisher hadn't sent many early copies out yet, and we're contacting those readers to let them know about the misinformation in the draft they read."

"Misinformation?" Skepticism marks Serena's expression. "Aunt Roselle had her finger on the pulse of everything. She was rarely wrong, but if you say so."

"Well, she was wrong about my father," I say with a confidence that can't be real until I know more about the charm we found. "Whatever she thought she heard my parents arguing about that night, she didn't. And writing something like that based on unconfirmed speculation is both reckless and potentially slanderous." I offer an indulgent smile since we have come to terms that meet my satisfaction. "But lesson learned, right?"

Serena lifts her chin. "Lesson learned."

"I want to be clear. I've already spoken to the publisher. The only way this book gets published is if these changes are made, and once I approve it."

"I'm surprised you're allowing it at all."

"You're a good writer and a smart journalist. That's clear. With the exception of the erroneous information about my father being unfaithful," I say, pausing, as if giving her the chance to contradict me, but looking at her like she better not, "we loved the book."

"I appreciate that."

"Adding personal accounts from my family will elevate your book from being an unauthorized biography, something we publicly condemned and tore apart, to one that has our full support. Also, delaying publication makes sense so we can dovetail the release with the dedication of the new Joseph Allen Atlanta History Museum. I'm assuring you a *New York Times* bestseller."

I give her a Queen Bee smile, sweet as honeycomb, but with a little sting. "This is the part where you thank me, by the way."

"Thank you," Serena says wryly. "You've got it all figured out, huh?"

I'm not sure if it's resentment or admiration in her voice. She's free to feel either. I don't care what she *feels*. I care what she does. And now I've got her in check.

Checkmate.

I'll never hear that word without thinking of Ezra, without seeing two kids in his living room with a big board and heavy pieces, ebony and ivory, between us.

"I need to go." I smile and start down the steps. "But we'll be in touch."

Once in Mama's Benz, I call Ezra through the car's elaborate dashboard.

"Tru?"

The hope in his voice breaks my heart because I know I'm probably going to break his, too. Unless... I've only allowed myself to consider the possibility that it's not Ezra's child a few times. All the maneuvers I've had to make over the last day—the conversations with Governor Rafferty, threatening the publisher, persuading and putting Serena in her place under my thumb—every move I made was carefully calculated, a bet I couldn't afford to lose. This game required my complete focus. I couldn't let myself consider what was happening with Ezra, but hearing his voice, it all falls on my heart at once, a stratum of hope and hurt and dread and fear.

And love.

"Yeah, hey." I heave a tired sigh. "I have good news."

"You do?"

"Serena is removing the lies about our parents from her book."

His silence surprises me. I expected instant jubilation, triumph. Not this waiting silence, like he's not sure what to celebrate.

"This is good news, Ezra," I tell him unnecessarily.

"Of course it is. I was just thrown off because I didn't expect it to be this easy."

"Easy it was not."

"I can imagine," he says. "Can we talk? I mean about us? Not all of this?"

He'd said Aiko was trying to get a doctor's appointment. Does he know yet?

"Ez, what—"

"Face-to-face," he says, his voice as level as screed concrete and giving less away.

It can't be good. If it wasn't his baby, wouldn't he just tell me now? Or maybe she didn't have the appointment yet. Or maybe they found out it was a false alarm. Anything good he'd tell me right away, but he wants to see me—wants to convince me, persuade me. *Love me* into doing something stupid. I'm so weak for this man, but that I will not let him do. I draw the lines clearly for myself. If the baby is his, I won't stay. My heart will break every step away from him, but it would be an act of self-preservation. If the baby is not his...

It hurts to hope this much. Hope is a bird that can soar or be shot down mid-flight.

I pull into my mother's driveway. "I'm at home. We could meet here."

He pauses, and when he speaks again, his voice has deepened, has heated. "I've missed you, Tru."

I've missed you, too rides the tip of my tongue, but I bite it, let the silence after his words stretch out.

"We've had some developments here, too," he says when it's

obvious I'm not going to respond in kind.

"You spoke to your mom?"

Another silence. Me making sure what was written in that biography never makes it to the shelves is different than confirming that it wasn't *true*.

"How did she explain her charm being at the lake house if your family had never been there?"

"My family hadn't, but she had with your mom, I believe."

"Oh." Relief courses through me, bursting out in a laugh. "That's right. Mama would take her friends there sometimes for girlfriend weekends. I didn't think she had started before your mom left, but I guess she had. Probably their mah-jongg group."

"You'll have to ask your mom."

"Okay." I suppress the nervousness that rises every time I think of Aiko's pregnancy, of knowing the answer. "Then I'll see you in a little bit."

He draws a deep breath. "I love you, Tru."

I can't say it back again. I won't yet. Not until I know my heart is safe and my hope is not in vain.

"I'll see you soon, Ezra. Bye."

It's hard to hang up, to break even the smallest connection to him, but I do. How the hell will I let him go if Aiko is having his baby? God, the bitter irony of it. I can't even get my period to come back, and she got pregnant *twice* by the man I love without even trying.

In the kitchen, Mama's cooking. Raw meat and fresh vegetables crowd the counter. I set my purse on the island in the center of the room and walk over, give her a squeeze, which she returns.

"You're cooking already?" I turn to lean against the counter so I can see her face.

"I wanted to make something good." Mama glances at me, her eyes dark and sober under the vibrant head scarf hiding her hair. "You'll be home for dinner?"

I assess the food. Pork chops, string beans, corn on the cob, sweet potatoes.

"All this for just us?" I ask.

"Just us." She blows out a breathy chuckle, blinks, licks her lips when they tremble. "Some days it gets bad, missing your father. I know it sounds silly, but it helps when I cook his...his favorite things."

That feeling I usually try to hide from seizes my unsuspecting heart.

Grief. Desolation that Daddy will never walk through that door. Never call me *baby girl* again. Tears sting my eyes.

"I miss him, too," I whisper. "All the time. I keep wondering when it stops hurting."

"For me, it won't." Mama scrubs dirt from the sweet potatoes, not looking at me. "I lost the love of my life, and it blasted a hole in the world. It doesn't so much stop hurting as you just get used to the pain, remember how to wake up in the bed alone. Oh, you have to learn everything all over again like a baby learning to walk because I forgot how to live without that man."

There are a million things I want to say, want to ask, but she's never spoken this openly about her grief and I'm afraid anything I say would make her stop.

"Sometimes," she continues, "I go into his office and pull out those stinky cigars he used to hide."

"You knew about those?" I ask, my question, my stunted laugh, teary.

"He knew I knew." She chuckles, snapping the ends of the string beans. "We had no secrets, Tru."

Her probing stare turns on me. "How did it go with that Washington girl?"

The reminder of our present drama jerks me from the past.

"Good." I turn around to help snap the ends from the beans. "She's agreed to the conditions I laid out."

"So she's taking it out of the book? The lies about your daddy and Ruth?"

"Yeah. The publisher won't release it if she doesn't. And I have final approval."

"You're something else, girl." Mama laughs and shakes her head.

My conversation with Ezra tickles my thoughts. Not the hard parts that he and I have to sort through for our future, but the mysterious parts about our parents' pasts.

"Ezra and I went up to the lake house the other night."

"So things must be moving right along," Mama says, her smile teasing.

"Things *were* moving right along." I grimace. "They may be grinding to a halt, but that's another issue. When we were there, I found that star of David charm Mrs. Stern used to wear."

Mama's hands go still under the water, and her whole body seems to freeze. Slowly her hands start moving again, but she doesn't speak. So I do.

"Ezra didn't remember his family ever going there, so he asked Mrs. Stern about it."

She turns her head, stares at me for long seconds. "And what did she say?"

"Ezra didn't tell me everything, but she said she was there with you," I say, rushing my next words, feeling on the edge of a knife I can't see. "I said you would have girls' trips sometimes with your friends, and it must have been something like that."

I pause, swallow, wait.

"*Was* it something like that, Mama?"

For a second, I think she won't answer, won't even acknowledge my question. Then she turns the water off, dries her hands on a dish towel nearby and faces me.

"No. It was just Ruth and me." Defiance and dread vie in Mama's eyes. "The reason I was so sure Joseph never had an affair with Ruth is because I did."

"W-w-what?" For once I don't care that I stuttered. What she's saying is incomprehensible, but as echoes from that night taunt me with the truth, makes so much sense.

Damn you, Ruth!

Let me explain.

You can't explain this!

"It was a hard year," Mama says, looking down at her hands, caressing the small diamond Daddy gave her when they married. She always refused his offers to upgrade. "Your father was busy, working, gone all the time. So was Al. It's no excuse. Ruth and I just...we were there for each other. I never would have thought..."

She shrugs. "It happened. I *let* it happen. The day Joe died was the hardest of my life. The day he found out about me and Ruth was the second."

I'm dumbstruck. Congealing in my shock and clenching a cluster of string beans in my fist.

"I broke his..." Tears trickle over Mama's cheeks. "I broke his heart and it took years to mend it. I wasn't sure I ever could. He didn't leave. He was *somebody* by then in his own right here in Atlanta. Maybe he was concerned about appearances, but that wasn't your father. I like to think he didn't leave me because he couldn't stand to live without me.

Loved me so much he had to figure out forgiveness."

The kitchen, Mama's confessional, is completely quiet. Even the refrigerator holds its breath while she gathers her thoughts and I gather my scattered wits.

"We didn't plan it," Mama says. "But she was miserable here and missing her family. I was resentful, felt like I was carrying all the load with your father gone so much, and I missed him. Missed being…touched, seen."

Mama huffs a short breath.

"We were careless when we went to the lake house. Stopped to grab something from the corner store up there. Al found the receipt, asked questions…" She gives a sad laugh and shake of her head. "Ruth is a terrible liar."

She hasn't looked at me while she told the story, but now her sad eyes find mine. "Love is not a tidy thing, Kimba. It can't ever be perfect because none of us are. Someone at some point will make a mess. The test of that love is how you clean it up. Your father stayed and we cleaned it up together."

Mama turns back to the counter, snapping string beans again.

"I'm glad you were able to stop Serena Washington," Mama says. "That night, the four of us agreed we would never tell. We all had things to lose. This would be a scandal now. But then?"

Mama bends a meaningful look on me. "*Back then?* Our lives would have been ruined. I would have told the world what I just told you if it meant clearing your father's name, though. For Ruth's sake, I'm glad we won't have to."

I have questions but asking them would feel like defiling an offering Mama made freely. She told me what she thought I should know, and that's good enough for me.

"I hated losing her," Mama says, smiling. "As a friend. We knew what happened between us was a mistake almost before it started, but sometimes when you're lonely and hurt, you'll try anything to feel better."

"Thank you for telling me." I swallow my curiosity and shock. "I think… I *suspect* Mrs. Stern told Ezra, too."

Mama grins and transfers the string beans from the sink into a pot. "Ruth and I always thought you two would find your way. I thought we had ruined it, but I guess fate had other ideas."

My laugh is bitter, hollow. "Fate has a sick sense of humor."

"Explain," Mama says, frowning.

"After all these years we finally found our way back to each other at just the right time when he's free, but his ex is now pregnant and I'm in perimenopause."

"Pregnant?" Mama searches my face. "What are you going to do?"

"He's on his way here. Aiko was going to the doctor, so he should know now if it's his or not." I slump against the counter. "Mama, if it's his, I can't do it. I can't watch her carry his baby while I'm not sure I'll ever be able to have one. Congressman Ruiz's campaign is my first truly solo, without Lennix. I want to get this right. I have to. I hope Ruiz would make a difference for people here in Georgia who need help. It's gonna be the fight of my life."

"Do you love him?" Mama asks softly.

I close my eyes, not wanting to answer that. Not having to. My heart answers for me, pounding Ezra's name into my chest. "Yes."

"This happened before you and Ezra got together?"

"Yes, but what if…"

A million what ifs crowd my mind and poison my soul.

If anyone gets hurt when things go south, it'll be you.

Mona was so right. This is about as south as things could go, and if I lose Ezra, the hurt will be unbearable.

"It sounds like you don't want right now," Mama says. "But you do want forever."

"That about sums it up. *If* there's any forever left when this is over."

"When it comes to love, some messes take longer than others to clean up." Mama's smile is wise. "Believe me—I know."

CHAPTER FORTY-SIX

Ezra

IT'S JUST A SLIP OF PAPER, BUT MY HAND TREMBLES HOLDING IT.

"God, I forgot about these," Aiko says, popping a large pill and chasing it with water. "You'll have to remind me to take them. Remember with Noah I couldn't ever remember my pre-natals?"

"Yeah," I say, my fingers, my voice numb. "That was a long time ago. They have apps now to remind you."

She crosses around the counter to the kitchen table where I sit holding the ultrasound. On the flimsy paper, a little form floats in its own starless galaxy. At the very bottom, tracking its orbit, are the letters and numbers that sink my heart.

7w2d.

Seven weeks. Two days.

The baby's mine. Any life that is just beginning deserves some celebration, but today, right now, it feels like my life is over.

At least my life with Kimba.

"I need to go out." I stand to leave.

"Out?" Aiko takes another sip of water.

I don't answer but gather my keys from the dish on the counter.

"I didn't do this on purpose," she says. "If that's what you think."

"I know that. Please don't make this worse."

"Worse?" She approaches me cautiously like I might run with her sudden moves. "Why worse? We're a family. Noah will be so excited about a little brother or sister."

"Yeah. He will." I laugh hoarsely. "Good news for everyone, huh?"

She glances from the keys to my face. "You're going to tell her?"

"Yeah, not that she'll actually…"

Give me a chance. Stay.

Kimba probably won't do either of those things and I can't blame her. Gravel lines my throat and I can barely move. It's the weight of anxiety, but I'm too stubborn, too determined…too damn in love with Kimba to give up yet. The odds are squarely against me, but I have to try.

"I don't want to do this alone, Ezra." Aiko's brow crinkles. Tears leak from the corners of her eyes.

"You're not alone. You have Noah and me."

"Do I?" She searches my face. "Have you?"

"You have my friendship and my promise to be the best father I can ever be to this baby."

"And what if Kimba won't accept it?" I hear the hope in her voice and have to squelch it.

"Even if Kimba won't have me, that's still all I can give you, Ko." I squeeze her hand. "But that's a lot. It will have to be enough, because it's all I have."

Everything else belongs to Kimba, whether she wants it or not. Whether she'll keep it or not.

Aiko nods, blinks at tears and tries a smile.

I bend to catch her eye. "You know I got you, right? I won't let you do this alone. It's my kid, too."

"Aren't you the teeniest bit excited, Ezra? You did always want another baby."

I manage a nod. There is a distant part of me that will at some point find joy that I'll be a father again because I love children so much. I'm sure once things settle with Kimba, however they go, I'll get excited for the chance to be someone else's dad. Today, there's no room for excitement. Dread and hope have taken up equal residence in my heart, and I have no idea who'll get to stay.

When I pull up in front of Janetta Allen's home, I don't get out of the car right away. I sit in this moment between hope and hell, between the possibility that Kimba can live with this, can stay for this, and the certainty that she won't. Knowing she's inside, wanting to see her as much as I'm dreading this conversation, it's not a place I can stay very long.

She answers the door almost as soon as I ring the bell. We stand there for a few seconds just watching each other, a wary wanting springing between us. One side of her hair is pulled back, exposing the high beveled bones of her face.

"You look beautiful," I tell her.

She is dressed for what, in her world, constitutes battle. The crisp linen dress is starkly white against the rich copper of her skin, with tiny sleeves fluttering at her shoulders like petals. It's not the clothes that give that impression of *don't fuck with me*—it's the confidence she wears inside. She'd probably give the same impression no matter how she was dressed. I assume her attire was carefully chosen with Serena Washington in mind.

"Thanks." She steps back and waves me in. "We can talk in here."

It's the front room, similar to the one Mrs. Allen had in their old house. No one sat on that furniture or actually breathed in there. This is an upgrade, a much more opulently outfitted room, but it feels the same—like I can't breathe.

Or maybe that's because of the news I have to share.

Kimba sits on one of the cream-colored sofas and gestures to a seat across from her, a queen holding court. So formal. I won't let her strip this of intimacy, of feeling. This is the most real thing I've ever had, and if I lose it, I won't pretend it doesn't hurt. I ignore her suggestion and sit beside her as close as I can. She flicks me a wry look and scoots back until she's in the corner of the couch.

"You said we needed to talk?" she asks, her words as crisp as her dress.

"Yeah, I..." Is there any way I can say this that makes it sound better, that gives me a chance? "Aiko's appointment was this morning."

She nods. "I figured as much. And?"

"Seven weeks along."

I see the devastation in her eyes before she can mask it, a flash quickly snuffed. "Okay. Thank you for letting me know."

"Tru, we can still—"

"I can't, Ezra," she says on a harsh breath. "Before you ask me, I cannot."

I reach for her, but she stands, steps out of my reach. I follow. She's my magnet, and even when I try to resist, I'm drawn to her. This is supposed to be our second chance, and I'm not giving up on it, on us, without fighting for it.

"Can we at least talk about this?" I ask.

"There's nothing to talk about." She settles on the edge of another cream-colored settee.

"The hell..." I grind the words to dust between my teeth and try to compose myself. I'm used to being in control, but she makes me crazy. She drives me mad like a drug. A hallucinogen that convinces me we belong together, that we could work, that she could love me enough to stay. To fight.

"Don't do this to us, Tru. Not again."

She closes her eyes, and tears spill over her cheeks, breaking me inside. I'm hurting her, which kills me, but I can't stop. I have to try.

"What do you need me to do?" I ask, swallowing a million pleas. "How do I prove to you this could work?"

"You have a family."

"I want you!" It comes out loud, a declaration blaring through the deserted house. "I want..." My voice breaks, my pain in accord with hers. "I'm only half without you. You have to give me this chance."

"I can't." Her mouth and her hands tremble. "Don't ask me to watch another woman carry your child when I might never be able to."

"I don't care." I take her face between my shaking hands. "I have Noah and I'll have this baby and I have my students. I don't need anything else but you. Do you think I care if you can't have kids? I don't."

"It's more than that." She shakes her head, pulling free of my hands. "Having a baby together—it's intimate. Something you and I may never experience. New feelings for Aiko could develop. Old ones could return. You never know how you'll feel."

"I do. I know exactly how I'll feel. I fell in love with you when I was six years old and that love has only grown. It will only grow."

A watery laugh cracks into a smile on her lips. "Ezra, don't you get it? I'm jealous. I'm possessive of you. I'm angry that she gets this with you and I don't. I can't *live* with all of this and do what I need to do. I can't do my job, can't pursue my dreams, can't focus on any of that when I'm so terribly focused on you. On whether you might love her again."

"I won't."

"Or might fuck her."

"*I won't.* I'm moving out. I told you I would."

She's quiet at that, and hope starts rising in my chest again. She bites her lip and looks me square in the eye. "I got my period."

"Okay. What does that mean?"

"I've been taking homeopathic remedies the last month or so to see if I could get my period back. It came back today."

"You have a window, right?" The muscle in my jaw spasms. "Are you thinking of...of letting someone else...of trying to get pregnant?"

Without me?

"I don't want to be pregnant right now," she says, shaking her head. "I need to give Congressman Ruiz my focus and attention. We're going to make history. I want to be at my best, and pregnant at thirty-seven and fighting menopause, I'm not sure I'll feel my best. I might, but it's not what I want to do. Not right now. I don't want to turn my life upside down because my body decided to flip some reproductive hourglass."

"I get that."

"I want this on my terms." She takes a deep breath. "I'll consult with my doctor to see if my eggs are any good. If they are, I'll freeze as many as I can and they'll be my safety net. So if at the end of this campaign I decide I want to have a baby, I'll have options."

"And me? Us?"

"If you still want—"

"If I still...what the hell does that mean? I love you. Of course I'll want you, want to do this with you."

"We'll see." She bites her lip, swallows. "But I think at least until the baby is born, we go our separate ways."

"No." My denial is a glass hurled into the wall, shattering. "You think you're jealous, possessive. The thought of you meeting someone out on the trail, *fucking* someone, falling for another man, someone less complicated, easier, with less baggage... I can't live with that. I can't go back."

"Maybe we don't go back and we don't move forward." Her laugh is hollow. "Daddy used to say sometimes the most powerful move you can make is to be still. I've learned that in the last few weeks."

"How so?"

"Running from my family name, from expectations, running from my grief over Daddy. All this time I thought my candidates were running, but maybe I was the one running all along. Maybe we just…hold."

"What does that mean? Are you saying we'll be together?"

"For now," she says, looking at me with tears in her eyes. "No. I can't."

"And will you be with someone else?" I'm holding my breath, holding my heart out to her, offering her the chance to break it.

"No," she laughs and swipes at the tears on her cheeks. "I don't want anyone else. Only you."

I want to be your last.

"I think we…hold and see what happens," she says. "Just hold while I elect Georgia's first Hispanic governor and you support Aiko the way she needs and be there for Noah the way he needs. And we haven't even discussed how your book will change everything. Once it's published, you'll be in demand in a way you've never been before. Mark my words, it will change your life."

"And once the governor is elected and the baby is born and I've taken the book world by storm?"

She smiles. Not a wide smile that makes any promises, but one that says what she intends. "Then we'll see."

I hate this plan, but at least she's not giving up on me, and most women would. I reach for her, and this time she doesn't pull away. She huddles into my chest, wrapping her arm around my waist. I cup her face, splaying my hand over her jaw and lowering my head for a kiss. Between our lips, I taste tears, hers and mine. I taste our dreams, our hopes, our fears. We kiss until we're both breathless and gasping. She grips my shirt for dear life, like she might fall if she lets go. I swallow more pain at the thought of being separated from her again even if it ultimately proves to be temporary.

"I love you, Tru."

In synagogue, we'd whisper the Baruch Shem because it's part of a prayer reserved for angels considered pure, a blessing we're not worthy to offer to God. That's how I tell Kimba I love her because I don't deserve her—don't have any right to ask her to wade into this morass of my life, but I'm begging her to.

"I love you, too," she whispers back, tears running unchecked down her face and her voice hiccupping on a broken breath. "I don't know what will happen, but I know you are the love of my life, Ezra Stern, and I'll never feel this way again."

"Promise?" I ask, brushing my thumb across her lips.

Her smile is sad, but I'll settle for it for now, like all the other things I have to settle for...for now. "I'll do better than a promise."

She hooks our pinky fingers together. "Pact."

I chuckle through the lump in my throat. "Pact."

CHAPTER FORTY-SEVEN

Kimba

*W*E LOST.

I read the text message a second time. A third, letting the words toll in my head like a church bell.

Felita: Should I call? You want the details of the vote?

I glance around the depressing hotel room with the dated décor in the Alabama town where I'm sleeping tonight. I have a meeting with a local voting rights organization tomorrow morning. How am I supposed to inspire, encourage them when the very legislation that could destroy their efforts just passed?

Me: No. I'll call you in an hour. I need to eat.

The overcooked chicken and underseasoned vegetables, already unappetizing, hold even less appeal now, but I've only eaten a bagel today. The better I eat— whole grains, fresh vegetables, avoiding processed foods—the better my chances of freezing quality eggs and maybe having a baby when I'm ready. I glare at the little bag that holds my syringe and medication for the injection I have to give myself. I'm good at a lot of things. Apparently giving myself a hormone shot isn't one of them.

It's so easy, the nurse said.

Anyone can do it, she said.

But I hate needles and sticking one in my hip is the last thing I want to do.

I strip off my dress and toss on yoga pants. I'm sifting through my overnight bag, looking for a top to wear, when Ezra's scent hits me. A corner of red cotton peeks out from beneath my toiletries.

His YLA T-shirt.

I found it in my overnight bag after our trip to the lake house. It must have gotten mixed in with my things. I've made no attempt to send it back to him and find myself packing it every time I go on the road. I'm keeping at least this for myself. I toss my bra across the room and pull Ezra's shirt over my head. The well-worn cotton instantly transports me to a different time and place. Not a dingy hotel room, but to his bed, where he could make love to me all night and hold me until the sun rose.

I pull the collar to my nose and inhale.

A ring of fire squeezes my heart, burning, aching, forcing tears from the corners of my eyes.

I miss you.

On a day like today, when I lose, even worse, when the people I'm supposed to be *fighting for* lose, I want to go to him. Abandon this self-imposed separation and let him hold me. My phone, screen darkened, beside the rubbery food, silently dares me to call. I ignore it and reach instead for the little pouch. I can't bear the thought of sinking the needle through my flesh right now. It shouldn't be hard, I know. I'm a badass, I get it, but I'm a badass who hates needles and having to inject myself with one is my worst nightmare. It'll be the last thing I do before I go to sleep.

I poke a fork at the food room service delivered and wrinkle my nose. It's not great, but there's an echo in my empty stomach and a throbbing in my head.

I've taken four mediocre bites when my phone lights up with a message.

Mateo: Down another four points in the polls. When are you coming back?

Can this day get worse?

Me: Don't worry about the polls. They're preliminary. We haven't even really started. The election's a long way off. I'm back tomorrow. I'll be at headquarters by noon.

I hope he doesn't respond, and he doesn't. We knew this would be a tough race and that our odds are long, but the reality of this uphill climb gets to us all sometimes. I took valuable time away from the campaign to come to Alabama and fight this shitty voter suppression legislation.

And lost.

Now we're down in the polls and Mateo's side-eyeing me, probably second guessing his decision to hire our team. Wishing he'd gone with his first instinct, bet on the good ol' boy Anthony.

Okay. I'm spiraling.

Lennix could get me out of my head, but she's so close to delivering and has a lot on her plate. I hate to bother her. I could call Viv or Kayla. Even Mama, but I already know there's only one voice I actually want to hear. And tonight I'm just weak enough to call.

He picks up on the first ring.

"Kimba?"

Ezra's voice is dark liquid poured over my nerve endings, making me shiver, soothing me in the space of one hot breath.

"Hey, Ez."

The rush of air on the other end sounds like relief, disbelief. Joy.

"Are you okay?" he asks. "We haven't spoken and I—"

"I know. I'm sorry I haven't called."

A beat of silence fills up with all the things we could have said to one another over the last four months.

"You've been busy," he says. "I understand."

"So have you." My smile belies the ache in my heart. "You turned in the book?"

"Uh, yeah. It's all behind the scenes, preparation stuff right now."

"How's Noah?"

"He's good." A smile enters his voice, the one reserved for his son. "Same Noah. Looking for new and inventive ways to rule the world."

I laugh, force myself to ask the next question. "And, um…Aiko? How's the pregnancy coming along?"

Another beat of silence, filled with all the things keeping us apart.

"She's great. The baby's growing. Healthy."

I want to ask if the baby has kicked yet. If he was there for that, if he felt it. If it's a boy or a girl. If Aiko has that famous glow. If this is bringing them closer…again, reminding them why they spent the last decade together.

Making him love her?

But I don't ask any of those questions in case I can't live with the answers.

"You sure you're okay?" Ezra asks. "Do you need me? I can come—"

"Yes, I need you, but no, you can't come."

"Tru," he groans, my name torture on his lips. "Baby, where are you? Tell me what's wrong."

"Just a crap day," I say, my words going watery. "I'm in this poo butt town fighting bullshit legislation that would promote voter suppression. And we lost. People who really needed this win don't get it, and I feel... I feel like I let people down, you know?"

"You didn't. I know you did all you could do."

Right, and the worst part is when it's not enough. So many times it's not enough. Tears prick my eyes and it feels good to cry for someone other than myself; to step out of my own problems long enough to consider all the people and communities who'll be affected when they purge those voter rolls.

"Shit," I say, my voice wobbling. "Why are people so... God, I hate this."

Tears run into the corners of my mouth as I think of the poor, elderly women on that committee I'm addressing tomorrow; the ones who have experienced the worst of discrimination. I sniff, appreciating the silence he allows me. He told me once I could take off my armor with him, and even though he can't see me, I'm naked, vulnerable in a way no one ever sees me. I hope it's all the hormones I'm taking and not my actual emotions.

"You know what I love about you, Kimba?"

I need to hear this so bad. "What?"

"You save all your tears for the things that set you on fire inside. Anyone who's ever thought you were cold never got to hear your passion for people, never got to see you fight for them when it's inconvenient or even a lost cause."

He's right. I do save my tears for the things that matter most. That's why I cry for him.

"Ez, I miss you so much," I say, my resolve crumbling.

"Tru, dammit, where are you?"

"Alabama."

"I can come. That's not far."

"No." I breathe in all the reasons he shouldn't come. Breathe out my desire to have him with me. "I'll be back in Georgia by noon tomorrow anyway."

"Atlanta?"

"No, we're set up out of Athens right now. It's easier for Mateo's family."

"Do you know what I would give to have one night with you?" There's a desperate need in his voice that drops a hook in me, pulls me from drowning. I'm caught. I'm his, but it's not time. But, God, I'm tempted.

"Is it a boy or girl?" I force myself to ask, needing to remind myself why *I* need to wait.

"Tru, don't."

"Boy or girl, Ez? You should know by now."

His breath releases on a tired stream. "It's a girl."

I lick at the fresh tears collecting in the corners of my mouth and glare at the little bag of needles and hormones, my weapons to fight for what comes easily to so many other women.

"You're happy, of course," I say, keeping my voice as even as I can.

The line goes quiet with his held breath. He doesn't want to say the wrong thing, the thing that would drive me away. Further away.

"Fair's fair," I say, my voice deliberately light. "If I'm honest with you, you have to be honest with me. You're happy?"

"Tru."

"This is why, Ezra. This is why you can't come to me, why we can't be together right now. I...I'm happy *for* you. I just can't watch."

He clears his throat, and when his voice returns, it's husky, raspy, stripped. "What about you? Have you been back to the specialist?"

"Yeah." I swipe at my cheeks. "I'm taking shots now. Hormone shots so I can freeze my eggs."

"What? You're...you're freezing your *eggs?* What does that mean? How many times do you do it? Are there side effects?"

"Whoa, buddy," I chuckle and settle on the lumpy bed, laying back. "That gun was loaded."

"Sorry." He blows out a quick breath. "I just didn't know."

"Because I'm over thirty-five, I'll have fewer viable eggs. So I do multiple rounds to increase my chances of a pregnancy. And since I'm in perimenopause, my chances are diminished even more. Fortunately, once the eggs are frozen, they don't age, so I can...you know. When I'm ready. And if I think I might want more than one baby, well, I have to do it more times."

"Do you think you want more than one baby?" he asks, the

curiosity in his voice barely-checked, straining on the leash.

The chaos of Kayla's house, five kids singing together, fighting, looking out for each other comes to me. Saturday mornings with my siblings, cleaning the house, eating macaroni and cheese.

"I think I might," I say with a little surprised laugh.

"This could be..." His words break and then rush ahead. "Tru, this could be *ours.*"

I haven't allowed myself to think of it that way, that what I'm doing now might be my only hope to have kids...with him. That it may be the foundation for *our* family. Until we get through this season, through Aiko's pregnancy, I won't think that way.

"I better go," I tell him, pulling his shirt over my face so I can absorb the vestiges of him in its fibers. "I have an early morning."

"Call again if you need to. I'd like that." He sighs. "I need it, Kimba."

So do I. We'll see...

"Goodbye, Ez."

I hang up before he says he loves me because there's no way I'll be able to stop myself from saying it back. Saying it louder. Meaning it more than maybe I ever have.

I sit up, walk over to the table, pick up the little pouch.

Tru, this could be ours.

This time when I try, the needle goes right in.

CHAPTER FORTY-EIGHT

Ezra

"IT'S JUST ME!"

Mona's voice booms from the kitchen, and my new daughter Mai, swaddled in my arms, jerks at the sound.

"Hell." I rock her a bit until the little pinch between her eyebrows levels out. She settles again, her rosebud mouth rooting even in her sleep.

"Jack?" Mona calls. "Where are you?"

"Mo!" I whisper-hiss. "In my office. How 'bout that inside voice?"

She appears at my office door, dressed in a hot pink flowing dress and wearing dangerously high heels for a woman I've rarely seen out of Chucks. Her locs are swept up and pinned with a matching flower behind her ear.

"Sorry." She covers her mouth. "I'm still getting used to having a baby in the house."

"So am I," I say, offering her as much of a grin as my tired body can produce. "You have on makeup and fancy shoes. What gives, Janet? Obama coming to town? That's the only man I've ever known you to dress up for."

"Very funny." She walks over to my desk and lays the back of her hand on Mai's forehead. "Fever broke?"

"Yeah." I kiss Mai's hair, inhaling the smell of baby shampoo. "Hers did, but now Aiko's sick."

"You're kidding? You guys can't *buy* a break. How's Noah?"

"Apparently immunologically resistant to every strain of sickness. I told him it's all the vitamins I've been force-feeding him for years." I nod to her attire. "Where *are* you headed?"

"I have a date." She fiddles with an earring shaped like a fan and doesn't quite meet my eyes.

Fiddling? Mona?

"Have I met this guy? What are his intentions toward you?" I ask, only half-joking. I do feel like her protective big brother, even though we're the same age. She hasn't dated much since her divorce and I don't want to see her get hurt.

"You haven't met him, and that dumb second question is why."

"Seriously, where'd you meet him, Mo? Tinder? Bumble? Show me his profile."

"Church," she says, lifting her chin and looking at me pointedly. "He's a deacon at my mama's church. No jokes, please, about my weed or my wine or my vibrators or how I'm not—"

"No jokes. I haven't even met him and I already know he's not good enough for you."

Her eyes widen and then soften. "Awww. Thanks, boss."

"Besides I'll be living vicariously through you." I look at the mess on my desk and Mai in the crook of my arm. "It's gonna be a rough night. This is the longest she's slept in days. I don't expect it to last. Every time I try to put her down, she wakes up, and I need to finish my part on these grants before the book drops next week and the tour starts."

"Look, I can cancel this. Jamal and I can go out any time."

"Jamal, is it?"

She rolls her eyes and her lips twitch. "I'm serious. I'll text him."

"No way. School's finally out and you've been carrying a lot of extra load for me lately. Go. Have fun. I'll be fine."

"You sure?"

"Positive."

"I know it's a lot," she says. "But bright side is school's out and, as much as I know you'll hate leaving Mai with Aiko alone, it will be good to have some time to yourself out on tour. These last few months have been brutal."

New baby. Finishing the school year. Preparation for the book release.

Missing Kimba. All the time. Every minute of every day.

"Speaking of school being out," Mona says, pulling out her phone, "I have something that might make you laugh."

"A laugh I could use." I consider the laptop in front of me and the color-coded spreadsheet. "Before I dive into this."

She walks around and lays her phone on the desk so I can see. "Keep the volume low so we don't wake Mai," she says, already grinning. "You're gonna love this."

It's a video on Instagram of our step team's latest choreography in YLA's courtyard.

"Does that say a hundred thousand views?" I look from her phone to Mona's smiling face.

"We've gone viral, Jack. Soon *Ellen* might want us. Wouldn't that be perfect timing with your book coming out?"

"I'm so proud of them." I shake my head. "They keep amazing me."

"Right?" She presses the home button on her Instagram app, and I do a double take at the post that comes up.

"Oh, shit," she mutters, biting her bottom lip.

It's Kimba with some guy. Some tall, Idris Elba lookalike. He's probably around my height, but bulkier. His hand is at her waist, and she's laughing up at him. Her hair is pressed straight and spills around her shoulders, bare in a formal strapless dress.

We haven't talked much since she called from Alabama. The occasional text, a phone call at Christmas. Usually initiated by her. This is her plan. Her terms, and I'm trying my best to respect what she says she needs. I know there was a part of her afraid my feelings would change, deepen for Aiko as we went through the pregnancy. She couldn't have been more wrong. If anything, over the last few months, Aiko and I remembered why we were friends in the first place. I get why Kimba wanted to wait. Our situation was complicated and difficult and unstable, but I've gotten through it counting on our promise that there wouldn't be anyone else.

Who is this good-looking motherfucker?

"What the hell?" I grit out, grabbing Mona's phone from my desk.

"That's nothing," Mona says hastily, trying to get the phone back from me. I stand and walk Mai and me out of her reach. "Ezra, don't overreact."

"You've seen this?" I tear my eyes from the screen, from Kimba's bright smile to Mona's guilty expression.

"It's not a big deal."

Reading The Shade Room's post, it seems like I'm not the only one who thinks it might be.

Be still our woke hearts! Kimba Allen, political badass, and Israel Hammond, professor, activist, author and thirst bucket-worthy, out together for a night on the town? We full-time stan for this hook-up.

I've heard of Israel Hammond, but have always seen him as a...thinker. Not this burly man. And I've never thought of him with Kimba.

"Is this real?" I ask Mona, shooting her a sharp look. "Kimba said..."

She said she didn't want anyone else, but that was nearly a year ago. She's probably tired of waiting—not that I asked her to. I assumed this was as difficult, as lonely for her, as it is for me.

She doesn't look lonely in this photo.

"We haven't talked much lately." Mona takes her phone from me carefully, like it's a loaded weapon. "But I do know her life is crazy right now. Not only did her firm take on Congressman Ruiz and Keith, but there's a few other key races she said needed support. She's stretched really thin."

"I know."

"So are you. Once election season is over—"

"I know." My jaw aches I'm holding it so tight. "You don't have to reassure me, Mo. I get it."

It's quiet, her looking at me and me looking at Mai.

"Don't keep Jamal waiting," I tell her, my voice even. "I don't want you to be late."

"Ezra, it's nothing."

"Right. You better go."

She dips to kiss Mai's cheek. "I'll check on you guys tomorrow."

"Thanks," I say, giving her a smile that *I* know *she* knows isn't real.

Mona's heavy sigh speaks for her before she heads out toward the back exit.

As soon as the kitchen door closes behind her, I pick up my phone, my finger hovering over Kimba's contact. I look down at Mai as if she might stop me before it's too late. "I'm gonna regret this, huh, little girl?"

I dial anyway.

It rings four times and I'm formulating the message I'll leave on Kimba's voicemail when she picks up.

"Ezra?"

Her live voice throws me for a second.

"Uh, yeah. Tru, hey."

I sound about as awkward as I felt at our middle-school dance. I just call her out of the blue like this? Like we talk every day? We don't. We haven't.

"Everything okay? Noah? The baby?" She pauses to clear her throat. "Aiko?"

"They're sick. I mean, Mai's been sick, but her fever broke. Aiko just got whatever Mai had, I guess. Noah's Teflon."

"Of course he is." Her laugh is low and husky, familiar and missed. "And you? Are you okay?"

"Yeah. I'm fine. Who's Israel Hammond?"

That was not subtle.

"Oh. Well, Iz and I—"

"Oh, it's Iz? That's what you call him?"

That was not low-key anything.

"That's what *all* his friends call him, yes," she says, her voice slowing, stiffening. "Did you want to ask me something, Ezra?"

"I saw a post on Instagram."

"The Shade Room? Yeah. I heard about it. Somehow, I didn't peg you as a Shade Room kinda guy."

"I'm not." I pause, give myself a second to get my shit together better. "Are you seeing him? Or...do you want to see him?"

"I'm not seeing him, no. Our interests intersect, and we've known each other for years. He has a girlfriend."

"The Shade Room didn't mention that."

"He's very...private." She chuckles. "I actually think he's a little self-conscious about it. She's younger than he is and used to be his TA back in the day."

I'd feel like an idiot if it wasn't for the fact that my impulsive, jealous phone call means I get to talk to her.

"I pre-ordered your book." Her voice is warm. My arm holding Mai is asleep. I'm so exhausted I can barely keep my eyes open, and I still have a shit ton of work to do before I can sleep, but I'd stay on the phone with Kimba all night if I could.

"Thanks. That's you and my mom. One step closer to a bestseller."

"I'm excited for you. Proud of you."

"How's the campaign going? Or campaigns. Mona says you're running a few."

"Well, obviously, Congressman Ruiz is our main concern, but we did take on a few smaller races. Nothing we can't handle."

"Seems like a tight race. I mean between Ruiz and Colson."

"Very much so. One of the tightest, hardest I've ever been in. Colson's tough and plays dirty. We're in the fight of our lives."

"I have no doubt you'll figure it out."

"I hope so. And you? How are things there? Besides the sickness."

"Good." I hesitate. "I found a house nearby."

The silence from the other end comes alive with a dozen questions she doesn't voice, but I know are there.

"It needs a lot of work," I go on, "but it's just one street over so I could still be around for Noah and Mai, close to the school."

"Oh. That's…that's great. I didn't realize you—"

"I told you I would move out."

"I know you did."

"I miss you." The truth makes its way up from the deepest parts of me and shows in my voice. "It's almost unbearable sometimes."

"I know," she whispers, her voice cracking. "I miss you, too. I—"

"Kimba, what the hell?" a female voice demands from her side of the call. "You just leave the field in the middle of a battle to take a call? We need you."

I'm such an idiot. I got jealous and called, pulling her away from the very thing she told me she needs to focus on.

"I'm sorry," I say quickly. "I'll let you go."

"If I can't leave a meeting for two minutes without things falling apart," Kimba says flatly, "what the hell am I paying you for, Felita?"

"Well, your two minutes are almost up," Felita replies, the tension in her voice easing some. "And then I start charging overtime."

Kimba chuckles. "Get back in there. I'm coming."

"Mateo was asking for you," Felita says. "Just wanted you to know."

"I said I'm coming." Kimba waits until a door clicks closed. "Sorry. I should probably—"

Mai's wail cuts off whatever Kimba started to say. I look down into miserable blue eyes. She's tired and probably hungry by now. With Aiko sick, too, I'll use the milk she expressed that's in the fridge.

"That's quite a set of pipes she's got," Kimba says. "I better let you go. I have to go anyway. Apparently, the world burns down if I leave a meeting."

Mai's lungs shift into another gear.

"Shhh." I bounce her and speed walk to the kitchen to get the milk. "Tru, maybe we can—"

"Kimba," a deep voice says from the other end.

"Mateo, hey."

"I could use your weigh-in on this if we don't want to be down *another* five points tomorrow." There's a bite to his voice, and I want to tell him to handle his own damn five points.

"Right," she says. "I'm coming now."

I hear the door close decisively.

"I really have to go, Ez."

"I get it," I say, opening the refrigerator in search of the bottles I know Aiko left, but I can't find. Mai's wailing doesn't let up, so I speak louder to make sure Kimba hears me. "I just called because I miss you like hell. When this is over—"

"Yes," she says, her voice low and tired and sad. "When this is over."

CHAPTER FORTY-NINE

Kimba

"WELL, WE GAVE IT OUR BEST SHOT," I TELL MATEO RUIZ.
"That we did," he says, his eyes solemn.

I squeeze his hand and lean forward with a grin. "I told you we were gonna make history."

The sobriety that has hung around him all night as he fully grasped what he has achieved lightens, and he smiles. "There's no question—I couldn't have done this without you."

"It was an honor to be on your team, *Governor*."

Music reaches us through the walls of the hotel, and he proffers his arm to me. "I guess I better report to the dance floor. They're playing my song."

When we step out into the hall, his wife and family are waiting, along with a security detail. His wife watches him with such pride, it touches even my politically jaded heart. I allow them to walk ahead, to make their entrance into the ballroom where they're greeted by wild, almost deafening applause. That's the sound of people who have witnessed history and pulled off what was practically a political miracle. I'm humbled to have been a part of it.

I use a different door than the one that led to the stage. The governor's inaugural ball has assembled Georgia's most powerful, influential citizens all in one room. I make my way to the table designated for my friends and family. Piers, Carla, Felita and the rest of my team convene there, and we begin our own private celebration.

"Excellent work," I say, toasting them all with my glass of champagne. "You are the best of the best, and I wouldn't want to do this with anyone else. Let's keep making history. Let's keep making a difference."

"Let's keep making money," Piers interjects with a laugh.

"I have no objection to that either." I smile over the fragile rim of my glass. "Girl's gotta get her paper."

"So what's next, boss?" Carla asks, sipping her champagne.

"Believe it or not…" I sigh. "We need to start shifting our focus to President Cade's re-election campaign."

"Already, huh?" Piers asks, biting into a fancy pig in a blanket.

"It'll be a lot different than electing him the first time. Now he has an actual governing record that everyone will want to pick apart," I remind them. "But Maxim Cade is a once-in-a-lifetime candidate. The man himself will be our greatest resource."

"Excuse me," a deep, familiar voice drawls from behind me. "Can your brother get in on this celebration?"

I turn to grin at Keith and study him with pride, not just because he looks so handsome in his tux, but because he comported himself so wonderfully during his own campaign. Because he's standing with his wife, who looks genuinely happy and has for some time.

"Congressman Allen," I tease. "I do believe congratulations are in order to you, too."

"I literally couldn't have done it without you, sis." He looks from me to my team who helped him, too. "Without all of you. I can't thank you enough."

"I'm sure I'll think of a way you can," I say.

They all laugh along as my mother, Kayla, and her husband Lawrence walk up and take their seats at the table. Carla scoots over so Mama can sit beside me.

"It's a great night for the Allen family," Mama says. "What is it your father always said? Big moves make big waves. Do big things. Make big waves."

She looks at me and then to Keith, who sits with his arm draped over the back of Delaney's chair. "He would be proud of you."

She shifts her eyes to Kayla. "Proud of you all. Not just for tonight, but for how you're living your lives, serving others. That is the Allen legacy."

The emotion etched into Keith's and Kayla's faces pricks my heart. I blink back tears. I've found myself close to crying more over the last year and a half than I have my entire life. Probably all the hormones I've had to inject into this body, but I hope it's not a permanent state of affairs.

"It is a great night for the Allens," Keith says, his grin growing even wider. "Not only am I going to be a congressman, I'm going to be a father again. Delaney's pregnant with our third."

Everyone at the table claps and exclaims and pats my brother on the back. Joy and jealousy wrangle in me. I lift one and squash the other, offering my brother and Delaney a genuine smile.

"I'm gonna be an auntie again, huh? That's incredible. I'm so excited for you guys."

"Laney says if I think being a congressman means I don't have to change diapers," Keith says, leaning over to kiss his wife's cheek, "I can think again."

We all laugh, but my smile is starting to hurt. At the fertility clinic, I have a freezer full of eggs and no guarantees. Now that the campaign is over, I need to figure out what I want to do with them.

"You look so pretty tonight," Mama leans over to tell me as everyone at the table returns to their dinners and conversations.

"Thank you, Mama."

Lorette styled my hair into an elaborate diadem of curls. Lotus created my cayenne-colored off-the-shoulder gown specifically for this occasion. Its mermaid design sighs around my curves, curves I've had to work hard to keep in check the last year and a half as my weight fluctuated, the hot flashes flared and the mood swings swung, all while managing the nation's most hotly-contested gubernatorial campaign.

A year and a half.

My entire adult life has been measured in runs, in races. Mayors. Governors. Senators. President. I've never regretted the personal sacrifices I made for each campaign. I saw it as a call to service, putting people in positions to make a difference.

Tikkun Olam.

Repair the world.

Ezra went about it his way, and I've gone about it mine.

Ezra.

Heat coats the inside of my throat and the plate in front of me blurs on the table through a sudden film of tears. A sense of purpose has driven me every step in every race, and it's always been enough. More than enough. It's been fulfilling. For the first time, as happy as I am to have done my part, this victory feels hollow somehow.

"Tell me something," Mama says, her voice pitched low enough for only me to hear.

I turn my head to stare into her wise, dark eyes.

"All you did to make these other folks happy," Mama asks. "When is it Kimba's turn?"

I glance around the room. Mateo and his wife stand in a receiving line, accepting everyone's congratulations. Kayla and Lawrence eat from each other's plates, checking their phones every few minutes for messages from the sitter. Keith and Delaney laugh and talk softly, basking in the glow of his victory and their baby news.

For the last eighteen months, this night has glowed at the end of the tunnel, a beacon that kept me on task and focused. This night was my reward. *He* was my reward.

"You're so much like your daddy," Mama huffs, but softens it with a smile. "Needed everything to be done his way. Had his lists and goals and it needed to go the way he planned it. Let me tell you what I told him. Life don't care about your plans. Life will make a mess of your plans, honey."

Mama squeezes my hand. "Haven't you waited long enough? Hasn't he? Are you ready to clean up that mess yet?"

I've spent my whole adult life cleaning up other people's messes. For the greater good, yes, but I've become adept at covering naked asses, spinning bad decisions and making indiscretions go away. I've never met a mess I couldn't handle...until Ezra Stern. It's easier to deal with someone else's mess than it is to clean your own. Hand me someone's problem? I can fix it. But when Aiko got pregnant with Ezra's baby, that was not just their future on the line. It was mine. *My* happiness in the balance. *My* heart on my sleeve. I glance at Mama, but she's not looking at me. She's caressing that tiny ice chip diamond Daddy gave her more than forty years ago, so small you can barely see it from a distance. She's lost the love of her life.

Will I lose mine?

"I have to go." I stand and spread my farewell around the table. "I'll see you...when I see you. I got shit to do."

Carla's startled glance bounces from me to the stage. "But Congressman...*Governor* Ruiz has a speech planned. He'll acknowledge you, bring you up on stage. We talked about this."

Bring me up on stage. Acknowledge me. I don't do the things I do so people can pat me on the damn back. The only thing Ruiz can do for me is keep the promises he made when he campaigned. And the only man I need to hear call my name is not in this room.

"You go," I tell Carla, grabbing my clutch from the table. I look to Piers, Felita. "Or one of you. I don't care."

"You're really leaving now?" Felita asks, a frown gathering between her brows. "The speech is later in the program. You don't want to wait? What do we tell the governor?"

I glance at Mama, warmed by the knowing approval in her eyes, in her smile. This may be my greatest move yet.

"Tell him I waited long enough."

I don't know where Ezra lives.

I got off his old exit only to realize I don't know where his new house is, or if he's even in it. He said he was renovating a house "nearby," but I can't plug "nearby" into Google maps.

A lot has changed for him over the last few months, least of which may be a new house. As I predicted, his book was a huge success, hitting all the lists. I was in the thick of managing multiple campaigns, but I did see him on a few morning shows. Texted him my congrats. His book is in airports. There's a Netflix documentary in the works about the YLA story. New baby. New book. New success.

New house?

Absent of a better idea, though I'm sure there is one, I park in front of their house. It looks like no one is home, but then the front door swings open.

"Shit." I resist the urge to duck down behind the steering wheel like a stalker.

Aiko walks out onto the porch, hand in hand with a tall man...who is not Ezra. I recognize the guy who stood awkwardly by the door with Aiko's luggage the day she dropped the bombshell about her pregnancy.

Chaz.

I wish I could disappear, but I just sit perfectly still, hoping my mother's Benz will miraculously become invisible before they notice it.

"Kimba?" Aiko asks from the driveway where a car, presumably Chaz's, is parked. "Is that you?"

Great.

I open the door and poke my head out, smiling as if it's perfectly normal for me to be sitting outside her house dressed in formal wear.

"Hi." My wave is as stiff as my smile. "I was just wondering if…is Ezra home by any chance?"

"He might be." Aiko smiles, tilts her head to the side. "I can't say for sure since he doesn't live here anymore."

"Oh. Right. Could you maybe…direct me?"

"Next street over." She points to the right. "Fourth house on the left. Gray with red shutters."

"Uh, thank you." I smile at Chaz. "Good…seeing you again."

His wry smile mocks us all.

I climb back in and pull away before this becomes any more cringeworthy. Ezra's house is easy to find. The shutters are red and his Rover is in the driveway. I get out of the car and stand in January cold for a moment, searching my mind for the perfect thing to say.

"I'm ready?" I ask out loud, leaning against the car. "Sorry I took so long. Let's do this."

I keep trying out opening lines all the way from the car, down the driveway, up the steps and onto the porch. When I ring the doorbell, I still don't know what I'll say, but I know I can't wait any longer.

"Kimba."

Ezra's tall frame fills the doorway. I can't see beyond him into the house, but I also can't tear my eyes from his face anyway. Stubble shadows the ridge of his jaw. His hair is a little longer than I've seen it in awhile, the coarse curls dark and springy. His eyes under the porch light – volatile blue. The emotion emanating from him, a tempest in a thumbnail, barely contained.

"Can I come in?" I ask.

"Uh, sure. Yeah." He steps back, allowing me entrance. A modern chandelier of wood and blown glass hangs from the foyer ceiling. There's very little furniture in the sitting room off to the right – a couch and a television. A mismatched coffee table.

"You just moved in?" I ask, my question slicing through the tension.

"Few months ago. I didn't want to choose the furniture…by

myself."

He holds my stare and I bite my bottom lip, look away. I'm always in control, but I feel completely out of my depth right now. What if he *has* found someone else? Even though Aiko seems to be with Chaz, who knows if Ezra remained single? He's still staring at me, his eyes intense, alert. His posture, deceptively indolent, leaning against the wall with his arms folded. But there's so much tension in his broad shoulders, in the tight muscles of his neck.

Unsure what to say next, I step farther down the hall to inspect photos on the wall. There's a series of collages. The first holds pictures of Noah, as to be expected. Lots of them with Ezra and a baby girl who could only be Mai.

There's no pain in my heart seeing her, at first swaddled in Ezra's arms and then growing bigger, rounder. Eventually standing on her own, her smile bright with a few tiny teeth. There's no jealousy or resentment. How could there be? With her midnight blue eyes, sulky-sweet mouth and dark curls, she's so obviously, like Noah, an extension of Ezra.

And I fall in love with her on sight.

"She's beautiful, Ez," I breathe.

"She is." He comes to stand beside me, slips his hand into mine. I squeeze his fingers, but still can't look away from the little dark-haired cherub Noah holds like a priceless piece of art. Ezra runs a finger over a picture with both his children. "He's great with her."

I nod, still processing the strength of my response to his daughter. My eyes drift to a collage of photos on the wall beside the one with him and his kids. At first, I don't recognize the two children in the photos. They're obviously older pictures, not shiny and glossy like the others. It's easily a dozen of them. A girl and a boy at the park, on swings. Riding bikes. Eating dinner, surrounded by family. And at the center, them as babies in a bathtub.

"It's us." I can only gather enough air to manage those words. "Ezra, it's—"

"Us." He smiles and points to the photos on the wall. In one, it's a Saturday evening meal, one at my old house. Our parents are there, my father and mother holding hands. Kayla, Keith. Ezra and me.

"Where did you find these?"

"My mother's attic, garage. She has a lot more. These were just some of my favorites." He pauses, turns his head to stare at my profile. "Are you here to stay?"

I don't look away from the two babies at the center of the collage, caught mid-splash in the tub. A lifetime. We've known each other all our lives, yet missed so much. Wasted so much time. Not anymore.

"If you still want me."

The words have barely left my mouth. He pulls me into him, pushes me to the wall. His body cages mine, protective and aggressive at once. I slip my hand into a gap between the buttons of his shirt, finding velvet over stone beneath. He squeezes my ass with one hand and clasps my neck with the other, tipping my mouth up and open. His kiss is deep, craving, the press of his shoulders and chest and hips and thighs a delicious weight that pins me in place so he can take all he wants.

God, how I've missed this—missed *him*. The textures, the taste and scent of him. He feels and tastes and smells like *mine*. I reach between us to palm his cock, sliding my hand up and over the hard, extended length of him.

"Let me give you a tour of the house," he pants into my neck. Grabbing my hand, he drags me up the stairs. "There's a kitchen, a half bath, a rooftop patio and some other shit."

He crosses the landing, rushes us down the hall to a large bedroom and pulls me into his arms.

"Tour's over."

I drop my forehead to his shoulder and laugh, trying to catch my breath. "I don't get to see the rooftop patio?"

He sets his thumbs under my chin and pushes up until our gazes lock. "After."

"After what?"

His eyes go black-blue and he licks the arch of my neck, sucks my earlobe, cups my breast, brushing the nipple to hard life. He takes my mouth, the kiss a drugging, thorough exploration that makes my head spin.

"I want you so bad," he says, his breath coming harshly. "My dick is telling me to take you right here on the spot."

He gives me a head-to-toe heated perusal, licking his lips. "But you're my gift. I also want to take my time unwrapping you, spreading you out on my bed."

"As long as you're inside me in the next five minutes, I don't care which option you take. It's been a long time, Ez. I need dick, not options."

"Bed then."

Holding his hand, I walk backward toward the large bed, never taking my eyes off him. It's been so long since we were in the same room, much less alone. The bedroom is barely lit by one single lamp. When my knees hit the edge of the mattress, I reach behind me to undress.

"No." Ezra gently turns me around, sliding his hands over my bare shoulders and arms, settling at my hips. "I want to."

The hiss of his breath through his teeth mingles with the hiss of the zipper as he lowers it, peeling the brocaded silk back so air kisses and pebbles my bare skin. The dress slouches at my hips and then surrenders, falling to the floor in a spill of decadence around my ankles. He traces the bare curve of my ass in the skimpy thong, my thighs. He slips his fingers under the lacy scraps at my hips and slides the underwear down. I step out of it and he caresses the inside of my thigh.

"On the bed."

His deep voice breaks the quiet in a rumbly rasp, and I climb on the bed, waiting for him. My breath comes heavy. My stomach muscles clench, anticipating his hardness. Fully clothed, he stretches out and pulls me on top, straddling his hips. He urges me up farther until my thighs bracket his face, my pussy hovering over his mouth. Our eyes connect, never breaking contact when the slightly callused pads of his fingers spread me open.

"Such a pretty pussy," he whispers, close enough that his breath mists the wetness of my most private place. A sanctuary I've reserved for him, for just this moment since the last time we kissed.

The first swipe of his tongue forces the air from my lungs, wrenching pleasure from my core and streaming through my legs.

"Dammit." I flatten my palms against the wall over the headboard. My knees tremble as he laves me again and again and again, the languid, steady sweep of his tongue and lips there nearly too much. My knees pull in against a pleasure that's almost unbearable, but he grips my ass, pressing me harder into his mouth, giving me no respite from the hungry kisses he lavishes on me.

My forehead drops to the wall between my palms and I rotate my hips in rhythm with the glorious work of his tongue. He passes his thumb through my wetness, caressing my clit with each stroke and then tracing the puckered track between my buttocks, pressing there.

"Can I?"

I nod, pushing back, anticipating penetration in the place too rarely touched. His thumb slips in, big, intrusive, perfect. My breath hitches at the tantalizing pressure, the sublime fullness. His other hand reaches up, cupping my breast while he pumps his thumb inside. I gasp, a shiver working itself through my body with sudden force. He slides his other hand down, leaving my breast, gliding over my belly, and finds the bud of throbbing nerves. He works me into a frenzy with the pressure inside and the delicate, unrelenting stroke across my clit. I churn my hips into his touch, caring about nothing but this urgency blooming inside me. It overtakes me, washing over every nerve ending with tsunami force that wrenches a sob from me. The orgasm uncoils, loosening my limbs and leaving me spent.

He slides from beneath my limp body, gently laying me flat onto the bed, turns me onto my back. Slack-jawed, arms and legs limp, I slit my eyes open. His eyes burn over my face, down the length of my body. There's so much barely leashed passion in his expression, in his eyes. I force my arm to move, reach up and smooth the muscle ticking in his jaw, brush the artfully sculpted bow of his mouth with my thumb. He turns his head into my hand, kisses my palm.

"I love you," I whisper, watching his long lashes fall, his eyes close as he absorbs the words, allows them to water the dry places I recognize because I've been dry without him, too. I've been lonely. I've been, at times, uncertain how this would work, how it would end. And now— love, relief, reunion.

He stands, stripping efficiently at the foot of the bed, tossing the jeans and shirt away. He's the same as I remember, muscles hewn from rock, skin cut from swathes of velvet, but having been so long without him, there's a novelty to his form. A freshness to his male beauty that I'll never take for granted again.

He slots lean hips between my spread legs. When he looks up, his face still wet from the time and care he took ensuring my pleasure, his eyes connect with mine, searing a thousand unspoken promises into my heart. There's a knowing between us, an intuition of body and soul and mind that I've never had with anyone else. At his first thrust, a hard, sure possession, I know I never will. He doesn't pull back, but stays buried inside me, his temple pressed to mine. He angles his head until only a breath separates our mouths. He closes the space, kissing me fiercely as he pushes in deeper. I wrap my legs around him, linking my ankles at the base of his spine. He moves, one sure thrust after another, slowly building the momentum between our bodies. Sweat beads, drips as he never lets up, the only sounds in the room our grunting and gasping and panting and urgent whispers of *more, faster, harder, please don't you ever stop.*

Finally, he groans into the curve of my neck, spilling into me, a hot flow of love and unleashed passion. I want it all, tightening my arms and legs around him like he's wisps of smoke that might drift away, like I could lose him if I'm not careful. The percussion of our hearts, mallets in our chests, slows. Our love-slicked limbs are a tangle of copper and bronze. I run my fingers through his hair, trace the muscles in his belly, caress the sinew at his hip, the corded arms. I hold his hand. My body is sated, but my heart hungers for him still, for unbroken contact. I want him until I'm full and running over and exhausted with affection. I can't stop touching him, making sure he is real and here and mine.

Still only mine.

Our bodies have cooled when he rolls away.

"No," I protest, my voice raw and husky. "Don't go yet."

"I'll be right back." He leans down and kisses my forehead.

I close my eyes and pull the duvet up and over my shoulders, relishing the warmth, the scent of us in the sheets. When he gently turns me over to face him, he's on his knees beside the bed, elbows propped on the mattress.

"Hey, handsome," I say sleepily, caressing the line of his brows, the bridge of his nose.

"Hey," he replies, his lips quirking, even though his eyes remain serious. "I want to talk to you about a few things."

"Okay." I drag myself up to sit with my back against the headboard and the covers tucked beneath my arms. "Talk."

"We kind of jumped right in," he says, linking our fingers on the sheets. "But I want to talk about what happened while we've been apart."

A chill skitters across my skin, stiffening my back and tensing my muscles. Is this where he confesses he *did* give in to temptation and sleep with Aiko once, twice, three times?

"What happened?" I ask, keeping my voice even and just the right degree of curious.

"I did what I needed to do," he says, studying the sheets. "I wanted to be there for Mai and Noah and Aiko, of course."

I gulp at the tears threatening, grit my teeth and brace for disappointment.

"I stayed there until Mai came, stayed for the first few months so I could be around to help as much as possible. Changing diapers, midnight feedings—the whole thing."

My heart clenches into a fist at the picture he paints of their family, their baby, their life together while we were apart.

"But we needed our own places to establish a new normal," he says. "Especially for Noah. He needed to see that separation to understand how our relationship was changing."

"Look," I say, deciding to just address my worst fears. "If you need to tell me that you…slipped…that you and Aiko—"

"I'm trying to assure you there *is* no me and Aiko," he cuts in, holding my eyes in a steady stare. "Not beyond Mai and Noah, and a long friendship. I knew what I wanted then and I know what I want now."

I don't ask, afraid to ask, to assume, but look away, hold my breath and wait.

"You." He squeezes my hand, tugs my fingers until I look into his eyes. "I only want you."

A relieved breath escapes the tight line of my mouth. "And Aiko? What does she want?"

"At first," he says, his mouth a wry curve, "she didn't know. It was hard for her to think of us differently, but she had no choice. She knows I'm in love with you, and she had to accept that she and I would never be what we were before."

"And?"

"And she gets it now." He chuckles, shaking his head. "Chaz helped."

"I saw him at your house. Your old house. I went there first."

"They're together. Chaz started coming back around when she was still pregnant. Now they're dating, sickeningly sweet, the whole nine."

"Well, that's unconventional."

"At no point has Aiko ever been conventional."

"And how is Noah adjusting to all of this?"

Ezra shrugs broad, naked shoulders. "He's pretty mature, unusually intelligent and open in a way that most kids aren't at his age. I think it helped that we never had a conventional relationship, never married. It has been an adjustment not seeing him quite as much. I mean, I'm around the corner, so I still see him every day, all the time, but it's different when you don't live under the same roof. He's with me a few days and with Ko the others. It works, but I'm always checking in with him, getting him to talk and tell me how he's doing."

I watch the man I love, the man I've known since he was a child, an awkward boy finding himself. I know him so well, and never have I seen him more in need of a pocket to shove his hand into.

Except he's nude.

He clears his throat, and some of the red that used to crawl over his cheeks all the time colors his neck. "So I thought now that my…situation is settled and the governor's race is over, maybe we could discuss our future."

I open my mouth and he rushes on before I can speak.

"First of all, if you want a baby, I do, too. Natural. Frozen eggs. IVF. I don't care. I want to make you happy, Tru."

I stare at the rugged symmetry of his features, the prominent nose and sculpted lips. The dark wing of his brows over African violet eyes. The cap of clipped curls. I remember this man as a boy, the awkward, lanky, too-big-for-his-body parts boy. He had to grow into the beauty of his face. I've seen the arc of his life, how he developed over time. Emotion scalds my throat and my lips tremble. Before I even knew how babies were made, I imagined ours.

"I would love to…" He clears his throat again. "I was hoping you'd consider…oh, hell."

He reaches to the floor and pulls up a black velvet box. My wide eyes connect with his, and we both swallow hard, on the cusp of something I wasn't sure would ever happen. He opens the box and I'm so shocked by what's in there, I laugh.

In the slit where a ring would normally be is the tab of a can.

"I was hoping you'd consider," he repeats, "marrying me again."

Again.

The years fall away, and we're those kids standing under an elm tree in the Sterns' backyard, laughing at shattered glass and sealed by vows we didn't understand. It's painfully sweet, that memory wrapping around my battered heart. As sweet as a million moments we shared before we could possibly grasp how rare and precious it was, what we had. We were each other's light and solace.

Hazak, Hazak, Venithazek.

Be strong, be very strong, and we will strengthen each other.

The prospect that we finally could live that out, that we could finally be partners for the rest of our lives and fulfill the promises we made in the shade of that tree, brings me to tears.

"Don't cry." Ezra brushes at my cheeks but can't stem the flow. "Tru, I—"

"Yes," I manage to whisper, barely able to see him through a scrim of tears. "I will marry you again."

He had to know I'd say yes, that I could never refuse him, but he looks shaken, a long sigh of relief rushing from his chest. He slowly pulls the tab from its velvet bed. It's bigger than a soda tab, but still barely fits when I extend a trembling hand, and he slips it as far as it will go onto my ring finger.

"Guess we'll have to get a replacement, fast." He chuckles.

There has never been a race, an election, a campaign, a win that has made me feel this way. It's the kind of contentment only found when you stand still. When you *stop* running long enough to run into yourself—to collide with your future and release the past. The path to this moment is paved with a million "ifs." If our parents had never argued, never fallen out. If the Sterns had never moved. If Ezra and I had found each other sooner. But every possibility changes *this* moment—shifts the path that has made us who we are at this very second. And I can't help but think when we were born on the same day, when we were made together, our path was set, even with its delays, detours and disillusions. We are made of choices and losses and triumphs and, yes, some happenstance. Ezra and I were made for this moment, made for each other exactly as we are now.

And looking into his eyes, I wouldn't change a thing.

EPILOGUE

Ezra
One Year Later

"Study your queen so you can give her what she wants without asking."

Nipsey Hussle,
Musician, Activist, Entrepreneur

CHRISTMAS AT THE STERNS' IS AN UNUSUAL AFFAIR.
A cohesion of traditions and religions and families. There's a Christmas tree that almost reaches the ceiling and stockings hanging over the fireplace. A menorah resides in the window and a mezuzah scroll guards nearly every door, courtesy of my mother. For dinner, we ate turkey and stuffing and macaroni and cheese and collard greens. Mrs. Allen's fried chicken made peace with Mom's fish and challah bread. Potato latkes, steamed rice and dumplings rounded out the meal, a hodgepodge of dishes to satisfy any palette. Chopsticks nestled between the forks and spoons.

Seated around our table? Three grandmothers- one Jewish, one Vietnamese, one black. All those nationalities convene in Noah and his little sister Mai, who squirmed the whole time to get away from the table so she could see her new puppy. Aiko sat with Chaz and Mama Tran, who added her legendary pho to our holiday menu. Mom and Stanley actually left New York. It's Stanley's first time in Atlanta, and he wants to see the King Center and have chicken and waffles before he leaves. As Atlanta sight-seeing goes, that's a pretty low bar that we can easily clear. Remarkably, as soon as Mrs. Allen and Mom saw each other, it was like old times. Not...secret affair old times, but talking in the kitchen while cooking, cackling over memories, sharing photos of grandchildren and catching up with the changes twenty-five years have wrought in their lives.

They've both lost their husbands. My mother has a new one. So much has changed since that first night when they bathed their babies together. After dinner, they insisted on cleaning up, and their incessant chatter, their laughter and reminiscing drifts through the house as we settle into board games and dessert. Our mothers even threatened to throw together a game of mah-jongg.

"Well, we survived our first Christmas," Kimba says, walking up beside me at the fireplace, taking my hand. "I mean, I'm not sure you can call it just Christmas when there's Baptists, Buddhists and Jews, but you know what I mean. The holidays."

"It's not the holiday we have in common." I look at our family, full of varying religions and practices. "It's each other. *We're* what brought us together."

Kimba nods, a contented smile on her face. Hard-earned contentment. We have taken a journey that would break most couples, but we aren't most.

We're soul mates.

As fanciful as that may sound, I believe it. Religion, politics, beliefs—all the things that form a person's worldview—none of them are as strong as what binds me to her: the connective tissue of our souls.

"Everyone's occupied," I whisper. "Let's go up to the roof."

She looks at me, one brow raised. "Should we sneak off when we have a full house?"

"We should sneak off *because* we have a full house." I bend to her ear. "I've barely kissed you all day in this asylum. These people are crazy."

She laughs, her lips, bare and pretty and full, spread into a smile. Hand in hand, we climb the two stories to reach the roof. The view from here is what sold me on this house. The Atlanta skyline, light-speckled buildings glittering at night like diamonds on a bed of black satin. A line of skyscrapers reaching for the stars, as aspirational as the people who live here. Kimba turns on the fairy lights. I light the firepit, pull out two champagne glasses and a bottle from the ice bucket behind the bar.

"You planned this, huh? Having your way with me on the roof?" She grins, nods to the bottle. "And you know I can't have that."

I turn the bottle so she can see the label. "It's sparkling cider, and yes, I've been fantasizing about having my way with you on the roof all day."

I fill the glasses and take one of the couches, sinking into the soft cushions. She grabs blankets from the nearby hutch and settles in front of me, her back pressed to my chest, and pulls the blankets over us.

"You cold?" I kiss the curls she's left loose and free tonight, handing her a glass of the honey-colored liquid.

She wiggles against me and drops her head into the curve of my neck and shoulder. "I'm fine for now."

"How do you think dinner went?" I ask, linking our fingers and resting them on her stomach.

"As well as can be expected with all we had going on." Her shoulders shake against me. "Your ex and her boyfriend were there with the children you had together. Our mothers were in the same room for the first time in twenty-five years since they broke off their *affair*. And your stepfather is here. It's just...all so weird. I thought Aiko getting pregnant was some Jerry Springer shit."

The richness of our laughter floats over the fire, out to the stars.

"Mona would have loved this," I tell her. "She would have been shaking her head and making fun of us all night."

"I hope she's having a good time. Meeting your boyfriend's family, it's a lot."

"She and Jamal have been dating for so long. It's about time she met his family."

"They've been dating off and on," Kimba corrects, "not exclusively for that long. I don't blame Mona for being cautious. She's been hurt before. She needed to know Jamal was serious."

"I'm happy for her." I hold up her left hand, study the square diamond I put there nearly a year ago. "I'm happy for us."

There was no long engagement. Why would there be? We were both sure. We married on Valentine's Day, barely a month past Governor Ruiz's inaugural ball, and started trying for a baby immediately. Actually before immediately.

"When should we tell them?" Kimba asks, pressing our hands to her flat stomach.

"I'd like to wait as long as we can."

"Why?" She tilts her head, catching my gaze over her shoulder. Her dark eyes, fringed with a thick veil of lashes, make me lose my train of thought. Make me lose my mind. They always have.

"Why do you want to wait?" she asks again, nudging her elbow into my ribs.

"It's our secret. I want to keep it just ours as long as we can. It's been a lot of work and some disappointment. I just want to savor it for a bit."

She swallows hard, disrupting the smooth line of her throat, and tears swim in her eyes. This isn't our first pregnancy. We lost one, so early we barely had time to celebrate, but it still hurt. Trying to have a baby when your body is hormonally resisting it in every way is difficult. Kimba manages the hot flashes and other symptoms of perimenopause with homeopathic remedies and yoga as much as she can, but there's no denying her body is marching in that direction. And we're fighting to get our babies before it's too late. We wanted to try naturally first, even though we have eggs frozen and waiting. The doctor was surprised that, considering the perimenopause, we were able to conceive not once, but twice.

"Let's tell our family in a few weeks," I propose. "And after the first trimester for everyone else."

She clears her throat, blinks to clear her eyes of lingering tears. "That sounds good. I'll tell Lennix and President Cade, of course."

I frown. Kimba is a political superstar. Race after race, she proves that, and the phones at Allen & Associates never stop ringing. I don't interfere, but I'll protect her from the candidates who would put their interests above hers, their campaigns over her health.

I'll protect her from herself.

"We need very clear instructions from the doctor, Tru," I say, tucking a curl behind her ear, kissing the curve of her neck. "I know you want to re-elect the president—"

"There is nothing I want more than this baby, Ez." She looks up at me, her eyes sober and settled. "Nothing. If I need to curtail my involvement in the campaign, I will. I promise I'll do everything the doctor tells me to."

I cup her breast, even fuller now that she's pregnant, brush my thumb over her nipple, and wait for the inevitable catch of her breath. "And what about what I tell you to do?"

She turns so her knees rest on either side of my legs, so she's straddling me. "Are you really trying to fuck your wife out in the open on this roof?"

"Wouldn't be the first time," I laugh, grabbing a fistful of curls and bringing her lips to mine in a fierce, tongue-tangling kiss. When the kiss slows, I roll my palms over the taut muscles of her back, over the swell of her ass, the supple line of her thighs. I would know her anywhere. The shape of her, the smell, the taste. Through the years, those things will change, but this living thread that has connected us since birth, it's inviolable.

"After this baby, you want another?" I ask. "We have eggs."

She laughs, a throaty, happy sound that wraps around me more warmly than this cashmere blanket. "We have eggs, Dr. Stern. After this one, let's see what my body has left. I'm down to try again."

I'm greedy. I wake up each morning starving for everything I can get from this life, from this woman, and want to offer everything I have to give. We spent two decades apart and for the rest of our lives, I'll be making up for lost time.

She looks down at me, the laughter dying. "But if not, we have Noah and Mai. I know they're not mine, but I love them like they are. I really do, Ez."

"I know you do." I lift the little tab suspended from the chain she wears around her neck, a symbol of our two weddings, of a lifelong love.

"You know Mama thinks Daddy set this all up, right?" she asks, catching my fingers at the necklace. "That he requested I present the awards, selected you, to bring us back together."

The memory of Joseph Allen, a giant in this city, taking time to talk for hours with me that day, furiously scribbling my dreams on a napkin as our coffee grew cold, is vivid in my mind. I unpacked my heart to him that day, and there's no way he could have seen what lay in my heart without seeing his daughter Tru.

"I wouldn't put it past him." My smile fades. "Maybe he wouldn't have if he'd known what you'd have to endure, living through someone else having my child."

Kimba drops her forehead to mine, slips her fingers into the hair at my nape.

"He wouldn't have changed a thing. Daddy knew firsthand how messy love can be," she says, her words wistful, certain across my lips. "Mama told me that love isn't tidy, and she's right, but all the mess we had to wade through to have this, to have each other, was worth it."

Nothing life has thrown at us so far—not a twenty-year separation, not Aiko's pregnancy or any of the challenges that come with negotiating such a complex blended family like ours—have managed to crack the foundation we laid for this marriage starting the day we were born.

Noah's laughter, Mai's squeals, the clack of mah-jongg tiles – the symphony of our life together—clamors from below. A cacophony that from the outside looking in probably seems discordant and sounds like a mass of noise. But to us it makes sense, all the notes fitting together. Harmony where there could be chaos. The tastes, the sounds, the stories, gathered from distant lands, borne by our blood, blended in our bonds.

Forever.

Want MORE of Kimba and Ezra?
Click this link to receive their BONUS EPILOGUE!

https://www.subscribepage.com/queenmovebonusscene

I'd love to chat! I'm in my reader group on Facebook every day. That's where I connect with readers most. Join me there!
http://bit.ly/KennedyRyanBookGroup

Author's Note

As I was writing, I had a few early readers wonder if I'd made up the Crown Act Kimba discusses. I didn't. It's a real thing and so very vital in the fight for workplace parity, not only between men and women, but to protect people of all ethnicities and traditions against systemic bias.

Learn more about the Crown Act here:

https://www.thecrownact.com

And as for the book Kimba gives to Noah, Ezra's Big Shabbat Question, it's an actual book written by Aviva L. Brown. She writes books about Jews of Color, different types of Jewish families, and every day Jewish life.

Sign up for the Blue Box Press/1001 Dark Nights Newsletter
and be entered to win a Tiffany Lock necklace.

There's a contest every quarter!

Go to www.1001DarkNighs.com to subscribe.

**As a bonus, all subscribers can download
FIVE FREE exclusive books!**

The Kingmaker
All the King's Men Duet, Book 1
By Kennedy Ryan

"This story sets a new bar in the genre... Exquisitely written, meticulously researched, tender, yet oh-so steamy--this is the Mary Poppins of Contemporary Romances: practically perfect in every way." -- Natasha Is A Book Junkie

Power. Passion. Betrayal.

Raised to rule, bred to lead and weaned on a diet of ruthless ambition.
In a world of haves and have nots, my family has it all, and I want nothing to do with it.

My path takes me far from home and paints me as the black sheep. At odds with my father, I'm determined to build my own empire. I have rules, but Lennix Hunter is the exception to every one of them. From the moment we meet, something sparks between us. But my family stole from hers and my father is the man she hates most. I lied to have her, and will do anything to keep her. Though she tries to hate me, too, the inexorable pull between us will not be denied.

And neither will I.

THE KINGMAKER is the epic and powerful first installment in the All The King's Men Duet by USA Today bestselling and RITA® Award winning author, Kennedy Ryan.

* * * *

My father would lecture me until his face turned blue.
He'd send the authorities searching for me.
A man I met only once before tonight, a stranger whose last name I just discovered an hour ago, has me alone on a nearly deserted street in a foreign country at three a.m.
It may not be wise, but I'll be damned if I would be anywhere else

right now. Not safely tucked into my top bunk at the hostel knowing Maxim was out there wanting my company. We've been wooing each other with tiny touches and furtive brushes and lingering glances. I'm not sure how much longer I can stand it.

"So you thought of me, too, huh?" His grin is rakish on the handsome "somebody" face. There's a Kennedy vibe about him. Not just the dark, dappled hair, or the tall, fit body, or the confidence in his shoulders. It's his ideals and the iron will barely hidden beneath the casual manner. I'm not fooled. This man is not casual. He bleeds ambition. I wonder if he tries to hide it—to blend in with everyone else. It's laughable to think he could camouflage his driven nature and be something that he's not. Be domesticated when he is indeed, like Kimba said, a wolf.

"You're probably already too conceited for me to answer that." I grin back and start walking again.

"Tell me." He says it like he means it, grasping my arm gently and halting our steps again. "You thought of me?"

Words rise and fall in my throat. I could tell him that I didn't realize it until right now, but he was a bar no other guy ever cleared. That it had nothing to do with how handsome he was, or his formidable body or dazzling smile. That the moment he stepped between me and that dog at the protest, something inside me recognized him as more than the rest.

I can't say any of that, so I answer with only a solemn nod. There's a wild flare in his eyes, like that ambition, that will I see tucked beneath his easy demeanor, roaring to life. He places a hand on either side of my face, his palms to my cheeks, and caresses the sides of my neck.

"Can I kiss you, Lennix?"

The question lights a fiery thread that binds us to one another, and it burns so strong, so hot, that words seem superfluous. How could he not know I want that, too? He has to know I hunger for this kiss, but I nod again.

He slowly backs us up a few feet to where the cobblestone street meets a wall. We're partially hidden in the shadow this building casts. There's stone at my back, the Amstel river glittering ahead, and Maxim's body flush against mine. I feel every hardened ridge of him perfectly fitting to my body. His fingers slide into my hair. He looks down at me, and though his face is painted in shades of night, I see those gem eyes, gleaming bright and green, staring at my mouth.

He doesn't ask again if he can kiss me. He just does, bending to test the texture of my lips with one swipe of his tongue and then another, like I'm a lollipop he wants to know how many licks it takes to get to the center of. He probes at me, seeking something I want to give. I open and take him in completely, tasting that last glass of whiskey and him. God, *him*. I want to crawl down his throat. My hands climb his shoulders and rove into the thick hair falling around his nape, all the while I tilt my head to get and give as much as possible.

If a kiss has a color, this one is the muted shades of the sky overhead, a ménage à trois of midnight and indigo and moonshine silver. If a kiss has a sound, this one is the concert of our breaths and sighs and moans. If a kiss has a taste, it tastes like this. Hunger flavored with yearning and spiced with desperation. With bites and growls and tender licks and soothing whimpers. Perfectly served portions of sweet and scorching.

About Kennedy Ryan

A RITA® Award Winner and *USA Today* Bestselling author, Kennedy Ryan writes for women from all walks of life, empowering them and placing them firmly at the center of each story and in charge of their own destinies. Her heroes respect, cherish and lose their minds for the women who capture their hearts.

Kennedy and her writings have been featured in *Chicken Soup for the Soul*, *USA Today*, *Entertainment Weekly*, *Glamour* and many others. She has always leveraged her journalism background to write for charity and non-profit organizations, but has a special passion for raising Autism awareness. The co-founder of LIFT 4 Autism, an annual charitable book auction, she has appeared on *Headline News*, *The Montel Williams Show*, NPR and other media outlets as an advocate for ASD families. She is a wife to her lifetime lover and mother to an extraordinary son.

Find out more about Kennedy at https://kennedyryanwrites.com.

Discover 1001 Dark Nights Collection Seven

Click here *for more information.*

THE BISHOP by Skye Warren
A Tanglewood Novella

TAKEN WITH YOU by Carrie Ann Ryan
A Fractured Connections Novella

DRAGON LOST by Donna Grant
A Dark Kings Novella

SEXY LOVE by Carly Phillips
A Sexy Series Novella

PROVOKE by Rachel Van Dyken
A Seaside Pictures Novella

RAFE by Sawyer Bennett
An Arizona Vengeance Novella

THE NAUGHTY PRINCESS by Claire Contreras
A Sexy Royals Novella

THE GRAVEYARD SHIFT by Darynda Jones
A Charley Davidson Novella

CHARMED by Lexi Blake
A Masters and Mercenaries Novella

SACRIFICE OF DARKNESS by Alexandra Ivy
A Guardians of Eternity Novella

THE QUEEN by Jen Armentrout
A Wicked Novella

BEGIN AGAIN by Jennifer Probst
A Stay Novella

VIXEN by Rebecca Zanetti
A Dark Protectors/Rebels Novella

SLASH by Laurelin Paige
A Slay Series Novella

THE DEAD HEAT OF SUMMER by Heather Graham
A Krewe of Hunters Novella

WILD FIRE by Kristen Ashley
A Chaos Novella

MORE THAN PROTECT YOU by Shayla Black
A More Than Words Novella

LOVE SONG by Kylie Scott
A Stage Dive Novella

CHERISH ME by J. Kenner
A Stark Ever After Novella

SHINE WITH ME by Kristen Proby
A With Me in Seattle Novella

From Blue Box Press

TEASE ME by J. Kenner
A Stark International Novel

FROM BLOOD AND ASH by Jennifer L. Armentrout
A Blood and Ash Novel

QUEEN MOVE by Kennedy Ryan

On Behalf of Blue Box Press,

Liz Berry, M.J. Rose, and Jillian Stein would like to thank ~

Steve Berry
Doug Scofield
Benjamin Stein
Kim Guidroz
Social Butterfly PR
Honey Magnolia PR
Kasi Alexander
Asha Hossain
Shelly Shotel
Chris Graham
Jessica Johns
Dylan Stockton
Richard Blake
and Simon Lipskar

CPSIA information can be obtained
at www.ICGtesting.com
Printed in the USA
LVHW011758070820
662641LV00003B/472

9 781952 457036